Destined for Love

by

Emma Kaye

Destined for Love

Cover Art by *Debbie Taylor*

The Wild Rose Press, Inc.
PO Box 708
Adams Basin, NY 14410-0708
Visit us at www.thewildrosepress.com

Publishing History
First Tea Rose Edition, 2018
Print ISBN 978-1-5092-2200-1
Digital ISBN 978-1-5092-2201-8

Published in the United States of America

"Are you proposing, Miss Evans?"

Her eyes widened. The heat that had suffused her arm spread to her cheeks. "I...I... No, of course not!" She tried to step back, but he stumbled after her. Her bum hit the arm of a chair, and she barely caught herself before falling. His grip strengthened and leant her his support. Given how unsteadily he stood, she wondered how he managed.

By propping himself up against her body, that was how. They came into full contact. His body pressed up against her, her breasts crushed against his chest. She fought to keep her breathing steady. His gaze fell to the rise and fall of the swell of her breasts straining against the pretty fabric of her gown. She forced her gaze away from his mouth and cleared her throat.

His head shot up to look her in the eye. The grin widened. He circled his arm around her waist. Holy crap, he was going to kiss her. She shouldn't allow it. She should push him away. Instead, she ran her hand up his arm, loving the hard play of muscles in his bicep as he pulled her closer. Just a little more and she could push against his chest, but she couldn't seem to make her hand move. At least, not to push him away. Instead, she caressed his arm and ignored the inner voices warning her she was being an idiot.

She'd never claimed to be anything else.

Dedication

To my family. You all mean the world to me.
I love you.

To my readers. Thanks for taking this trip through time
with me.

To the Scribes. You're the best. Love you.

To Allison Byers and everyone at The Wild Rose Press.
Thank you for all your hard work.

Acknowledgements

Companion story to the award-winning time travel romance, Time for Love.

(Note - This book takes place during the same time frame as Time for Love. It tells the story of the sister, a secondary character from Time for Love)

Chapter One

Current Year, March 29

Charlotte Evans's head pounded. Terror beat against her ribs as her heart attempted to escape her chest. Her eyes refused to open. *Where am I? What the bloody hell happened?*

The *slap-slap* of footsteps grew louder, stopping just before she feared they'd stomp on her. She tried again to open her eyes. No luck. She couldn't move, her body sluggish and unresponsive.

A male voice whispered near her ear, "We need to hurry. She's starting to wake." Cool fingers wrapped around her wrist, lifting her arm at an awkward angle. The stink of onions wafted across her face as the man breathed heavily.

A familiar humming noise buzzed in her ears, but the source eluded her. The darkness beyond her eyelids flickered. She couldn't for the life of her figure out why, but she seemed to be lying on the cold, hard floor. A sharp pain pierced her left hip. Her entire body ached.

Where in the world was she? Last she remembered was meeting with Mr. Sawyer at the London office of Griffin International.

His call had shaken her to her core. It couldn't be coincidence that he contacted her the very same day she found her sister. And he thought she'd actually *want* to go back to the nineteenth century? After all these years?

Stumbling through that time portal when she was ten had been an accident, but a happy one that had saved her life. Going back wasn't an option. After telling him in no uncertain terms to leave her the hell alone, she'd walked away.

Funny. She couldn't remember leaving the office. Last thing she recalled was reaching for the door handle. Then everything went black.

Pins and needles crept up her legs. She needed to get up.

Her next attempt to open her eyes was successful. Lights flickered but didn't go out completely. She traced the buzzing noise to the fluorescents that dropped down from the ceiling.

She rolled over and managed to rise onto her hands and knees. The contents of her stomach threatened to spill. Jagged stones jammed into her. Scratch marks gave the impression the floor had been carved out of solid rock. It seemed natural, yet—not.

"Too late, I see," a voice she recognized spoke clearly from across the room.

"Mr. Sawyer?" The words surged out as a croak, her throat rough and scratchy, like she hadn't used her voice in a long while. "What's going on? Where am I?"

"You collapsed this morning. The air must not agree with you," he said in an amused, breezy voice. "You really should be heading home. Don't worry. I'll see to it."

"My brother can pick me up." Fear threatened to choke her. He couldn't mean what she thought he did, could he? "I'll call him."

"That's not exactly what I meant. You remember our conversation? You don't belong here. It's not your time. The portal will send you back to 1818 where you belong. I'm sure you can come up with some explanation of where you've been all these years."

She gasped and tried to catch her breath. "I told you I'm not going back. This is my home now." Her gut roiled in protest every time she moved. She crawled to the wall and slumped into a sitting position, breathing heavily through her nose. A strange odor permeated the air, like someone threw kerosene onto a campfire.

"I'm afraid you *will* be returning. We had hoped for your cooperation. You should be eager for this chance to return to your family. Don't you miss them?"

"No," she said bitterly. "My family, my *real* family, is here. My parents died in a car crash a few years ago, but I have my brother Steven. He's here. In London. He'll worry about me if I disappear. I told him I was going to see you," she lied. "He'll put two and two together."

"We both know that's not the whole truth."

"It's the only truth that matters," she spat back. "Why do you want me to go now, after all this time? It's been fifteen years! I have a life here. I barely remember the past."

Her eyesight finally focused. She studied the room. Well, room wasn't really the right word. Cave was more appropriate, though it was the most high-tech cavern she had ever seen. The floor had been evened out but still retained a lumpy, uneven texture with pebbles and dirt littering the floor. A steel case filled with computers lined one wall. To her right, the air rolled in distorted, shimmering waves that sent a chill through her body that pulsed to the same rhythm of the portal.

She fought against the panic trying to consume her. Tight spaces were bad enough—she'd learned to fight through her fear with deep breathing techniques mastered through years of practice. But being underground—and here in particular? Her worst nightmare come to life.

The only thing that kept her from a full-blown panic attack was the smug look on Sawyer's face. She'd never have thought the squat, balding mouse of a man in his rumpled suit could have the ability to screw her life so royally. Yet here she was.

Air wheezed through chapped lips. She gulped, trying to force moisture down her parched throat. She had been here once before. The worst day of her life. She shook her head to get the image of her sister's broken, blood-soaked body out of her mind. That Alex had survived was a miracle.

Oh, God. Alex. Had Sawyer found her too? Was she, even now, waking up underground somewhere about to be forced through another time portal?

If she was, surely Sawyer would have used that information to gain Charlotte's compliance. If he told her Alex had already been sent back, what choice would she have but to go find her? Judging by her current situation, he was the kind of man to use any and all means at his disposal.

She had to assume her sister was alive, in *this* century, and awaiting her call. She had to find a way to get to her. To warn her about Sawyer and find a way to get on with their lives. In this time. Because there was no way she was going back to those traitors, that so-called family who had betrayed them both.

Of course, considering all the heavily armed men surrounding her, her wishes might not exactly be taken into consideration.

****

Her stomach slowly settled to the point she could move without retching. Her head pounded a little less, but without that ache, the discomfort in her hip became more pronounced. She was going to have one hell of a bruise.

Two men cradling machine guns guarded the opposite end of the room, near the door and farther away from the distortion. Their hard faces continuously scanned the room and skipped over her as if she didn't exist. Her eyes narrowed. They'd regret dismissing her so easily.

She returned her attention to Sawyer and the young man who seemed overly concerned with her state of health. He grabbed her wrist again and shone a light in her eyes—until she regained enough strength to shove his hands away. He stumbled backward in surprise.

"Oomph." He grunted as his backside hit the ground, hopefully on the same pebble that had been lodged in hers, she thought vindictively.

"Hey! I'm just checking to make sure you're okay," he whined.

"Okay? You want to make sure I'm okay? If you hadn't drugged me in the first place, you wouldn't have to check." She turned to Sawyer. "And you haven't told me why it's so bloody important I go back all of a sudden."

"We're cleaning house, so to speak. The company

has decided it's time that you, and a few others, return from whence you came."

A tiny bit of her tension eased. If he had Alex, he most definitely would have said so.

"Most were quite happy to go. Times are hard. They were pleased to go back to lives that were so much less complicated." He shoved a variety of items into an old-fashioned looking sack as he spoke. "It won't be without difficulty, however. I'm sorry to say we have information that a woman was—will be?—murdered not far from where you'll be arriving in the past. Of course, the article may not be about you." He tapped his chin as if pondering an interesting puzzle. "Hmm. Perhaps I have changed that event simply by warning you of the possibility." He shrugged and continued his task.

What the bloody hell was the bastard going on about? Murder? A tremor ran through her from head to foot.

He shook out and then folded a simple, and if she recalled correctly, serving class dress before shoving it into the sack. Petticoats and a corset followed.

Oh man, he was serious.

"This is crazy," Charlotte said against gritted teeth. She inched up the wall to a standing position. Her eyes flicked to the touchy-feely guy and quickly away. He had a gun in his belt. Could she possibly grab it? If she didn't act soon, she'd be in real trouble. The walls were closing in on her. A full-blown panic attack was on its way if she didn't do something. Fast.

"Are you going to put this on, or am I going to have to help you?" Sawyer asked, the serious expression on his face countering the depraved flirtatiousness of his tone.

Charlotte took the sack gingerly and looped it over her arm. "A little privacy, if you please?" she snapped.

As soon as the two agency men turned, she grabbed the gun. The man whipped around and backhanded her across the face, but she had the weapon. She flipped the safety off and leveled the weapon at eye height. Her vision blurred. Her hands shook from fear. She had fired a pistol only once in her life, and she hadn't done all that well with it.

"Back up!" she screamed. A trickle of blood from her split lip dribbled down her chin. The copper taste mixed with the sourness of terror fouled her tongue. Time moved extra slowly, and the most minute details itched for her attention. The satchel swung from her elbow and banged against her knee. She should drop it but couldn't take either hand off the gun. It trembled enough with a two-handed grip. The portal now loomed at her back like a storm cloud threatening to engulf them all.

Movement at the corner of her eye caught her attention. The soldiers near the door had their weapons trained on her. She aimed at Sawyer, and he waved them off. "Stand down, Charlotte. Don't be stupid. There's no way you can get out of here. The only thing to do is cooperate and go home."

"Never." A flash from the side caused her to swing around. Too late. The man grabbed her arms and forced them to point toward the ceiling. In a roar of sound and light, the gun went off.

A large chunk of stone fell from the ceiling, the man took the worst of the blow, but fragments struck Charlotte hard on the cheek and shoulder. She was knocked back amidst a cloud of dust and debris. She ran, her arms thrown over her head. She could barely see six inches in front of her.

There wasn't enough time to stop when a slight shimmer told her she headed into the portal—and straight into the childhood nightmare she left behind fifteen years ago.

Chapter Two

March 29, 1818

Pain and terror consumed her. Every nerve ending sprang to life in a torrent of agony as her body was set afire. She remembered the feeling like it was yesterday. The memory may have faded with time, but it all came rushing back in a flash. Fortunately, it was over quickly, just like the last time.

She crashed to the floor, curled into a ball. Trembling and retching, she worked her way into a sitting position. She waved her hand in front of her face. Nothing. The portal trembled beside her. She inched as far away as possible. Huddled against the wall, she breathed shallowly through her nose. Dust and mildew made her nose itch with the urge to sneeze. The jagged, uneven floor reinforced the knowledge she was no longer in the same cave she had just left so unwillingly.

A draft brushed her left side. Fresh air. Out. She needed to get out. Her brain skittered to a halt. She needed air.

Pressure on her arm reminded her of the satchel Sawyer had forced on her. She tugged until the bag lay securely in her lap. Groping the ground around her, she touched metal a few inches from her leg. The gun. She stuffed it into her bag.

She got onto her hands and knees and made the slow, careful climb to the surface. She scraped her shoulders repeatedly as she crawled up the steep path. Boulders jutted out from all sides. Left, right, top, right again. She couldn't keep a straight line to the top. Her tender arms were likely covered in bruises already. She had tumbled down this tunnel as a child, right through the portal at the bottom. Memories fought to overwhelm her as with every inch the walls closed in, tighter and tighter.

Her breath gushed out in harsh gasps. *I'll be out soon. Out soon. Out. Out.*

Just as she thought she could take no more, the way opened up, and she emerged into the cavern where she and her sister had once been held captive. Still black as pitch, but the icy air flowed more freely around her. Sounds echoed in the stillness. She inched along the wall until it disappeared, and she stumbled into the tunnel that would take her to the surface.

After a few minutes, a faint glimmer of light ahead gave her hope. She rushed forward, heedless of the tiny pebbles bruising her legs. She would feel them later. Now she was consumed with getting outside.

She rose to her feet and ran the last few steps, gulping great big breaths of air—clean, cold, glorious air.

Bushes partially concealed the exit, but she was able to make her way out into a clearing without any struggle. Snow covered the ground, an inch or so thick where it drifted against the bushes but receding to a light dusting along a road through a fairly thick stand of trees in one direction and across rolling hills in the other.

When her breathing returned to normal and her pulse stopped its mad dash, she turned her attention to figuring out her next steps. She settled for taking inventory. Thank God they hadn't managed to take away *all* her things. Her purse was gone, which was a shame, but she did escape with a pocketknife and the watch her parents had given her when she passed her A levels. The few pound notes she had tucked in her pocket were useless now, but she shoved them back into her jeans. The small bottle of hand sanitizer hooked to her belt could be useful.

The satchel contained the dress and undergarments she had seen, but it also contained a surprise at the bottom. Unshed tears burned behind her lids as she picked up a beautiful gold, heart-shaped necklace with a brilliant teardrop emerald dangling from the base and her name etched on the front. She flipped it over and read the tiny letters of the inscription, *We Love You, M and F.*

She had no idea why she kept the stupid thing. She had no wish to remember her birth family. Except Alex. Their mother had given them the matching necklaces shortly before they were taken. She had nothing else to remember her twin sister by, so she'd kept it out of a desperate wish to keep her alive in some manner.

Her hands trembled with cold as she secured the necklace around her neck. Easiest place to carry it where it wouldn't get lost. If nothing else, the gem would fetch a pretty penny. Now that she knew Alex was alive, she didn't need the jewelry quite so much.

The dress was poor quality, with rough fabric in an awful flowered pattern. No help for it though, she had to put it on. Nothing she wore was suitable for this time. Her jeans would cause all sorts of commotion if someone caught her walking around in them. And she appeared to be stuck here for a while.

Going back right away was out of the question. Even if the cave hadn't collapsed entirely on the other side, Sawyer would be sure to keep people on the lookout for just such an attempt. Who knew what he'd do to her if she barged back through now.

Of course, staying here wasn't necessarily safer if Sawyer's story about a murder was true. But what choice did she have?

If only he'd shown her the article he talked about. Maybe she could avoid that fate somehow. After scaring the crap out of her, the least he could have done was give her details. How the bloody hell was she supposed to avoid being murdered if she had no idea when, how, or who did it?

The best she could do was get away from the portal. And that meant putting on the beastly clothes Sawyer packed for her.

She traced the lines of the stiff corset. Maybe she could make do without that nightmare contraption. Her own bra would be much more comfortable.

Shivering with cold, she struggled into the dress. The fit was entirely wrong without the stays. She sighed. Oh well, it had been worth a try. She undressed again and put on all the authentic undergarments she had tried to do without. It wasn't as difficult as she anticipated. Servants required complete freedom of movement and didn't have help to tie-up intricate laces. If Sawyer had given her the lady's gown her birth family's station demanded, she wouldn't have been able to manage. Thank God for small mercies. She drew a woolen cloak over her shoulders, wishing for her down jacket abandoned somewhere at Griffin International headquarters. She rubbed her hands together for warmth.

Finally dressed, she took a good look around. She was only ten years old the last time she'd been here. She didn't remember much, having been in an enclosed carriage and blinded by fear at the time. But the woods didn't ring any bells, so she had the vague feeling she hadn't traveled through them.

She slipped on her shoes and struck out through the trees in the opposite direction she thought she had come from all those years ago. She did not want to go into London, where her family had been back then.

Hopefully there was a town nearby. Whether the road was public or private, she didn't know, but surely it would eventually meet up with an inn or stable. People had to switch horses for long journeys, and inns were like the petrol stations of the day. The moon and stars would light her way, but she didn't relish the idea of sleeping out here in the cold and dark. If she couldn't find shelter, who knew if she would survive 'til dawn.

****

It took her a few hours to walk to the nearest town. Midnight had come and gone by the time she saw signs of people. Chilled through and shivering with frozen feet and sopping wet shoes obviously not meant for tramping through the snow, she almost danced with delight at sight of habitation.

It wasn't so much of a town as an inn, probably a stopping point for mail coaches and other travelers. The building was large and appeared to be on the popular side. As late as it was, people ran in and out. A coach had just arrived, and a man disembarked. He jumped the final step and rushed into the inn. Charlotte wondered briefly why they would be traveling so late but was too tired to think much about it.

Realizing how dreadful she must look, she made her way around to the back door. She had no money, but maybe she could sell her necklace. It should more than pay for shelter for the evening.

The inn's staff rushed around like mad, worried frowns on each and every face. Odd for so late in the evening. She stopped a young maid. "Is something wrong? Why is everyone so upset?"

"Oh, it's horrible. A young miss is in a terrible way. The doctor just arrived and is seeing to her now." The girl gasped. "What happened to your face? Were you in an accident or set upon by thieves?"

Charlotte raised a hand to her cheek. She had almost forgotten the blow she had taken to the face. She must look worse than she thought to elicit such a response. "I had a little accident. I look worse than I feel." Wanting to take the focus off herself, she asked, "What's wrong with the girl?"

"Can't breathe. It's awful, the poor child."

"A child?" Charlotte asked in concern. She was almost at the end of her second foundation year at London Central Hospital. Maybe she could help—Lord knows what a doctor from this century would do for someone having an asthma attack.

"Yes, Viscount Tyndale's daughter, such a sweet little girl. You'll have to excuse me, miss." She rushed off.

Charlotte considered the general air of anxiety of everyone who passed by and decided to see if there was anything she could do. She had considered going into pediatric emergency. She loved children and couldn't wait to have one of her own. In the end, she couldn't stomach the idea of seeing children in pain day after day and was continuing her education to become a general practitioner.

She managed to find her way to the main entrance. A maid carrying a tray of tea and coffee walked carefully up the stairs. Charlotte followed. Maybe the tray was on its way to the child's family.

The maid stopped at a room crowded with people rushing in and out. Charlotte peeked through the open door. No little girl anywhere. The man who had rushed out of the carriage when she first arrived attempted to calm a large, blonde Adonis pacing the length of the room.

"I do not want to hear there is nothing you can do for her," the man said, his quiet voice commanding the attention of everyone in the room. The naked anguish in his tone tore at her heart. Nothing she could do for him. Best find the girl.

The next door down was slightly ajar. A little girl with blonde hair and large brown eyes, surrounded by extra thick lashes spiked with recent tears, tossed about in a large featherbed, grunting and wheezing. She clutched a ragged stuffed bunny to her chest. The idiot doctor hadn't even left someone with her. Poor thing must be scared to death. Charlotte swiftly approached the bed. "Hi there, sweetie. Not feeling well, huh?"

The girl glanced up, startled. "Who?" She barely got the question out.

Charlotte leaned close and put her ear to the child's chest. She couldn't hear all that well without a stethoscope, but the child was clearly having an asthma attack. Her pulse raced. Fairly bad, but not too far gone yet. Even so, without modern medicine what could she do?

She thought of the coffee in the room next door. Coffee, there's an idea. She slipped into the next room and, unnoticed by anyone, poured a large cup of coffee from a tray near the door. She took a sip, *whew, strong, but not too hot*. Good. She hurried back to the child.

"Here, sweetheart. Take a sip of this." The girl looked wary but was in no position to protest. She made a face at the first taste of the bitter brew. Charlotte forced her to drink the entire cup.

Just as the girl finished, the doctor showed up. "What in bloody hell do you think you are doing?"

"I was just giving her a little something to drink." She widened her eyes and affected as innocent an expression as possible while she backed away.

"Who are you, and what are you doing here?" The agitated father strode into the room. He beelined straight to the bed and perched on the edge by his daughter's hip. He barely spared a glance for Charlotte, but she couldn't keep her eyes off him.

He was about six foot, with thick, gorgeous blond hair. Maybe mid-twenties. She couldn't see the color of his eyes, but she would lay bets they were as intense as he appeared. Maybe brown like his daughter's. A shiver coursed through her. She wasn't sure if it was from fear or anticipation. The man struck her as someone she wouldn't want to cross, but she wasn't entirely sure whether that was the cause of her nerves or an awareness so intense she had never felt anything to match it.

The doctor glared, face red, lips tight. Shit. The father had asked her a question, and she'd been sitting here contemplating the color of his eyes.

"My name's Charlotte Evans. I was just trying to help." She kept her eyes cast down, her attention on the little girl.

Good, her coloring had improved. She inched closer and flashed her best you can trust me smile. "How are you feeling, sweetie? Is it a little easier to breathe now?"

The girl smiled shyly and nodded.

The father spared a quick glance for Charlotte. She had been wrong about the eye color. They weren't brown. They were a clear cobalt blue that sent sparks straight to her core. Charlotte shook her head and forced her gaze away from the father to concentrate on the daughter.

She skirted around to the opposite side of the bed and sat. She took hold of the girl's wrist and started counting. A little fast, but the girl probably wasn't used to the amount of caffeine she had just swallowed, so it wasn't too troubling.

"Just what do you think you are doing?" the doctor asked in outraged tones.

Fear clouded the girl's eyes, and her little hand clenched shut. Charlotte stroked her arm reassuringly.

"Be still," the father barked at the doctor, making a cutting motion with his hand. "You are upsetting my daughter."

"Yes, my lord," the doctor responded with a little bow, but if looks could kill...

"Will she recover?" the father asked.

"Oh, she should be fine. Can I ask you a few

questions?" Charlotte asked.

"Yes, you may."

She got as complete a history as she could with the doctor hemming and hawing behind her the whole time. The little girl, Prudence was her name, had woken up about two hours ago, crying and breathing fast and shallow. Lord Tyndale had sent for the doctor immediately, and Charlotte had seen his arrival. The doctor had barely glanced at Prudence before pronouncing there was little he could do and the girl would surely die.

Lord Tyndale's gaze softened, and he smiled whenever he gazed at his daughter, but his face was a mask whenever he turned away. The agony he had experienced that evening was plain to see in his tired eyes and slumped shoulders. Her heart melted.

She placed a hand over his and squeezed. A bolt of electricity shot up her arm at the contact. Her voice was a trifle unsteady as she tried to reassure him. "She'll be fine. Honest. In the future, whenever you see any signs that she's having difficulty—coughing, wheezing, that kind of thing—give her a cup of coffee, the stronger the better. The caffeine will help open up the passages in her lungs."

"Will she always suffer so?"

"It's a little early to tell. She may grow out of it. Some kids do. But she also may develop a full-blown case of asthma. If that's the case, she'll have to deal with this her whole life." If she were at home, she would tell him it was controllable, but she just didn't know what they could do with the medicines available in this century.

"How do you know all this?"

"I'm a doc… I, uh, my brother has the same difficulty. I'm used to it. My lord," she added awkwardly as an afterthought.

"My lord, why are you listening to this—this *girl*? She will surely do great harm to your child," the doctor exclaimed. A hint of panic tinged his voice.

You should be worried about your job, you jerk. His emphasis on *girl,* as if that were all the reason anyone needed to ignore her, raised her hackles.

"You told me my daughter was likely to die tonight, yet five minutes in the company of this *girl* and she appears better." The fire blazing in his eyes this time made Charlotte glad she was currently on his good side. "You may leave, Doctor."

The doctor turned red and, spluttering beneath his breath, slammed out of the room.

"Quack," Charlotte muttered.

"He is the finest doctor in the county. However, I must admit I was not pleased with his attentions this evening. Thank you for helping my daughter." He nodded in her direction then smiled at Prudence. "How are you feeling, my dear?"

"Better, Father. Thank you." She smiled shyly, her eyes drooping as she struggled to stay awake.

"She's doing much better now," Charlotte whispered. "It would be best if she got some rest."

"Yes, of course," Lord Tyndale said. He squeezed Prudence's hand. "I shall be in the room next door if you need me." He motioned for Charlotte to precede him out of the room and followed her into the corridor. "This way, if you please." He indicated his room next door.

"Someone should stay with her a while," she

pointed out.

He motioned with his hand, and a woman slipped into the child's room.

Nervously, Charlotte walked into his room, wishing she had been able to think up a decent cover story for how and why she was there in the first place. She'd have to wing it. She faced him and jumped back in surprise at how close he stood.

He inspected her from bottom to top, his gaze lingering on her worn out shoes, drifting up her servant's clothing and then stopping on her bruised and battered face. He lifted a hand, and she flinched as he swept a lock of hair away from the cuts on her cheek. "Who did this to you?" he asked, his voice quietly menacing, anger clear on his face.

She shrugged. "It was my own fault really. I can be a bit clumsy at times." She kept her gaze down and shuffled her feet. For some reason, she didn't like lying to him.

"I see. You don't need to tell me, but perhaps I may be of some assistance?" Lord Tyndale asked, his face back to the careful mask he had shown before in his daughter's room.

Maybe she had been mistaken about him being angry. Hard to judge when his emotions flitted across his face so swiftly.

"Are you employed at this inn? I don't believe I have seen you here before."

"No. I just got here. I was hoping to find work, actually. If you really want to help me, a kind word to the owners would be wonderful." She needed to find a job soon which was going to be difficult without any recommendations or history. A few words from a titled gentleman would go really far.

"I am pleased to meet you." He nodded. "I will gladly speak to the proprietors if that is your wish. We can discuss it tomorrow. You must wish to clean up. I will secure a room for you and request a hot meal and bath delivered."

"Please don't go to so much trouble." It sounded heavenly, but she wasn't sure whether it would be a good idea to accept. She didn't want to become indebted to the man.

"Nonsense, I insist. I am in your debt." He strode to the door and motioned to one of the many servants littering the corridor, waiting to see if the lord needed anything else before retiring for the evening. After a few quiet words he returned to her side. "Please, follow Amelia. She will lead you to your room. I will see you in the morning."

He obviously wasn't going to take no for an answer so she gave in gracefully. "Thank you," she said and smiled. "I'll just peek in on Prudence first. If you don't mind, I'll check on her a few times during the night to make sure she's okay. She should probably have a bit more coffee in another hour or so."

****

Miserable from stomach cramps and a pounding head—after-effects of the drug Sawyer had given her, probably midazolam since her memories were a bit fuzzy—Charlotte sank onto the feather mattress in her room. Add on the unaccustomed hike to get this far and she was knackered. She lay back, her arm draped across her eyes.

She'd had plenty of time to think while she walked but still had no idea what to do. She was in a world of trouble.

The portal wasn't an option. At least not right away. Even if Sawyer and his goons weren't guarding the other side, her screw-up with the gun caused enough damage it would take weeks to make the portal passable. She could only hope Griffin International lost interest in the portals after a while and lowered their security. If she stayed within a reasonable distance to the portal, she could try again in a month or so. Give them enough time to think she no longer posed a threat.

She snorted. Some threat. She'd screwed things up for them to be sure but landed exactly where they wanted her to be.

Now she was stuck in a time she'd never thought to see again. Never *wanted* to see again. Not after what her father did.

She had to focus on her current predicament. There was no use going over old hurts. She was in trouble now. What should she do?

Striking blue eyes drifted through her thoughts. Lord Tyndale in a rage was quite a sight to see. Scary, except for the fact he'd been in a rage over the welfare of his child. Seeing what parents suffered through when their kid was hurt always tore at her heart.

He was obviously a devoted father. An admirable trait.

She examined the room—nice, clean, decent size. Tyndale hadn't skimped when seeing to her comfort. He meant what he said about feeling in her debt.

Maybe she shouldn't be shy about using that? Not to take any unfair advantage of him, of course. But she could help him and his little girl. She couldn't call up the pharmacy and order a round of steroids, but she knew enough about homeopathic remedies that she could make a difference in Prudence's welfare. Surely a devoted father wouldn't care about references when he saw for himself the improvement Charlotte could make in Prudence's health? He obviously wasn't impressed by mere credentials if the way he spoke of the doctor were any indication.

She struggled to a sitting position and leaned forward with her elbows on her knees. The fact of the matter was, she had no place to go. She had no references and no family to turn to. At least, no family she could rely on to provide help.

She was so screwed.

Would it be wrong to take advantage of Lord Tyndale's gratitude? Surely not if she was able to provide a valuable service. She was much better qualified to take care of Prudence than anyone in this century could possibly realize. In fact, wasn't she obligated by her oath as a doctor to see the child was given the best possible medical care? And wasn't she the best qualified?

Just because she found herself in a rather desperate situation didn't make Prudence's need and her own qualifications any less real.

She shoved off the bed. Prudence's room was only a few steps away. She needed to check on her patient before she slept.

Her door squeaked as she inched it open. She grabbed the knob and kept it from making any more noise. It was the middle of the night, and she had no wish to wake everyone in the inn. The night had been tough enough for everyone already.

She tiptoed down the hall, wincing each time a

floorboard groaned. Candle sconces along the wall lit the way. Thankfully, she didn't have far to go. She eased Prudence's door open and stepped inside.

A maid slumped over in the chair next to Prudence's bed. Charlotte lay her finger upon the pulse beating steadily in the little girl's neck. Without a watch she couldn't get an accurate count, but experience told her it was only slightly faster than desired. Not unexpected after the amount of coffee the girl drank. If necessary, she'd sneak her watch out for a more accurate reading. But she wasn't going to risk showing off any of her modern items if she could avoid it.

A rumbling snore issued from the poor maid. Charlotte shook her shoulder gently and put a finger to her lips as the maid startled awake. She indicated that she would take over, and the maid smiled gratefully. Poor thing had dark bags under her eyes, and Charlotte was aware the unfortunate girl would hardly be allowed to sleep late in the morning. Servants weren't afforded such luxury.

She made herself comfortable in the chair the maid vacated and ran through her plans once more. In the morning, she'd present herself to Lord Tyndale and ask for a job as his daughter's maid or governess. Hopefully, they didn't live too far away. If they did, well, she could always stay with them for a few months and then find a way to return so she could make an attempt at the portal. She had a good life in the future. She wasn't willing to give it up without a fight.

Chapter Three

James Tyndale stared at the mystery woman asleep in the chair alongside his daughter's bed. He'd lambasted the poor maid he'd instructed to sit with Prudence throughout the night when he ran into her in the common room moments before. He'd have to apologize later. Apparently this girl—Miss Evans—had taken the maid's place at some point during the night.

Miss Evans's head and upper body lay on the side of the bed, one hand limply draped across his daughter's wrist. Exhaustion and fear for his daughter had prevented him from noticing much about the woman the previous evening, so he studied her now.

Her long brown hair tangled about her shoulders and mostly covered her face. She'd given an impression of delicate beauty the night before, but the bruises and dirt he'd remarked upon had made it difficult to get a true notion of her visage. His fatigue and worry over Prudence's welfare had precluded anything more than the vague recognition that the woman had been treated poorly.

She had a trim figure, though the clothing she wore did not fit properly. The skirt barely covered her ankles, and the top stretched awkwardly across her shoulders. That could have something to do with her current uncomfortable-looking position, but he seemed to recall the dress's unsuitability from the night before.

He switched his attention away from the intriguing young woman to study Prudence's precious face. She slept soundly, her mouth open the tiniest bit, her sheets kicked off, and her arm stretched awkwardly behind her back. How she slept in such uncomfortable positions was beyond him. Yet sleep she did. Relief weakened his legs, and he sat on the edge of the bed, on the opposite side from the young woman.

She jerked upright in her chair, her eyes wide and frightened as her gaze darted about the room. She stilled when she caught sight of him, then pulled herself into a more dignified position.

Soft light filtered in through the drapes, setting her face aglow. A bruise marred the smooth skin of her cheek. The dark red of a healing wound at its center. The mark of a fist, perhaps? A surge of anger swept through him. He'd never been able to abide those who beat on the fairer sex.

He crooked a finger in her direction and indicated the door. Miss Evans ran her gaze over Prudence before nodding. A good sign. This woman considered his daughter's welfare rather than blindly following his command.

She could be useful.

When they'd both stepped out into the corridor, he eased the door shut behind him.

"I wish to thank you once again for coming to my daughter's aid."

She nodded. Once. A matter of fact gesture as if she received such praise on a regular basis.

"I believe I know of a more suitable position for you than toiling away in this inn. Would you care to hear more?"

"Yes, I'm interested."

"Then, please, follow me. I have obtained a private room to break our fast."

Prudence's nursemaid, Theresa, approached from the far end of the corridor. A tray for Prudence held before her. He opened the door, and she slipped past with a respectful curtsey. He'd sent his coachman to fetch her first thing this morning. Perhaps if he'd kept her with them on their return journey rather than sending her on ahead, she would have alerted him to Prudence's distress earlier. He wouldn't make that mistake again.

Miss Evans followed him downstairs in silence.

The table in the room he'd purchased for the morning already held a veritable feast. He sighed. He'd requested a simple meal, but the innkeeper insisted on impressing him. He'd have been more impressed if he'd managed to follow instructions.

****

The delectable aromas of breakfast had Charlotte's stomach rumbling the minute she followed Lord Tyndale into a private parlor. Sleep had overtaken her before she could partake of the meal he'd promised the evening before.

Tyndale frowned at the great array of food displayed before them. She couldn't begin to imagine what displeased him. Everything looked delicious. She almost sighed with relief when he gestured toward the table and held out a chair.

"Please, make yourself comfortable."

She sat in the offered seat, and he took his own place at the head of the table.

Her stomach growled. Thankfully, he didn't appear

to notice. Or at least, he was polite enough not to mention it.

He did, however, motion for her to help herself. She forced herself to make only a modest selection and not gorge herself. The inn had certainly pulled out all the stops. She closed her eyes to savor a sweet, melt-in-your-mouth bite of honey cake.

For a while, the soft clinking of their silverware was the only noise in the room. She observed him through her peripheral vision as she ate.

She hadn't been mistaken about his good looks the night before. In fact, a few hours' sleep had made a marked improvement in his appearance. His hair was combed back neatly, and the rough stubble from the night before had been shaved away.

He'd managed much better than her. A desperate attempt to finger comb her hair as they'd made their way into this room was a lost cause. She could do only so much without an actual brush. Sawyer hadn't included any toiletries in the sack he'd packed for her.

Her hands cramped from her death grip on the silverware, just thinking about what Sawyer had done to her. She forced the muscles of her fingers to relax and set the fork and knife down gently beside her plate.

Lord Tyndale cleared his throat. "You mentioned you seek employment?"

"Yes. I only recently arrived and find myself without…" What could she tell him? Lying always got her in trouble, but the truth wasn't so easy. Fat chance he'd give her a job if she claimed to be a time traveler. He'd have her kicked out in the cold faster than she could diagnose a sore throat. She shrugged.

The motion sparked a sharp pain along her

shoulder blade and down her back.

She must not have done a good job hiding her wince, because his eyes narrowed. He scanned her face. "Perhaps it would be best if you tell me how you received your injuries." He leaned forward, his elbows propped on the table. He pitched his voice low and soft. She guessed he meant to be comforting and reassuring, but the effect was hot and sexy. "I can protect you. If your husband did this, it will be more difficult. However, a few words in the right ears and…"

Charlotte shook her head, appalled at the conclusion he'd reached. "I'm not married." She refused to consider too closely why it felt so important that he know this. It just was. She gingerly touched the cut on her cheek. She'd taken care of it the best she could, even used some of her hand sanitizer, so she knew it was clean. But it was also likely a hundred shades of purple by now. "I don't need protection. I do need work. You mentioned you had something in mind?"

He didn't look convinced, just stared at her a long moment. She forced her hands to remain folded in her lap and resisted the urge to fix her hair or squirm under his perusal.

"Should you change your mind…" He gave her a moment, then continued, "Very well. I would like to hire you as my daughter's governess for the time being. I assume you can read and write?"

"Of course I can," she burst out. She straightened in her chair. Good posture had been drilled into her from a young age, but the haughty glare she sent his way demanded that extra steel in her spine she reserved for chauvinistic doctors and recalcitrant patients. "I'm quite sure my education surpasses that which would be required to teach an eight-year-old."

She'd amused him. She could see it in the tiny lines that crinkled at the corners of his eyes and the slight uptick of his mouth. She clamped her mouth shut on the rest of the tirade she longed to blast at him.

"Good. That's settled then. Though I trust nothing of your situation will come to haunt me or hurt my daughter in any way. She must be your top priority." The worried father had returned. He ran a hand through his blond hair, which fell just shy of ponytail length.

He was the epitome of the handsome rakes her birth mother had warned her would seek her out when she made her debut. Dating in the twenty-first century was bad enough. Thank God she never had to deal with that nonsense in this era. Her first trip through the portal had seen to that.

Now was not the time to get that train of thought stuck in her head. She squeezed his balled up fist that rested on the table, then yanked her hand away in a flash. She almost forgot where she was for a moment. She'd pushed memories of this time so far out of her mind for so long, she'd forgotten how formal people were now. Random touching between a governess and lord wasn't exactly common practice. Unless she wanted more out of this arrangement than just a job.

That was one complication she definitely didn't need. Putting the idea in his head was a bad idea. She was in a risky enough position as it was.

She cleared her throat. "I can help her. I can't cure her, and I can't guarantee that she'll grow out of it, but there are breathing exercises I can teach her. Once we figure out her triggers, we can…" Despite a lot of time spent with worried parents, she couldn't decipher the expression on his face. "What?"

"Did your brother survive his condition?"

"My brother?" Oh right. That's the lie she told last night to explain her knowledge. What to say? "He learned to deal with it, and so did I."

The door squeaked open behind her. Tyndale's brows rose inquiringly. "Can I help you, Stone?"

She twisted in her seat for a glimpse of this Stone person, but with a quick, "Sorry, Tyndale," the door clicked shut.

Something about that voice rubbed her the wrong way. A strange reaction to two short and surly words, but she hoped the man would be gone before they left the room.

"My neighbor," Tyndale explained. "He likely wants this room for himself and is now sorely disappointed I am in possession of it. Had someone else occupied this space, he would likely have insisted he be given precedence, and the room cleared for his use."

"Yet he has enough respect for his neighbor to stand down?"

Tyndale laughed. "Hardly. Enough fear, more like. He's a coward at heart, and I've never taken kindly to cowards." He pushed his chair back. "At least he has sense enough to know it now."

"Now?" Meeting over, she rose along with him.

"A story for another time. I wish to be on my way. Is Prudence well enough to travel? I live within an hour of here."

"I'll check on her. But she appears to have weathered the worst of it last night."

"Then gather your things. We leave in an hour."

The tingling warmth of his hand at the small of her back caused a hitch in her breath. He smelled of clean soap and the wildness of the forest. She stopped herself just shy of leaning in for a better whiff.

Uh oh. What had she gotten herself into?

****

Gabriel Stone tore out of *The Rambling Inn*, straight through the yard and stomped to his carriage.

"Timmons," he yelled. He scanned the area for his most trusted servant. Barely a second passed before the old retainer shuffled out from behind the barn. "What took you so long?"

Cantor waited by the horses' heads, gripping the lead rope and smirking. He thrived on others' discomfort. One of the facets of his personality that made him so useful.

With a careless wave of Stone's hand, Cantor sprang to open the carriage door and let down the steps.

"Timmons, follow me," he ordered.

Timmons darted glances left and right, clearly unsure whether this was a test of some sort.

"In." Stone normally encouraged fear in his servants. He had no patience for it today.

The luxurious comfort of his favorite coach did nothing to calm the turmoil in his heart. Instead of the soft cushions and expensive privacy curtains, he noticed the fabric had begun to wear thin at the edges, and a misshaped lump forced him to shift in his seat. His mood soured further with the knowledge he did not have the wherewithal to refurbish the conveyance.

Timmons perched across from him, wringing his hands together and waiting in silence.

The dread that knotted his stomach from the

moment he'd spotted his neighbor, Lord Tyndale, escorting that young woman into the private parlor twisted his gut. He must be mistaken. She couldn't possibly be who he thought. Spying at the door had not garnered him the information he needed. Plus, he'd risked notice. Bad enough to be caught snooping by that brute, Tyndale. If *she* recognized him…well, he didn't want to contemplate that possibility.

He'd have Timmons do his dirty work.

"Lord Tyndale has hired a new governess for his daughter," he told Timmons. "Find out all you can about her and report back to me. I must continue on my way to London but will return by the end of the week."

Timmons's square face pinched as he considered his new mission. "What you want with 'er?" He rocked forward, hands twisted in his lap. "The little chamber maid, Ann, says as 'ow the girl showed up outta nowhere, middle of the night. Worked some magic with the Tyndale girl. Doctor's all fired up 'cause she made 'im appear a fool before the viscount."

"Did you get a good look at her? Did she see you?" An edge of panic tinged Stone's voice. What if she recognized Timmons?

Unlikely. The past fifteen years had not been kind to his servant. Timmons stooped over considerably, and his skin sagged, weighed down with age. What remained of his hair had gone completely gray. Yet, the man was deceptively strong and could be relied on to do as told, otherwise Stone would have been rid of him long ago.

He cleared his throat. It wouldn't do to have his servant think he was truly worried. He took a calming breath.

"I didn't see no one," Timmons said. "Servants just talking 'bout 'er."

Stone breathed a sigh of relief. Perhaps he worried about nothing.

The girl had been but a child. Even if she recognized his servant, she had never laid eyes on him. The twins had slipped away just as he'd arrived at the cave that day.

Yet a frisson of unease skittered up his back.

The girls had been present upon occasion when he visited their father, Marcus Creswell, the Earl of Downing. He was not a complete unknown to them.

His hands clenched into fists. He'd suffered significant financial difficulties due to the crusade to end slavery all those years ago. If only he'd acted sooner, the risk he'd taken kidnapping the earl's twin girls might have done some good. Instead, by the time his threat was taken seriously, the earl's support of the anti-slavery bill had gained too much momentum. It had passed, and Stone's holdings had suffered for it. His pockets were to let, and he struggled with recovering his wealth to this day.

That was soon to be put behind him. However, he could not afford any hint of scandal to touch his name. If the baggage really was one of the Creswell girls, he would simply take care of her before she ruined everything.

"Find what you can." He explained who he believed the girl might be, ignoring his servant's whitened face and shaking hands. "You can rely on Cantor to help. If needs be, we shall take care of her."

"Take care of 'er?" Timmons squeaked out. "What—what do you mean, m'lord?"

"If it turns out she is one of the Creswell girls, we shall arrange a suitable *accident* and finish what we started fifteen years ago."

Chapter Four

Charlotte stared out the carriage window at the huge monstrosity of a building Lord Tyndale called home.

She could just barely remember her own country house. This dwarfed even that imposing structure. Of course, she'd been a child last time she saw her ancestral home, so it probably seemed bigger than it was. Which made this enormous place even more impressive.

Or maybe pretentious was a better word.

What in the world could a couple with one child need with such a huge house? She pictured Lady Tyndale as some high society miss who cared only for appearances.

Stop it. She had to stop jumping to conclusions. Whenever her nerves were on edge, she turned nasty and judgmental.

Tyndale had been gracious and kind. His daughter was a doll. There was no reason to think his wife was anything other than a lovely woman. Probably drop dead gorgeous too. The kind of woman who did everything to perfection.

After all, Tyndale could have his pick. Rich, handsome, and a title to boot, women probably threw themselves at him. Even being a married man with a child wouldn't be an impediment. He could have mistresses out the wazoo for all she knew. Regency men weren't renowned for their fidelity in marriage.

Seriously. She had to stop. She really should get to know these people before deciding she knew all about them.

The coachman opened the door and stood by to help her down. She placed her hand gently in his and descended the small set of steps he'd lowered for her use, kicking her skirt out of the way as she did.

The long skirts took some getting used to, but she was getting the hang of it. Growing up in London in the future, she was able to avoid them for the most part. Avoided anything that reminded her of the past, actually. Not hard to do. But her body seemed to remember exactly how to deal with the inconveniences of her former, and temporarily current, time in history. She didn't want to get used to it. She wanted to go home. Steven was likely frantic by now.

"Are you all right?" Tyndale had dismounted his horse while she gaped at his home. He stood at her side, watching her.

"Yes, of course."

He turned away to lift Prudence out of the carriage. He swept her up in his arms and swung her around. She giggled and squealed, her sweet face lit up from within. The little girl had been extraordinarily quiet on the hour-long ride from the inn, but Charlotte already knew she could easily grow to love her. What little the girl said was either super polite or extra cute in that way young kids have.

Charlotte trailed after Tyndale and Prudence on the approach to the front door. She really had very little to recommend her as governess. If the lady of the house decided she didn't want Charlotte around, she'd be screwed. Yes, the men of this time controlled just about everything, but children were still largely in the woman's domain. Nerves somersaulted in her stomach.

They entered the large front hall. Charlotte did her best not to gawk. Their footsteps rang out along the lightly veined, cream-colored marble floor. Tyndale spoke quietly with a serious older man in formal black livery who managed to maintain a respectful conversation with his lord while somehow directing several footmen about their duties with subtle flicks of his hand. Impressive.

"Worthing. May I introduce Miss Charlotte Evans. I have hired her as Lady Prudence's governess. Please see that Mrs. Sterling prepares a room. Is Lady Tyndale in the solarium?"

Charlotte smiled and dipped into a brief curtsey to acknowledge Worthing's nod of greeting.

"Yes, my lord," Worthing replied to Tyndale's question. "Miss Crawford visits with her. She brought the viscountess a new flower that needed to be planted at once."

Prudence caught Charlotte's attention. She'd been happily standing at her father's side, bouncing on her toes—until a second ago. At Worthing's statement, she became perfectly still, the smile dropped from her face to be replaced by a mask of polite interest. Charlotte would consider the stuffed bunny lucky if Prudence didn't decapitate the poor thing, she held it in such a tight grip.

While Tyndale continued a discussion with Worthing on various visitors who'd stopped by while he was out of town, Charlotte dropped to a crouch next to Prudence. "Are you all right, sweetie?" She tilted her head and tried to look as trustworthy and comforting as possible. Something was obviously bothering the child. Charlotte wanted to know what.

Prudence just nodded.

"Well, I'm pretty tired, myself." Charlotte faked a yawn behind her hand. "Any chance you know what room I'll be in? I'd love to drop off my things and rest a moment." She let her satchel drop to the ground as if it were too heavy to lift anymore. The soft thud of the gun hitting the marble made her wince. Thank goodness she'd wrapped it in her shirt. The bullets had gone into a little pocket sewn into the inside. She wasn't taking any chances with the thing, but it might prove useful at some point, so she wasn't about to get rid of it. She didn't need to shoot to make a point.

Prudence's mask only slipped slightly, but Charlotte caught the brief tilt of her lips. Charlotte nodded at the little girl before straightening.

"If you don't mind, my lord, I'd like to get Miss Prudence up to her room and make sure the trip hasn't tired her too much." Instant guilt at the widening of his eyes and alarmed expression on his face made her cringe. She hadn't meant to worry him. But Prudence was her first priority.

"Yes, of course." He made a gesture, and servants scurried like ants into their hill.

A stern, older woman dressed entirely in gray swept into the hall from a small corridor Charlotte hadn't noticed. She popped up out of nowhere as if beamed in.

"Ah, Mrs. Sterling. Please escort Miss Evans and Prudence to their rooms. Miss Evans is to be my daughter's new governess. See that she has everything she requires." He faced Charlotte. "After you have seen to Prudence, please report to the solarium. I should like to introduce you to Lady Tyndale."

Charlotte curtsied. "Yes, my lord."

He strode from the room, so Charlotte and Prudence followed Mrs. Sterling up the wide sweeping staircase. A long hallway with several turns followed, then another set of stairs to the third floor.

Prudence's room fit the huge house. *It's a wonder the child doesn't get lost in here.* Delicate furniture littered the enormous room. Some of it in miniature as you'd expect in a child's room, but others, while of the same wood and style as the rest, would have fit better in an adult's room. Charlotte doubted *she* could reach some of the toys on the top of the armoire, let alone Prudence.

Colorful rugs covered the floor from one end to the other. A whole section was dedicated to dolls and other playthings. Prudence dashed immediately to her four-poster bed, swept aside the curtain and picked up a ragged doll that had seen better days. She placed her bunny in the spot of honor on her pillow.

Charlotte figured the doll must be another of Prudence's prized possessions. It had just as much wear and tear as the bunny, which she'd kept close to her side the entire trip.

Mrs. Sterling's hand on her arm kept her from following Prudence into the room. Charlotte turned toward the woman with a smile. She needed to make friends if she were going to stay here while she figured out what to do. "Yes?"

"I will show you to your room now." She made a

sweeping gesture with her arm, indicating Charlotte should follow her.

Charlotte hesitated. Prudence seemed so lost. She sat on the edge of her bed, hugging the doll to her chest. Her face was buried in her doll's hair. *What was she thinking?*

"Thank you, Mrs. Sterling. Do you think I could look at that a little later? I'm still getting to know my charge. I'd like to make sure she's settled in before I see to myself."

A rod seemed to melt in the older woman's back. Charlotte wouldn't exactly say she smiled, but there was a lightening of her features that seemed to indicate approval. "Yes, I understand. Right you are. Theresa can see you to your room when you are ready." Mrs. Sterling nodded toward the young pregnant woman who had been with them on the journey from the inn and now hovered nearby. Mrs. Sterling took a step back, pulled the door shut, and left them alone.

Charlotte took a deep breath and continued into the room. A rocking chair sat to one side at the head of the bed, so she took a seat. The ache in her shoulder twanged as she leaned back, reminding her that the whole incident in the cave had happened only yesterday. The long walk to the inn, followed by a sleepless night taking care of Prudence had certainly taken their toll. She fought the urge to sweep aside the gauzy material bunched around the bedpost and take a nap right then and there. The bed itself was of the same delicate, light wood as the rest of the furniture and in excellent condition. Huge, for a little girl's room, but pretty. The sheet puffed up around Prudence where she perched on the edge. It looked heavenly.

But first, she'd escorted Prudence up here for a reason. She wanted to know what was bothering the little girl. Physical issues first and then try to earn some trust before she asked any deeper questions.

"How are you feeling, Prudence? Do you mind if I call you Prue? I've never been much for formality, myself."

Prue nodded, so Charlotte kept up a steady stream of nonsensical chatter as she checked Prue's breathing and heart rate. She didn't appear to suffer much lingering effect from her attack, though she coughed on and off. Charlotte suspected she had the beginning of a virus, which could have been the trigger of this most recent episode. Her father would know if her problems tended to coincide with illness. Charlotte would ask him later.

Prue continued mostly in silence, but she guided Charlotte to a child-sized table in the corner and showed off her drawings. They sat in companionable silence for a while until Charlotte realized she better let Tyndale know how his daughter was doing. He was probably worried.

"I better go see your father. All right, Prue?"

Prue continued to draw a fanciful fairy with long flowing hair and a swirling pattern on her wings. She used charcoal, so it was in black and white. Charlotte wondered what the picture would be like if she had a box of crayons. It seemed a shame to confine her imagination.

When Charlotte made to leave, Prue grabbed her hand. Charlotte squatted at her side to see what she wanted.

"This is for you." She lifted the fairy picture off her

desk, holding it out for Charlotte.

The sting of tears made her blink. Prue had signed the bottom with a little heart. It probably didn't mean much, they barely knew each other, but Charlotte felt it deep in her heart.

"Thank you. It's lovely." She took the picture gingerly between her thumb and forefinger, afraid to smudge the delicate lines. "Now I have something for decorating my room." Dammit. She was already getting attached.

Maybe this wasn't as good an idea as she first thought.

****

Charlotte made sure Prue was settled in with Theresa before making her way downstairs in search of Tyndale. She didn't have to go far before she ran into a servant willing to point her in the right direction.

Surprisingly, he was still in the solarium with Lady Tyndale and their guest. She'd figured he'd have gone on to something else a long while ago.

She wasn't getting a good feeling about this Miss Crawford. Not one person she met was able to say the woman's name without a slight grimace—quickly hidden. And Prue had turned sulky the second she knew the woman was in the house. She considered retracing her steps and checking out her room instead of reporting to her new boss.

But she needed to relieve a worried father's mind. She'd promised to let him know how his daughter was doing, and that was her job. Not her favorite part of the job, but a necessary one. She couldn't put her ethics aside, even in her present situation.

She paused at the solarium doors, pressing her ear

close to listen for any indication of what she was about to walk into. Nothing. It was likely as large a space as everything else in this house. Listening at the door was no indication of whether they were in there. They might just be on the opposite side of the room. She'd never hear them.

The door stuck so she shoved it with her shoulder. It crashed open, slamming into the wall with a resounding bang. She cringed in the doorway. Staring at her with mixed gazes ranging from annoyance to amusement stood Tyndale and two women she'd yet to meet.

The older woman must be Miss Crawford, though miss seemed a stretch given her age. She was a tall woman, with dark blonde hair streaked with gray and the perfect posture Charlotte remembered so well from the ladies of this day. Despite the ramrod straight stance, the welcoming expression on her face endeared her to Charlotte instantly.

Lady Tyndale on the other hand... At the least, she was a perfect match for her lord. Her golden blonde hair was piled in a mass of curls on top of her head. Her flawless complexion would have made the execs at any cosmetic company drool. The empire waist gown showed off her tiny little figure to perfection. But the hostile frown twisting her mouth seemed unwarranted and set Charlotte's back up immediately.

She twisted her fingers in the pocket of her gown. She had to resist the urge to smooth her hair and cover her bruised face. Lady Tyndale somehow managed to peer down her nose at Charlotte despite the fact she stood a good half foot shorter.

"I'm so sorry. The door stuck. I..." she drifted off.

There really wasn't anything to say. Her cheeks burned with embarrassment. The red probably a lovely addition to the mottled purple, green, and yellow of her battered face.

Tyndale held a hand over his mouth. Not enough to hide his twitching lips completely. He waved her in without a word. He'd probably burst out laughing if he attempted to talk.

She stiffened her spine and stalked forward. She faced all sorts of people at the hospital but she had never felt so self-conscious as she'd done in the past day and a half of being back in the era of her birth. She consoled herself that it had nothing to do with the people. Who wouldn't be disoriented and out of place after traveling through time?

She swept a curtsey at the small group. "I beg your pardon, Lady Tyndale. I hope I haven't inconvenienced you or your guest." She nodded at each woman in turn. "Lord Tyndale had asked that I report to him after seeing to Lady Prudence's welfare." She faced him. "She's doing well. I left her to get some rest."

Lady Tyndale's frown transformed into a smug smile, while Miss Crawford grinned, and Lord Tyndale's amusement fled altogether.

What the hell did I say?

The older woman spoke up first. "Oh, my dear. That is so lovely. I haven't been called a Miss in... Well I can't say how long." She gave Charlotte a kindly smile. "I am afraid you are mistaken. I am Lady Tyndale, Lord Tyndale's mother." She swept her hand out toward the younger woman. "May I present Miss Julia Crawford, the daughter of one of my late husband's business associates?"

Charlotte's cheeks blazed even hotter, but the knot in her stomach eased just slightly. "I beg your pardon."

Tyndale cleared his throat. "Mother, Miss Crawford, may I present Miss Charlotte Evans? She is the young woman of whom I spoke earlier. I don't know what I would have done had she not seen to Prudence's welfare last evening."

Lady Tyndale pressed a hand to her chest. Tears glittered in her eyes. "You have our utmost gratitude. When Tyndale told us what happened…" She swayed, and Tyndale rushed to her side. She gazed up at her son with a smile.

"Are you all right, Lady Tyndale?" Ah, the years of swooning over everything. Charlotte was so happy to be back. Not.

"Yes, of course." She continued to rest her arm on her son, but he no longer supported any of her weight. More emotional support than anything else. Lovely.

"I am so relieved," Miss Crawford spoke up.

Charlotte tried to be subtle as she studied the woman that made everyone in the house cringe. She stood close to a stand holding a beautiful flowering bush that Charlotte couldn't name. One white-gloved hand rested against her flat stomach. She touched the other to her full lips, then trailed her hand down along her neck, where she picked up a delicate gold chain and followed its path to where a large diamond pendant nestled between her breasts. Charlotte struggled to keep the smile from her face. Oh, the woman was good. She managed to appear concerned while calling Tyndale's attention to her feminine assets.

That whole necklace maneuver was one she'd often used herself, though never in the guise of expressing concern. Her ex-boyfriend had sworn that was what drew him to her in the first place. It wasn't until her parents died and left her a significant sum that his gaze strayed to her bank account rather than her bosom.

Miss Crawford approached Charlotte. "You are so very clever to have known what to do." She clapped a hand to her mouth with a gasp. "Oh my! But what has happened to you, poor dear?" She poked the bruise on Charlotte's cheek, none so gently. "You look just dreadful." The edges of her mouth trembled.

Charlotte suspected it was with the effort to hold back a grin, but someone could mistake her to be on the verge of sympathetic tears. She cast a glance at Tyndale and his mother. He appeared to be eating the whole act up, but the lines between his mother's eyes creased slightly. Charlotte suspected Lady Tyndale wasn't as easy to fool as her son.

"I do hope the doctor saw to it?" She gave a delicate shudder. "I am afraid I have so little tolerance for pain of any kind. Thank goodness there are men like Lord Tyndale to come to my aid when necessary." She fluttered her eyelashes at his lordship.

"I'm quite all right, thank you." Charlotte took a step back. "It was nice meeting you all. I didn't mean to interrupt, so I'll just head on up to my room and get settled."

"Your room?" Miss Crawford's voice whipped out. All traces of a smile gone.

Tyndale nodded. "Yes. Miss Evans has agreed to be Prudence's governess."

The smile on Miss Crawford's face was obviously forced. "How nice. I wasn't aware you were searching for a new governess, my lord. I know several suitable women from my days at Miss Price's academy for young ladies." She sashayed over to his side and tapped him with her hand. "You could have but asked. You know how much I adore Miss Prudence."

Lady Tyndale quickly stifled her cough, but Charlotte heard it nonetheless. She had a feeling she was going to like the lady. Hopefully the feeling would be returned, because from the expression on Miss Crawford's face, she suspected she was going to need someone on her side.

****

Miss Evans scurried from the room. Under normal circumstances, James would have had the doctor attend to Prudence upon returning home. Yet somehow, knowing the new governess was with his daughter, he felt confident his little girl would be well. As the minutes had ticked by and no one came to fetch him, he'd relaxed, though he'd been unable to interest himself in his mother and Miss Crawford's discussion of rare flowers.

Unfortunately, his inattention had been remarked upon. His mother joked, but Miss Crawford was most definitely displeased. She made several cutting remarks followed by such a sweet smile he was left doubting whether he'd heard her correctly. Quite at odds with the young woman he thought he knew. Perhaps his decision to court her had been made in error. She demanded a great deal of attention, which he was unlikely to be able to provide. Perhaps they weren't as well suited as he'd initially believed.

"Are you certain she is a wise choice for overseeing Miss Prudence, my lord?" Miss Crawford asked. "You know so little about her."

"I liked her," his mother chimed in. "And my granddaughter obviously does as well."

He raised his brows at that remark. "Why do you say that, Mother?"

She released his arm and began fussing with one of her flowers. "Didn't you see the picture she held?"

"No, I'm afraid I did not."

His mother's hip bumped into a potted plant, causing it to tilt at a dangerous angle. He leapt forward, catching it just in time to save it from crashing. Dirt cascaded over his hand and spilled to the ground. Miss Crawford leaped back with a squeal, but not in time to prevent a spray of soil from splashing against her skirts.

He set the plant back in its place and did his best to shake the soil back into its pot. "Don't worry, Mother. I'll have Mrs. Spencer send someone in to clean up this mess."

"Oh, dear," his mother said.

He furrowed his brow at his mother's expression. She was trying to appear serious, though he could tell she wished to laugh. She often found amusement in situations others of their society deemed serious. He sighed. The dirt.

He slowly shifted his gaze to Miss Crawford. She stood as if in shock, staring down at what he considered a minuscule amount of dirt dusted over the bottom portion of her dress.

His mother apparently gained control of her desire to laugh. "I am so sorry, Miss Crawford. Oh dear. I think you should see to that right away. Shall I summon my abigail for you? She is a wonder. She can have you presentable in no time."

Miss Crawford tore her gaze away from herself. A

flash of ire lit her eyes, but it was gone so quickly he could have mistaken it. She shook her skirt, sending dirt trickling to the floor and smiled at them. "Think nothing of it, Lady Tyndale. Accidents *will* happen."

He had his suspicions on the nature of this *accident*, but he kept them to himself. He was pleased to see Miss Crawford didn't take herself so seriously that a little dirt would discompose her. He detested the ladies of the *ton* who seemed unable to cope with the smallest of inconveniences.

She brushed an errant curl off her shoulder, drawing his eyes to the round of her breasts straining against her bodice. She was a striking woman. Who could blame her if she were a bit vain about her appearance?

"I really must be going," she said. "I only intended a short visit to provide company to your mother while you were away, my lord. I was quite surprised to see you home so soon."

"I thought I had mentioned last week that Tyndale and my granddaughter would be returning today, Miss Crawford." His mother swatted at the leaves of a plant that had been doused with the soil, sending more dirt onto the floor. "I must have been mistaken."

"Did you? I'm afraid I did not recall. So silly of me." She gave a soft, throaty laugh that sent the men of the *ton* thinking of ways to make her repeat the sound. "Well then, I shall leave you to enjoy your son's return."

He held out his arm. "Let me escort you out."

She tapped his arm lightly. "Nonsense. We must not stand upon such formality. I have interrupted your day enough already. Please don't worry yourself over my account." She pressed herself closer and smiled up at him. Her breasts brushed against his arm, and his gaze dipped to their gentle swell. "Although I appreciate that you do. I shall be sure to see you many times before your birthday. I do so look forward to your house party."

The overwhelming scent of lavender made his eyes water as he bent over her hand. A sneeze threatened, but he fought it back until she'd disappeared beyond the doors. He pulled out a handkerchief and wiped his nose. "Is there a polite way of asking a woman to desist in pouring large quantities of scent over her person, Mother?"

She burst out laughing. "I'm afraid not, my son. Perhaps she will learn moderation when she is greeted by your sneezes each time she steps near."

"One can hope." He leaned against a stone bench nestled among several of his mother's favorite flowering trees. "Now. Tell me why you felt it necessary to throw dirt upon our guest."

She lifted a hand against her chest in mock horror. "I did no such thing." The corners of her mouth twitched despite her feigned innocence. His mother's sense of humor often outweighed the proprieties.

"No. Of course not." He sketched an exaggerated bow in her direction, unable to suppress the smile on his own lips. "Nevertheless, we have managed to scare away our guest, and I fear I have much to do. My steward has poked his head in here more times than I can count since my return. Is there anything you require prior to my departure to the confines of my study?"

She shook her head before turning to her plants. "No, darling. I shall be fine. However, I would like to speak with this new governess you have brought home. You don't mind, do you?"

"I am sure she will be delighted."

Chapter Five

A fortnight later, James closed his accounting books with a sigh and leaned back in his leather desk chair. He rubbed at eyes tired from the strain of calculating figures for the past several hours. Dusk settled in the garden outside, crickets chirruped, their noise a background hum that soothed. He missed their peaceful chatter after time spent in the madness of London. He much preferred to remain at his country estate, but at times, duty demanded his presence in the city.

Had he not been called away; Prudence's health would not have been put at risk. Thank goodness he had not seen any hint of a recurring problem the entire two weeks they had been back.

No. It was his selfishness that had exposed Prudence to the rigors of travel to the city. There had been no reason to bring her along. It wasn't a long journey, and he'd only needed to be away for a week, yet he'd been reluctant to leave her at home. She always cried terribly when he was called away, and he hadn't wanted to face her tears. And, truth be told, he would have missed her dreadfully.

Still, had he left her at home, perhaps she wouldn't have suffered such horrible difficulty with her breathing. He could only be thankful Miss Evans had happened upon the inn at the right moment.

Her appearance remained a mystery. Where had she come from? An unknown to the inn staff, she had not come off any of the carriages that arrived that evening. He had done what he could to learn more of her situation, to no avail.

His mother appeared to approve. She was, in general, an excellent judge of character, though for some reason, she had taken an instant dislike to Miss Crawford. Perhaps she felt no woman could compare to Harriet.

She'd be right. His gaze roamed over the masculine furnishings of his study. Rich brown leather covered the furniture, blending in with the dark mahogany of the desk and molding. Harriet had selected each piece herself when she first entered this home as his wife so he would always have a space to call his own.

His gaze moved to the fireplace and her portrait above the mantel. He'd had it commissioned over Harriet's protest. A sign to those who entered his domain that he truly loved his wife. That her money had been a blessing in their marriage, not the cause of it.

Not that anyone ever believed him.

He pushed away from his desk, stood, and strode over to the hearth. Her kind sherry-colored eyes watched over him. The artist had done a fine job of capturing the essence of his wife.

Her light brown hair was swept up with a few stray locks escaping to soften the lines of her face. Harriet always hated that her hair refused to conform to whatever style her maid designed for her. He'd loved it. It gave him an excuse to trail his fingers down her cheek as he tucked the errant locks behind her ears.

Miss Crawford never had a hair out of place. This suited him. He did not wish her to be a constant reminder of the woman he'd lost.

He sought a wife. True. But he did not seek a replacement for Harriet. Rather he wished to find a mother for Prudence. Someone who could teach her everything she needed to know to successfully traverse the waters of the *ton*. His mother could provide all the motherly love his child could ever need, but she lacked the knowledge of society, not having been born to it.

He did not wish his daughter to be treated as he'd been.

A knock sounded at his door.

"Enter."

The door eased open, and Miss Evans poked her head inside. "Mrs. Sterling said you wished to speak with me?"

"Yes." He gestured toward a set of chairs facing the fireplace. "Please, be seated." He waited for her to make her way over and take her place before dropping into the other chair.

He studied her face. The swelling had receded, and the bruising reduced to a motley collection of yellows and grays. The firelight sparkled in her green eyes as she studied the fire, waiting for him to begin the conversation. He'd noticed that about her. She had a patience he'd not experienced in many women. She didn't insist on filling all silence with a steady stream of nonsensical chatter.

What he hadn't noticed was her beauty. With her injuries healing, he could appreciate the light dusting of freckles across her cheeks. The gentle pout of lips that seemed made for kissing.

Her wardrobe had improved considerably as well. The dress was an old favorite of his mother's. She often gave her old clothing to the servants, but this gown had always been a particular favorite. She must like Miss Evans more than he'd realized to part with it.

"Tell me how my daughter fares."

As Miss Evans discussed his daughter at length, he couldn't help noticing the improvements in her appearance. His mother's dress, a soft blue with wide vertical stripes, complimented Miss Evans. It had been altered in some ways. He was certain the bust had been let out, and if he wasn't mistaken, some fabric had been removed in that area as well. This dress was much too low cut for his mother, though he had to admit he quite liked the alterations on Miss Evans.

He found his gaze continuously drifting down to her chest. He forced his gaze toward the fire when he noticed her fidgeting with the neckline.

Damnation. Caught ogling his daughter's governess. He could not afford to make her uncomfortable. Prudence not only suffered less health issues but appeared happier as well. She was quickly growing attached and would not forgive him if he chased her new friend away with his lecherous thoughts. Nor would he forgive himself.

He came to with a start when he realized she'd ceased speaking. How long had he sat there in silence?

"I apologize. I am afraid my mind wandered."

"That's fine. You've been locked away in here for weeks as I understand." She stared into the fire for a moment. "Maybe you should take a little break tomorrow? Prue would love to spend some time with you." She chewed on her bottom lip. He had to force his gaze away once more. "She's worried you're upset with her about her illness."

"What?" He leaned forward, elbows on his knees. "How can she believe such a thing? What did you say to her?"

"I explained to her that you have been extremely busy and assured her she need not feel guilty for not feeling well at times."

He frowned. "You didn't tell her that I'm not upset with her?"

"I told her how very much you love her, and that sometimes responsibilities tear us away from those we love. It doesn't mean we love them any less." Her hand twisted in the fabric of her gown. "I don't know that she was reassured. She needs her father."

"Of course. I shall make myself available for whatever you plan for the day tomorrow."

She nodded and left.

The enticing sway of her hips held his attention until she eased the door shut behind her. The woman was a distraction he didn't need. He must accustom himself to her presence. So far since his return, he'd been so engrossed in his duties, he'd been a veritable hermit in his own home. He'd have to change that.

There had been an increase in tension between him and his daughter lately. He'd assumed it was a product of his worried mind.

His business in London had not gone as well as he'd hoped. Then to have the aggravating trip end with his daughter's illness... It was entirely possible his daughter had misinterpreted his foul mood for displeasure with her.

He would rectify this impression immediately. He

could not bear his daughter's unhappiness. He'd go to her now.

Then he remembered that he'd ordered Miss Evans to report to him after Prudence was asleep. He plucked a crystal decanter filled with his favorite scotch from among a dozen other liquors he kept handy. Since immediate action was not possible, he'd consider how best to approach his daughter.

He'd talk to her, of course. Tell her how much he cared for her. But would that be enough? It never had been for her mother. He needed to suit his actions to his words.

A little help would not be amiss. His mother reported that Prudence felt comfortable in the governess's presence. Inviting Miss Evans to accompany them tomorrow could ensure Prudence's comfort. Surely he could keep his gaze off her delectable body while his daughter was present.

****

The next morning, Charlotte hovered outside Prue's door. The little girl twirled around her room, dancing with her doll. She wore an older gown that fell above the ankles and looked like it had been through the wringer. Theresa had done her hair up in a complicated sort of braid. Charlotte was pleased to see her instructions had been followed so well.

For today, Prue and her father would have a little fishing expedition at a small brook not too far from the home. Easy walking distance. And Prue had said fishing was one of her father's favorite activities.

Charlotte's father had often taken her and Steven out on a small jon boat he'd kept tucked up against the side of the house. She hadn't appreciated his effort at the time, but the way he'd treated her as if she could do anything her brother could do had taken a while to take hold.

When she first arrived in the future, she believed her place was to get married and be a good wife. It took years before she realized she could do anything she set her mind to. Admittedly, her newfound freedom sparked a rebellious streak that wasn't easy to curb. But her parents' love had remained steadfast throughout her teenage years, and she'd settled down. Her choice to become a doctor and do something meaningful with her life was the best of her life.

Prue wouldn't have those same opportunities, but it was important to Charlotte to make sure the girl understood her true worth. Tyndale appeared to value his daughter above her marriage possibilities. She hadn't realized that was possible in this time, but she was certainly glad of it. She liked the viscount.

It would be good for him to spend time with his daughter doing something he enjoyed. And Prue had proved to be very interested in the outdoors. Not that it mattered what they chose to do. Prue would love any activity that meant spending time with her father. He'd been very busy since they'd arrived, and Prue said it wasn't all that unusual.

Prue spun on a dime to face Charlotte with a grin. "Is it time?"

Charlotte nodded. "Yes. Are you ready?"

She dropped her doll on the bed, then ran to Charlotte with an eager nod.

They held hands as they skipped down the corridor. Charlotte was much more used to the huge labyrinth of a house than when she first arrived. She'd had plenty of time to investigate the largely unused rooms while Prue spent time each day with a procession of instructors. Reading, writing, history, and language, as well as the arts like dancing, singing, piano, and painting. All the accomplishments necessary for a lady of this day to succeed in society.

Charlotte remembered the same from her younger days. The piano was the only hobby she continued when she fell forward in time. Her adoptive parents had continued to get her lessons once she expressed an interest. They'd even purchased a cheap upright piano so she could practice.

Those memories had to be shoved aside. Even when she managed to find a way home, her parents wouldn't be there. She missed them terribly, but she and Steven had managed to move on with their lives after the crash. As their parents would have wished. She couldn't afford to wallow in self-pity.

It didn't take them long to reach the study where they were to meet Tyndale. Prue fairly bubbled over with excitement. Her sweet, talkative nature had returned very shortly after she learned Miss Crawford had left the house on the evening they arrived. She really didn't like the woman and clammed up whenever she was nearby.

Charlotte couldn't blame her. The woman had visited once or twice over the past couple weeks and had certainly made a lasting impression on Charlotte. Lady Tyndale had requested Prue be present at each visit, with Charlotte to attend her. Her role more that of a bodyguard than a governess.

Miss Crawford didn't have a genuine bone in her body. She pretended a great interest in Prue but obviously couldn't stand children. Charlotte suspected Lady Tyndale brought Charlotte and Prue into the visits to avoid having to face the woman on her own. She certainly devoted most of her time during the visits to playing with Prue, rather than entertaining her guest, leaving Charlotte to make conversation with the witch.

Of course, the witch dropped all pretenses around Charlotte. She couldn't decide if that was better or not. At least she didn't need to suppress her gags at the sugary sweetness that spewed forth from the woman's mouth when Tyndale or his mother were within earshot.

But, then again, she had to deal with full-blown nastiness. The woman spent half the visit pulling apart everything Charlotte said or did. And Charlotte was in no position to respond in kind. Biting her tongue wasn't easy.

By this time, Charlotte's cuts and bruises weren't nearly so bad. She was recognizable at least. Miss Crawford hadn't been pleased to see Charlotte wasn't normally as messed up and pathetic as she had appeared on the first visit. Suppressing her laughter at the scowl on the witch's face hadn't been easy, but she had to play it smart. The witch could make life miserable for Charlotte if she put her mind to it. And getting fired would be a disaster to her plans.

This position was perfect for her purposes. She had a nice place to live, plenty of food, and Prue was a delight. Plus, it had the added benefit of being within a reasonable distance from the portal.

Not that she had any clue what to do in order to go home. If only she had someone she could talk to about the whole situation, but that was impossible.

"Father!"

Prue's exclamation brought Charlotte's thoughts back to the present. Tyndale swung Prue up and tossed her in the air. The girl squealed in delight. He put her down gently and held her out at arm's length.

"And just what do you have planned for the day?" His gaze shifted to Charlotte for the answer.

"I thought you and Miss Prudence would like to get out of the house on such a lovely day." The snow she'd slogged through when she first arrived was completely melted, and it was remarkably warm for April. Perfect for fishing. She gestured toward the wide-open doors to the garden. Flowers were just beginning to bloom, lending their sweet scent to the soft breeze. "I've arranged for your fishing gear to be hauled down to the pond. We dug up some worms the other day, so everything's all ready for a nice afternoon of fishing."

"Fishing?" He put his hands on his hips. His brows scrunched together in an annoyed frown. "I'm not taking my daughter fishing."

He was still facing Charlotte, so he missed the hurt that flashed across Prue's face before she put her mask into place. If he asked the girl what she wanted to do, she'd probably give a teenager's *whatever* type of response.

"Yes, you are." Charlotte mirrored his posture, her chin up as she skewered him with her gaze. "You're going to forget any nonsense about fishing being an inappropriate activity for a girl, and you're going to take your daughter fishing. You'll teach her to hook a worm and reel in a fish and enjoy yourself doing it. But first…" A deep breath helped to calm her nerves. She was taking a risk, but she couldn't stand the disappointment on Prue's face. "You're going to apologize to Prue."

His mouth gaped open. He stared at Charlotte for a second before switching his gaze to his daughter. He must have seen some of her disappointment despite Prue's attempt to mask it, because he immediately knelt on one knee to get eye to eye with her. "I'm sorry, Prudence. I didn't think you would enjoy fishing. Did you really wish to go?"

She nodded.

"It's settled then." He stood and took Prue's hand. As they headed to the door, he said over his shoulder, "What are you waiting for, Miss Evans? We're going fishing."

****

Charlotte scooped another worm out of the jar of dirt and expertly hooked it onto Prue's hook. The fish were definitely nibbling. Every other cast required a new worm. Slime and dirt covered her hands. She grimaced. Her father had made sure she was capable of hooking her own worms, but she'd never enjoyed the process.

She handed the rod back to Prue then stepped down to the edge of the water to wash her hands. Tyndale guided Prue's cast, whooping with delight when the line soared over the water and landed with a plop next to the downed branch that provided good cover for hungry fish. She clapped her hands before plunging them into the cold running water of the brook that fed into the pond.

The icy water made her shiver, but she endured the cold to scrub her hands, hopefully getting most of the muck off. Her skirt dipped forward with her bent posture, dampening the front of her gown. Shoot. At least she wore the servant garb Sawyer had provided. She hadn't wanted to risk one of Lady Tyndale's pretty cast-offs.

She had hoped to spend the day exploring the grounds. Someone had mentioned that there was a system of caves bordering the edge of Tyndale's property. They'd pointed her in the right direction, and she'd planned on scoping it out while she had time to herself. Find out whether they were connected to the portal cave, and how long it would take to get there. It was apparently much closer going across the property than following the road.

Instead, Tyndale roped her into this family outing. She had no idea why. Was he nervous about being alone with his daughter, or was he interested in spending time with Charlotte?

Her stomach tightened and her heart fluttered. Not good. She was already extremely fond of his daughter. Getting attached to him as well would be beyond stupid. She needed to get home, and falling for a nineteenth century lord would only cause her heartache.

She straightened and made her way back up the bank to the basket of food Mrs. Sterling had prepared for them. Prue would be getting hungry soon.

Her stomach rumbled as she pulled a delicious selection of food out of the basket and set it up on the table some of the footmen had set up a dozen or so feet from the water. They didn't have paper plates, but she was pleased to see they hadn't packed the fine china. All that delicate porcelain and cut crystal they used at regular meals made her nervous. One piece probably cost more than she could make in a year as a governess.

The slow, faint squish of footsteps in the damp

grass alerted her that Tyndale approached. She calmed her racing pulse and continued to set the table as if she had no idea he was even there.

"This looks wonderful. Thank you for arranging it."

She finished placing the last fork and turned. Thankfully, he kept a respectful distance. She didn't know if she could take it if he tried to seduce her. Well, she could take it. Leap into it, more like. Which, as she'd already told herself a million times, was a bad idea.

He gestured toward Prue who perched on a flat rock by the edge of the water, her gaze intent on the end of her line. "I believe she's enjoying herself. Do you agree?" He ran a finger under the edge of his collar. His gaze darted between her and Prue.

Charlotte was suddenly struck by his insecurity. Her heart melted. "Yes, she truly loves being outdoors. The activity doesn't really matter. She'd be ecstatic no matter what we were doing so long as she was with you."

His smile widened, revealing dimples in his cheeks. "I never thought to invite her to fish with me. I assumed she would prefer to draw or play piano."

And... he ruined it. "Women's activities—right. You know, women enjoy many of the same things as men. And can do them just as well. You shouldn't restrict your daughter's potential just because society says a lady should do one thing and not another." She swung back around to fiddle with the table. She needed to get a grip. Yelling at the boss wasn't a good idea.

He grabbed her arm and swung her back around to face him. He didn't look angry, just confused. "What are you going on about? I simply wished to thank you for bringing my daughter and I closer together. I've noticed a tension between us lately. My hope was that you might be able to shed some insight into the cause."

Her shoulders slumped. "I'm sorry. It's just…" She paused. How could she explain herself without sounding like the modern girl she was? "I've noticed the tension as well. You just need to spend more time with her."

"More time?" He swiveled his head to watch Prue. "Shall I have her attend my meetings with my estate manager?" He faced Charlotte again. "Or should I seek her help in balancing my books?"

Charlotte flushed at his scornful tone. "When she's older, yes. But since she's only eight, I'd say no for now." She smirked at his dumbfounded expression. If he was going to act like an ass, she'd treat him like one. She forced herself to appear calm and slowed her words as if speaking to a child. "If you would like my help in coming up with ideas, we can discuss it another time." She swept her hand out to encompass the table. "You may not have noticed, but it is time for your mid-day meal."

He frowned at the table as if noticing for the first time. "Why are there but two place settings?"

"I did not realize I was to accompany you, so only had enough prepared for two."

"And yet there is food enough for ten. You will join us."

"Then you won't go hungry. But I'll be eating at the house. Have fun." Before he could stop her, she sped away toward the mansion. She played with fire, disobeying an order like that, but she was enjoying their outing a little too much.

****

A knock sounded at the door to Lord Stone's study. "What?" He stabbed his signature onto the letter he'd been writing and then threw his pen onto the desk blotter.

This interruption better be important. He'd been home less than a day, and it hadn't been a good one. Creditors plagued his doorstep, and the business deal he'd left to attend to in London had fallen far short of expectations.

Timmons inched the door open. "M'lord? I have news regarding the—uh—project you wished me to investigate while you was gone." He jerked a nervous glance at Mr. Lyman, then stared at the ground to await Stone's response.

He flicked a hand toward Lyman, who immediately rose and left the room.

Timmons wrung his hat in his hands as he stood before the desk. He shifted from foot to foot and directed his words toward his toes. Stone had to lean forward to hear what his servant reported. A sure sign it wasn't to be good news. "Speak up, Timmons. I can't hear a word you say."

"It's the girl, m'lord."

Stone's heart sped up. He'd nearly forgotten the woman he'd spotted before his twice-blasted trip to London. "Was I correct? Is she one of the Creswell twins?"

At Timmons's nod, the fringes of Stone's eyesight dimmed. He clutched the edge of his desk until his fingers creaked with the strain. *This can't be happening.*

"Yes, m'lord. There's no mistaking it. She claims the name Charlotte and looks exactly as Lady Downing did at a younger age."

He struggled to calm his rapid breathing and appear as if the news was nothing to cause alarm. "Have you learned anything from whence she came? It's been fifteen years since her disappearance. Where has she been all this time?"

Timmons shook his head. "I could find out nothing prior to 'er appearance at the inn. It's as if she appeared out of nowhere."

A wraith sent to torment. Yet a spirit would not bother him for she was meant to be dead. He gulped. "To date, no one has appeared at my doorstep demanding we pay for the crimes of fifteen years past. Has she let slip any mention of her past?"

"I spoke with my cousin who's been with the viscount these past three years. 'e's not heard nothing 'bout 'er history. Staff like 'er. Say she's kind to all. Speaks little of 'erself."

"We cannot afford to allow her to tell our secret."

"Could be she don't remember none of it? I don't see no earl's chit playing servant could she avoid it."

Stone rubbed at his bottom lip. Timmons had a point. Why would the girl not return to her father? The Earl of Downing would care little for the scandal that would ensue were his daughter to return to him, alive and well.

"It matters not. Take care of her. Finish what we started all those years ago. She cannot be allowed to expose me."

Chapter Six

James's study door slammed open, and Sebastian strolled in. James relaxed and shot his younger brother a grin. He hadn't expected to see the young scamp anytime in the next few months. Last he heard, Sebastian was gallivanting around London trying to make a reputation for himself.

"Creditors chase you out of London again?" he asked with a smile. He knew better. After they discovered the dismal state of their finances upon their father's death, Sebastian would never be so foolhardy.

True to James's thoughts, Sebastian snorted. "Hardly. I am here to deliver a new stallion to our stables. Fortenoy was a bit loose in the purse, so I bought Whiskey off him so he could escape dun territory."

James whistled. "He must be under the hatches. I've had my eye on Whiskey since I first saw him at the hunt in September." Fortenoy had some odd training techniques for his mounts including whistled commands and regimented exercise schedules, but there was no denying the man had a knack for prime horseflesh.

"I know." Sebastian flopped into a chair, crossed his arms over his chest, and flung his muck-covered boots onto the corner of James's desk. "A gift for your birthday."

James stared at his brother's feet until Sebastian got the hint and dropped them to the floor with a thud.

"Thank you, little brother. Yet my birthday is not for another month."

Sebastian popped up. He swiped two snifters and the brandy decanter off the sideboard and poured a healthy portion in each. "Fortenoy couldn't wait. Consider Whiskey an early birthday present then." He lifted a glass of the amber liquid to his mouth and took a deep gulp.

"Are you sharing, or are both glasses for yourself?"

Sebastian smacked his lips. "I must confess to a most terrible thirst." He lifted the second glass and waved it under his nose. He paused, ready to drink then laughed and gave the tumbler to James. "I suppose it would be impolite to enjoy your excellent brandy without a toast." He waited until James held his drink aloft. "To my dearest elder brother on this most auspicious of days. Happy birthday!"

James tilted his glass in recognition and took a small sip. "I thank you." He set the nearly full glass down and waited for his brother to come to the point. Nothing short of an emergency would drag his brother away from the joys of London during the season. He did not appreciate the quiet of the country as did James.

"I'm afraid I won't be able to attend the festivities in honor of your birthday. Another reason I am here tonight."

"What pressing business will keep you from the joys of Mother's annual house party in my honor?"

Sebastian snorted. Neither one of them enjoyed the types of *festivities* their mother planned for them each and every year, yet they never missed one out of respect. Was he not considering marriage in large part to put her mind at ease and cease the endless invasions of his home by all the marriage-minded females of his mother's acquaintance?

"A business trip that cannot be avoided." He grinned unrepentantly. "I leave early in the morning. I fear I will not even have the opportunity to meet the new governess. I hear she came to you under some rather unusual circumstances."

Just the mention of Miss Evans conveyed her image instantly to mind. Not that she'd been far from it since their first fishing trip when she'd bent over at the riverbank to wash her hands. He hadn't been able to help admiring the curve of her arse and the image stayed with him. They'd gone on many such trips in the ensuing weeks—repeated tests of his resolve not to pay any undue attention to Prudence's governess.

"She did. Yes." Was his new hire fodder for the London gossips already? "How precisely did you learn of the fact?"

"I stopped in the solarium to visit with Mother before bothering you."

Relief loosened the tension in his shoulders. He'd been unaware how tight they'd become until he felt the release. "I see. And did Mother share any other interesting tidbits you wish to question me about?"

"Mother? No."

He took a fortifying gulp of his brandy before asking, "Then who?"

"Rumor has it you're to offer for Miss Crawford before the season has ended." Sebastian raised his brows. "Is this true?"

"Would it bother you if it were?"

He shrugged. "I could do worse for a new sister. She is a pretty little thing. How does Prudence feel about her?"

At mention of his daughter, James smiled. His brother doted on her nearly as much as James himself. "What? You didn't visit with her as well before coming to see me?"

Sebastian chuckled. "I surely would have done so. However, I was informed by Worthing that she has already retired for the evening, along with her governess."

He forced himself not to think of Miss Evans preparing for bed. "You traveled here from London to discuss a rumor about Miss Crawford?" He unclenched his fist to pick up his drink. "Were those the only rumors that surfaced?"

Sebastian sunk into his chair. "No, brother. I'm afraid not."

****

Charlotte trailed her fingers over the keys of the grand piano in the manor's music room. It was as cozy a space as could be found in the house and one of her favorite spots.

Prue was with her grandmother for the next few hours on one of their frequent trips into the nearby town. Lady Tyndale liked to take Prue when she visited with friends.

Charlotte enjoyed the older woman's company, though conversation often turned dicey. The lady was determined to learn all about Charlotte's past and had the tenacity of a pit bull.

Little tidbits tended to slip out when she wasn't paying close enough attention and fuel Lady Tyndale's theories. Like the name of Charlotte's childhood piano teacher who was apparently a well-known music instructor to many of the best families of London society. So while Charlotte refused to confess her birth family name, Lady Tyndale had grasped onto the fact that Charlotte's family was of the highest *ton*. She assumed a scandal had separated Charlotte from her family and hinted that she was sympathetic to the plight of ladies who'd experienced the bite of society's cruel barbs.

She wasn't far off. Her birth family was high in the ranks of English society, but it certainly wasn't a scandal that kept them separated. Even if the reason was scandalous.

The ivory keys called to her. She sat on the bench and tickled out a few scales and then launched into *Minuet in G Major*, the last song she'd learned before her studies to become a doctor limited the time she could spend on proper lessons. Nowadays, she mainly utilized her small keyboard as an outlet when she had a particularly bad day and needed to take her mind off things for a while. The calming effect of losing herself in an intricate piece of music was worth its weight in gold on those days.

After about half an hour, she sensed she was no longer alone. As the last lingering notes died away, she swiveled on the chair to face the open door. The door she'd made a point to close so as to not disturb anyone who happened by.

No one watched her from the door jamb. She wrinkled her brow and swept her gaze around the room.

James lounged on the couch against the far wall. His arms spread across the back of the sofa, his long legs stretched out before him. The minute her gaze swung in his direction, he leaned forward, elbows on his knees. "You were so engrossed in your playing, I didn't want to disturb you."

She pushed back a strand of hair that had fallen out of the neat bun she'd twisted at the base of her neck. "I can't believe I didn't hear you enter." She lowered the cover over the keys and stood. "I was finished anyway. I'm sorry if the noise disturbed your work."

"Not at all. I enjoyed it." He rose when she did. "I have decided to put aside my work for the rest of the day." He rubbed his eyes.

Strain from long hours spent at his desk showed on his face. Lines creased the otherwise smooth expanse of his forehead and crow's feet crinkled. Shadows smudged below his eyes.

She needed to figure out how to give him an unobtrusive eye exam. Even a slight visual impairment would cause his eyes to tire after prolonged reading. And the lighting these days was less than ideal. Candlelight might be romantic, but it wasn't a reliable source for clear vision.

"I'd like to hear how Prudence fares. Would you care to take a stroll with me through the garden? The weather is fair."

Did she have a choice? "That would be pleasant." She always took a walk at this time of day, whether she had Prue with her or not. A brisk turn around the grounds at least got her pulse going, even if she wished she could head to a gym for a decent workout. Her pulse would likely skyrocket all right, but from Tyndale's presence rather than any decent exercise. A gentleman to his core, he'd keep his strides short and slow to allow her to keep up with him while maintaining a calm, ladylike pace.

She missed her gym. She did what she could when she had private moments, but they were pretty few and far between. Forget running and working up a true sweat. She'd scandalize the whole lot of them. She was already something of an oddity, and she desperately needed to fit in for a while until she could figure out a way to go home.

Tyndale led her through the house and out the wide double doors leading to the garden from the ballroom. She usually took the door from the kitchen, but of course Tyndale wouldn't go that way.

She had a lot more leeway as governess than if she were a kitchen maid or somesuch, but she was still a servant, albeit in the upper hierarchy of the house. Especially this home because Prue's care was deemed the most important task. Plus, the rest of the servants assumed she was born into the aristocracy since many governesses came from noble families who were down on their luck.

She stifled a laugh. Down on her luck was the understatement of the year.

"Did I say something to amuse you?"

Shoot. Must not have covered that up as well as she'd thought. "No, I'm sorry. My mind was wandering."

"I see my charm has been grossly overestimated— by my mother," he said with a grimace. "And I always trusted her to be a reliable judge."

She giggled. Her hand flew to cover her mouth, but she couldn't stop the sound completely.

He grinned and winked.

Brilliant. The dimples in his cheeks grew more pronounced with his happy expression. Her knees almost buckled when he sent the full force of that grin-wink combination her way. She twisted to the side, thankful a large terra cotta pot overflowing with purple and white flowers gave her an excuse to turn away. Lady Tyndale had moved the potted plants from her greenhouse just yesterday because the weather was so fair.

She bent close and tilted a delicate purple blossom up so she could inhale its fragrance. He paused at her side. He maintained enough distance to remain decent, but she could still feel the warmth of his body at her back. She could imagine how shocked he'd be if she stepped back and pressed her rear into his crotch.

It took a moment to gather her wits and calm her racing pulse. She was dangerously attracted to Lord Tyndale.

These thoughts weren't at all like her. She'd dated her last boyfriend for six months before sleeping with him. She barely knew James and was sorely tempted to have her way with him in the garden.

There was no way that could end well.

****

James barely managed to keep his hands off Miss Evans as she sniffed a flower. This situation was untenable. He had hired her to take care of Prudence but couldn't stop imagining her filling another role in his household.

Well, not in his house. In his bed.

His mother would have his head.

He had to think of Prudence and all the reasons he would never begin a relationship with anyone who might bring unwanted attention their way. Hadn't Sebastian's report of resurfaced rumors proved that point? He cleared his throat. "I have enjoyed my outings with Prudence these past few weeks. I never would have considered fishing as an activity we could enjoy together."

Miss Evans straightened. "She loves it."

"I would appreciate any other suggestions you might have."

"I would simply suggest you take her along on any activity you enjoy." She shrugged. "It doesn't have to be anything elaborate. She just wants to spend time with her father."

"Her tutors tell me she excels in all she does. Can I trust they are telling me the truth? Or are they attempting to keep their jobs?"

Her smile lightened his mood. "She's a very intelligent little girl. I can't think of anything she hasn't taken to immediately."

Pride warmed his heart. "Thank you."

They continued to stroll along the walkway through the formal garden. He liked the more informal kitchen garden himself, but guests always raved about his mother's flowers. She took a lot of pride in the wide variety of blooms. Those plants that couldn't survive outside had a special spot in her solarium. Blooms were few and far between at this time of year, but there was a certain elegance to the beds that he enjoyed. And in a few short weeks, this spot would be bursting with color.

"The garden is lovely. Lady Tyndale has led me through here several times to show off her favorite flowers."

"She loves this garden." He flicked a bug off the

leaf of a bush bordering the walk.

They wended their way around the various beds and back up near the house. "The best view is from the balcony off my bedroom." He pointed up and squinted against the glare of the sun. Something seemed off. Pots filled with flowering blooms from his mother's greenhouse lined the brick balustrade, perfectly spaced so a flower was always within a few steps. He counted. One, two, three. The fourth display veered out of line and angled dangerously outward over the garden, teetering on the edge. Had the gardener knocked the plant backward yesterday when his mother had the new flowers planted? A grating sound of brick on brick assaulted his ears. The planter wobbled.

Movement from the corner of his eye pulled his attention down. Miss Evans crouched near his mother's favorite rose bush, plucking a lone weed out of the soil. Right below the rocky planter.

He leaped forward and swept her into his arms. He ignored her yelp of surprise as he yanked her away from the wall.

Not a moment too soon. The pot crashed, splattering the area where Charlotte had stood mere seconds before. He wrapped his arms around her, holding her close in his embrace. Her heart pounded in time with his. Her body molded perfectly within his arms. He lowered his face to the top of her head. Rested his cheek on top. Her hair smelled of cinnamon.

A sharp sting pierced his leg. Blood outlined a gash in his trousers below the knee. Shards of broken pottery littered the area at their feet. The moist, earthen smell of the soil filled his nose.

She could have been killed. He grasped her upper

arms and held her at arm's length. He ran his gaze up and down her body, searching for signs of injury.

"Charlotte—Miss Evans—did you sustain any harm?"

All color had leached from her face. Fine tremors ran up and down her arms. She stumbled backward a step. He kept a firm hold and led her toward a bench several feet away. He eased her down and sat back on his haunches to be sure he hadn't missed a sign she was hurt.

His trouser leg rubbed against his cut. He winced.

"I'm fine." She brushed her hands against her skirts, took a deep breath, and lifted her head to look at him. Her eyes widened. "You're bleeding."

All at once her demeanor changed from shaken to stern and in charge. She grabbed his hand and maneuvered them so she stood in front of him with his back to the seat. With a slight poke to his chest, he fell backward onto the bench.

She knelt on the dirt path at his feet. With quick, dexterous movements, she rolled the fabric up to his knee, exposing a two-inch gash on his leg. Her poking and prodding made him wince, but he kept still, too shocked to react.

He shifted on the bench. His body had a completely inappropriate reaction to the sight of her kneeling before him. He tugged on the bottom edge of his coat to cover his lap more thoroughly.

After a moment, she rose, brushing the dirt from her knees. "It's merely a scratch, but it needs to be cleaned, and a bandage would be a good idea. Merely to keep it clear of ger—uh, dirt." She frowned but quickly wiped the expression away when she glanced from his leg to his face. "Shall I send for someone, or can you make your way to the kitchens? I'd like to clean the cut right away."

"I can walk." He stood to prove his point. He was not some child that needed to be coddled and led by the hand. He strode toward the house. As they entered, he called for a servant to fetch water to his study. Charlotte added her own request for freshly laundered linens.

The water and linens arrived within minutes. He gestured for privacy and soon enough he and Charlotte were left alone. She immediately set to work cleaning his cut and wrapping it in the linens. "Is this all necessary? 'Tis but a scratch." He tried to focus on the piddling pain of the cut and ignore the soft stroke of her hands upon his leg or the way her hair fell forward as she bent close to his body.

"Even a scratch can cause an infection if not taken care of properly. Trust me. I know what I'm doing." She smacked his hand where he scratched at the edge of the linens. "Stop that and stop being a baby."

The irritation in her voice left him feeling as though he'd been chastised like a young boy. He raised his brows. "It's been a long time since I've been spoken to like a child."

She gasped. Her hand rose to her lips. She stumbled back. "I'm so sorry." She curtsied, her head bent forward, staring at the ground. "I forget my place sometimes."

He liked her better when she spoke out. He didn't need another servant bowing and scraping before him. "Do not be sorry. I give you leave to speak as you wish. I wouldn't have it any other way. I can't have you afraid to come to me if you fear I won't like what I hear."

She dipped another quick curtsey. She still kept her eyes averted. "Yes, thank you, my lord." She rubbed her hands on her skirts, then gathered her supplies. "I'm finished here. I'd like to change the bandage tomorrow, if that's all right."

"Fine."

She fled from the room.

Chapter Seven

Charlotte paced the length of her bedroom. Remembering her place in this society became more and more difficult the longer she spent here.

How could she have been so stupid? One did not go about treating a viscount as if he were a child. Especially one who held such power over her. If he were displeased, he could ruin any chance she had at decent survival in this time.

But she couldn't help but relax in his presence. He didn't act toward her as if she were a lowly servant beneath his notice. He didn't look down on her as women in this time so often were. She actually felt as if he respected her.

She doubted it were possible though. At least not to the extent she needed, deep in her heart. Best she keep that in mind.

What she needed to do was focus. Over a month in this time and she was no closer to figuring out a way to return home. She needed a plan. Surviving wasn't enough, but she had no idea what to do next.

Steven must be beside himself with worry. Her stomach dropped whenever she thought about what her brother must be going through. What had he done when she didn't turn up for dinner? Was he even now searching for her, putting up posters and pestering the police?

What if it was even worse than just the worry? Could he be considered a suspect in her disappearance? The police usually investigated the family first, didn't they? And Steven was all the family she had left. She crossed her fingers that he didn't have any trouble with the law over her. There wasn't much she could do about it if he did.

There was her sister to worry over too. What had Alex thought when Charlotte failed to call as promised? Everything had looked so bright for a moment there. Her sister was alive and well, not dead like she believed for so long. She'd been all set to hop a plane and reconnect. They'd been so close as children—virtually inseparable. Coming here was like losing her all over again.

Charlotte prepared for bed as she thought through the problem. At least now she had time to figure it all out. She'd been rushed, obviously, as the ceiling tumbled down around her before she sprinted through the portal. She hadn't assessed the damage, but it certainly seemed like a significant amount. Was the portal even usable? What kind of importance would Sawyer place on repairing the damage? Would he begin immediately, or place it on the back burner?

He'd seemed determined to send back everyone who'd passed through those portals in the past fifteen years.

That there had been others came as a huge shock. How many people had stumbled through those portals—portals with an s. Another shock. And how many lives had Sawyer ruined, again, by sending them back through? She wasn't buying his bullshit that everyone had been eager to return. Even if she hadn't been sold to a devil who planned to kill her, by a father who was supposed to love and protect her, she'd created a new life for herself. Why would she trade that for a life she barely remembered?

She sank onto her feather mattress. Not quite what she was used to, but pretty comfy. The comfort didn't make much difference though. She hadn't slept well since she arrived. Not just from worry over her situation, but she wasn't used to going to sleep until she was drop dead exhausted. Her hours at the hospital were insane, and she worked her bum off during her shifts.

Prue took a lot of her time during the day, but she also had tutors and a nursemaid. Charlotte didn't need to cook or clean or any of the things that normally took up her limited free time. What the hell was she supposed to do with herself?

She'd been running into Tyndale more and more frequently in her quests to keep herself from going stir crazy. Tonight's excursion in the garden hadn't been their first leisurely stroll to talk about Prue. And they'd both insisted she go with them on their father daughter fishing expeditions. Sometimes they happened upon each other and walked along in a companionable silence.

A silence punctuated by an acute attraction she found harder and harder to resist. He was a good man, a good father, and she couldn't help but notice. The fact he was bleedin' gorgeous didn't escape her radar either. There was something so hot about a man in breeches and a cravat. Maybe because she was used to men in scrubs. The difference was striking.

Her ex couldn't hold a candle to Tyndale.

She cringed just thinking about Arthur. The prat. Best decision she ever made was kicking him to the curb three months ago.

Well, she was the one who moved out. Their flat was not worth fighting over, and finding a new place hadn't been at all difficult. Had Arthur even noticed when she failed to show up for work? Probably not, self-absorbed arse that he was.

She'd be lucky if the hospital gave her a chance to justify her absence when she found a way home. How exactly could she explain her disappearance? She couldn't tell the truth. Damn. Another lie to concoct.

Add that to the to do list she had building in her head because she couldn't write it down. Not easy for a woman who liked nothing more than crossing off completed projects.

A leather-bound journal Lady Tyndale had gifted her lay open on her nightstand. Every day, she jotted down random thoughts, careful not to even hint at the reality of her situation. But she needed the process of writing to clear her head. She itched to be free with what she wrote, but what would someone think if they discovered such a list?

She snorted a laugh. Right. That would be something. She could just imagine Tyndale reading it. Her to do's sounded nuts to her own ears.

Find her way back to the time portal. Travel into the future. Get past Sawyer and his goons. Make up a lie about where she'd been. Get her job back.

She lay back and tugged the sheets and quilt up to her chin. The room was drafty and the air cool, even though it had been a beautiful spring day. The temperature dropped quite a bit at night. She ruminated on all the comforts she missed from the twenty-first century.

She was going to crank up the heat in her flat when she got home.

If she got home.

****

Rain drilled against Charlotte's window. The steady pinging startled her from her nightmare. Her nightgown clung to her chest, plastered there with sweat. Her chest rose and fell as if she'd been performing CPR for hours. Had she called out in her sleep? She lay still, taking deep breaths to calm her racing pulse.

When no one rushed through the door, she figured she must have made it through the terror of her nightmare without screaming.

The dreams had plagued her more and more lately. Ever since she got here, actually. Not every night, but frequently enough.

And no wonder. After stumbling through the cave in the pitch dark, any sane person would have nightmares. Having almost died in that cave fifteen years ago ensured it.

The roar she remembered from that day had turned to laughter. The sound lingered long after the images of the dream drifted away. The laugh echoed in her ears still. She never saw his face, hadn't seen it then either, but the sound from her dream was burned into her brain.

She got up and poured water from the cream and white porcelain pitcher into the wash basin under the window. The shock of the cold water splashing into her face helped relinquish the lingering effects of the dream and succeeded in waking her fully. She washed as best she could with the chilly water and got ready for the day.

The rain made it impossible to tell what time it was, but she guessed it wasn't too late, or someone would have come to her room to see why she neglected her charge. The servants in a manor this big were never lazy. Their day started at the crack of dawn and didn't end until the family was tucked snugly in their beds at night. She had it easy in comparison.

She selected a cheerful yellow dress with a pattern of roses along the hem out of the small wardrobe. Lady Tyndale had insisted on supplying her with a decent sized wardrobe. Thank goodness the lady was so generous, because the one outfit Sawyer had seen fit to give her was a mess. As a young lady's governess, she did have to project at least a modicum of style. Thankfully, given her state when she met Tyndale, no one questioned her lack of proper attire.

It didn't take her long to get dressed, and only a little time to tame her long hair into a tidy bun. She wasn't planning on going anywhere, so she left off wearing a bonnet. Another few minutes to brush away the stink of morning breath and she was ready.

First stop—Prue's room. She inched the door open and peeked inside. Her charge lay curled under the covers, so she eased the door closed as quietly as possible. It must be fairly early then. Prue had a natural internal alarm that had her up by seven a.m. rain or shine. Charlotte would use the time to sneak down to the kitchen and grab a quick breakfast. If she didn't make it down there before Prue was up, Theresa would have to haul her meal up the stairs along with Prue's.

Charlotte hated putting her to the trouble. The servants' stairs were rather narrow, so carrying a loaded tray wasn't exactly easy. Theresa was used to it, of course, but Charlotte didn't like making a pregnant woman do a task she could do so much easier.

The kitchen fairly buzzed with activity. More than normal.

"What's going on this morning? Why so busy?"

Mrs. Bailey glanced up from where she busily prepared pastry. "Morning, dear." She gave Charlotte a big smile before returning to her work. She directed several of the kitchen maids toward their tasks while crimping the edges of the sweets she prepared. "The guests start to arrive tomorrow. We've lots to prepare. You didn't forget all about the party now, did you?" She cast Charlotte an inquiring look.

She slapped her forehead. The party! "I forgot all about it. I can't believe it. It's all Prue's been able to talk about the past few days, but it went completely out of my head. Is there anything I can do to help prepare?" She'd asked the same question when she first learned about the upcoming house party but had been turned down flat. Maybe now that they knew her a little better, they'd be more comfortable having her pitch in.

"That's very kind of you, miss, but we'll do all right. Everybody knows just what to do. You just see to our little lady." She waved toward some covered dishes set up on a table in the corner. "Just go on and grab yourself a little something to break your fast. Miss Prudence will likely be up right soon and asking for her governess."

"Can I grab her tray? No sense calling Theresa down for it when I'm already here."

Mrs. Bailey waved her flour coated hand and shooed her away. "Already sent it up. You go on now."

Charlotte grabbed some food she could easily eat on the go and left the kitchen. She wanted to help but was nothing but a nuisance getting underfoot as they bustled about.

Prue was munching on a biscuit when Charlotte made it up to her room a few minutes later.

"Miss Evans! The guests arrive tomorrow for Father's birthday celebration." Prue hopped up and down in her seat. Crumbs flew from her mouth as she talked. "Father has invited my friend, Lady Regina Atwater. It's been ever so long since I've seen her."

Charlotte smiled. "Wonderful! You'll have a great time."

Prue grabbed Charlotte's hand. "You'll stay with me, won't you?"

How could she resist that sweet little face? "Of course. I'll be right here whenever you have need of me." How was she going to leave this child when the time came?

****

Later that evening, Charlotte peeked through the open door into Tyndale's study. Normally, he'd still be hard at work at this time of day, but he wasn't at his desk. She clutched the clean linens she carried. He might not have much time for her, and she didn't want him to put her off if she had to skip out to find bandages.

She hovered in the doorway. Should she stay and wait? Leave and come back later? After working up the nerve to come here, realizing he wasn't even around was a bit of a letdown. Better to wait. The cut needed tending, and she might not have the courage to seek him out again.

She stepped farther into the room. The huge painting of his wife stared down on her with a sweet smile. Her smile seemed to invite the sharing of confidences. Charlotte could almost imagine sitting on the sofa, her legs tucked up beneath her, telling everything to the lady's portrait.

Stupid.

"My wife."

Charlotte jumped at Tyndale's voice coming from the depths of the sofa. She hadn't noticed him lying there. "I'm so sorry. I didn't realize you were resting in here."

He snorted. He lunged upward to sit hunched forward, elbows on knees. He gestured at the painting. "You were admiring the painting of my wife?"

"Yes." She nodded. "Prue speaks of her often. She must have been a lovely woman. I'm sorry for your loss."

"I'm glad to hear Prudence remembers Harriet at all. My daughter was so very young when her mother died."

Charlotte inched over to a chair and perched on its edge. She chewed on her bottom lip. Was she about to step over a line here? Probably. But she was responsible for Prue's welfare, and that was more important than keeping her nose out of the viscount's business.

If she were lucky, he'd understand. If not, well, she'd figure something out.

"I wanted to talk to you about Prue and her mum, actually."

He straightened and placed an empty rocks glass

onto an end table at his side. "Is something wrong?"

Crap, she hadn't realized he'd been drinking. It was obvious now that she saw the glass. His eyes were bloodshot, his hair messed. Plus, he didn't rise to his feet when she entered the room. That was a first.

"Maybe now's not a good time. I can come back in the morning." She stood, now hoping he was so drunk that he didn't think to stop her.

He lurched to his feet and grabbed her arm when she turned to leave. Even as unsteady as he was, his grip was gentle. The warmth of his hand, rather than force, restrained her because she was loathe to break the contact.

"What's wrong with Prudence?"

She sighed. She'd stepped into it. Too late to back out now. "She's fine. It's just that I'm getting the impression she's a bit worried that you're thinking of getting married again. She's under the impression you're sacrificing yourself for her sake, and it's upsetting to her." She tried to ignore the hand that still gripped her just above the elbow. It wasn't easy.

His thumb stroked back and forth along her upper arm, below the shawl she had draped over her elbows. The touch of his hand on her bare skin sent warmth soaking into her. He stood much closer than strictly appropriate given their relationship. He swayed dangerously, each movement bringing him closer.

"Married?" He grinned, an unsteady quirk of the lips that set off the dimple in his right cheek only. "Are you proposing, Miss Evans?"

Her eyes widened. The heat that had suffused her arm spread to her cheeks. "I...I... No, of course not!" She tried to step back, but he stumbled after her. Her bum hit the arm of a chair, and she barely caught herself before falling. His grip strengthened and leant her his support. Given how unsteadily he stood, she wondered how he managed.

By propping himself up against her body, that was how. They came into full contact. His body pressed up against her, her breasts crushed against his chest. She fought to keep her breathing steady. His gaze fell to the rise and fall of the swell of her breasts straining against the pretty fabric of her gown. She forced her gaze away from his mouth and cleared her throat.

His head shot up to look her in the eye. The grin widened. He circled his arm around her waist. Holy crap, he was going to kiss her. She shouldn't allow it. She should push him away. Instead, she ran her hand up his arm, loving the hard play of muscles in his bicep as he pulled her closer. Just a little more and she could shove against his chest, but she couldn't seem to make her hand move. At least, not to send him away. Instead, she caressed his arm and ignored the inner voices warning her she was being an idiot.

She'd never claimed to be anything else.

Chapter Eight

"Tyndale?" Lady Tyndale's voice shocked her out of her haze like a shot of adrenaline. "James, are you in there?"

James hopped back. Charlotte grasped the back of the chair she leaned against for support. A chill swept down her front at the loss of his warmth. She shivered. She sank into the chair, facing the smoldering fire in the grate.

James dropped onto the sofa. He picked up his glass and filled it with some brownish liquor. "Yes, Mother. I'm here." He grimaced as he took a large gulp.

Lady Tyndale swept into the room, pausing only briefly to scan the area and locate her son. Her stern expression relaxed into a smile as her gaze fell upon Charlotte. "Miss Evans. I didn't realize you were still up."

Charlotte opened her mouth to respond with some inane platitude, but James interrupted. "We were discussing Prudence, Mother. Did you need to speak with me?"

"Quite obviously, I did, Tyndale. Otherwise, I would not be wandering around the house calling your name."

Charlotte hid her snicker behind her hand. Lady Tyndale was a force to be reckoned with, that's for sure. The lady plucked James's glass from his hand.

She brought it to her nose and frowned. "Whiskey. How you can drink such an abominable liquid, I cannot imagine. It is no wonder your brother is so often in his cups when he visits." She whisked the glass and decanter away from James and placed them on a table near the door. With a flick of her hand to some invisible servant in the hall, the drink disappeared.

"I should be getting back to Prue," Charlotte said.

"Nonsense, dear." Lady Tyndale waved her hand in dismissal of the idea. "I have been meaning to speak with you about the upcoming festivities." She settled on the couch next to James. With a light slap to his shoulder, she motioned for him to sit straight. With a priceless grumpy little boy expression, he did as requested.

Charlotte stifled her giggle and resumed her seat. She schooled her face to show polite interest and forced her gaze away from James to focus on his mother. "Yes, my lady. Is there something you wish me to do?"

Lady Tyndale beamed at her. "Such understanding. It is a pleasure to speak with someone with your intelligence." She paused as Worthing directed a maid into the room with a tea tray. Lady Tyndale got ready to pour the second the tray was laid before her. "Thank you, Sally. That will be all." She poured as Sally curtsied and left. "Here you go, dear."

Charlotte accepted the cup, shocked that the lady of the house saw fit to serve a governess. "Thank you, my lady."

James simply watched, a quizzical expression on his face. His mouth tilted down in a slight frown of concentration, his brow furrowed. He looked as clueless as she was regarding his mother's behavior.

"I can see that you have been a tremendous influence on our little Prudence. She's come out of her shell, so to speak, since your arrival. I want to thank you for the excellent care you've given her."

"It's been my pleasure," Charlotte said. She didn't have to fake the sincerity or warmth in her voice. She had grown very fond of Prue in such a short time. "Miss Prudence is a lovely child. I fear I can take little credit for her—I've known her such a short time."

"And yet she has become a happier child these past few weeks. I feel certain that has been your influence."

Charlotte didn't know what to say so she just nodded, waiting for Lady Tyndale to make her point. All this buttering her up made Charlotte nervous.

"There will be several events during the next several days at which I would enjoy having Prudence present. Normally, Theresa attends with her. However, I would appreciate it if you would take her place this year."

"Has something happened to Theresa? I'd hate to ruin her fun." Charlotte hid her scowl. She'd hoped to use the free time to make a trip to the caves. If she had to hang around the party, she wasn't going to sneak away any time soon.

"Theresa is fine. So sweet of you to worry." Lady Tyndale sipped her tea. "No. I just feel that Prudence enjoys your company so thoroughly and could benefit from seeing your example in a social situation such as the house party. And you can help her learn to handle herself in any uncomfortable moments. Theresa, while a wonderful nursemaid, is unable to deal with many situations."

"Whatever are you getting at, Mother?" James

asked.

Charlotte wondered the same.

Lady Tyndale replaced her cup on the tray and clasped her hands in her lap. "The other children, James."

He frowned. "Are you saying Prudence has had trouble with the neighboring children?"

"No. Of course not. It's the children of the *ton* that worry me." She grasped Charlotte's hand. "You'll understand, I'm sure. Children born of privilege are not always the kindest of people."

Charlotte snorted. "Children of any social class can be mean. Are you saying that Prue's being picked on? Bullied?"

Lady Tyndale tapped her hand and sat back. "I knew you would understand immediately. Children can be cruel. Especially when there are no adults nearby to chastise them for their misbehavior."

"Surely Theresa can oversee…" Charlotte trailed off. Now she got it. Theresa would have no problem chastising a servant's child but would be hesitant to say anything to a child born to a higher class. One wrong word said by the child could cost Theresa her job. "I understand. Are you so certain I would have any sway?"

"You, at least, would be willing to step forward to protect Prudence."

"Why does Prudence need protection?" James asked. He leaned forward, crowding his mother until she answered him.

"You know why, dear. The same reason you did."

****

James threw the sheets back and leaped out of bed.

He'd spent the last hour tossing and turning. Time to give up hope of a decent night's sleep. His mother would be less than pleased with him come morning, but it was her words that kept him up.

Damn. He'd hoped for better for his daughter. The thought that she suffered from the vicious taunts of other children enraged him. Being the whipping post for society's cruelty hurt. He'd dealt with as much his entire life.

He'd thought himself past caring. And for himself, he cared not. But for Prudence...she already suffered from Harriet's loss. He couldn't bear any more unpleasantness coming her way.

His clothing from the evening lay across the foot of his bed. Albert knew better than to wait up for him when he was in his cups. His mood rarely accommodated being fussed over by the elderly valet. One of the benefits of maintaining the same valet over the course of a lifetime. He knew when to stay and when to go.

It took James less than a minute to throw on the wrinkled clothing and head for the door. The urge to see Prudence spurred him on. Did a father's worry ever end? He'd never expected to feel this way when he learned Harriet was *enceinte*.

The short stub of a candle he'd grabbed flickered as he made his way up the stairs and down the long hall to his daughter's bedroom. The light wouldn't last long. He should have selected a newer candle. This one had burned almost to its end.

A whisper of sound made him tense. A shadow slipped into his daughter's room, and the door eased closed, blocking his way. Was Prudence all right? Her nursemaid was under strict orders to fetch him directly should there be any cause for worry.

The warmth of the door handle surprised him. Had someone paused before entering, their hand lingering on the handle as they decided whether to enter or not?

He inched the door open. Only enough to spy inside. He shielded his meager light so as not to disturb Prudence were she asleep. His daughter slept soundly on most occasions, yet the light of a candle falling across her eyes could wake her instantly.

A figure perched on the bed's edge. Whispered voices refused to reveal the person's identity, but he recognized the profile as Charlotte's. Some of the tension eased in his shoulders. There was no panicked edge to their voices. Were something seriously wrong, he'd have known.

Prudence was awake however. He heard the high pitch of her giggle as Charlotte tickled her.

He nudged the door open wide enough to allow his entrance. Prudence glanced up at the squeaking of the hinges.

"Father!" She sat, one hand reached out in his direction.

He rushed to her side. She placed her tiny hand in his and smiled up at him.

"I did not expect to find you awake, little girl."

She frowned. "I had a bad dream, Father. I couldn't sleep so Miss Evans came to sit with me."

A mass of hair had escaped from Prudence's braid. It tangled wildly about her head. Charlotte swept a lock off Prudence's forehead and tucked it behind her ear. "Just for a few minutes." She peered up at him. "Did you wish to sit with Prue for a while, my lord? I can step out into the corridor until I'm needed."

He shook his head. He didn't want her to leave. "You may stay." He sat near the headboard, his knee knocked against hers. She shifted in her seat as if burned. Perhaps it wasn't entirely appropriate to sit on the bed with her, even in this most innocent of situations. He should consider that he might cause her some discomfort. Did she worry over her reputation?

She'd have to have some connections to society, any society, to have that concern. "Why don't you tell us a story, Miss Evans?"

She blinked. He'd caught her off guard.

But she recovered quickly. She tapped a finger to her chin and tilted her head. "Hmm. What kind of story would you like, Prue?"

Prudence fairly danced in her bed. "The little lost princess from the future!"

The light was faint, but Charlotte's blush was still evident. Curiosity egged him on. "I don't believe I've heard that tale before. Please, do share it with us, Miss Evans." Given her evident discomfort, the proper thing would be to suggest a different story, yet a perverse interest in what would cause such a reaction in the calm, steady governess urged him to ignore his better judgment.

And so she began a fantastical story about a future world of such wonders as could never be imagined. The hero of this journey was the princess, who was equal in all ways to a man, and in many ways superior, as she had knowledge of future inventions that defied belief. He found himself as drawn to the story as Prudence. When Charlotte fell silent, he clapped along with his daughter and expressed his admiration for the intrepid princess.

Yet the story was left unfinished. "And when does the princess meet her prince? Does he find the princess and save her from her trials?"

She shook her head. "The princess doesn't need saving."

He smiled. "Perhaps not, but how can she live happily ever after without a prince to marry?"

"Marriage is not the only path to happily ever after. The princess enjoyed her life as it was and wished only to return."

He frowned at her frosty tone. He sensed he'd angered her but couldn't imagine how. "Surely all women long for a family of their own? Without a husband and child to care for, her life would be without purpose."

"There are other things to life than marriage and babies." She leaned past him, her breast grazing his leg, as she kissed Prudence's forehead. "Goodnight, Prue. Sleep tight."

She didn't so much as glance at him as she swept out of the room. What the bloody hell had just happened?

****

Charlotte stomped out of Prue's room. Aggravation refused to allow her to contemplate returning to her bedroom. No way was she going back to bed in the mood she was in. She'd never fall asleep.

She wanted to throw something. Preferably at James's head.

And he had absolutely no idea that he'd just been a complete ass. The confusion on his face when she stormed out was clear. She couldn't blame him. After all, he'd been raised in this century. If events had been different, she'd have believed every stupid word he'd uttered. So many people, even in the future, still believed them.

That thought infuriated her even more. The idea that she could have believed her sole purpose in life was to get married and make babies with some idiot lord who saw her as little other than an incubator chilled her to the bone.

She needed to get out of the house. The wallpapered walls closed in on her as surely as the rough rock passages of the portal cavern. She sucked in breath after breath of stale air. She needed a cool breeze and the freedom of the yard.

The house was locked up for the night, but she knew where Mrs. Bailey left the key to the kitchen door. She would let herself out and be back before anyone could be disturbed by her absence.

She struggled with the lock. She'd left in such a hurry she hadn't brought a candle with her. Moonlight filtered through windows at the ends of the upstairs corridors, but here in the back corner of the kitchen, she could barely make out the key hole.

Finally, the key slipped into the lock, and she won her freedom. At least for a short time. A leisurely stroll through the kitchen herb garden wasn't what she needed. She strode straight through and out the gate at the opposite end. A worn path led down to the stables with branches leading off it—one to a small orchard, the other to the pond where she'd set up James's fishing date with Prue.

Throwing rocks into the water might give her some satisfaction so she veered off to the left and down to the muddy bank. She gathered a number of stone pebbles and skipped them across the water. The moonlight flooded the area, providing more than enough light for her to see.

She threw a rock. *Splash.* That was for living life as a mere extension of a man. Another. *Splash.* That was for James believing a princess was nothing without a prince.

She sank down cross-legged at the edge of the water and took a deep calming breath of the crisp spring air. Mud seeped into the fabric under her bum. She was the idiot, not him. How could she blame him for believing in something he'd been taught was true his whole life? Had she remained with her birth parents, she'd have believed it too.

And what good was she doing Prue with her tales of the future and equality for women? Prue wouldn't have the same opportunities she had. All she was doing was setting the poor girl up to be unhappy with her lot in life. She was trying to teach her she didn't need a man to be happy. That she could be anything she wanted to be.

But it was all a lie. At this point in time, Prue couldn't be anything she wanted to be. If she tried, she'd be ostracized. She might manage to eke out a living or, more likely, live off a pension her father would set up for her. But she wouldn't be allowed to become a surgeon or fly a plane—planes had yet to be invented, and no one was going to allow a woman to cut them open.

So if she filled Prue's head with visions of making a living at some fabulous job, she was setting her up for disappointment.

What should she do? She couldn't bring herself to tell Prue her greatest achievement in life would be to provide an heir for some viscount or earl. She had to find some happy medium. Teach Prue to be true to herself, but within the framework of this society.

Because when she figured out a way to get home, Prue would be left with this society. And from all the hints Lady Tyndale had dropped, there was some scandal in the family's past that continued to rise up and bite them in the arse once in a while. Charlotte may not have planned on this trip to the past, but since she was here, she best make the most of it.

As a governess she was theoretically preparing Prue to be an attractive mate for an appropriate man. Charlotte viewed her job as helping Prue to find future happiness. Finding a man to love and have a family were worthy goals. She had to remind herself of that. Hadn't she spent two years with that loser, Arthur, because she'd dreamed of a happily ever after for herself? One that involved a loving relationship and family, as well as a satisfying career.

She needed to teach Prue to seek different qualities in a man than people would advocate for now. One who respected her and let her be herself. Not just some guy who had the right title and proper bloodlines.

She didn't think James would object if she went about it the right way. He truly cared about Prue's happiness. He was a good father. Just restricted by his upbringing.

So she had that all planned out. Great. But how long was she going to be here? She was no closer to figuring out how to get home than almost two months ago when she first arrived.

She'd taken care of her immediate need for food and shelter, then the rest had gone by the wayside. Not that she didn't want to get home. She may have enjoyed a moment here or there, but this wasn't her home anymore. Her home was in the future. With Steven and Alex. With her job at the hospital and hot, running water.

She needed a plan. Or at least a plan for how to come up with a plan. She laughed at herself. How convoluted was that. Keep it simple, stupid. Start with something easy and work her way around to solving the problem.

Tomorrow she'd find time to slip away before all the guests arrived. Stock the cave with supplies. Prepare to go back through the portal. Bring a lantern and attempt to see through to the other side.

She hadn't exactly been at a hundred percent when she came through. Drugs and fear had clouded her judgment. Not to mention she hadn't had the leisure time to inspect the portal.

She shivered. The pain she'd have to go through to return home turned her stomach. But she had to deal with it. What choice did she have? There was no other way to return.

She nodded to herself. It was just the beginnings of a plan, but all she had for now.

She leaped up and brushed herself off. There was no point in wallowing here in self-pity. The breeze that had been so welcome when she burst through the kitchen door now seemed icy and unfriendly. Her light linen night rail wasn't meant for running around the English countryside in the middle of the night.

Chapter Nine

The next day provided no time for Charlotte to slip away from the house. All hands were required to finish last minute preparations for the guests' arrival. Mrs. Sterling kept everyone busy. No idle hands.

Charlotte left Theresa to help Prue get ready to greet everyone while she helped Mrs. Sterling and the upstairs' maids. They had everything pretty well under control, but an extra set of hands came in handy. The poor woman was as stressed as she'd ever seen her. Guilt wouldn't allow Charlotte to sneak off while so much remained to be done.

At long last Mrs. Sterling declared them ready. But by that time, the first guests had arrived, and Charlotte had to take Prue down to greet them with Lady Tyndale and James. That wasn't so bad. Since this was a country party rather than a ball, the arrivals were spaced throughout the day. She read and played games with Prue in James's study and every once in a while sent Prue out to say hello to the newest arrival.

Miss Crawford arrived in all due splendor, of course. Then stuck like glue to Lady Tyndale's side, greeting all the guests as if she were the lady of the house rather than merely a guest herself.

Prue's mood drooped when Miss Crawford arrived, but she rebounded quickly. She didn't, however, let go of Charlotte's hand, and proceeded to drag Charlotte to the greeting line as well. So it was quite the happy family that greeted the majority of guests. Charlotte tried not to smirk at Miss Crawford's chagrin, but it was tough. The woman sniffed like she smelled something terrible whenever Charlotte stood anywhere within her vicinity. Charlotte almost laughed when Lady Tyndale offered her a handkerchief.

"Have you taken ill dear?" Lady Tyndale asked. She slipped a white lawn square out of her sleeve and handed it to Miss Crawford. "I do hope you feel better. I would not want you to miss any of the festivities. Perhaps you would feel better if you rested a while? I shall send someone to wake you in time to dress for dinner."

Miss Crawford had no choice but to accept graciously and head to the room assigned to her for the duration of the party.

As soon as she was out of earshot, Lady Tyndale complained to Charlotte. "I thought she'd never leave. The nerve of the child. She is not mistress of Tyndale Manor yet." With that, Lady Tyndale stalked off to confer with Mrs. Bailey over a small change she wished to make to the evening meal.

Prue was not to attend dinners during the party, so Charlotte finally found some relative peace and quiet after the last guest arrived, and Prue was released from greeting duty. She retired to her room, exhausted. All hope for scouting out the portal was put on hold until after the guests left. She might have been able to sneak away before the event began, but now that it had started, she wasn't going anywhere soon.

She needed to do something with the supplies she'd gathered though. She was to share her room with other governesses, and she didn't entirely trust that her things would remain untouched. She'd hidden all the modern items from her satchel the day she arrived to avoid the risk of getting caught with any of it. How would she explain?

Besides items not yet invented, she had some valuable stuff in there. Most of the Tyndale staff were trustworthy, but her necklace alone was likely worth more than most of the people here earned in a year, maybe even a decade. It definitely wasn't something a working class girl like herself would be expected to own. If she were caught with such an expensive piece, they'd likely think she stole it from her previous mistress. Her lack of references would suddenly seem suspicious and lead to the assumption she fled persecution for theft.

So when she'd explored the huge house, she'd done so with an eye for a good hiding spot. One hadn't been all that hard to find. The attic was a graveyard of relics from days gone by. None of the staff ventured up there according to Mrs. Sterling.

James had packed all his wife's personal belongings himself and sealed them in that attic space before instructing the staff to leave it alone. The place was thick with dust and cobwebs. With such a large house to clean, the servants weren't going to bother with an attic they'd been told was off limits.

Charlotte, of course, had never been given those directions. She cleaned the space and made it into a getaway for herself. Including a handy-dandy hiding spot among the rafters. She'd considered stuffing her sack in one of the chests of his wife's old clothing but had reconsidered when she realized it was highly likely

Prue would one day wish to rifle through her mother's old belongings. She once had a child come into the A and E after accidentally shooting himself with his grandfather's gun found in the basement. The deadly weapon had to be stashed somewhere Prue couldn't possibly get at it.

Her newly gathered supplies were another thing though. No danger there. She took everything up to the attic and tucked it away in a shadowy corner. No great need for secrecy.

When she returned to her room, her fellow governess had already climbed into bed. Charlotte groaned. Not only had the woman stolen the only comfortable place to sleep in the small room, but her snores made the water pitcher vibrate on its pedestal. Her room was packed tight. A lady's maid lay on a pallet on the floor, and she was pretty certain at least one other servant was assigned to share her room for the duration of the party. She clapped a hand over her nose. Lack of personal hygiene was a definite issue in a room this size.

Charlotte anticipated another sleepless night. She seemed to be racking those up lately.

****

The next day dawned bright and clear, but Charlotte's head felt as if it were filled with cotton. She'd been right in thinking sleep was going to be hard won last night. The party had only begun, and Charlotte already couldn't wait for it to be over.

She dragged herself out of her tiny corner of the mattress, silently cursing Gertrude, her temporary roommate, as the woman hummed while she dressed. Thankfully, the woman was quick. If she'd had to listen to her discordant warbling any longer, she might have thrown something at her. Not the best way to make friends.

She washed and dressed as quick as she could manage. Theresa would get Prue ready for the day, but Charlotte had to accompany her downstairs. Excitement at being a part of the party had probably woken the sweet child hours ago. Getting her to go to bed the night before had been a chore. She never slept in, let alone when she had something she wanted to do so badly. And the little girl could barely contain her glee at being included in the riding party and picnic this afternoon.

Charlotte groaned as she slipped button upon button into the holes on her riding habit. She had to admit that she looked good in the tight maroon fabric, but seriously, she'd never seen so many buttons in her life. She'd never appreciated zippers quite so much.

Prue perched on the edge of a chair when Charlotte arrived in her room. To anyone who didn't know the child, she appeared entirely collected, but Charlotte could sense her agitation. She fairly vibrated off the soft cushions of her seat.

"Looks like you're all ready to go for a ride."

Prue bounced to her feet. "Oh, yes. Father says we're to have a picnic on the far hill. Grandmother wishes to enjoy the warm weather. I may even hold Muffin's reins, while a groom holds my lead line."

"It's a gorgeous day. Perfect for a picnic." Charlotte's pulse picked up its pace. She'd known there would be a picnic at the end of their ride today, but she hadn't been told what direction they were headed. That hill was fairly close to the cave entrance. Maybe she could find a moment to herself to do a little investigating.

They made their way down to the stables where guests interested in joining in on the pre-picnic ride had been instructed to gather in the morning. Those who didn't want to ride would take carriages to the picnic spot in the early afternoon.

Charlotte figured they'd have a full house and was surprised to find only a handful of guests waiting for their horses to be saddled. None of the children were around.

James strolled out of the stable, and her breath caught in her throat. Damn, he looked good in his tight breeches and a blue riding jacket that brought out the color of his eyes. At ten, she'd been too young to appreciate how well the fashions of this age suited the figure of a strong man.

She could definitely appreciate it now. She'd done her fair share of drooling over Colin Firth in *Pride and Prejudice*, but watching on TV fell way short of seeing the real thing. James was definitely the real thing.

"Father!" Prue exclaimed and ran to him.

Charlotte smiled at the girl's exuberance, her heart warming at the pleased expression on James's face. He was a good father. One of the many qualities that had made Charlotte fall in love with him.

Her heart skipped a beat, and she whipped her head around to stare blindly in the opposite direction.

Love? What a disaster. She had no business falling for James. Lord Tyndale— When had she begun thinking of him as James? Nothing could ever come of it aside from heartbreak.

She struggled to get herself under control. How could she act normal after such a realization? Bloody hell. She was now officially one of the biggest clichés on the books.

Governess falls for charge's father.

She was an idiot.

Besides the fact this wasn't a made-for-TV movie where the rich employer fell for the down-on-her-luck nanny, there was the slight issue of her being in the wrong century. She may have been born here, but she'd grown up in the future. That was where she belonged.

"Miss Evans?" Prue placed a hand on her elbow.

Charlotte schooled her features and smiled down at her young charge. "Yes?"

Prue frowned up at her, confusion wrinkling her young brow. "Are you well, Miss Evans? Father called for you several times, but you didn't respond."

Charlotte jerked her head up. James stood a foot away, the same concern on his face as his daughter's. "Oh. I'm so sorry. I...I was lost in my thoughts. How rude of me. Did you need something?"

"I inquired as to your riding ability," James said. "Would you care to accompany us on horseback, or shall you wait for the carriages?"

Prue's smile was so hopeful, Charlotte couldn't resist, even if she wasn't entirely eager to get back up on a sidesaddle. But it was like riding a bike, right? "I have to admit it has been a while since I've ridden, but I was quite accomplished when younger. I would love to ride, if it's not too much trouble."

"I'll have a horse saddled immediately." He made a gesture, and one of the grooms ran off into the barn.

Prue bounced up and down. "Can we go straight away once Miss Evans's horse is ready?"

James frowned and scanned the yard. "I'm afraid

we must wait a few more moments, Prudence. Miss Crawford wished to join us this morning. She appears to be a few moments late."

Prue's little shoulders sagged, and Charlotte's heart twisted. What exactly had the witch said to have the child react in such a way at the mere mention of her name? Charlotte had asked several times but had yet to get a satisfactory answer. She put a comforting hand on Prue's shoulder. Fine tremors swept through her, and Charlotte gave a little squeeze.

Lady Tyndale chose that moment to stroll up to them leading a sweet-looking sable brown mare. "Tyndale, darling. Miss Crawford will not be down for quite some time. I'm afraid there was a mishap with her riding habit. There was quite a large tear in the train. She couldn't possibly ride until it is fixed."

"I trust someone has been sent to assist her?" he asked.

"Of course, darling. But I do suggest you begin the journey to the hill without her. I've seen to it she'll be comfortably situated in a carriage to join us at the picnic when she is feeling quite the thing."

When Tyndale turned to see to Prue's horse, Lady Tyndale bent low to whisper in Prue's ear, just loud enough for Charlotte to hear. "I'm afraid it was all my fault. I may have stepped on the dear thing's hem. So clumsy of me." She put a finger to her lips. "Shh. Not a word to your father." She patted Prue on the cheek and winked at Charlotte.

Prue's happy smile would have been enough to make Charlotte appreciate Lady Tyndale's gesture, but she couldn't help thinking how much more pleasant her own morning would be without having to deal with that harpy's tongue. It also increased her chances of sneaking off to locate the entrance to the cave as well. Without Miss Crawford digging her claws into James and demanding all his attention, he'd spend more time with Prue, leaving Charlotte time to wander off.

She could only hope.

The rest of the guests made quick work of mounting their horses and starting out. Lady Tyndale led the way with a quick wave to James that they'd all meet up at the picnic spot.

James took extra care getting Prue up on a sweet little pony called Muffin. He watched Max, his head groom and Theresa's husband, with an eagle eye while instructing Prue to listen carefully to instructions. Once the groom pronounced Prue all set, he double checked her saddle and spoke quietly with her while observing how she handled the reins and kept her seat.

"We're going to go nice and slow. Max will lead Muffin and give you a lesson along the way. Pay careful attention to him, now."

"Yes, Father." She nodded gravely, schooling her face into a somber expression, but even from across the yard, Charlotte could see the happy gleam in her eyes.

Another groom led a beautiful, dappled gray horse toward Charlotte. "Ooh." She clapped her hands in delight.

"Here you go, miss. Miss Bea will treat you right, she will. She's a real gentle lass." He looped the reins over his elbow and cupped his hands to create a step for Charlotte.

"Thank you, John."

She started. She'd been so engrossed watching Miss Bea that she failed to hear James come up behind her. He stood at her elbow and motioned for John to step back.

John bowed and stepped to the mare's head to keep her steady.

James stooped low and linked his fingers.

She'd have done better with John. She was so conscious of the warmth of James's hand seeping through the thin leather of her borrowed boots, she tangled her skirts trying to hook her leg on the saddle. She blushed with embarrassment.

"Did I mention it's been a while since I rode?" she said as she attempted to put herself to rights before trying again.

"I believe you did." He stood so close she could smell the sweet buttery scent of the scones that had been served with breakfast. "Let me help." He smoothed the twisted fabric of her skirt so it hung correctly once more. That his hand brushed up against her hip, she forced herself to ignore.

The butterflies in her stomach thought that was a bad idea and refused to let her relax. Thankfully she managed to control her instinct to turn in his direction and press herself against the length of him. But she was sorely tempted.

His hand brushed her calf as he linked his fingers once more. "On three. One. Two. Three."

On three she used the upward thrust to leap into the saddle, settling herself onto the horse before attending to her skirts. James's hand lingered on her calf—to keep her steady?—while she got herself arranged. Her heart thundered in her chest. She gripped the reins tight so he wouldn't be able to see the trembling in her hands.

She smiled down on him, trying to play it cool. "Thank you."

"You're most welcome."

The fire in his eyes told her he was as affected by their casual touching as she was. If she didn't know her heart was already entangled, she'd be tempted to take advantage of their attraction. Talk about no strings attached. She certainly wouldn't need to worry about running into him unexpectedly at the mall once she returned home.

She was not cheered by the thought.

****

James kept a critical eye on Max as his head groom carefully instructed Prudence on how to manage her horse. She had, of course, had a number of lessons before today, but she'd never traveled out of the stable yard.

A glow of pride lit him from within. She was shaping up to be quite an accomplished rider. Harriet would have been proud of their daughter.

Finally confident that Max had everything under control, James turned his attention to Charlotte riding beside him. Not that his attention had ever completely left her. At least a portion of him was always aware of her anytime she was near.

It was damned distracting.

What would Harriet think? Would she begrudge him his interest in another woman? Funny, he'd had no qualms when he decided to court Miss Crawford, yet here he was wondering what Harriet would think of Charlotte. Would she approve?

Were Harriet alive, he believed she would have liked Prudence's governess. The two women had many similarities, though his Harriet had a more delicate constitution. Some had called her a wallflower. They hadn't seen how Harriet blossomed when they were alone. How her true personality shone through without the overbearing nature of society stifling her.

Charlotte was unlikely to allow anyone to stifle her nature. Society's dictates seemed of little import to the woman. He admired the way she stood up for Prudence's welfare no matter the obstacle—one reason he was pleased to have her accompany Prudence throughout the house party. She would see to it his daughter suffered no ill effects from the rumors society insisted on dredging up whenever in her presence.

But Charlotte's current position in his household and her attendance on Prudence was not what made the guilt rise up in him like a snake prepared to strike. No, his interest in other positions he envisioned for Charlotte were what caused such conflicting emotions within him.

"How do you fare, Miss Evans? You appear to be adjusting well to the saddle." She may have been away from horses for a good while, but her instruction must have been top notch. Her seat was excellent, her handling of the reins just as should be.

She was a mystery. One that he was quite determined to solve.

"I'm well, thank you. Perhaps a bit tired, is all."

He nodded his understanding. Though riding was as natural to him as breathing, he could well remember the days when he was loath to get in the saddle for the aches and pains it caused his arse. "Would you care to walk for a spell?"

Her deep sigh was answer enough. He began his

dismount before she confirmed her wishes.

"That's a brilliant idea. Thank you."

He led Whiskey to a decent sized patch of green on the side of the path, confident the animal would remain with his snack until called upon to venture forth once more. In the short time since Sebastian gifted the stallion to him, he'd learned the horse was a glutton.

Charlotte remained perched on Miss Bea, a frown on her lovely face. She twitched her skirt to free it from her saddle, twisted, and leaped to the ground with ease.

Impressive, but he was less than pleased. He felt cheated. Damned if he hadn't wanted to help her from the horse. There were so few acceptable reasons to lay his hands upon her person, he wished to take advantage of each and every opportunity. Well, she'd put that hope to rest right quick. Damn.

He stepped back before she noticed him hovering over her like a lovesick swain. "Do you need any assistance with Miss Bea? Shall I hold her reins for you?"

"No, thank you."

His gaze swept along the curve of her hip and the soft swell of her breast as she stretched to tug the reins over Miss Bea's ears. The fit of his breeches strained where before they'd been comfortably loose. He swung toward Whiskey and concentrated on the sweaty odor of heated horse flesh to get his mind off Charlotte's delectable figure. His body remembered too well the feel of hers pressed up against him.

A moment he'd relived in his dreams.

Only in his dreams his mother had not arrived at such an inopportune moment. No, his mother hadn't entered his dreams of Charlotte at all.

Did Charlotte have similar dreams? He hadn't been so foxed not to have noticed her reaction. Had they not been interrupted, he fully believed she'd have allowed him to kiss her.

This line of thought was not helping to calm the heat raging through his body. He was lucky his riding coat covered his manhood, or he'd cause Charlotte a great deal of discomfort.

"It's lovely," Charlotte said, her voice coming from directly behind him.

What? Lovely? He swung to stare at her, surely she wasn't referring to his manhood?

But she wasn't even looking his way. Her gaze was riveted on a slight opening of the trees on their right. The rolling hills stretched out before them. The sight was, indeed, lovely. Not that lovely was the first word he'd want used to describe himself, but he suddenly wished her gaze had been trained on him and not the view.

Sunlight filtered through the trees, casting a glow upon her face made brighter by the beauty of her smile.

"Lovely, indeed."

She turned to him, and the smile faded from her face, replaced by an awareness that he hadn't been speaking of the view. A rosy blush suffused her cheeks, and she cast her gaze toward the path, her heavy lashes covering the brightness of her green eyes.

"I never apologized for my behavior the other night."

The blush deepened. "No need. You'd had quite a bit to drink."

He stepped closer until their bodies were a mere hairsbreadth apart. "Not that much. Merely enough to pursue what I wanted despite knowing the inappropriateness of my actions." A curl of hair escaped the neat confines of her bonnet, and he captured it between his fingertips. The soft, silky texture called out for him to pluck the pins from her hair and let the sweet masses escape. Instead, he brushed the hair behind her ear, tracing the delicate skin with the tip of his finger.

A slight sigh escaped her open lips, and her eyes flew up to meet his gaze. He could swear his hunger was reflected in her gaze. Or was that just what he wanted to see?

He should step back. Instead, he rested his hand along the nape of her neck, keeping her head in place as he lowered his face to hers. The first touch of her lips hinted at the ecstasy to be found in her arms. Soft, warm, and welcoming.

When she didn't push him away in anger, he attempted a bit more. A thrill shot through him as she returned his kiss. He had to taste her. He swept his tongue along her bottom lip, teased the seam of her mouth asking her without words to open to him. She hesitated, and he repeated the motion.

With the smallest of moans, she opened her lips the tiniest bit. A roar of triumph surged through his veins. He kept his body rigidly in control. He ached to drag her against himself, to feel the heat of her all along his body, but he forced himself to remain apart.

She was skittish. Enjoying the kiss, but anything more could cause her to flee and perhaps even avoid being alone with him in the future. And he desperately wanted to be alone with her more often. This was just the beginning.

He hoped.

Chapter Ten

Fear of falling finally snapped Charlotte back to her senses. If she didn't break away from the magic of James's kiss, she was going to collapse to the ground. Her legs were hard pressed to keep her upright.

She tried to ease out of the kiss, but that proved futile. James's grip on the back of her neck was gentle, yet impossible to break. She backed off, but he simply applied a slight pressure, and the kiss heated to boiling once more.

The problem was, she didn't really want to pull away. She wanted to move closer.

Bad idea. She was stuck at Tyndale Manor for who knew how long. She was already in love with her boss. Sleeping with him would take her to a whole new level of screwed.

She moved her hand, which had been inexplicably stroking his bicep, in between them. She meant to shove him away, but instead she gripped his lapel to keep him in place.

Damn it. Her body was not cooperating.

James swirled his tongue in her mouth, and her knees threatened to buckle again. They had to stop.

She pushed against his chest. He resisted for barely a second, then gave in with the grace she'd come to expect from him.

His hand lingered at her neck, teasing the hairs that

refused to stay in the bun she'd so carefully tucked all her hair into this morning. Delicious shivers ran down her body. She could still taste him on her tongue.

Tasted like more.

She cleared her throat. "Umm." Brilliant. What a way with words.

He smiled. "Yes. I'm at a loss for words myself. Perhaps words are superfluous to the moment."

A slight pressure at her neck almost brought her back into him, but she resisted. How she had the strength she didn't know. But she did. "This is a bad idea."

"I beg to differ."

The heat from his gaze could have scorched her, and she lost her train of thought. "What?"

"I believe it's a wonderful idea." His gaze drifted down to rest on her lips. He cupped her jaw, stroked her bottom lip with his thumb.

She resisted the urge to take his thumb into her mouth. Completely not the signal she needed to give off at the moment. She let her mouth fall open slightly to aid in her quest for enough air to sustain life. Her lungs were fit to burst, her heart thundering in her chest.

Finally gathering up her strength, she took a step back.

And bumped up against Miss Bea.

Thankfully, James took the hint and didn't pursue her. He turned to his own mount. He whistled, and the horse picked his head up from the snack he'd been making of a clump of grass. "Mayhap it's time to continue on to the picnic. Prudence will be waiting on us."

Prue. Right. What had she been thinking? "Yes,

that's probably best." She grabbed onto Miss Bea's reins like they were a lifeline and put one step in front of the other, ignoring the man walking silently beside her.

Words bubbled to the tip of her tongue, but she couldn't let them go. Her face flamed at the idea of voicing any of the thoughts currently on her mind. Where did he see this going between them? Did he have any feelings for her other than lust? Did he enjoy their kiss as much as she had?

She was pretty sure the answer was a resounding 'yes' to the last question, but she had no idea about the others. And she couldn't bring herself to ask. Did she really want to know the answers?

If he did have feelings for her or actually wanted to have some kind of relationship with her other than employer to employee what would she do? What did she want?

Her mind spun with the possibilities. Bloody hell. How had everything gotten so complicated?

And why did she feel so awkward, yet he could shake it off like nothing? She snuck a peak at him under her lashes.

The color in his face was a trifle high, but the path they hiked had a steady rise to it. She found herself breathing a little heavy as she kept pace. That could account for his heightened color and the sweat glistening along his brow. She swept her gaze down to take him all in. Okay. So maybe he wasn't completely unaffected. As he walked, he made an uncomfortable looking shifting motion with his hips. The long front panels of his coat hid the evidence, but if she had to guess, an erection was making this trek less than pleasant for him.

She twisted her head away so he wouldn't see her grin. She shouldn't be pleased, but damn, she was suffering from her own arousal, and it was nice to know she wasn't the only one.

He cleared his throat. "Ah, I see we have arrived at our destination." He gestured toward a clearing in the trees. "Wait a moment, Miss Evans—Charlotte, if I may?"

She nodded. Given their recent make-out session, she figured being on a first name basis should go without saying. Then again, this was the Regency, not the twenty-first century.

"Call me James." He paused. "When we are not in company, I should say."

She snorted silently to herself. Yeah, she could imagine what Miss Crawford would say if she heard Charlotte call him by his given name. Such impertinence! She'd likely suggest a whipping and turning her away without references.

She made to move on, but he put a hand on her arm to stop her. It was the barest of touches, but it stopped her dead in her tracks. She liked the warmth of his hands upon her and after the kiss they'd shared, could well imagine how his hands would feel on other parts of her body.

Stop that! she chided herself. She didn't trust her voice, so she raised an eyebrow in question.

"I feel I owe you an apology. I trust you understand that you are under no obligation to return my advances. Your position in my employ will not change should you tell me to go to the devil."

Her eyebrow rose higher. The cursing for one. For

the other, she had never expected him to say he was sorry for kissing her. "I believe you."

With a nod, he continued. She followed only a step or two behind.

She did believe him. Her position as Prue's governess was safe as long as Prue needed her. He wasn't the type to use his position of power to pressure her if she chose to ignore this attraction between them. He'd probably just let it go.

She should be happy about that.

So why wasn't she?

****

"Are you okay, sweetie?" Charlotte tucked Prue against her side and cradled her, though Prue held her little body stiff.

Fire lit Prue's eyes as she glared at the group of giggling girls, their maids standing nearby with various expressions of worry and adulation.

"They're stupid. I hate them all."

Charlotte put a finger under Prue's chin and forced her to look her in the eye. "Don't say that. Tell me what they did, and we'll see if we can't work this out."

Prue's chin trembled, and Charlotte wanted to take a swing at the little brats herself. Similar urges had plagued her all throughout the picnic. Most of the kids weren't bad. Prue's friend Regina was actually a darling child. No, it was one or two spoiled little devils who were plain mean-spirited bullies.

She forced herself to view the situation from all angles as Prue told her the teasing words of her playmates. And yup, the same names popped up as the ring leaders. Little Lady Catherine Bellgrove and Lord William Hepworth.

Ugh. Both kids came from families high up on the social ladder if the maids were to be believed. And those maids were less than useless. Those kids shot rainbows out of every orifice as far as their caregivers were concerned. What a nightmare.

"They actually said that?" Wow. Making fun of a girl's dead mother. That was low. And from the way James cherished his wife's portrait, she'd swear he had loved his wife, deeply. Still did, she was pretty sure. And why did they care anyway? Wasn't marrying for money the norm around here?

"I'm sorry, what?" Now she was confused. Dragging an accurate story out of an upset eight-year-old wasn't an easy task.

"They know about Grandmama," she whispered.

Charlotte peered down at Prue's stark white face. "What about your grandmother?"

"That—that she worked in a *brothel* before marrying Grandpapa."

Holy crap. Her mind blanked for a second. Couldn't be. She thought back on all her interactions with James's mother. True, the lady was a bit unorthodox for the times, but a prostitute? She couldn't see it.

Yet Prue sure seemed to believe it was true. Even if she likely didn't know what a brothel was, she evidently knew it was a bad thing. And was seriously upset about it if Charlotte was reading the little girl's grim expression correctly.

Charlotte smoothed Prue's hair back away from her face and tucked a stray strand behind her ear. She squatted down so they could look each other in the eye. "You listen to me. Don't you worry about what they're saying. Your grandmother is a wonderful woman who loves you with all her heart. That's all that matters. And I know it's hard not to hate those kids when they're saying such mean things, but I'll tell you what. I feel sorry for them. And I think they're just jealous."

"Jealous?" Her gentle brown eyes were stretched wide, her mouth hung open the tiniest bit. "They have no scandal to their names. Why would they be jealous?"

"Look around, Prue. Where are their parents?"

Prue scanned the area, pairing parents with kids. Catherine and William's parents had not attended the picnic. Charlotte was well aware they'd elected to stay at the house with a few of the older members of the house party. They'd barely acknowledged their children other than when they first arrived and paraded them in front of the others as their pride and joys, then relegated them to the care of their nursemaids.

Prue shrugged. "I know not."

"And where is your father?"

"Over there." She pointed to where James sat on a blanket, Lady Crawford at his side. The witch had latched onto him the minute she arrived, but before that he'd spent most of his time with Prue. Every few moments he glanced toward them and smiled. His thoughts obviously never far from his daughter, even while Lady Crawford tried her best to monopolize his attention.

"Uh-huh." Charlotte smiled. "Your father is here and paying attention to you. *You're* here because you're his world and he wants to be around you. *They're* here because your father and grandmother invited them so you'd have someone to play with."

Prue's face lightened. She was beginning to

understand what Charlotte was telling her.

"So I should let them say whatever they want to me?"

"Hell, uh, heck no."

Could the child's eyes get any wider? Charlotte fought off a blush. She had to be careful about cursing. She didn't do it often, and even when she did, her curses were pretty mild, but here, even the weakest curse was a monstrous thing.

"You can stick up for yourself. Tell them to mind their own business. Or ignore them and tell me what's going on." At the hopeful expression on Prue's face, she said, "Why don't we stay a little closer together. That way I can hear what's going on. Send me a signal if you want me to step in."

Prue nodded eagerly, the sadness of a few moments ago banished. She popped out of Charlotte's reach and raced back to the other children.

Bang! Shards of wood exploded from the tree near Charlotte's head. She yelped and ducked to the ground. *What the hell?* Was that a gun shot? Ridiculous. Who'd be shooting at her?

Piercing screams filled the air around her. Something was wrong with her arm. A stinging pain spread from her shoulder down to her elbow.

James shouted a warning. Next thing she knew, he was on top of her, yelling orders at everyone.

"Prue? Where's Prue?" She struggled to get to her feet. She had to find Prue. What if she were hurt?

"Prue's fine. She's fine. Stay down." James's voice was gruff, his hold implacable. She couldn't move an inch.

The ground trembled from horses pounding the

ground and shrieking in fright. Two of the grooms struggled to keep the normally peaceful animals in check. James yanked her back into the line of trees as one escaped and thundered past the spot they'd crouched but a moment ago.

It all happened in an instant but seemed to move in slow motion. She searched frantically for Prue and found her only a few yards away, the head groom, Max, shielding her with his body. Theresa seemed in charge of the group of nursemaids, instructing them to keep their heads down and their bodies protecting the children. Sobs of fright came from the maids as well as the kids.

James shoved her to the other side of a tree, then strode into the clearing and issued orders. People scattered to do his bidding.

She leaned heavily against the solid bulk of an evergreen. Her knees wobbled. The trunk was the only thing keeping her upright.

James grabbed her hand and squeezed. She started. She hadn't noticed his return.

"My lord?" One of the footmen ran up to them. "We gave chase, but the scoundrel was fleet of foot and escaped us. We're searching the area for accomplices, but Max feels certain if there were other poachers about, they've fled along with their friend."

James nodded. "Thank you, Sam. Gather all our guests together and see them safely back to the manor. See to the children first."

Sam ran off to follow his lord's bidding.

"Where's Prue?" she asked again. She couldn't make her out among the children getting to their feet near their picnic spot.

"I instructed Max to spirit her away the minute the way was clear. She should be almost back at the manor by now."

Her voice trembled as she said, "Good. That's good."

"Are you well?" James scanned her from head to foot.

"I…I'm fine. What happened?" She winced as pain lanced down her arm.

He took her elbow in a gentle grip. "You've been injured."

She twisted her neck and tilted her chin to locate the source of her pain. The maroon fabric of her riding habit was shredded from her left shoulder to her elbow. Slivers of wood dotted her arm with blood dribbling from each small cut. *Damn.*

"Oh, dear. I'm afraid this outfit is ruined."

"That is immaterial. We must return to the manor and have the doctor see to you immediately."

No. Way. No nineteenth century quack was getting anywhere near her arm. The relatively minor injury would end up infected, and next thing she knew she'd lose her arm. *Nuh-uh.* "Don't worry. It's nothing more than a few scratches. I'll take care of it myself."

James pursed his lips, displeased to say the least.

****

James scowled at Charlotte's shoulder. He wanted to yell at her for her stubborn refusal to send for the doctor but bit his tongue. Instead, he sat at her side while Theresa assisted him in removing slivers of wood from Charlotte's arm.

Theresa cast him a disapproving glance, her sense of propriety offended at him attending Charlotte in such a personal manner.

The hell with that. He wasn't leaving. In fact, he wished Theresa to the devil so he could be alone with Charlotte.

He dropped yet another piece of bark and skin into the bloodied water in the washbasin Theresa held. His hand shook. He fought back his nausea, wishing he could strike the image of that bullet striking the tree so close to Charlotte's head. And Prue...a mere ten feet away.

Prue was fine. She was fine. He kept telling himself that over and over. If anything had happened to her...he refused to finish the thought. Max deserved a reward for the way he jumped to see to Prue's welfare. Theresa had also done her duty well, impressing him with the way she took charge of the other nursemaids and saw to the children's safety when others appeared ready to abandon their charges. Yes, both would be rewarded greatly.

Charlotte hissed. Theresa winced as he removed a particularly large and deep piece of wood from Charlotte's arm. Charlotte twisted to inspect her wound. "Was that the last of it?"

He inspected the injury. Bloodied, thankfully not torn as badly as he feared, and no sign of any other debris. He nodded. "Yes, I believe so."

"If you please, my lord, hand me the linen." Charlotte nodded to a pile of clean linen she'd insisted on gathering before allowing anyone near her wound. He placed the cloth in her hand. "Thank you."

With Theresa's help, Charlotte's shoulder was soon cleaned and wrapped.

Perhaps now he could get to the bottom of what

had just happened. "Theresa, please leave us." His study was scarcely a scandalous place to have a private conversation with his daughter's governess. They had met here often enough in the past. "I must speak with Miss Evans. I assure you she will be quite safe with me."

Theresa nodded, then gathered the mess they'd made and left, closing the door quietly behind her.

Once the door clicked shut, he asked Charlotte, "Why is someone trying to kill you?"

She gasped. Her head jerked up to meet his gaze. "What?"

Perhaps she didn't have any idea, but he was certain. He'd even instructed the staff to be sure someone was always on hand to watch over her whenever she left the manor. Discreetly, of course. He was certain she would not approve. "Someone is trying to do you harm. I thought the flowerpot falling as we were in the area the other day an odd coincidence, yet I had no reason to believe it was anything but an accident. But when someone shoots at you, there's no mistaking the intent."

She gathered the hair that had come out of her bonnet, removing and replacing pins to straighten her appearance. "I have no idea what you're talking about. Didn't Max say it was a poacher?"

He snorted. "Poachers generally avoid crowds. They certainly don't shoot into one."

"Then he must have been shooting at one of the guests." She stood. "I should go clean up." The shoulder of her dress was in tatters. The shards of wood had damaged it beyond repair, and he'd ripped the fabric further to expose her wounds.

He blocked her path to the door. "You can clean up in a moment. We need to discuss this."

She refused to meet his gaze, her chin up and tilted to the side, staring in stony silence over his shoulder.

"Miss Evans—Charlotte." He lowered his voice to a whisper and gently urged her chin up. "I know you're frightened. So am I. I want to help you, and I must know what this is all about in order to do so. Please, talk to me."

Tears glistened in her eyes. A muscle twitched near her eye. Yet she didn't break down. Didn't ask him to save her from her troubles. "I can take care of myself."

No doubt. He had never thought highly of strong women, but Charlotte had shown him how much there was to admire in a person who didn't need rescuing. He'd loved his wife, but she'd been weak. Unable to stand against the sometimes harsh views of society. A great deal of his energy had gone toward bolstering her, trying to prove his love. Charlotte would demand to stand on her own. Was there no middle ground?

"I feel assured that you can. However, why must you? You have become a valued member of this household. I would not wish to replace you." He winced at his inept handling of the situation. He sounded as though he only valued her for her position in his employ when the truth was so much more. "Prudence has come to care for you greatly." *As do I.*

He couldn't tell her so. A kiss shared in private was one thing. Were he to confess his desire for further intimacy, he would be putting her in a most difficult situation. Not to mention the sheer folly of creating such a scandal. His daughter would be subject to further upset.

She stiffened. Took a step back. "I understand completely if you must let me go. If, and I'm not so sure you're right, someone is out to kill me, I wouldn't dream of exposing Prue to any danger." She nodded. "Yes. You're right. I should leave immediately."

He reeled back. What just happened? "That's not what I meant at all." He ran a hand through his hair. How had this conversation taken such a turn? "You're not going anywhere. You're going to sit down and tell me the truth about yourself once and for all."

****

The truth? She suppressed a snort. He couldn't handle it. Shit. She couldn't handle it.

Fury and fright warred within Charlotte. Someone was trying to kill her? No. That was too much. Her hands shook. She pressed her hands into her sides to at least *hide* the trembling if she couldn't *stop* it.

She'd worked hard to keep her presence in this century a secret from anyone that knew her from her past. Yet—she was close to the portal. Near the caves. Had the person who'd tried to kill her and Alex back then set about to finish the job?

There were no cameras here, no television, no computers that made age progression shots of missing kids. Even if someone from her past saw her, she wasn't ten years old anymore. She hardly resembled the girl she'd once been. No one could recognize her. Could they?

No. Focus on the fury. The fright was too much.

"Excuse me? I'm going to do what?" She poked a finger into his chest. "If I decide to go, I'll go. Don't think you can order me around, My Lord High and Mighty."

The shock on his face was almost comical. Maybe it would have been if his astonishment didn't disappear so fast. He clacked his teeth together, a muscle twitched in his jaw. His eyes narrowed, and he stuck his hands on his hips, jutting his chest out and inhaling. She braced herself.

"A simple 'my lord' will do."

She blinked, picturing her face mirroring the astonishment she'd seen on his only moments before. Laughter quickly followed. His lips quirked, and she lost it. Maybe the stress got to her, but suddenly she could barely breathe she laughed so hard. She would have bent over, but her corset prevented any such movement and didn't help with the breathlessness.

His hand at her back guided her to a settee in front of the fireplace. He sat next to her, their thighs touching, his arm resting behind her on the couch back.

Her hysteria slowly subsided. She wiped away the tears of mirth and gave him a quick grin to show she had come back to her senses.

She meant to turn away but got stuck by the heat in his gaze. A mere inch separated them. Later, she'd probably curse the instinct that took over, but when she was rewarded by the sweet press of his lips against hers, and the fire that lit her from within, she couldn't get up the resolve to resist the temptation so close at hand.

He didn't seem to mind. And when she inched closer, his hand rose to cup her cheek. He tilted his head, deepening the kiss, and drew her onto his lap.

Glorious. She doubted she'd ever used that word in her life—too grand, too dramatic, and not her style—but right now she couldn't think of a single word that better described the pleasure that rushed through her.

His moan, and the hardness in his breeches, told her he agreed.

The door creaked open. "Lord Tyndale? Are you in here?"

Charlotte jumped off James's lap and scurried over to the opposite corner of the sofa. She peered over her shoulder and stifled her groan when she recognized Miss Crawford. By the daggers Miss Crawford shot out of her eyes, she hadn't missed what had been taking place.

Her expression morphed into a light smile, and she glided into the room as if noticing nothing. "There you are, my lord." She gave a little start. "Oh my. Miss Evans. I didn't see you there. We were all so worried about you. I trust my lord has summoned the doctor on your behalf?"

Charlotte had to give her credit. She was an amazing actress.

James shook his head. "Miss Evans has refused to see a doctor despite my urging her to do so." He stood. "Is there something I can do for you, Miss Crawford?"

"I hate to interrupt, but I have done my best to soothe our—" She bit her lip and tilted her head as if hiding a blush, though none appeared to redden her cheeks. "—your guests' fears, but I feel they would benefit from your strong, commanding presence. We would not be able to help feeling the situation is completely under control if you are present. I'm sure Miss Evans would agree the guests must come first."

Charlotte rolled her eyes. She couldn't help it. *Laying it on a bit thick, aren't you dear?* Of course, she couldn't say that out loud, but even thinking it made her feel a bit better. "Miss Crawford is correct. And I'm fine. Plus, I really should see to Prue."

"Tell her I'll be up to see her in a short while." James crooked his elbow for Miss Crawford. Not that he had much choice as she already hung upon his arm.

They swept from the room, and Charlotte was left with her thoughts.

And boy did she have a lot to think about.

Chapter Eleven

James didn't know how he made it through the rest of the day. The numerous birthday toasts at dinner made him feel like a prize stallion on display. The feeling wasn't helped by Miss Crawford attaching herself like a leech to his arm and making sure they remained the center of attention at all times. A few weeks ago, he would have been delighted. Now, he couldn't keep from comparing her to Miss Evans, and she fell short in every way.

His enchantment with her pretty face could no longer disguise her basic lack of respect for others, her appalling manners, horrible sense of humor, and complete lack of wit. How had he ever considered attaching himself to such a woman for the rest of his life? Thank goodness she hadn't witnessed his kiss with Miss Evans. Lord knew what the woman would do were she to suspect his interest had turned to his daughter's governess.

They took another turn around the drawing room. Miss Crawford's claws digging into his forearm. He forced himself to smile at her jokes, the non-offensive ones at least, and keep up his half of the conversation. Thankfully, the last didn't take much effort on his part. She'd been speaking for the past ten minutes non-stop. He'd ceased paying attention a good nine minutes ago. Come to think of it, he should probably take heed to what she was saying or he might find himself agreeing to accompany her during the game of charades planned for later that evening.

"I am certain you will agree that Mr. Lawrence is the superior painter. Lady Swinton had her portrait done and has recommended him highly for ours." Several guests sniggered at her overloud comment, one she obviously meant to be overheard.

Wait. Did she just imply… "Ours?" He scowled down at her and steered them into a private corner where their conversation would not be observed. "I am afraid I must disabuse you of the notion that we will at any point require a portrait of the two of us together, Miss Crawford."

Her spine stiffened. Her hand spasmed on his sleeve. "A poor choice of words in front of your guests, my lord." She averted her gaze. "I did not mean to pressure you into declaring your intentions too soon. Please forgive me."

He ran a hand through his hair. Damn. She wasn't entirely to blame for her conclusions. He had at one point seriously considered a proposal. And he'd been well aware she would respond in the positive. But these past few weeks had shown him quite clearly they would never suit. This needed to be made clear without further delay or there were those who might think a proposal imminent, and Miss Crawford's reputation would be tarnished when none was made.

"I'm terribly sorry, Miss Crawford, if I led you to—"

She dropped his arm and stepped away. "I see Miss Leighton signaling me from across the room. I had promised to play a round of whist with my dear friend.

Perhaps we may speak of this later, Lord Tyndale?" She didn't give him time to respond but sped across the room to a surprised Miss Leighton who jumped when Miss Crawford suddenly appeared at her side.

Later then.

He caught his mother's eye and made his way to her side.

"Do be more careful, Tyndale." She tapped his arm and raised a brow. "I gather the lovely Miss Crawford no longer holds your interest?"

He nodded. "I'm afraid I was wrong in thinking we might suit."

She put a hand over her heart. "Thank goodness. I never could stand the girl."

"I was well aware of that fact. Though I never did understand why you never said a word against her."

"Would you have listened?"

He analyzed his pursuit of Miss Crawford. A pretty face, acceptable family, and an eagerness to conform to his desires was all he'd noticed. Lust, yes. Love, not a hint. That had seemed sufficient. He'd had no desire to replace Harriet in his heart, and Miss Crawford stood no chance of doing so. Perfect.

Until he met Miss Evans and realized he could love another woman.

That he could love one more fiercely, more fervently than he'd ever loved Harriet should disturb him. But it didn't. He somehow knew Harriet would be pleased with his choice. That loving someone as worthy as Charlotte didn't diminish his first love.

Harriet had said as much. Once she realized she was dying, she told him that he would move on one day, and he had her blessing. He'd assured her he'd do no such thing. She laughed at him. "You'll see," she'd said, then dissolved into a fit of coughing, ending the conversation.

The guests drifted off to bed shortly after midnight. With his mother playing hostess, he escaped with the first of them. He should have gone straight to bed, but even though he'd checked on Prudence several times since the incident earlier, he would never get any sleep without seeing her safely in bed first.

The floor creaked as he made his way down the corridor to Prudence's room. Up ahead, a meager light shone through the crack in the door left ajar. He rushed the last few steps. Why was her door open? With all the guests in the house, he'd left strict instructions to keep her door locked.

He nudged the door open. Movement at eye level startled him. He ducked. Narrowly missed getting bashed in the head. He grabbed his attacker around the waist, lifting and heaving the unexpectedly light figure out of his daughter's room.

He raised a fist, then stared in shock at Charlotte. Chest heaving, she clutched a hand to her breast. "What the hell was that?" she asked in a hissing whisper.

After a reassuring glance to make sure their noise hadn't woken Prudence, and gesturing for Theresa, who hovered wide-eyed in the darkness, to lock the door behind him, he grabbed Charlotte by the elbow and guided her toward the stairs. "We can't talk here," he whispered. "Come with me."

All the rooms contained multiple guests who'd come for the party. Even Charlotte's room was packed tight with governesses and ladies' maids. They didn't have many options. He could think of no other place than his suite where they could speak in private.

He paused at the corner leading to his door, listening for any indication his guests might be up and able to witness him sneaking Prudence's governess into his room. That was one confrontation he had no interest in having.

All quiet. Half a dozen steps and he whipped the door open then dashed inside to the relative safety of his private domain.

She faced him, chin up, back against the wall. Her eyes wide, her lips slightly parted. The warm glow from the fire cast light and shadow across her face. What was she thinking? Had their kiss from that afternoon consumed her thoughts as it had his?

He meant to guide her toward the set of chairs before the fire, but when he stepped close, her light, cinnamon scent, and the soft, silky feel of her arm hit him hard with the memory of their kiss, and he couldn't resist trying to repeat the moment.

****

Charlotte's heartbeat tripled as James leaned into her. Her pulse warred with her head. She never should have allowed him to lead her here. This was a bad idea. Dangerous. She hadn't been able to—hadn't wanted to—resist him earlier with pain shooting down her arm and the threat of a killer on the loose. The comfort and excitement of his kisses were preferable to the uncertainty she'd been feeling. Now that the pain had subsided and she'd rationally concluded James was flat out wrong about someone being after her, did she really expect to be able to resist sleeping with her boss when his extremely comfy looking bed stood not three feet away?

And if she let him kiss her again, here, where no one would interrupt them, she had no doubt they'd end up making good use of their privacy.

Head over heart. She'd always been a practical woman, more's the pity. She put a hand on his chest, ignored his warmth and the steady beat of his heart. "Stop. We shouldn't."

To his credit, he stopped immediately. Her resolve weakened. Even in her century, being a female doctor didn't come easy. She'd had to fend off her fair share of men in powerful positions who thought it their right to treat a woman any way they wanted. James actually respected her wishes—one of the things she loved about him. Even if that love was futile.

She had to keep that in mind. This was going nowhere, and the more she fancied this man, the harder time she'd have when she finally figured out a way to return home, without him. She skirted him to take a seat in a high-backed chair near the fireplace, staring into the flames as she struggled to calm her traitorous heartbeat.

"I'm sorry. I didn't bring you here for that purpose. I do believe we need to discuss what transpired earlier today." His strained tone brought her head up in time to witness a grimace quickly hidden. He settled into the chair next to her.

"James," a sleepy voice whispered from behind her, from deep within the heavily curtained depths of the bed.

She spun in her chair, mouth gaping open. *Who the*... A pale white hand drew the curtains back to reveal the last person she'd have suspected. "Miss Crawford?" Her voice cracked, it rose so high at the end.

James's swiftly indrawn breath told her he was just as surprised at their unwelcome visitor.

"James! What is *she* doing here?" Miss Crawford's voice trembled. Even though she was partially hidden in the shadows of the bed, Charlotte could see that she wore only a shift tied loosely to reveal a wide strip of naked skin.

"You know what? Forget this. I'm out of here." If anything were to cool her libido, this was it. She had enough to deal with. She didn't need little miss nude's drama. She jumped out of the chair and made a beeline for the door.

Not quick enough. James grabbed her arm and pulled her against his chest. "Wait. This is not what it seems."

"Really?" she drawled. He was in for a surprise. "So Miss Crawford didn't sneak into your room in the middle of the night in an attempt to compromise herself and force you into asking her to marry you?" She'd read enough novels to be familiar with that particular trope. Used to be one of her favorites. Not anymore.

Eyebrows raised, jaw slack, he blinked like a patient woken in the middle of the night to have their blood pressure checked. She'd have laughed at his stupefied expression, but she wasn't even remotely amused.

Miss Crawford added nails to the chalkboard. "I demand an explanation, James. Just what is your governess doing in your room at this hour of night? This is highly improper, and I must let you know I will not stand for such behavior when we are wed."

James maneuvered Charlotte back to the chair.

"Please stay. I will attend to you in a moment." He spun around and marched toward the bed. "Miss Crawford. I must insist you leave my room immediately. I attempted to make my intentions clear this afternoon yet you—"

Miss Crawford leapt from the bed into James's arms. "Oh, I'm so glad to hear you say that. I must confess I was beginning to worry you would delay our engagement past the point of bearing."

Charlotte stifled a disbelieving laugh, and the witch cast her a scathing glare. Damn, but the girl was clueless. Or, at least, so convinced she would always get her way she hadn't noticed the tight set of James's shoulders or the furious puff of air he expelled as he attempted to withdraw himself from her tight grasp.

He finally threw off Miss Crawford's tentacles, sending the woman reeling back until she staggered to a stop against the bedpost. "Get out. I have no intention of marrying you. Had you not fled from me so hastily this evening, you would have known as much."

The door creaked, and someone gave a loud shriek. Charlotte swiveled toward the sound.

Miss Crawford's maid hovered in the hallway, the door wide open. She scanned the scene in James's bedroom, her eyes widened, and the color drained from her face when she caught sight of Charlotte.

Charlotte couldn't help a twinge of sympathy for the poor girl. She probably had strict instructions to catch Miss Crawford in James's arms and raise the alarm so the "lovers" could be caught in the act. Charlotte threw quite a wrench in that plan.

"Agnes." Miss Crawford gasped. "It's not what you think. Please, don't say a word to my parents."

With a subtle twitch of her head, she sent the maid scurrying backward. Agnes slammed the door. Her cries for Mrs. Crawford rang loud in the midnight silence as she ran down the corridor.

"Shit," James cursed.

Miss Crawford grasped a hand to her breast, clutching her shift tighter about her neck. "Oh, dear. What are we to do now? This is terrible. My reputation will be ruined. Agnes will never keep a secret from my mother. She's likely running to her room at this very moment. My father will insist you do right by me."

Charlotte itched to wipe the smug smile off her face. Had she really thought Miss Crawford an accomplished actress? Now she could barely contain her glee that her plan appeared to be working. After all, Charlotte was nothing more than a governess. From Miss Crawford's point of view, no one would care that Charlotte was also found in James's bedroom.

Forget that. She wasn't going to allow it, if for no other reason than Prue would suffer with such a wicked stepmother. Never mind the idea of James married to Miss Crawford made her want to scream.

Pounding on the door set her into motion. She leapt up, rushing to Miss Crawford's side just as the door burst open.

Miss Crawford's parents burst into the room. Mr. Crawford's face livid with rage, his wife barely hiding a smirk entirely too reminiscent of her daughter's. James looked ready to spit fire, his face almost as red as Mr. Crawford's, his hands clenched on his hips.

Charlotte forced herself between the two men.

****

The rest of his life flashed before his eyes as James

glared back at the angry father. This glowering animosity would disappear the second he agreed to marry Miss Crawford, but what once had seemed a promise for a bright future, now appeared doomed to abject misery for all involved.

Should he do what society would demand of him, or what his heart told him was the right choice?

The cage of society's moral hypocrisy closed his throat, preventing speech. Miss Crawford had created this situation to gain her own desires, yet he'd be the one forced to repair the damage to her reputation or suffer the consequences. If not for Prudence, he would be tempted to fling Miss Crawford's behavior in her parents' face and send them to the devil. But such callous behavior would cause scandal to taint his name as well, and children always suffered the consequences of their parents' flaws more deeply than the adults.

As often happened when he'd been a child faced with the disdain of his peers due to his mother's low birth and dubious past, his fists clenched. Blind rage at this duplicitous family surged through his veins. Society may be satiated with a tale of eager lovers leading to a quick marriage, but the Crawfords would know they'd played a dangerous game, and all would not go as smoothly as they'd no doubt planned. He stepped forward.

Charlotte's hand slapped to his chest brought him up short. Her other arm stretched toward Mr. Crawford, whose eyes narrowed and jowls quivered. Likely, he'd never had anyone dare stand up to him in such a manner. James had to admire her spirit.

"No need for violence, my lords." She gave them each a pointed smile and apparently satisfied she had their full attention, dropped her hands, and strolled over to place an arm across an astonished Miss Crawford's shoulders. She placed a silencing finger to her lips. "We should let Miss Prudence get some rest, poor child." She indicated the empty bed. With the curtains drawn closed, for all anyone knew Prudence could be cocooned inside.

Noise at his door gave evidence that they'd drawn a crowd. Too much to hope they could have managed this among themselves.

Charlotte appeared unaffected. She smiled and ushered everyone out of the room, shutting the door in the faces of his gawking guests. "So much excitement. I'm sure you all heard the ruckus?" With the arm not wrapped around the cause of the "ruckus," Charlotte plucked a cloak out of Mrs. Crawford's limp grasp and swung it up and around to cover Miss Crawford. "You'll all be happy to know that Miss Prudence is quite fine. All this uproar for nothing."

His mother charged through the crowd. "Prudence? Did something happen? What's going on?"

All James could do was force a relaxed expression on his face as if he weren't about to be forced into declaring his intentions for a horrible woman in order to save her from well-deserved ruination. Thankfully, Charlotte seemed to have the situation well in hand.

"Your granddaughter is perfectly fine, Lady Tyndale. No need to worry." She squeezed his mother's hand and then beamed at Miss Crawford. "I am sure you will wish to know all about Miss Crawford's kind act this night. Such a kindness toward Miss Prudence."

Miss Crawford gave a forced smile, though her brow furrowed in reflection of the confusion they all felt. She gave a shaky laugh. "I hate to keep everyone from their beds. Perhaps we can continue this discussion in private?"

"Nonsense. Such modesty, a real credit to your upbringing. You must be so proud of your daughter, Mrs. Crawford."

Mrs. Crawford stuck her nose in the air. "Naturally."

"But what happened?" his mother asked.

"With all the excitement today, dear Miss Prudence had great difficulty sleeping. She became quite scared and naturally wished for the reassuring comfort of her father's presence." Charlotte stepped away from his room, leading everyone toward the stairs where the guests could take the adjacent corridor back to their individual rooms.

James followed, marveling at the way she managed a group who would normally never take orders from a governess.

"I tried to convince the dear child to wait until morning, but she eluded me and made her way from the nursery. Without a light to find her way, she became lost and wandered near Miss Crawford's room. I had not thought to search for her there. Dear, sweet Miss Crawford—" Charlotte's smile was sickeningly sweet and as insincere as any that had ever touched Miss Crawford's lips. "—heard Miss Prudence's cries and rushed to help. Lord Tyndale wasn't in his room, so she sat with Miss Prudence until he returned. When I couldn't find my charge, I sought out Lord Tyndale. We heard Miss Crawford's sweet voice singing a lullaby and found her easing dear Miss Prudence's fears. That's when Lord and Lady Crawford came searching for their daughter."

Charlotte beamed at the crowd staring at her with their jaws trailing along the floor, his own included.

His mother clapped her hands, then enveloped Miss Crawford in a tight embrace. "Such kindness," she exclaimed.

"Yes." He grit out the lie. "I'm greatly impressed by your daughter's kindness to mine." He gave the Crawfords a short bow. "And to repay that kindness—" He smiled. Finally, an end in sight. "—I'll allow you all to return to your rooms and return to your rest."

The guests laughed and slowly made their way to their rooms.

He breathed a sigh of relief and turned to give Charlotte his heartfelt thank you for rescuing him from Miss Crawford's repugnant trap.

Empty corridors stretched in either direction. She was gone.

Damn.

Chapter Twelve

"Why do they stay so late? Should not they have left yesterday as so many of the others? Why do they hang about?"

Charlotte secretly agreed with Prue, but that wouldn't help the girl deal with the pushy busybodies who wanted to know all the details of three nights ago. The viscount's guests smelled a scandal and weren't happy with the watered down, boring explanation they'd been given. Charlotte and Lady Tyndale had been forced to run interference for days. Luckily, the children's activities were separate from the adults, so for the most part they'd been able to keep Prue away from the worst of it.

"They'll be gone soon enough. Have a little patience." Easier said than done. Charlotte peeked over the railing at the mess of people milling around in the entry. She wanted to get a broom or something and shoo them out the front door. It was only a little past noon though, so really not that late at all. The realization didn't help.

Mrs. Sharple, one of Mrs. Crawford's sycophants, peered up at the balcony. The light of recognition lit her eyes.

Charlotte whipped her head back out of sight.

"Oh, Miss Evans." Mrs. Sharple trilled in her irritating high-pitched whine. "Do send dear little Miss

Prudence down so we may say our goodbyes."

Prue's eyes bugged out of their sockets, and she whipped her head back and forth. "No, please. I don't want to. She'll pinch my cheeks." Tears welled, threatening to spill over.

"I'm sorry, Prue. But I really think you ought to go down." She cursed Miss Crawford ten ways to Sunday for making this necessary. "It's the polite thing to do. And if you don't, Mrs. Sharple is likely to make a scene." The wretched woman had already spent half the morning continuing her mission of implying there was more to the story Charlotte had invented the other night. It wouldn't take much to tip the woman into stating outright that James had compromised Miss Crawford. The truth was inconsequential when the possibility of seeing her friend's daughter marry a title was on the line.

Prue sniffed. "Yes, Miss Evans." She dashed at her tears, squared her shoulders, and took hold of Charlotte's hand.

Pride warred with a desire to shield Prue from the coming confrontation. She kissed Prue on the forehead. "I'm proud of you, Prue."

At her words, Prue stiffened her spine and squeezed Charlotte's hand.

They made their way down the stairs with a whole host of guests scrutinizing their every step. Mrs. Sharple's smile cracked like ice in warm water, but she held out her arms as if to take hold of Prue when they reached the hall.

Charlotte stepped forward to get in the way. She tipped her head in a gesture just shy of disrespect. "Leaving so soon, Mrs. Sharple? Miss Prudence was just saying how sorry she is to see the party come to an end." She rested a hand on Prue's shoulder. "Weren't you, dear one?"

Prue smiled and curtsied. "Yes, Miss Evans. Have a safe trip home, Mrs. Sharple."

Charlotte kept herself between Prue and Mrs. Sharple, though the older woman repeatedly tried to make her way to Prue's side. But Charlotte could well remember how this game went. She'd attended any number of intimate social events in this time with her original family, and there had always been people trying to play up to her to get into her parents' good graces. Such was the life of the daughter of an earl. As the daughter of a viscount, Prue would deal with much the same.

She had a hard time resisting the urge to laugh when Mrs. Sharple grit her teeth in obvious frustration.

"I'm sure you have many duties to attend to this morning, Miss Evans. I'd be happy to watch over dear Miss Prudence until your return."

"Not at all, Mrs. Sharple. I am completely devoted to my charge. Why, I have come to love the dear child so much, I would positively ruin anyone who dared to hurt her. In any way." She gave her most saccharine sweet smile, waited until the threat appeared to register in Mrs. Sharple's flushed cheeks, and then said to Prue, "I believe your father wished to speak with you this morning. After how kind Miss Crawford was to you the other night, he knew you'd wish to bid her a very special adieu. Good day, Mrs. Sharple."

She swept Prue before her and hightailed it out of the hall. Several people snickered discreetly into their handkerchiefs. She ignored Mrs. Sharple's loud, "Why that little…"

Holding in her own mirth wasn't easy. By the time she and Prue closed the library doors behind them, they'd had enough. They burst out laughing and sank onto the couch facing Prue's mother's portrait.

"I am pleased to see you both enjoying this morning. I can't say as I've found anything remotely amusing today." James plopped down on the couch next to Prue, who immediately relaxed into his embrace and rested her head against his chest.

"You should have been there, Father. Miss Evans…"

James raised his brows and gave Charlotte a piercing stare over Prue's head as his daughter gave a blow by blow of her conversation with Mrs. Sharple.

Charlotte blushed as Prue called Mrs. Sharple a particularly vulgar word. She couldn't recall ever using that phrase in front of Prue, but as her governess, it was her job to make sure she spoke like a lady rather than a smart-mouthed little hoyden. "Watch your language, Prue. Your father's going to think he's not getting his money's worth out of me."

Prue startled upright. "Oh, no, Father. Miss Evans is quite wonderful. Lady Catherine uses such colorful language all the time." She mimicked the other girl's manner, " 'I shall trounce that fool maid,' or she'll call the Pastor's wife, who dared tell her not to take a loaf of bread meant for the poor, a mutton-headed harridan."

James grimaced. "Lady Catherine said all of that, did she?"

Charlotte waited, curious to see how he'd handle this. She'd been having a hard time coming up with a socially acceptable way to tell Prue how to deal with the bullies of her world. She could well remember the tight line her mother used to tread between insulting someone who could do her social damage and allowing them to walk all over her. At only ten years old, she could clearly recall some of her peers' attitudes of superiority.

"Lady Catherine Bellgrove is not someone on whom to model your language and certainly not your behavior."

Short and sweet.

Prue relaxed her stiff posture. "I beg your pardon, Father. Miss Evans has told me so. I sometimes forget. My last governess always said the Bellgrove family was to be greatly admired."

"Then Miss Evans is a definite improvement over your last governess. You must learn to look past a title and see the person. Our place in society lends itself to certain privileges yet does not make us better than those without. In fact, it very frequently makes us less as our peers deem themselves above common decency. I hope to never find you guilty of such behavior as is common among children such as Lady Catherine Bellgrove."

"Yes, Father. We are very lucky to have Miss Evans. We want her to stay with us always, don't we?"

Charlotte bit her lip to keep the tears at bay. Warmth spread through her chest. Prue certainly knew how to wrap her father, and her governess, around her little finger.

"Yes, indeed."

James's eyes gleamed in the light from the fire in the hearth. The warmth in his gaze let her know he appreciated Charlotte for more than her teaching skills. She shivered and glanced away.

"You should marry her. That way, she would never leave us."

****

James cringed at Prudence's declaration and Charlotte's shocked, and less than pleased, expression.

He, on the other hand, wasn't as displeased at the notion as he'd have thought. In fact, the idea warmed him in a way he hadn't felt in years.

Charlotte's face turned red from the insistent cough his daughter's announcement had set off. "Are you quite all right, Miss Evans?" he asked with concern.

Prudence pushed away from him toward her would-be mother. "Miss Evans?" She slid close and peered into Charlotte's face.

Charlotte held up a hand and gasped out, "I'm fine. Give me a moment." The coughing slowly eased. She wiped tears from the corners of her eyes and took a deep breath. She took Prudence's hands in her lap. "Prue, I'm sorry, sweetie, but I can't marry your father. And I can't stay with you forever. We've talked about that."

Did she mean that? Or was she saying what she thought he wanted to hear? He frowned. What did she mean, she couldn't stay? "Are you going somewhere, Miss Evans?" His voice was colder than he intended, but she'd shocked him more than his daughter.

Her head jerked up. Her eyes wide. She licked her lips. "I, well, Prue won't need me around forever. I know my position here is temporary."

The idea did not sit well. He opened his mouth to demand a further explanation, but Prudence interrupted.

"But that was when you first arrived. Now that Father loves you, and you love him, we can be a family."

The door burst open, and his mother dashed into the room.

"There you are, Prudence! Lady Atwater is about to leave, and she wished to say her goodbyes. Come along, dear. No need to come with me, Miss Evans. This proud Grandmama wishes to show off her darling granddaughter one more time. All the other guests have departed. I'm sure Tyndale can keep you company until I return."

Prudence ran to her grandmother and then skipped out of the room with a huge smile.

The door shut with a bang that echoed the rapidly pounding beat of his heart. Love? Yes, he loved her. Did she love him as well? "What in the world have you been discussing with my daughter?" He brought his gaze around to find Charlotte staring at him, mouth hanging open, color high in her cheeks.

"What have I said to Prue? What have I—" Her words choked off.

Bloody hell. The color blossomed, her chest heaved, and her eyes bulged.

"I may have chosen my words poorly." He gulped. Blast. He held out a hand to ward off the coming storm. "I was merely wondering how Prudence concluded that we are in love with one another." The more he thought the word, the more he liked the sound of it. True, he had some concerns over society's acceptance of his marriage to a governess, but he'd swear Charlotte came from a good family. Very likely peers.

Even if he were wrong, someone like Charlotte would certainly be a better mother to Prudence than some silly, scheming society chit like Miss Crawford.

"I discussed no such thing with her." Charlotte sat ramrod straight, hands clenched tightly in her lap. She kept her chin averted, so all he could see was the rapid beating of the pulse in her neck. "Have you?"

"No. Of course not. However, my mother chose a most opportune moment to usher Prudence out of the room. Seems an odd coincidence. I would not put it past her to have been listening at the door."

She finally faced him. "Huh. Yeah, your mum has been dropping hints that she'd consider the match a good one. I didn't think she'd go so far as to mention it to Prue though."

"She may not have. Prudence is an observant child." Would she grasp his meaning?

Her hand stopped mid-motion as she attempted to tame an errant lock of hair. He completed the act for her, the soft, silky strands smooth against his fingertips. Her cool skin a contrast to the heat of the fire. He breathed in the delicate scent of cinnamon he associated with her.

"What, exactly, are you trying to say? That you love me? Or are you insinuating that I'm the one in love with you."

Was she holding her breath? Waiting for his answer? "I rather hope her entire statement to be true." She remained perfectly still. Didn't even blink. Was that a good sign or a bad one? Life had been much easier with Harriet. He'd known her his entire life, her moods easy to ascertain and generally revolved around pleasing him. Charlotte was a different story. He had no idea what was going on in her mind as she stared at him.

Take a chance, or hedge his bets? He might never

have such an opportunity again. He'd never been one to take the easy road.

He slid from the couch to perch before her on bended knee. "Miss Evans. Charlotte." He placed a hand over hers, clenched tightly on her lap. "I have come to care for you, perhaps more than is wise. I fought against my growing affection to no avail. I believe we are well suited. What I don't know about your background, I feel confident you will confide in me when you are ready." He took a deep breath, stared deep into her crystal clear green eyes, and asked, "Will you marry me?"

****

Charlotte's mind reeled. Marry him? Was he crazy?

How could he ask her such an outrageous question? She didn't belong here. No matter her feelings for him, for Prue, for Lady Tyndale—she couldn't stay. She choked back a sob at the sudden realization of exactly how much she did care for the entire Tyndale family.

A slight tilting of James's lips indicated he expected a positive response to his proposal. She'd be crazy to turn him down. And he knew it. No matter how often it happened in romance novels, titled gentlemen didn't regularly propose marriage to their daughters' governesses.

Plus, he'd been deeply affected by his mother's lack of pedigree. The fact he'd ask a lowly governess to marry him showed he must care for her greatly. Her heart twisted.

Everything she could possibly want was being dangled before her. Except—the timing was completely wrong. Like, two hundred years, wrong.

"I…" What was she supposed to say? What could she say? Her mouth dried as if wads of gauze were stuck to her tongue. Just as it always did after a particularly stressful patient. "I can't."

She ripped her hands from his clasp and jumped to her feet. She paced before the hearth, inhaling the woodsy scent that brought back memories of her childhood. The family hanging out around a blazing fire. She'd play the piano while Mother knit and Alex attempted to master her water colors. When Father and Gregory would often join them after reviewing estate matters, Father would listen to her playing and declare how talented she was with barely a wince, and *ooh* and *ahh* over Alex's terrible painting. He'd been such a good liar. She'd never guessed what he planned on doing to them.

All those good memories were trashed when he sold her and Alex to the monster who almost killed them. If not for the time portal…

The portal. She couldn't stay here. Eventually someone would figure out her connection to the Creswell family. If James was right about that shooting, someone had already figured it out. She should have considered the possibility herself a long time ago. She'd just gotten so caught up in life at the Tyndale estate.

And now this. She scrubbed her eyes, ruthlessly forcing back tears. Her heart was crying out for her to say yes to James. So tempting.

But she couldn't. Even if this century wasn't so dangerous to her, she had a life to return to. A career. A brother.

Steven must be insanely worried by now. She'd

been gone almost two months. What must he be thinking? Was he searching for her, or had he given her up for lost?

"You can't?" James stood, blocking her path, forcing her to a halt. "You said you weren't married. Did you lie?"

"Married?" She laughed. "No. I'm not married. Who had the time?" Or the inclination. She'd broken up with Arthur not long before this crazy trip, but even though they'd discussed marriage, she hadn't really believed it would ever happen. A part of her had known he wasn't the guy for her.

A larger part of her knew that James was.

She was so screwed.

"Then why can you not marry me? Do you finally wish to tell me the story of how you came to be in such a sorry state the night we met?" He crossed his arms across his chest and stood still.

Tell him? Why not? He'd never believe her, and when he concluded she was out of her bloody mind, he'd regret his rash declaration of love. Maybe even kick her out of the house.

That would be fun. But maybe that would be the kick she needed to go explore the caves and find her way back to her real world.

"Fine. You want to know the truth? I'll tell you." She took a deep breath, held it for a few seconds, then let it out in a rush. "Part of a cave wall fell on me after I fled from a man intent on sending me through a time portal back from the twenty-first century to a past that I had escaped when I was ten. Unfortunately, my ill-advised gunshot aimed at scaring the men away from me, because I had absolutely no interest in returning to the eighteen hundreds, caused part of the cave we were in to collapse, and in running for my life, I fell through the very portal I intended to evade."

James's eyes had widened as she spoke, almost comical in his astonishment. She could just imagine the thoughts spinning around in his brain at the moment.

"Are you referring to the caves on the edge of my property? The inn is near that locale. Is that why you were there that night?"

"The caves." Seriously? Not at all what she'd expected. "That's what you want to know?" She shook her head. " 'Time portal' or 'twenty-first century' don't elicit any curiosity whatsoever?"

"The ridiculousness of those claims makes them unworthy of a response. An injury incurred in a cave that borders my property does. I know those caves well, having explored them as a child with my brother."

"I'm pretty sure you don't have to worry about a liability suit, so what do you care?"

He bent to stoke the fire and added another log. "Tell me more about this cave-in. I personally have not been back to them since my father forbade my explorations." At her raised eyebrows, he explained, "I became trapped in one when I was but eleven. It was two days before I was found. My parents experienced a great deal of anguish during that time. The caves can be dangerous, with several entrances, some of them interconnected and difficult to navigate." He shrugged. "Despite not having explored them in quite some time, I don't believe they have become a common area for strangers to visit. Why were you in there to begin with?"

She laid out her complete life story. She skipped

over details about her birth parents, just stating that they'd had a falling out when she was ten. She told him a man intent on killing herself and Alex had trapped them in the caves, but they'd managed to escape through the portal. And how she'd believed Alex died only to discover just before she was forced back to this time that she had survived. She talked about Steven and how worried he must be. How close they'd always been and how with their parents' death, they were all each other had. She needed James to understand why she couldn't stay in this time. Why she had to get back. To her family. Her *real* family.

"I'm afraid the blow to your head was more severe than we guessed. It has addled your brain to a frightening degree." He pulled her against his chest and stroked her hair. "I shall send someone for the doctor immediately. Perhaps there is something to be done to ease your suffering."

The comforting scent of his freshly laundered cravat, mixed with a musky aroma that she'd come to associate with James, lulled her into a brief return hug. Until what he was saying penetrated the fog that always enveloped her brain when in his arms.

She shoved at his chest, sending herself back a step as even with her best effort he didn't budge. "Suffering? Suffering? The only suffering I'm doing is being forced to listen to your condescending little 'I'm here to help' act."

He crossed his arms over his chest and glared down his nose at her. "I will give you the benefit of the doubt that this is the injury speaking."

Ooh, her fists itched to punch his annoying face. Instead, she grabbed his hand. "Fine. I'll prove it to you. Follow me."

****

"Where are we going?" James winced at her tight grip. Her nails dug into the back of his hand. Was she doing that on purpose? She couldn't have actually expected him to believe her story, could she? Unless he was right, and her brain had been addled by the cave-in.

Thank the lord all the guests had left. No one remained to witness the spectacle of Viscount Tyndale being dragged through the house by a governess.

Wrong. His mother hid her grin and gave him a jaunty wave as Charlotte dragged him past. He grimaced in response. This whole state of affairs was completely undignified.

But he didn't put a stop to it. He let Charlotte lead him wherever she wanted. She'd attempt to prove her ridiculous time travel fantasy, and when she failed to do so, she'd have to conclude that all was not right in her mind. Then he would be free to summon the doctor and find out what care was possible in such a situation.

She paused at the steps to the attic.

"I hid everything up here."

"Fine. I shall review this 'proof' of yours, but only if you promise me you'll allow me to call the doctor should I still feel one is warranted." He raised an eyebrow and refused to be moved by her tugging on his hand.

"Brilliant idea. Trust me. You're not going to want to call anyone after you see what I have up here." She dropped his hand and scurried up the steps.

He followed at a more dignified pace. When he reached the door, he peered inside the dimly lit area to see her making her way through a cloth covered pile of furniture in the far corner. He smiled at his mother's old rocking chair, remembering the stories she used to spin for him late into the night when he couldn't sleep.

Charlotte reached into the rafters near the wall and hauled out several rag-covered items. A covered bundle disappeared into a hidden pocket among her skirts, but a medium sized bag was held up in triumph.

He frowned. What was the point of dragging him up here if she planned on hiding something from him? The sack in her hand now held little interest compared to the object hidden in her pocket. If she thought to hide it from him permanently, she would be sadly mistaken. The idea that she hid these items up here all this time did not sit well with him.

She beckoned him to stand with her in the shaft of sunlight filtering through the window high up on the far wall. She wiped a hand across her cheek, leaving behind a streak of dust.

He restrained himself from brushing the smudge aside. He couldn't imagine she had anything in that disreputable satchel of hers that might relieve his fears for her well-being. Yet he'd promised to look, so with a sigh he took what she held out to him.

"This is just what I had on me when I was forced through. Bastards had already taken my purse. They were trying to get me to strip out of my modern clothes when I got the drop on them."

"Who tried to force you to disrobe?" he asked, not bothering to hide the outrage in his tone.

She laughed. "Of course that's the part that pisses you off. Don't mind the kidnapping, forcing me through a time portal, or anything else I've said. Get me naked, and all a sudden I've got your attention."

He forced a grin, though the thought of what else might have happened that she wasn't telling him plunged his mind into turmoil. "As it would any male of the species."

She smiled and nodded to the satchel. "Go ahead. I'm looking forward to seeing your reaction."

He upended the sack and poured the contents onto the nearest flat surface. A puff of dust rose around their faces. They both coughed and waved their arms to clear the air.

"You might want to have Mrs. Sterling clean it out up here. If Prue ever wants to go exploring, she shouldn't dig around in all this dust with her asthma."

He nodded, squinting through the remaining dust at the strange grouping of objects on the table. Breeches and a shirt, both of odd material and questionable fashion sense took up most of the space. Interesting though they were, his gaze was drawn to a bracelet of sorts with the smallest timepiece he'd ever seen.

"My watch." She held it up for him to see more clearly. "Battery's still going strong. Have you ever seen a clock this small? Your pocket watch is huge in comparison. And notice there's no mechanism for winding it like you'd have on anything you own."

He brushed off her comments. Interesting, yes. But not proof. "And yet timepieces are not uncommon. Who knows but some enterprising clock maker has developed just such a thing."

She grunted. A most unbecoming sound for a young woman, but he fought the desire to laugh at her consternation. She'd been so sure he'd fall for her outlandish tale after such skimpy evidence. Ha.

"Fine. Ignore what's right before your face. What

about the clothes? Or the pocketknife?"

"Unusual, yes. However, my mother might be the correct one to ask about matters of fashion. I pay no mind to such things other than to select among the clothing my valet deems suitable for any given occasion." The fabric was not something he was used to. The breeches were tough with strange metal bits sewn under a brass button. The shirt fabric was silky to the touch, and he caught a faint whiff of flowers as he set the blouse to one side to expose the other contents.

An oblong object that when unfolded, revealed a knife and several other tiny tools. What use any would be, he could not say, but he spent several minutes opening and closing the intriguing device.

He almost hated to disappoint her when he caught her hopeful stare. "This is all immensely interesting, my dear, but hardly enough to convince me that you are a traveler from another time."

She rolled her eyes. "Fine. I didn't really want to show you this last one. It's dangerous, and if I could have figured out a way to get rid of it where no one would ever find it, I would have." She dug into her pocket and removed the object that had gained his curiosity when she initially hid it from view.

The weight, when she placed it in his hands, was surprising. He hadn't expected such heft.

He unwrapped the bindings under her watchful gaze. Then stared in confusion.

Chapter Thirteen

Charlotte bit her lip as James unwrapped the gun she'd stolen from Sawyer's flunky. She wasn't exactly an enthusiast, but even she knew they didn't have guns like this one in this time.

Judging by the expression on his face, she'd been right to assume this would be the piece of evidence that tilted his belief in her favor. But his lack of response was beginning to be a bit worrying.

"Well? What do you think? Believe me now?" She bit her lip. Damn it. She needed to learn to control her sarcasm. She needed him to believe her. He needed to understand why she couldn't say yes to his proposal even though her heart desperately wanted to.

"This is remarkably like a dueling pistol, yet I've not seen its like before." He lifted his chin, darted a quick glance at her, then returned his attention to the gun. "How do you come to have this?"

"I stole it."

His head jerked back. "What?"

"I had just been kidnapped, and they were trying to send me through the portal. I saw a chance, and I grabbed it." She rubbed her head where the collapsing cave had left a small scar. Her brother had instilled enough gun knowledge in her head so she could tell James the manufacturer and caliber. "I hid the bullets under here." She scooped them out from under a covered table a few feet from where she'd hidden the gun. "I didn't want to take a chance of anyone finding it and killing someone by accident."

He nodded. "A wise decision. My hunting weapons are kept under lock and key at all times. Tell me more."

She gave him as many details about the gun as she could. Showed him how to load, how to shoot. A few forgotten pound notes fluttered to the floor. He picked them up, studying them with a slack jaw while she told him more about the future—cars, hot and cold running water, phones, everything she could think of that would amaze someone from this century.

After a while, she asked, "You never answered my question. Do you believe me now?"

He nodded slowly and with a heavy frown. "Yes. I can't deny these items are not of my time. I apologize for doubting your word." He stepped closer until they were toe to toe. "Do you forgive me my ignorance?"

Her heart beat a little faster. Her breath quickened at his nearness. She had to clear her dry throat twice before she could respond. Her words released on a sigh. "Yes, of course."

"Good." He leaned in and touched his lips to hers. They were soon locked in a passionate embrace.

The clatter of bullets falling to the ground startled them apart. She breathed heavily, clutched a hand to her chest, and stumbled her way to a nearby chair. Dust puffed up around her as she sat. She sneezed half a dozen times before wrinkling her nose and deciding the chair wasn't worth it. She jumped to her feet.

She ended up back in his arms. Not a bad place to be. Safety, passion, love. She could have it all by merely staying right where she was. But could she do that to Steven? Could she do that to herself? She'd worked hard to make a life for herself in the twenty-first century. She wasn't ready to give that up. Not to mention someone was out to kill her here. She might not even survive to enjoy the love she felt for James.

"I must admit to being stunned by this revelation," James said.

She snorted. "Understatement of the year. I'd be shocked if you weren't."

"Too true." He grinned, and her heart flipped. "None of this changes the fact that I wish for you to be my wife. And assuming you are not married in this future time of yours…?"

"No. Not married."

"Then I repeat my proposal. Charlotte Evans, will you marry me?"

She rested her forehead on his chest. She couldn't look him in the eye with the response she intended. Her will was too weak, but she knew what she had to do.

"No. I'm sorry. But no."

He stiffened, then stepped away. "I see. I thought I knew your heart. It appears I was mistaken." He pivoted on his heel and stalked away.

She fell to the chair, put her head in her hands, and cried.

****

James stormed into his office, slammed the door shut, and made a beeline for his decanter of whiskey. He tossed back a quick shot, then refilled the glass and took a smaller sip.

"I take it your conversation with Miss Evans did not end well?" his mother asked.

He whirled around to find her sitting on the sofa.

Right where he'd asked Charlotte to marry him the first time. He forced the scowl off his face. One didn't frown at Mother. "I didn't see you sitting there. I apologize." He tilted his glass her way. "Would you care for a dram?"

"Really, James. Resorting to drink already? Must you give up on what you want so easily? I thought better of you." She smoothed her skirt across her lap with particular focus, then murmured, "Or perhaps I was mistaken as to the extent of your feelings for Miss Evans."

He downed the remaining liquor. It didn't burn nearly as much as his mother's accusation. "Not care? I proposed marriage! I offered to share my life with her, my fortune, my title… Any other woman would say yes for the latter alone." He paced the length of his study. When had the room shrunk to such a miserly space? Barely ten strides and he was forced to turn. At no point could he escape his mother's reproachful gaze.

What would she say if he told her of today's revelations? He rested his palm against the hard bulge of the gun he'd stashed in his pocket. He had the proof right here. He opened his mouth to explain, but the words wouldn't come. Somehow it felt like a betrayal of Charlotte's trust. Instead, he said, "She doesn't love me, Mother. What would you have me do, force myself upon her?"

"Nonsense. Of course she loves you. Regardless of title, what woman could stand against your charm when you choose to display it?" She patted the space beside her. "Sit down."

He recognized an order when he heard one, so he made haste to do her bidding, albeit after a quick refill.

He poured his mother a brandy as a show of good will.

She took it with a nod of thanks and took a delicate sip. "Listen to your mother. You will have to admit I know more about love than you."

Hopefully she didn't notice the grimace he quickly wiped from his face. Any reminder of her past was a sore spot for him, but he loved his mother too much to let her know how much he knew or how much pain that knowledge had cost him as a young man amongst his peers.

She raised a brow and peered down her nose at him. "Forget that line of thinking, my son. I am referring to my relationship with your father. I loved him dearly, you know. And he loved me to distraction." A tear glistened at the corner of her eye. "You are just now experiencing that depth of emotion. In the beginning the passion it engenders can be quite confusing and difficult to understand."

Despite the ten years since his father's death, she couldn't mention the former viscount without shedding a tear or two. The love the two shared had been considerable. His parents had never been happier than when they were together.

He'd believed he had that with Harriet. "I loved Harriet."

She put a hand on his knee. "I know you did, darling. But—"

When she didn't continue, he pressed. "But?"

"Harriet was a lovely woman. Graceful, beautiful, and with the sweetest nature one could ever ask for in a wife. But...she wasn't the one for you."

He reared back. His mother had never said a negative word about Harriet during their courtship or marriage. And in the years since her death, she'd built Harriet up to be a paragon of womanhood with whom few could compete. He tried to summon some semblance of rage at her words, but all he managed was a vague annoyance that she would bring her up now as a means of doubting him.

"I don't mean anything against Harriet. Nor do I doubt your love for her. But Miss Evans—Charlotte—is different. She challenges you, makes you think, makes you be a better man. With her at your side, well, there's no limit to the happiness you could achieve. I wish that for you. And for dear Prudence." She stood and pointed her finger so close his eyes crossed. "Don't be an idiot and let her get away." She swept out of the room taking her brandy with her and directing the footman to close the door.

He put his head in his hands. His mother was right. He'd given up too quickly. He jumped to his feet. Damned if he'd let Charlotte go without a fight.

A knock at the door stopped him from sprinting to the attic in search of the answer he wanted from Charlotte. "Enter."

"My lord. A messenger has arrived with a message from Mr. Tyndale." Worthing held out a silver holder bearing a folded paper.

"Thank you." He frowned at the note. The soft click of the door told him he was alone once more. What could Sebastian want? He couldn't ever remember his brother sending a message in this manner before. He flipped the page open. No seal, no address, just his name written on the outside and a measly three lines written within.

Must speak to you at once.

Come to London immediately.
Sebastian.

What the bloody hell could he want? The handwriting was sloppy, like the note had been written in a hurry. His brother must be in desperate straits to make such a request.

He threw open his study door and motioned for Worthing. "I'll be leaving for London shortly. Have an overnight bag readied. If I elect to extend my stay, I will send for Albert to follow in the morning. See that my carriage is ready by the time I get back down. I have a matter of some urgency to see to first."

Confidant his staff would arrange all precisely as needed, he took the stairs two at a time. He did not wish to leave matters with Charlotte as they now stood. If he couldn't gain her acceptance of his proposal in the limited time allotted this afternoon, he'd convince her to follow him to London on the morrow and woo her until she agreed to be his forever.

****

Charlotte wiped her nose. The light had faded, and shadows ruled the room. She didn't know how long she'd sat crumpled in this chair in the dusty attic. Prue had likely eaten her supper by now.

Light glinted off something at her feet. Her necklace. She picked up the delicate gold chain. She'd stashed the necklace with its gold heart and perfect teardrop emerald in the attic among the rest of her future things. She hadn't been able to come up with a reasonable explanation for having such an expensive piece that wouldn't cause more questions than it answered.

Guess she didn't have to worry about that now that

she'd come clean with James. She clasped it around her neck, settling the heart under her dress, between her breasts.

The attic door flew open. She jumped. James marched over to tower above her. "This is a unique situation. Neither of us knows exactly how to deal with the issues we face." He took hold of her limp hand. "We can figure it out together."

She shook her head. "We can't work this out. This is not just a case of moving from my father's home to yours. Or even moving across the ocean to America. This is not a long-distance relationship. I don't belong in this *century*. I have a career at home. I'm a doctor. What am I here? Your daughter's governess? Your wife?"

The hurt on his face almost stopped her. Almost. Part of her wept at the harm she caused, but her brain told her this was for the best. She didn't want to stay, so take away the option and she wouldn't have to wrestle with the choice.

"If I were to stay, I'd forever be *your*—" She waved her hands in the air around her head. "—Fill in the blank. Not me. And should I just leave my brother and sister to wonder what the hell happened to me? Steven's probably out of his mind with worry. I'm all he has. And I'd just found Alex. I can't do that to them."

"You care nothing for me then? For Prudence? How do you think she will fare when you return to this future of which you think so highly?"

She winced. There was no arguing with him on the matter of his daughter. Prue wouldn't take it well when she left. And with only the doctors of this era... No.

She couldn't afford to think that way. Asthma could be managed. Prue's wasn't even that severe. Provided she took certain precautions, she should be fine. She might even grow out of the condition within a few years.

She'd miss the little girl something awful though. She blinked back tears. Would she miss Steven and Alex any less?

Maybe. She'd come to think of Prue like a daughter. Prue and her father would always hold a special place in her heart. Would she be able to get on with her life if she left them behind?

Did she have a choice?

Sure, she could be quite happy living here with James, Prue, and Lady Tyndale. But for how long? How long before she resented not being able to use her hard fought skills as a doctor? How long before she couldn't stand the patriarchal society that said she was good for nothing more than as a prop to her husband and a mother to his children. Had she grown up in this century, she may have been able to accept that, but now she expected so much more.

"I care for you both. Deeply. That doesn't change anything. I'm sorry."

He closed his eyes. Took a deep breath before opening them once more. "I must leave for London this evening. Come with me. Or follow in the morning. I can leave Max with instructions to see you safe to my London townhouse as soon as you make ready. We can discuss this further."

She shook her head. "No. There's no point. I've made up my mind. I have to at least try to make my way back home. I haven't had a chance to come up with a plan yet, but I'll think of something. Now that I know your feelings, I won't lead you on to think there's any possibility we might end up together. It's just not going to work."

James's lips thinned into a tight, white line. A pulse throbbed in his temple. She had to admire his restraint. He fairly burst with the need to say something he deemed inappropriate to say to the opposite sex. This reaffirmed her decision that a relationship between them would never work. If he couldn't bring himself to say certain things to a mere woman, how could she ever feel like he viewed her as a human being rather than a member of the weaker sex?

"This discussion is not over. I wish I had no need to leave this evening, but I am concerned for my brother. His message was unusual. I must attend to him immediately."

"I hope he's all right." She did. She was causing James enough heartache. She had no wish for him to suffer any further.

"Just remember…" He grabbed her and hauled her in for a scorching, yet brief, kiss. "…I fight for what I want. And I want you, Charlotte."

"But I don't want you." She forced out the lie, her throat threatening to choke off the words, her stomach burning in a tight-knit knot of remorse.

"We're going to have to work on your lying. You're not very good at it." With a smirk and a curt nod, he stomped off.

Chapter Fourteen

James squashed his irritation as he approached his London townhouse. Sebastian wouldn't have called him all this way if it weren't important. His brother had no way of knowing of his proposal to Charlotte, or her rejection.

He leaped out of his carriage before John had the chance to open the door. It didn't take him long to reach the front door, but Gideon beat him to it. That brought a brief smile to his face. He'd be hard pressed to beat Gideon at his post, even at such a late hour as this.

The smile didn't last. "Is Sebastian in the study?" he asked.

"No, my lord. Mr. Tyndale is out for the evening."

James stopped dead in his tracks halfway to the open study doors. "He's out for the evening? What then is the urgent matter that called me here?"

"I'm sure I do not know, my lord." Gideon selected a card off the pedestal at the front entrance, used to hold correspondence, calling cards and such. "I believe this is the invitation for the event he planned to attend."

James strode back and plucked the card out of Gideon's hand. "Lord and Lady Downing? I have never met the earl, though of course I know of him." He studied the creamy white paper, expecting some clue as to what made this event so important. "Why would Sebastian attend a ball when he made it clear my attendance was needed in town tonight and no later? I expected him to be here wearing a hole in my rug with his anxious pacing."

"Mr. Tyndale made no mention you would be coming to town."

"No?" Stranger and stranger. "I will seek him out. Is Loring about?" He'd left his own valet at home, not expecting to need him on such a short trip. At Gideon's nod, he said, "Send him to my room at once. I will follow my brother to this ball but must dress appropriately." He cursed the delay. His brother's missive had appeared urgent, though how important could the issue be if his brother were out gallivanting at a debutante's ball?

Loring wasn't quite as skilled as Albert had been in his prime, but he had James dressed and ready in half the time. He elected to walk to the ball. The distance was short, and he didn't wish to get caught up in a crush of carriages that would be fighting to drop off and pick up their passengers at the front door. If he had to attend events such as this, he much preferred to leave the carriage at home whenever possible.

The house was ablaze with candlelight, and as suspected, the commotion at the front door was intense even though the ball was well underway. It took him longer than he liked to gain entrance.

Once inside, he searched for his brother immediately. He cursed the press of bodies that made it difficult to find the one he sought. Dancers swirled upon the dance floor alternately hiding and revealing those scattered around the edges. He scanned the dancers for sight of his brother. Perhaps his emergency wore a ball gown. Were his brother to have fallen in love, he very well might consider it a pressing matter.

His thoughts returned to Charlotte. Yes, love in its first stages was definitely compelling. He itched to get back to her. The way he'd left her created a sour taste in his mouth. He didn't like leaving her with their conversation unfinished.

The lump of her gun in his pocket struck his side as he strode about the room. Perhaps he should have left it at home, but it wasn't the sort of thing he wanted any of the servants to happen upon. His reaction had been bad enough. He didn't want to think what some of the servants might think.

He had to get his mind off Charlotte. He squinted through the mass of people toward the opposite side of the room. Thoughts of her possessed him to the point he imagined he spied her among the dancers. Yet she was safe at his home, under the watchful eye of several of his people.

There she was again. This time he was certain. The crowd obscured his vision once more, but it was she. He strode directly across the floor. Dancers whirled out of his way. They must have sensed his mood.

What the bloody hell was she doing here? And how had she managed to make her way to London from the country? His staff was under strict orders to keep her safe. They would not risk his wrath by taking her to London without his say so.

People cleared out of the way of his determined strides and provided a clear view of Charlotte. Beautiful. He'd not seen her dressed in such a fashion. It suited her. Someone took her hand, and James scrutinized the bear of a man at her side.

He increased his pace. The look that passed

between the two caused anger to writhe in his gut. As if they knew each other well. And were in love. Another impossibility. His Charlotte couldn't possibly know this man.

The stranger had caught sight of him and turned his head, exposing extensive scarring along his left side. This was a man James wouldn't normally care to fight, but the way the man clasped Charlotte's hand had James itching to make use of the gun in his pocket.

That would have to wait. He needed answers first.

He stopped a foot before her. Her brows wrinkled in confusion. There was no recognition in the eyes he knew so well. He reared back.

The woman wasn't Charlotte.

****

The door burst open again. Back already? What more could she say to him?

Charlotte stood, placing a dusty old trunk of who-knew-what between them. She couldn't keep the shock from her voice when it wasn't James who interrupted her. "Miss Crawford? What are you doing here? I thought you left hours ago."

"I did." Her perfect hair was rumpled, her cheeks pale. She twisted her hands together tight against her stomach. "I returned to… Oh, I shall explain later. Quick, you must come with me." She raced from the room.

Charlotte darted after her. What was wrong with the woman? "Miss Crawford. Stop. What's going on?" They'd reached the grand stairway before she finally caught up. She grabbed hold of Miss Crawford's elbow and yanked her to a stop. "I'll not go a step farther until you tell me what's going on."

"Miss Prudence is in danger, and you want to stop to talk? I thought you cared for the little girl."

"Prue?" That got her moving like nothing else. She flung around to head back to Prue's room.

"She's not there. She's by the stables." Miss Crawford grabbed her hand and pulled her toward the stairs. "I'll show you."

Her confusion grew as she followed Miss Crawford down the stairs and out the front door. Where were all the servants? She'd never seen so few people about the great house. "Where is everyone? Is Max with Prue? Why was she at the stables?"

"I'm afraid I have no idea. A stable lad is with the child. I ran to the house to get help, but no one was about. I searched for the nursemaid, but Miss Prudence's room was empty. That's when I saw the door to the attic was ajar."

The story didn't make sense, but they were almost at the stables. A man she didn't recognize hunched over a figure lying on the ground. Prue! She tore out of Miss Crawford's grasp and ran the last few yards.

She stumbled to a halt. Max lay crumpled on the ground, not Prue. She threw herself to her knees at his side. Blood covered his temple, matted in his hair. She prodded the cut, quickly deciding it wasn't too severe. She checked his breathing, concerned he wasn't responsive when she called his name.

A rough hand grabbed her by the upper arm, yanking her off balance. With a painful yelp, she tried to wrest herself free, to no avail. "What are you doing?" She twisted to glare at her assailant and froze in horror.

She could never forget that face. The long nose, the thin, cruelly smirking mouth, the bloodshot eyes. She shivered and drew back in revulsion. Memories of him dragging her and Alex to the caves, of their desperate escape attempt that led to the portal, of her sister's prone, bloodied body. The man pinched her all the harder. "Ow." He was such a scrawny little thing, but his grip was like steel. She couldn't break free. He forced her hands together and bound them cruelly with thick, rough rope.

"There you go, Mr. Timmons. Just as discussed. I expect you will do as you promised and see that she never returns to Tyndale Manor?"

"Yes'm. She won't never be seen again. You can count on that."

Oh, how she'd love to punch the self-satisfied smirk off the evil woman's face. "Please tell me you didn't drag Prue into this."

Miss Crawford straightened the hair about her face. "Of course not. The little pest is likely sound asleep in her bed while the staff searches the garden for the necklace I claimed to have lost there."

Charlotte let her breath out in a *woosh*. Her shoulders slumped. The knot in her stomach eased the tiniest bit. Oh, thank goodness. She wouldn't be able to live with herself if anything happened to Prue.

"I put the fear of God into them. They won't give up for quite some time yet. By then, I will have found it all on my own without their help, and you shall no longer be a thorn in my side. James will realize we are meant for each other once you are no longer around to seduce him away from me. And when I am mistress of Tyndale Manor, you will be but a distant, unpleasant memory."

"You self-centered bitch. He doesn't love you.

You're going to get me killed, and you're never going to get what you want. You'll never be Lady Tyndale."

With her hands tied, and Mr. Timmons holding her back, she couldn't avoid the slap. Her head rocked to the side from the force. Timmons shook her and forced her upright. The metallic taste of blood welled up from where her teeth dug into her cheek.

"Liar! He will marry me," Miss Crawford screamed. "You ruined everything. But it's not too late. It's not. With you out of the way, he'll come back to me. Just wait and see." She smiled, drew her arm back, and struck once more.

"Now, now, miss. M'lord's wishing to speak with the lady. She'll get what's comin' to 'er, don't you worry. But I must needs take 'er to 'im in one piece first. And I best be going. I need to let 'is coachman know the deed's been done so as 'e can inform m'lord."

Miss Crawford drew herself straight, head up and chest out. She smoothed the lines of her dress and tucked a stray hair back into place. "Yes. Of course. I must be going as well." She swung around to march off toward the house but bumped into another man Charlotte hadn't seen sneak up on them. He grabbed her arm, restraining her when she tried to pull free.

"Unhand me. What is the meaning of this?"

"Milord wants to see you as well. Thank you in person."

Miss Crawford threw her head back and glared. "Don't be ridiculous. I must return to the manor before anyone misses me."

The man sneered, and a chill ran down Charlotte's spine. He had a nasty air about him. And the way his gaze roamed over her and Miss Crawford's bodies, she didn't want to think what was going on in his head. Finally, he shrugged and dropped Miss Crawford's arm, sweeping a hand toward a carriage waiting a few paces away. "Never you mind them all up at the manor. Milord insists, so's do I."

"Fine." Miss Crawford huffed. "Let us get this over with as quickly as possible. But I can assure you your lord will not be pleased that you treated me in such a manner."

"Don't you worry 'bout me none. Come along."

She tossed her head back and stalked in the direction he indicated, for all the world as if she had no idea of the trouble she was in.

Charlotte opened her mouth to scream, but Timmons's hand clamped down on her face, covering her mouth completely and partially cutting off air through her nose. She fought to breathe through the fetid stench of horse, and she didn't want to think what else.

"M'lord wants to know what you been saying 'bout 'im," he said, his lips distressingly close to her ear. "You ain't said nothin' to Lord Tyndale, far as I can see. Why? Where you been all these years, hmm?"

She grunted through his hand. Spots floated behind her eyes. She grew dizzy from lack of oxygen. Dangerously close to blacking out. If he didn't release her face when she sagged against him, she'd be done within minutes.

His grip eased suddenly just as she thought she might pass out. She heaved in great gulps of air, shook her head and tried to force the cloudiness from her brain. "I…" She swallowed. "I don't know what you're talking about. I have no idea who your lord is. I haven't said anything."

He spun her to face him. Eyes wide, mouth slack, his voice quavered as he asked, "You're one of them Creswell twins, ain't ya?"

Before she could gather her wits to say she wasn't, he pinched her chin, wrenching her face side to side. "Yeah, you are. I ain't wrong." He ripped her necklace off and held it up for a good look. He grinned. "I remember this. Planned on nickin' it fifteen years ago, but you got away from me first. No mistakin' you now. I'll give this to Cantor as proof to Lord Stone as I've got ya, *Charlotte*. Would ha' been better had ya changed that, too, Miss *Evans*." He cackled and shoved her toward the side of the barn where a carriage waited.

****

"Excuse me. I'm terribly sorry to disturb you. I thought you were someone else." Who the hell was she, and why did she look so exactly like his Charlotte?

"Do you mean Charlotte?" the woman asked in a voice much like his love's though James couldn't place the accent.

"Yes. I thought you…"

"I believe this conversation would benefit from a smaller audience. We shall gather your father on our way," the large man said to the woman.

Her father?

"Would you come with us, please?"

James nodded at the man's request. As if he would let them leave without getting some answers first.

They led him up the stairs to a small, private drawing room. The sounds of music and laughter followed them up the stairs but cut off abruptly when the door slammed shut behind them.

The dark-haired gentleman rounded on him immediately. "Who, pray tell, are you and what do you know of Charlotte Creswell?"

"Creswell?" She couldn't possibly be related to such a well-known family, could she? Impossible. "Nothing. I thought for a moment the young lady was my daughter's governess, but I realize I was mistaken." He bowed in Charlotte's lookalike's direction. "I beg your pardon if I startled you. It was not my intention. The resemblance is uncanny." He couldn't help his frown. The resemblance *was* striking.

"Is your governess's last name Evans?" the girl asked.

"Yes, it is." She knew Charlotte?

Lord Creswell, James knew him by sight though they'd never spoken, stepped forward. "I believe introductions are in order." He bowed slightly to James. "You are Lord Tyndale, I believe."

James nodded, surprised to be recognized.

"May I present to you, Lord Oakleigh." He gestured toward the man who stood so close to the girl. "And my daughter, Lady Alexandra Creswell."

His jaw dropped, and he gaped at Lady Alexandra. Charlotte had mentioned a sister named Alex but said nothing about them being twins.

"It sounds as though you know my other daughter, Lady Charlotte," Lord Downing continued. "Alexandra's sister. We have been searching for her for quite some time."

James listened in amazed silence as Lord Downing spoke about what had happened to Charlotte and Alexandra fifteen years ago.

"I had received threats against my eldest, Gregory,

but I was naïve enough to believe I could protect my family. I refused to bow down to the villain's demands. So I hired men to protect my son and continued as I had been. It didn't occur to me my girls might be in danger as well." Tears welled in his eyes but didn't fall. "They were taken from our garden. Their nursemaid brutally murdered." The man's eyes fell on Lady Alexandra and some of the haunted despair fell from his expression and his smile showed the love he had for his children. "About a month ago, Lady Alexandra returned to us. She brought hope that her sister is alive as well, and we have searched for her ever since."

Amazing. Yet another aspect of Charlotte's past that defied belief. He vaguely remembered hearing about the kidnapping so many years ago. He should have connected Charlotte's tale to the rumors from back then, but the memory had escaped him.

"Miss Evans said she had family in London, but she refused to tell me your name. I had gathered from some of her comments you had parted on less than amicable terms."

Lord Downing's expression made it clear he was unaware of any rift with his daughter, but James focused his attention on Lady Alexandra. What was she doing here? Charlotte believed her safe in the future. Would she be pleased or upset to learn her sister had followed her into the past?

No doubt she would be pleased. Did she not long to return to the future to see her sibling once more? If her sister was here… "She worried she would never see you again. She will be thrilled when she discovers you are in London."

"Not on good terms?" Lord Downing's confused

voice interrupted him. The man quickly dismissed his confusion with a shake of his head. "It is unimportant. Where is she now?"

"At my country estate. I asked her to accompany me to London, but she refused. I had an urgent letter from my younger brother requiring my presence in town." His concern for Sebastian surged forward. In all the confusion of seeing Lady Alexandra, his brother's request had flown from his mind. "I expected to find him awaiting my arrival at our townhouse and was surprised to find he intended to attend your ball. I arrived at your home and was further shocked to see Charlotte, or so I thought, talking to Lord Oakleigh, when I left her safe at my home."

"Safe?" Lord Oakleigh asked.

"Yes." Worry for Charlotte brought a frown to his face. "I am afraid there have been several attempts on her life since the moment she entered into my employ. I did not wish to leave, yet I had little choice. I left several men to guard her in my absence." Nothing short of his brother's desperate pleas could have tempted him away from Charlotte at this time. The need to know the reason burned within him. He started toward the door. "If you will pardon me, I would like to find my brother. His missive sounded quite urgent."

Lord Oakleigh blocked his exit. "You can find your brother in a moment. I want to know more about these attempts on Alex's sister."

James bristled at the note of command in the marquess's voice.

Lady Alexandra spoke up in a quiet yet determined sounding voice. "Why don't I have a footman escort your brother here?"

Before Lord Oakleigh could stop her, or even finish his sentence, "No, I think…" she was out the door.

****

"James! A young lady told me you were here. I almost didn't believe her. What dragged you away from Tyndale Manor?"

James spun to see his brother saunter into the room, his face a wreath of welcoming smiles. And surprise. Sebastian hadn't sent that letter. His stomach dropped. He'd been fooled. "I received an urgent message from you demanding my presence in London immediately. Please tell me this is all a lark, and you did indeed send the message."

Sebastian lost his grin. He stopped in his tracks and surveyed the room. "No. I did not." He bowed to Lords Downing and Oakleigh before returning his attention to James. "What's happening?"

"Where is Alex?" Oakleigh demanded, stepping in front of the footman who accompanied Sebastian, towering over the smaller man, his fists clenched at his sides.

"Alex?" Sebastian chimed in upon hearing her name. "Ah yes. I was given a message. Alex has gone to find Charlotte. Lord Stone provided a carriage for his use."

James cursed. Stone. His neighbor. Stone had been there the day he'd hired Charlotte on as Prudence's governess. James had assumed his pain in the arse neighbor had wanted the private room for his own use. Had he, in fact, been spying on Charlotte? Even then plotting to kill her?

Charlotte was in dire trouble. His head pounded.

He rubbed his temples. He needed to think clearly. "Who gave you a message? Did she look like Miss Evans?"

"Prudence's governess?" Sebastian scrunched his brows. "Is Prudence with you? A footman fetched me from the ballroom. As I came out, a young lady approached, told me you wished to see me, and asked that I deliver a message."

"Did she resemble Miss Evans?" James asked again.

"I have no idea. I've not yet met Miss Evans."

"Did you see where she went after speaking with you?"

Sebastian nodded. "Yes. She returned to the ballroom. She seemed eager to be on her way."

"It must have been her." Lord Downing stood. His face had paled. He appeared to have aged ten years in the few minutes since Sebastian entered the room. "We'll search the house first."

James nodded and filed out after the other men. Lord Downing organized his servants to search the house, while the rest of them scoured the rooms open to the public. Several friends waylaid him, but he brushed them off as quickly as possible without causing a furor over his rudeness.

They met back in the drawing room after a half hour of fruitless searching. Lady Alexandra had managed to slip out of the house despite the numerous people who'd been instructed to keep watch over her the entire evening.

Oakleigh looked ready to commit murder. "Where is she?"

The poor footman trembled under the lord's fury.

"I don't know, my lord. She instructed me to escort Mr. Tyndale here."

"I gave strict instructions she was not to be left alone, even for a moment. Was I not clear?"

"Yes, my lord. She was headed into the ballroom when I left her. She must have doubled back when I weren't lookin'. I'm right sorry, I am." He ducked his head, remorse overtaking the fear in his expression. "She's real nice. I sure would hate to see anything happen to her."

Oakleigh's eyes closed briefly, and he took in a deep breath. His hands flexed at his side as if he longed to wrap them around the servant's throat. "Find Lord Stone. Alert all the servants. If he is still here, he is not to leave under any circumstances. Bring him to me." When the footman left, Oakleigh faced the room.

Lord Downing sat next to the fire, his head in his hands. "How did this happen?" he asked in a whisper, his voice strained and tired.

James paced before the hearth. The fire had dwindled to mere coals. Even a blazing inferno could not have warmed the chill in his blood. "He must have sent that fake message from Sebastian to lure me away from my country estate in order to kidnap Charlotte. He then used her as a means of forcing Lady Alexandra to follow his demands." He shook his head. "Why is he doing this?"

"Obviously he's afraid the ladies can identify him as the man who kidnapped them fifteen years ago." Oakleigh turned to Sebastian, whose face had gone white as a sheet as he listened to the panicked men surrounding him. "Tell us again what she said."

"She simply said to let you know that Alex had

gone after Charlotte, and Lord Stone was providing the carriage." He screwed up his face in concentration. "She didn't tell me her name, so I assumed Alex was a man."

James paused in his pacing as a thoughtful look overtook Sebastian's face.

"Actually, she said to say it exactly as she did. Let me think." He closed his eyes and stood perfectly still, his mouth moving slightly. "She said Alex had gone to find Charlotte *at the cave*." He opened his eyes. "At the cave, does that help?"

James gasped. "The portal! That's it."

"What?" Oakleigh asked, his eyes alight with hope. "Do you know where they are?"

"Yes. Lord Stone's country estate shares a border with mine. I used to explore the system of caves there when I was a child. That's where Charlotte…" his voice trailed off, and he looked around. "What has Lady Alexandra told you about her life for the past fifteen years?"

Lord Downing spoke from his spot near the fire. "She told us everything. I gather Charlotte has confided her past to you as well?"

"Yes. And did you believe Lady Alexandra's story?"

Oakleigh answered, "Lord Downing and his family did, yes. I have to admit to some doubt."

James snorted. "Can't say I blame you. I had a time believing it myself." And he'd given poor Charlotte quite a time about it, too. "Time travel! The concept was too incredible to comprehend. Until she showed me her proof of course."

"Proof?" Oakleigh's brows rose, his eyes widened.

"How could she prove her story to you?"

He couldn't blame Oakleigh for his doubt. Without any evidence to support her claim, would he have come to believe Charlotte? "She had certain items that couldn't possibly exist. I found no explanation other than they came from the future. They defied belief." He waved the thought aside. "That doesn't matter now. When the girls were kidnapped as children, they were taken to a system of caves that lie along the boundary of my property and that of Lord Stone. He must have planned on killing the girls and hiding their bodies in the caves. Charlotte told me she and Lady Alexandra tried to flee but fell through the portal instead. Charlotte was forced back through that same portal two months ago. That is when I met her. Lord Stone or one of his servants must have seen her and made the attempts on her life. I am an idiot for not suspecting him in all Charlotte's troubles." He stopped pacing and stared at Oakleigh. "We must hurry. If he brought them to those caves, he must be planning on killing them."

"We shall have to make sure we get to them first," Oakleigh said as a knock sounded at the door.

"Enter," said Lord Downing.

A tall blond man dressed in evening clothes entered, followed closely by the butler, who carried several great coats draped over his arms. "We have searched everywhere. Lord Stone left less than an hour ago. I sent two footmen around to his townhouse to await his return there. If they locate him, I have instructed one to stay with him and the other to bring word back to us."

"Excellent," Lord Downing said. "Preston, please have the carriage prepared. We have an idea where he may have taken Alexandra and will leave immediately."

"Yes, sir," Preston responded. He placed the greatcoats on the back of a chair and left.

"I believe it would be best if you were to wait here," Oakleigh told Lord Downing, raising his hands to ward off any further comment from Charlotte's father. "Someone needs to wait here in case Lord Stone did indeed return to his townhouse. We also have no idea if Lord Stone has an accomplice keeping an eye on matters here. You have a house full of people, and your absence would be difficult to explain. Besides which we would not care to upset Lady Downing unnecessarily."

James spoke to his brother, "Sebastian, wait here with Lord Downing. If Lord Stone has returned to his townhome, I will need you to detain him. Make sure he does not have a chance to surprise us at the portal. We shall return as soon as we have Ladies Charlotte and Alexandra safe."

"I will contact some old *friends* of mine and see what I can discover about Lord Stone," the tall stranger said. "You should take this." He held out a pistol to Oakleigh. "It's primed and ready."

"Thank you," Oakleigh replied.

James didn't know much about the other man, but from the look that passed between him and Oakleigh, he was confident that every avenue for finding the ladies, no matter how unpleasant or unsavory, would be taken. Good.

He pulled Sebastian aside. "You trust Stone about as much as I do. Be careful."

Sebastian nodded and clapped him on the arm. "And you as well."

James turned to Oakleigh. "Let's go."

Chapter Fifteen

The walls crowded in on Charlotte, pressing her down into the cold, damp stone below her. Creatures rustled somewhere above her head. Any minute something might drop on her, use her as just another outcropping of rock. Not knowing what was going on around her was the worst part. After all, this wasn't her first time in this cave. She was in no danger of getting lost, there was only one passable way to the surface. Even as a child she'd been too big to fit through any of the tiny side passages.

She cursed and screamed until her throat was raw from the strain. Her cries were of no use. Even if someone heard her, she was unlikely to elicit help. She'd screamed bloody murder when they'd stopped at Lord Stone's estate so Cantor could continue on to London and inform his boss of her capture. She ended up locked in a room while Timmons "got a bit o' shut eye." The servants were all too afraid of Lord Stone to come to her aid.

The brief hope that Miss Crawford would come to her senses and somehow help her get away had been dashed almost immediately. The clueless woman had smirked at her throughout the carriage ride. She hadn't even blinked when Timmons dragged Charlotte out of the carriage. It wasn't until they arrived at Stone's estate that her demeanor changed. Cantor had slammed the door in her face and driven off with her screaming at him to take her home.

Tears leaked down Charlotte's cheeks, but with her arms tethered to her side, she couldn't manage to wipe them away. She couldn't stand Miss Crawford, but the poor woman didn't deserve whatever Cantor had in mind for her. Remembering the article Sawyer had mentioned months ago twisted her stomach in knots. Maybe neither she nor Alex had been the victim after all.

She twisted her knees up and to the side, just barely managing to reach the rope that bound her ankles. By the time she finished working the knot loose, the tips of her fingers were scraped and aching. The one benefit? The minor pain distracted her, at least a little, from the vast darkness of the cave that imprisoned her.

She stretched her legs out in front of her. A dozen pebbles lodged under her bum. Shifting was useless. All she managed was to move the tiny rocks so their sharp edges pricked relentlessly into her.

What was she going to do? She had to escape. She refused to die down here in the dark. Alone. Not when she had a chance for true love. If only James was willing to forgive her for being a blind fool.

And an idiot. Any sane woman would have jumped at the chance to marry a rich, titled man like James. What had she done? Said no. And why? Because she couldn't give up on the idea that she might someday return to her life in the twenty-first century—the appeal of which faded every day she spent with James and Prue.

She'd been plotting how to leave them from the moment she arrived. Now her departure had been forced upon her. But she wasn't going home. She was a stone's throw away, but no closer to returning than she'd been two months ago. There was no way she could make her way down to the portal with her arms tied and no light to guide her. She'd kill herself blundering into a wall or stumbling into a crevice between stones along the uneven ground.

Not to mention that the man who wanted to kill her was unlikely to apologize and set her free. Of all the rotten luck. After being gone for fifteen years, who happens to see her on her very first day back? That creep Mr. Timmons. The bastard who'd taken her and Alex from their garden when they were kids.

After all these years, she'd finally learned the name of the man her father had sold them to. Gabriel Stone. A baron. Probably one of her father's cronies.

She still didn't understand why. That question had consumed her for years, before she finally put it behind her and accepted the love her adopted family offered so freely. Eventually, she decided her father's betrayal was a blessing in disguise. Had he not been such a bastard, she never would have found herself in the future with a family that truly loved her.

And she'd been on the verge of reuniting with her beloved twin sister. Fresh tears threatened as she thought of Alex waiting by the phone for her call two months ago. What had gone through her head? Had she been able to move on, or was she even now tormenting herself with worry?

A sound filtered through the darkness of her thoughts. Had someone called her name? She held her breath and strained to make out any sound.

"Charlotte? Can you hear me?" A woman's voice.

So quiet she could barely make it out.

What would a woman be doing down here? Had Lord Stone sent someone to check on her? She snorted and struggled against her bindings. As if she could possibly get away. Maybe Lady Tyndale had somehow learned where she'd been taken? "Who's there?" Her voice sounded weaker than she liked, but her useless screams had taken some of the life out of her.

"Charlotte? It's me, Alex."

She started. Alex. Alexandra? Not possible.

"Where are you? Lord Stone's coachman is outside. We have to come up with a plan to get out of here." The voice gained slightly in volume. Sounds of movement accompanied the voice.

"Alex?" It couldn't be true. She was imagining her because she wanted to see her so very badly. "That's impossible."

"It's true. We spoke on the phone, remember?"

Her heart sank. She wasn't imagining things. That meant... "Oh no! He got you too!" Damn that bugger, Sawyer. He must have tracked Alex down and forced her back as well.

"I'm afraid so. Where are you?"

"I don't know. He didn't leave me a light, the bastard." Anger fueled her now, and her voice strengthened.

"I have a lantern. Let me know when you start to see the light, and we'll know I'm getting close."

She swung her head back and forth, searching for any hint of light. It took only a moment to see the faint lightening of the area around her. Yes. "I can see some light. Keep coming. You're almost here."

The light got stronger. Her eyes struggled to adjust

after such a long period in utter blackness. The outlines of the cavern became visible. The glow was strongest coming from directly across. Finally, the lantern floated into the small space, about waist height. It cast shadows on the figure that followed, hunched over and shuffling. Alex straightened to her full height with a groan that sent fresh fear through Charlotte.

"What's wrong? Are you okay?"

"I'm fine. It's just this stupid dress. Looks great, but not meant for spelunking."

Charlotte squinted at her sister and struggled to stand, but her bound arms threw her balance off. None of her dreams of reuniting with her sister took place in this bloody cave. She always imagined them meeting in modern times. And not once was Alex wearing a ball gown. Probably quite fine at one time, the gown was streaked with dirt, and the skirt ripped practically to shreds.

"Alexandra! It is you. But how?" Had that bastard Sawyer knocked her out too? Did this mean the portal had been cleared?

Alex dropped to her side and set to work on the ropes. They kept their silence as they struggled with her bonds. Charlotte soaked in her sister's presence and let that knowledge buoy her spirit. They'd been unstoppable together as kids. The second the ropes were loose enough, Charlotte wiggled out of them and threw her arms around her sister. Alex returned the embrace with equal enthusiasm.

Charlotte pulled away to get a good view of her sister's face. "I just can't believe it's you! I thought you were dead for so long. When I saw that web page, I almost fainted. Then I got trapped here and thought I'd lost all chance of ever seeing you again."

"It's a long story, and we've got to think of a way out of here, so I'll give you the quickie version."

Charlotte settled down to listen and work the feeling back into her limbs. Alex guessed it was somewhere around three in the morning, so she'd been here for over five hours.

"When you didn't call, I got worried. You'd said something about Griffin International, so I called them and was put right through to Sawyer. He told me how you were a client of Griffin's time travel division. That you'd been studying the Creswells and got trapped in a cave-in at the portal."

"What!" If she hadn't wanted to kill the jerk before, she was dying to do so now. "That bloody bastard! I wasn't a client, and I bloody well didn't come here on purpose. He drugged me and forced me to come back here. I caused a cave-in when I tried to fight my way out of there." She forced a deep breath and closed her eyes. "Just go on, tell me the rest. I'll tell you my sordid story later, when we have more time." She opened her eyes and nodded for her sister to go on.

"There was an article in a local paper about a woman who was brutally murdered near here. The body wasn't identified, but they were sure it was you. So I decided I'd come back to save you." She rubbed her face. The lamplight flickered over her features but couldn't hide her frown. "I was such an idiot. I practically begged to come back here. I played right into his hands. Made it so easy on him."

Charlotte put a hand on Alex's shoulder in an attempt at comfort. Sawyer must have learned from screwing with her. He'd resorted to manipulation rather than force. She didn't doubt he was very good at it. Honesty gave him more trouble than a pack of lies.

Alex cleared her throat. "Anyway. So I came through the portal."

Charlotte was more than a little impressed. Alex had been forced to use a portal in the United States and then figure out a way to get to London. Charlotte admired her courage.

"But I'd read enough romances to know women didn't just travel around on their own. So I dressed up like a boy and signed on as a sailor on a merchant vessel." Her voice faltered. She was leaving something out, but now wasn't the time to push, so Charlotte let it go.

"I've been searching for you since I arrived in London. Stone approached me at a ball and showed me your pendant to prove he had you. He threatened to kill you if I didn't come along. So I did."

Hopefully, they'd have time to discuss this when they got out of here. "So what now?"

"I have no idea. How about you?"

Not what she'd hoped to hear.

****

"We had better let the horses walk." Oakleigh grunted as he dismounted.

James followed suit, though he wanted to insist they keep going. "I can't bear the thought that something may have happened to Charlotte. Who knows how long he's had a hold of her." He cursed beneath his breath. "We fought the last time I saw her. She refused to marry me."

"It must run in the family." Oakleigh chuckled. "Alex is refusing to marry me as well, though she will eventually. She loves me," he said in a cocky tone.

James knew the feeling. He'd thought the same when he proposed—until Charlotte burst into tears and confessed to all. "Enough to give up her life, everyone and everything she knows and loves back home? Charlotte loves me, as well, but she has family and friends where she came from, and it's tearing her apart." He was a heel. How could he ask it of her?

How could he not?

The smile fell from Oakleigh's face. "Women do it all the time. They leave their father's home for their husband's. It's the natural order. Besides, I own a ship. I could take her to visit any friends she may miss. She knows that."

"You can't sail a ship to their home." *If only it were so easy.* "Besides, it's different in their time. They can reach out and communicate instantly with loved ones around the world." James snapped his fingers to emphasize his point. "They can travel distances much more quickly. A trip that would take us a month can be accomplished in less than a day with their technology. They can speak with someone across the ocean, without leaving their home." He shook his head. Oakleigh must think him insane. He would have thought the same if a stranger had spouted such nonsense. "The advancements science will make in the future are truly amazing."

Oakleigh snorted. "Impossible. Are you talking about this time travel nonsense? How can you believe in such a fairy tale? It is patently ridiculous to believe people can travel through time."

"It's not nonsense. Charlotte proved it to me." He remembered the gun that rested in his greatcoat pocket.

The hard lump slapped against his thigh as they trudged along. "She showed me technological inventions that couldn't possibly exist today. Once you get over the difficulty in believing the concept of time travel, it's the only logical explanation."

"Logical!" Oakleigh exclaimed. "How can you call time travel logical?"

"I have learned to trust Charlotte. Do you not trust Lady Alexandra?" But did he deserve Charlotte's confidence? No. Her family believed in Lady Alexandra implicitly. They had no need of proof to recognize her character. "Her family appears to trust her completely. They didn't have the evidence I had, and yet they believed her."

"Her parents are so happy to have her back they would believe anything she told them. They *want* to believe her. They *need* to. So do I." Oakleigh's breath released in a huff. "Yet I can't believe her. She has lied to me from the day I met her, all for good reasons I'll grant her. This is no different. I just don't know her reason—yet."

Perhaps he and Oakleigh had more in common than he'd first thought. Would he not have taken the same view had Charlotte failed to provide proof of her claims? "You'll never truly win her if you don't learn to trust her." What if he didn't get a chance to prove to Charlotte the depths of his feelings? He wouldn't be able to live with that. She had to be all right.

The silence stretched as they both lost themselves in their thoughts and regrets.

The slap of Oakleigh's hand against his mare's neck snapped James back to the situation at hand. "I think the horses are sufficiently recovered. Let's get going."

James gripped his reins in white-fisted hands. His horse grunted and tossed its head but burst forward to keep the rapid pace Oakleigh set.

James approved of the grueling pace. He only wished Charlotte had brought more of her future devices with her. Their modern conveyances would have come in quite handy.

****

"Well, good thing I came, huh?" Alex snorted.

Charlotte grimaced. The last two months were spent with no idea of what she should do, and now her brief hope that Alex would have some knowledge she didn't was dashed.

"Hopefully Nicholas and Lord Tyndale got my message and will be able to figure something out."

At the mention of James's name, Charlotte's heart skipped a beat. "Lord Tyndale? How do you know him?"

"He thought I was you and approached me at a party in London. He realized his mistake immediately, but we all went to a private room to find out what he knew about you. We've had people searching for you since I arrived in London.

"I wanted to leave some sort of clue where I had gone and who was responsible so I left a message saying I had gone to find you at the cave, and that I was using Lord Stone's carriage. I never told anyone about the London portal, but I was hoping maybe you did?"

Charlotte nodded. Yeah, that had been a fun conversation. "Yes, I did. We're actually on James's property. He got trapped in these caves once when he was a child, so he knows just where we are." Tears burned at her eyes. "He asked me to marry him, and I said no. Do you know what I've been thinking about most as I sat her in this damp, dark hellhole? I've been thinking about what an idiot I am. I had a chance to marry the man I love, and I said no. Do you think he'll ever forgive me?" She wiped her nose with the edge of her sleeve. He'd been so angry when she'd turned him down.

"I'm sure he will. Judging by the way he looked at me for that short time when he thought I was you, he's as much in love with you as you are with him."

Charlotte returned the smile Alex gave her. It was nice to hear someone else confirm James's feelings for her.

"Thank God you told him about yourself." Alex hesitated. "Did he believe you?"

"Yes. Well, not at first." Understatement. "But I had a bag full of modern stuff, so he didn't have much choice." She wouldn't forget the astonishment on his face when he finally started to believe.

"Nicholas didn't believe a word I said. He's infuriating. He never listens. I get so mad at him, but then he turns around and does something wonderful."

Ah, the missing piece of Alex's story. "Is Nicholas your boyfriend?"

"Yes. And I'm completely, totally, in love. I don't know what I'm gonna do."

Charlotte could sympathize.

Alex glanced up and shrugged. "Anyway, now's not the time. Lord Stone could get here any minute. We can't just sit here and wait. We have to come up with a plan."

"I'm afraid it is a little late for that, my dear."

They both gasped at the voice coming from the cavern entrance. An older gentleman she didn't recognize blocked the exit. The flickering light from the lantern he held aloft didn't do him any favors, emphasizing the deep lines and slack skin of his jaw. Timmons stood a step behind, a smug smile on his smarmy face.

"Where's your coachman?" Alex asked.

Charlotte was proud her sister kept her voice so steady.

Stone waved his hand, dismissing the importance of anyone other than himself. "He is watching the horses, of course. He is quite upset with you, Lady Alexandra. I have rarely seen him in such a temper." He gave a nasty sounding chuckle. "He is looking forward to dealing with you personally."

Alex's voice was harsh as she replied, "Your coachman is a pig and should be kept in a sty."

Charlotte bit her lip to keep from smiling at Lord Stone's frown.

"You are an unusual girl. Your father should have taken a whip to you and taught you to mind your manners."

At mention of her father, Charlotte stiffened. Was her father behind this? Had he learned of her return and sent his flunkies to kill her once and for all?

"What are you planning to do with us?" Alex asked.

"What I planned on doing all those years ago. But first, I want to know where the two of you have been hiding all these years and whom you have informed of my involvement with your disappearance."

Seriously? All this because he assumed she knew

more than she did. "I already told Mr. Timmons. I didn't tell anyone about you." Alex inched toward Stone, so Charlotte did her best to keep his attention. She flipped her hair out of her face and sneered at him. "Until you walked in here, I never saw your face. You had nothing to worry about, you idiot."

Stone fairly bristled with rage. "As unpleasant as your sister. It will be a pleasure to finally rid the world of the two of you." He whipped the gun toward Alex. Charlotte froze in fear. "Stop right there, if you please. You wouldn't want your sister to be lonely now, would you?"

Charlotte clasped Alex's hand when she eased back over. A shuffling sound echoed down the passage, and Stone's smile widened. "Ah, here comes Mr. Cantor." He waited for the coachman to reach the cave and stand tall, before instructing him, "Make sure the ropes are nice and tight. We don't want them slipping through our fingers again, now, do we."

She grimaced as Cantor rebound her wrists. She tried to flex her arms to gain some wiggle room in the bindings, but he caught on and yanked even harder on the rope. She winced as the rough fibers cut into her skin.

He made a number of crude comments as he bound Alex in the same manner. Her sister twisted her head to the side and did her best to ignore him, though Charlotte could discern her disgust even in the dim light from Stone's lantern. Cantor had placed his several feet away, out of reach.

When the last knot was tied, Stone led his coachman out of the cavern leaving them to utter darkness.

Chapter Sixteen

The knots of Charlotte's bound hands stubbornly refused to give. She struggled not to groan as Alex picked at them. The circulation was almost entirely cut off, the ropes had been tied so tightly.

It seemed forever before Alex exclaimed, "Gotcha!" and the bonds fell off.

Charlotte flexed her wrists. "Brilliant, thank you. Give me a second, and I'll work on yours." She hissed as she shook her hands. "Pins and needles. Ouch. Bastard tied the damn rope so tight I lost circulation in my hands."

"Mine aren't that bad. The pig was distracted by my cleavage. He actually drooled on me." Alex shivered. "Yuck."

"Okay, give me your hands." Charlotte worked on the ropes. She had them off within minutes. "There you go." She paused. "Now what?" She wished she could see her sister, but the bastard had taken the lantern.

"Should we try to make it to the portal?"

That's all she'd thought about for the past two months. She still didn't know the answer. "I don't know if we'd be any better off. They might just send us right back. Or shoot us."

"No, they wouldn't, would they?" The horror in Alex's voice hissed through the darkness.

"I don't know. They weren't about to let me walk

out of there. That's for sure." She pictured Sawyer with his smirk and armed guards at his back. "Would they have shot me if they couldn't force me back? I just don't know. They wanted me back here, not dead. Not to mention, I caused a decent amount of damage when I left. I doubt they'd be too happy to see me."

"Yeah, but we might be able to buy some time. Convince them to let us stay a day or two before they force us back. Lord Stone and his people might think we escaped the same way we did last time and leave. Then we could make our way back and find a way to Lord Tyndale's house."

"Or Lord Stone might stumble through the portal." Charlotte laughed. "That could be fun. Lord Stone and those creepy servants of his at the business end of a couple of machine guns. With any luck the soldiers would shoot first and ask questions later."

"Humph." Alex chuckled. "Why was Sawyer so determined to send us back, anyway? I mean, it's been fifteen years. It's not like we just stumbled through the portal yesterday. We grew up there—uh, then—uh, whatever. Did he explain it to you?"

"No, not really." Charlotte sighed. "He said something about *cleaning house* and sending people back to their own time. He tried to tell me everyone was happy to go." She snorted. "I certainly wasn't. They had to drug me, and it still took a cave-in to push me through."

"They were a bit more creative with me. They went full court press to convince me to go willingly. They dangled you as the carrot to lure me here, but of course, I thought I could always come back. I wonder what they were planning on doing when I returned."

"Maybe they didn't expect you to return." There had been no name given in the article Sawyer mentioned. Who's to say they hadn't believed it was Alex in the piece? She shivered. She'd lost her sister twice now. She didn't want to lose her again.

"He said I could save you, and I believed him. He gave me the creeps. I should have paid attention to my gut and known everything wasn't what it seemed. I'm an idiot."

Charlotte clasped Alex's hand tight and tried to rub some warmth into her icy fingers. "You wanted to save me. That makes you heroic, not stupid. And if you'd never come, we would never have seen each other again. Nor would you have met your Nicholas and had a chance of living happily ever after with the man of your dreams," Charlotte whispered the last.

"Do you think it's possible?" Alex asked.

"What?"

"Happily ever after. Is it possible for us to live here, in this time, and be happy?"

"I've been thinking about that." More than a little. Especially after James had asked her to marry him. Charlotte sighed. "I remember what it was like when we were kids. We were happy, but we didn't know any better. Had we been raised in this century, we would have accepted that our lot in life was to marry well and become dutiful wives and mothers. We were wealthy, so we wouldn't have had to face some of the harsher realities of this time. But now, we've been exposed to a different way of life. I don't know if we can go back so easily."

Charlotte blinked rapidly. She'd cried enough for one day. She sniffled. She wasn't going to let any new tears fall or she'd never stop. "I'm a doctor. I went to work every day and made a difference, saved lives. Here, I can diagnose illnesses, but I have very little chance of actually helping. I lack the resources, and in most cases, they wouldn't listen to a woman anyway." Could she stand by helpless while people died from things she could cure with rudimentary medicine in the twenty-first century?

"But you could find a way to help within the strictures of this time." Alex paused. "They have midwives. You could use your knowledge to help pregnant women. Think of the horror women go through to bring a child into the world now. You could make a huge difference."

"I would love that. *If* I were allowed..." She tried to keep the bitterness from her voice but failed utterly. "A woman's life isn't really her own here. I would need to have permission from my husband or father."

"Yeah. The idea of needing a man's permission to live my life drives me crazy. I've been taking care of myself since I was sixteen, and I resent the implication I'm not capable. I'm not even allowed to decide for myself who to marry." Another brief pause. "Do you think it's possible for a man of this time to accept us and not try to run our lives?"

"I don't know," Charlotte whispered. "My parents," she hesitated. Alex would think of the parents they shared. "My *real* parents always discussed anything major, like when my mum wanted to move but Steven, my brother, and I were still in secondary school and dad didn't want us to have to switch schools. They argued a while, and in the end, they waited a few more years. I guess this wouldn't be all that different. James knows what I'm capable of. I think he would be supportive as long as I found a way to help without causing a scandal. If Nicholas loves you, he'll want you to be happy. Surely you'll be able to work things out."

Alex released a breath on a long, drawn out sigh. "That's *if* he loves me."

"Of course we have to get out of this mess first." Charlotte's tone turned bitter as she continued, "And hope our father doesn't decide to sell us to some other monster the minute he finds out we're still alive."

"What!" Alex exclaimed. "You think our father sold us to Lord Stone?"

"I know he did," Charlotte practically spat out the words. It was his fault she'd grown up with the horrifying image of a bloodied Alex a recurring theme in her nightmares. "When we were kids, I heard Mr. Timmons telling Lord Stone our father had given us to him in exchange for some vote."

"That's not true!"

Charlotte listened in disbelief as Alex talked about how sickened their family was over their disappearance. The tale she told was so far from what Charlotte had believed, she had a hard time following her sister's words. News of their nursemaid's murder hit her hard. She'd had no idea the poor woman had been injured. Timmons had whisked her away so quickly, she'd barely had time to register what was happening to her, let alone what was happening around them.

Could it be true? Could she have been wrong about her father all these years?

"He's had a virtual army of people out looking for you since the moment I came back and said you were in trouble. Please, you have to believe me."

Tears choked Charlotte. Damn, she'd barely lasted a minute before losing her promise not to cry. "I don't know, Alex. I want to believe you, but I *heard* them."

"We were only ten. Maybe you didn't hear what you think you heard. Maybe it was just an expression, like *he practically handed them to me* because it was so easy for Mr. Timmons to grab us."

Charlotte sucked in a sharp breath. "Oh my God. Could I have misunderstood all this time?"

Charlotte's shoulders shook with her tears. She sunk into Alex's embrace, rocking back and forth as her sister patted her back.

"I've hated him for so many years. Everything I thought I knew has turned out to be wrong. What's next?" Charlotte gave a shaky laugh. "If Lord Stone doesn't kill me, I think I'll die from shock."

"Or cold." Alex let Charlotte go. "I'm freezing, and I'm getting a cramp from sitting for so long. I've got to move around a bit."

Charlotte shivered from the loss of shared warmth. "Maybe we can make our way to the surface," she suggested. "They might not have bothered posting a guard. If they did, maybe the two of us can overpower him. Anyway, I'm with you. We have to do something."

"Okay. Let's go together. Grab my hand."

Charlotte groped around in the dark until she found Alex's questing fingers.

"Now, grab on and follow me. I need my hands to make sure I don't bump into anything. The ceiling gets pretty low in spots."

She took hold of the fabric at Alex's waist and tightened her grip. She didn't want to lose their connection as they made their way around the cavern. She trailed her other hand along the rough rock wall they inched along. She shuffled her feet, fearful of stepping into a crack and twisting an ankle.

In due course, they arrived at the tunnel entrance. She fought to still her heavy breathing, closing her mouth and fighting for air through her nose.

They tucked themselves up against the jagged wall of the cave. Charlotte gripped Alex's arm when she got a good look outside.

Lord Stone stood not far off, issuing orders to his servants. "I need you to discover what the ladies know and with whom they have shared that information. I don't care how you find out. Timmons, you stand guard while Cantor *persuades* the little ladies to talk."

The creepy grin that crossed that wanker Cantor's face gave her chills.

"I will await your report at my estate. Once you are satisfied you know everything, I do not wish to have any additional problems with them. See to it they never bother me again. It is late, and I do not wish to be disturbed at too early an hour. I shall expect your report directly following breakfast."

"Yes, milord," Cantor answered, eager anticipation evident in his tone.

She tugged Alex farther back into the cave. "There's no way out. They're too close to the tunnel entrance for us to sneak by them. Maybe we can ambush them as they enter the cave," Charlotte whispered as they both crouched to avoid the low ceiling, hands feeling along the walls to guide them in the complete darkness.

They reached the low portion of the passage and

used the cave walls to balance. Her thighs burned by the time the walls fell away into the larger cavern where they'd been held captive. "Go right. I'll go left, and maybe we can surprise them before they have the chance to stand up straight." She cursed. "If only I had my gun. I think James has it."

"I weighted down my purse. I can use it as a weapon. I have a few other things up my sleeve as well. Do you have anything on you?"

"No," Charlotte replied. Thank goodness Alex had something to use. Charlotte had been caught without a thing. Of course, Mr. Timmons had confiscated everything she had when he stole her necklace and then had that nasty coachman frisk her. "It probably wouldn't have done any good if I had the gun anyway. I couldn't shoot the broad side of a barn." She laughed quietly, but without humor. "Steven tried to teach me how to shoot, and I just scoffed at him. I said I would never be able to shoot anyone, so why bother. I'll tell you something. I wouldn't hesitate to shoot Lord Stone or that creepy Mr. Timmons."

"Is the gun how you proved to Lord Tyndale you weren't lying about being from the future?"

"The gun, my clothes, my watch, and a few pound notes I had in my jeans pocket." Thank goodness. She never would have convinced James she was telling the truth if she hadn't had some measure of proof. "Sawyer and his cronies were about to strip me down and dress me in period clothing when I regained my senses and made my bid for freedom. I grabbed a gun, but the whole thing backfired, and I ended up causing the cave-in that forced me through the portal. At least I got through with my stuff."

"I wish I hadn't been so gullible. I just went along with everything like a good little puppet, and look at me now."

If only she could. A little light would be a nice touch. She forced herself not to think about what could be crawling around them, or on them, in the pitch dark. Her skin crawled anyway. Her wrists, arms, and ankles stung from where the rope had dug into them. Cleaning them would be a priority if they made it out of here. She didn't want an infection to set in.

Fabric ripped. Was Alex preparing bandages? Or had her dress caught on one of the sharp rocks surrounding them.

Shuffling feet rustled in the tunnel. Charlotte tensed. She hoped Alex was prepared, because she certainly wasn't.

****

Part of James wanted to head straight to his estate. Surely this was all a mistake, and Charlotte was safely at home where he'd left her. But he agreed with Oakleigh that wishes were a waste of time, and they'd do better to proceed directly to Lord Stone's estate. They considered going directly to the caves that bordered both properties but elected to approach the house first. Stone's servants had little reason to remain loyal to their lord. An offer of future employment, or threat of imminent dismissal, might work wonders at gaining the information they sought. No such luck.

The servants, in various degrees of undress, huddled together in the hall. Oakleigh's repeated questions returned useless information.

James stormed out the entryway. He sucked in a lungful of air to calm his racing pulse. Getting his thoughts under control was essential. Their next step would be the cave entrance closest to Stone's property. But James chafed at the prospect. They might waste hours searching all the entrances to the caves. Who knew how many sections existed? And several had their own entrance with no access to the others.

A noise out of the shadows to his right caught his attention. He squinted into the darkness. A young man stepped to the edge, where the light from the house barely provided enough illumination to reach his face. "I done seen the lady," he said, with a shifty glimpse toward the house. He gestured for James to follow him away from the light.

James didn't hesitate to approach the man—a stable lad, judging from his attire.

"She was here. Screaming like a banshee as Timmons dragged her into a carriage. Some of us tried to interfere, but Lord Stone is a hard master." The man gazed down at his worn-out boots. Frown lines creased his forehead. James guessed his age to be two score, but the worry on his face made him appear closer to four. Life at the Stone estate was not easy.

"Do you know where they took her?" Please. Please let him know the answer.

But the servant shook his head. "I'm sorry, my lord. Lord Stone does not explain himself to us. He keeps much to himself."

"Tell me your name."

"Rupert, my lord."

"Well, Rupert. I thank you for the information." Several pairs of eyes followed their every movement. "You know where my home lies?" At Rupert's nod, he continued, "Present yourself to my butler, Worthing, tomorrow. He shall see you properly settled in my employ."

A huge smile lit Rupert's face. He bowed repeatedly, bobbing up and down like Prudence's hobby horse. "Thank you, my lord. Bless you, my lord."

James dismissed him with a nod and sought out Oakleigh, who continued to question the servants inside. He took Oakleigh to the side and quietly explained what he'd learned.

"We need fresh horses," James said. "I have doubts that Stone's servants will see fit to lend us one of this estate's mounts."

"Then we shall not ask," Oakleigh said with a raised brow.

Oakleigh knocked out the head groom with a swift punch to the jaw. James couldn't help but admire the man's fighting skills.

He led the way to the back of the stable where Stone kept his top hunters. He didn't often socialize with this particular neighbor but had been inside the stables more than once.

They were debating which route to take to the caves when the sounds of a carriage reached their ears. James scanned the distance. Just enough time to find cover. He spotted a row of trees lining the drive to their left. "Over there." They maneuvered their horses into position.

Stone drove his cabriolet at breakneck speed. One of the reasons James generally avoided the man. He showed as little regard for people as he did his finest horses. Light from the lantern cast an eerie glow on the dust raised from the horse's hooves. Flecks of spittle at his mouth and lash marks on his sides showed he had been ridden hard that night, and his driver had little care for his welfare.

"They're not with him," Oakleigh said. "Shall we stop him, before he reaches the house and has servants to come to his aid?"

"Yes, I believe that would be the wisest course of action," James responded. He kept his voice calm though rage had him gripping the reins of his mount in white knuckled fists. He swung his horse around to block the road.

The cabriolet's horse lurched to a screaming stop, fighting the reins that kept him in place, eyes wide in terror at the specter suddenly blocking his path. James kept his mount steady as the carriage horse plunged violently up and down before him, eyes white rimmed with terror.

He whipped out Charlotte's gun and trained it on Stone's head as Oakleigh made his way around the frantic horse to grab Stone around the neck and drag him off the carriage.

James pulled back, and with nothing left to control the frightened animal, Stone's cabriolet streamed past them, likely on his way to the barn. Hopefully, the groom had gained enough sense to take care of the mistreated animal.

Oakleigh dropped Stone, who landed hard in a puddle of mud at his horse's hooves.

Stone clearly had no idea of the danger he faced as he stood and attempted to brush the mud from his clothes. "How dare you!" he roared. "You will be punished severely for your affront to my person. I demand you turn over your horse to me at once and go fetch my carriage."

James joined Oakleigh in laughter.

Stone's confident demeanor faded as he stared between the two men in the dim light available from the moon and stars overhead. "I fail to see the humor in this situation."

"We simply find it amusing that you demand our horses," Oakleigh said, "considering they are yours."

"Mine!" Stone spluttered. "You have stolen my horses! I shall have you hanged for this. I am a baron. You cannot get away with this atrocity."

"Oh, I believe we can," James stated.

"Tyndale?" Lord Stone asked, his voice suddenly weaker. "What are you doing on my property, with my horses? I am, of course, always happy to help my neighbors with any trouble they may experience. There is no cause for such tactics."

"I believe there is a very good reason, two as a matter of fact."

Oakleigh dismounted. The large man then grabbed hold of Stone by his now severely rumpled cravat. "Where. Are. They?" Oakleigh asked. Slowly. Deliberately. Heaving Stone closer with each word. Stone's feet just barely reached the ground. His mouth gaped open like a fish out of water, struggling for breath. "You had better tell me they are unharmed, or *I* will hang *you* myself."

****

As Cantor made his way toward them, light from his lantern filtered into the cavern. Charlotte could make out Alex's outline, her arms raised and ready to strike. *Hit him hard, Alex.*

He didn't even pause as he entered, so sure they'd

still be trussed up, easy prey. Alex swung, her bag catching him under the chin and sending his head crashing back into the cave wall. The lantern flew from his grasp.

Charlotte leaped forward to catch it before they lost what little light it shed.

Cantor fell to the ground with a heavy thud. He lay still.

She peered up the tunnel, no one in sight. He must have come alone, no doubt feeling he didn't need any help, or witnesses, to interrogate two bound women.

Alex grabbed the ropes and tossed one to her. "Tie his feet. I'll get his hands."

First, she grabbed his gun and stuffed it into her pocket, then she wrapped the rope around his legs, as tight as she could, leaving him no room to escape.

Alex finished with his arms. "Now what?"

"Let's head back to the surface. Timmons must be around here somewhere, and I'd rather deal with him up there than down here." She had to get out of there.

"Yeah, me too," Alex agreed.

When they reached the surface, Charlotte hid the lantern behind her skirts so Timmons wouldn't notice its light. The rising sun was just making itself known. They had no trouble seeing Timmons inspecting the inside of a grand carriage. She could just make out the ruined interior.

"Do you have any idea how to drive that carriage?" Alex asked.

"No, but I could probably figure out how to unhook the horses. Can you ride?"

"No, I never even got near a horse before coming here. I haven't had the time to learn to ride one."

Bloody hell. They wouldn't make it far if Alex couldn't keep to a horse.

A noise reached her ears. They hushed, listening to the approaching rumble of horses. Timmons whirled toward the sound, an expectant smirk on his face. Had Lord Stone returned?

Alex made a motion toward some nearby bushes, and she nodded. They didn't want to get trapped with the cave at their backs—they'd just escaped their prison. Charlotte was in no mood to return so soon. They tiptoed over while the approaching horses distracted their guard. Crouching behind a large evergreen bush, they peeked out to keep an eye open for a chance to escape.

Alex watched the road, so Charlotte kept an eye on Timmons. He lifted his hands in the age-old sign of surrender. What? She followed Alex's gaze to the road. A man with dark hair pointed a gun at Timmons. And next to him was...

"James!" she yelled. It was foolish, but she couldn't seem to stop herself. She burst out from behind her hiding spot so she could feast her eyes on him.

"Charlotte." Relief tinged his voice. He shifted toward her, and she caught sight of something hanging across the withers of his horse. She gasped. It was a person, covered in mud and shaking violently. James shoved him off the horse. Stone landed awkwardly, barely maintaining his footing as he clutched the horse's side. James had her gun in his hand, pointed at her kidnapper.

"Don't move, Stone." James swung his leg over the horse's side and dismounted. Charlotte immediately rushed into his arms. He pulled her close to his side, his warmth chasing her lingering fears away.

A high-pitched whinny startled them both. James's horse reared on its hind legs, pawing the air. He swung her out of the way, putting himself between her and the horse. He caught a glancing blow to his shoulder, and the gun flew out of his hand as he toppled to the ground. She dropped to her knees at his side. Was he hurt?

She should have grabbed the gun. Stone snatched the weapon that had fallen practically at his feet and straightened, his legs wide and arms out in front of him.

It all happened so fast. Charlotte threw herself to the ground beside James. He tackled her, crushing her beneath him against the hard earth.

Bang! She flinched. Oh my God. She couldn't see a thing.

James jumped off her, flinging himself away. He tackled Stone to the ground. They struggled for only a moment before James wrenched the gun from Stone's hand.

A low groan, like that of a wounded animal, caught her attention. What she saw stabbed through her heart like a knife.

Alex lay in the large man's arms. Blood oozed from her side. Charlotte panicked. Alex was bleeding.

"No, Alex, no!" she screamed. *No. No.*

Charlotte ran to her sister. Then froze. All she could do was stare. The man holding Alex in his arms watched her like he was the one dying. Nicholas? Must be.

She should know how to handle this, but her mind was a blank. This was Alex lying beside her. She was suddenly ten years old, her sister lying dead at her feet.

Screw that. She was a grown woman. A doctor. She could handle this. She had to handle this.

She lifted her skirts and tore through the thick linen, tearing off the least soiled piece she could find. Sterile bandaging was a pipe dream here. She pressed it to the wound in Alex's side. She knew what had to be done, but she couldn't do it here. In this world of bloodletting and poor hygiene, Alex would never survive. A doctor in this time wouldn't even attempt to keep her alive.

A doctor in this time. But she wasn't entirely from this time, was she? Perhaps…

"Charlotte." Nicholas's voice was gruff, strangled by tears. "She's dying. I've seen wounds like this before. She cannot be saved. Here. Does she have a chance of recovery in the future? In your time." He closed his eyes briefly before continuing, "In her time?"

"I thought you didn't believe her." Tears streamed down her face. "Here, apply pressure here." She placed his hand over the wound, and he pressed down gently. "No, you need to be firm. Don't worry about hurting her. She can't feel anything." She grunted as she made more makeshift bandages from her dress.

James moved around in the background. His presence a soothing balm that allowed her to think clearly for the first time in what felt like forever.

"I didn't, but I do now. Trust does not come easy to me. But she deserves my trust and my love. She doesn't deserve this. Do you know whether she can be saved?"

"Yes, but we have to hurry." Charlotte paused, two fingers pressed to Alex's neck. Her pulse was reedy, thin. They didn't have time to waste. "You'll have to help me get her to the portal. I can't carry her by myself."

Charlotte tied a bandage tightly to Alex's wound and picked up a lantern. Nicholas cradled Alex in his arms, her head lolling against his shoulder.

"Follow me," Charlotte said. "There are some tight spots. We'll need to work together to get her through them. You won't be able to carry her the entire way."

Whenever possible, she forced herself to pause and check on Alex. Her instincts screamed at her to rush toward aid, but if Alex died before they even reached the portal, what was the point?

Finally, they arrived at the spot Charlotte remembered from her nightmares. "The portal is down at the bottom of this decline." She pointed ahead of them.

The ground dipped steeply downward and was narrow enough that getting Alex down was going to present quite a challenge. How was she going to carry her sister and navigate the passage at the same time? "We have to figure out how to get her down there. I don't know if I can carry her all that way."

"You're not taking her. I am."

"What!" She glared at Alex's man. "You can't."

"Why not?" he asked.

"They may not exactly welcome us with open arms." She gave a quick explanation of her botched escape in the future—the gun, the cave-in…

"All the more reason that I attend to it," Nicholas asserted. "I shall convince them of their obligation to cure her. Now, I believe time is of the essence."

He ignored her spluttering and continued down the path. She could only pray he'd find safe passage.

Chapter Seventeen

James held his lantern aloft trying to keep track of Oakleigh's progress. He believed Charlotte, he really did, but he couldn't deny the portion of himself that expected Oakleigh's journey to fail.

The tunnel was tight. Oakleigh's shoulders brushed both sides, and he was forced to twist his body to make it through some narrow sections. How he maintained his hold on Lady Alexandra was anyone's guess, though James supposed if the situation were different and Charlotte relied on him to save her, he'd have found a way as well.

They were almost out of sight, and suddenly Oakleigh lurched forward—and disappeared.

Charlotte's keening cry forced him out of his stupor. He dropped to his knees at her side and wrapped his arms around her trembling figure. He strained to hear her mumbled questions.

"What if it's too late? What if they won't help?"

"If I've learned anything about Oakleigh this night, it's that he is not to be denied. If there's any chance to save Lady Alexandra, he will see it done." It killed him he couldn't give her a better answer. Truth was, they had no way of knowing what had just happened to Oakleigh and Lady Alexandra. Given what Charlotte had explained about the portal's guard, their friends could have been shot on sight the moment they appeared in the future.

He hoped not. And he most definitely wasn't going to let on that the thought had even entered his mind. "We'll know if he was successful in a few moments."

She turned to him, her face tipped up to his, tears streaming down her cheeks, her mouth set in a miserable frown. "How? What do you mean?"

"If the portal guard is unwelcoming, they will send Oakleigh and your sister back immediately. If Oakleigh is able to convince them to lend Lady Alexandra aid, they will not return for some time. I imagine, even with the wonderful powers of your future world, that it takes some time to heal from a wound of this magnitude. Oakleigh will not allow her to return home until she is adequately recovered."

Slowly, her frown eased. Until, with panic spreading in her expression, she asked, "What if she died before they could help her? What if the crossing killed her? She was so weak. She didn't have much time."

"Then Oakleigh will return here immediately." He pulled her back into his embrace and settled himself against the cavern wall, her head resting on his chest. A rock immediately made itself known against his posterior, but he ignored the discomfort so as not to disturb his beloved. "We'll wait here for a short while. If they do not return within the half hour, I feel we can safely assume Lord Oakleigh has found some way to force their hand and help Lady Alexandra."

Her shoulders continued to shake with silent tears. All he could do was hold her and pray his logic was sound.

With each passing moment, he felt more hopeful

their prayers had been answered. Eventually, Charlotte's crying stilled. He began to think she'd fallen asleep, until she suddenly sat and straightened her skirts. "I'm going."

He tightened his grip around her shoulders. "Going where?"

She twisted under his arm to face him, pointing back over her shoulder. "Home."

That word was like a dagger to his heart. Home. She still thought of the future as her home. Never-the-less, he couldn't let her go. "No. You're not."

"I beg your pardon?" Her back straightened, her chin rose, and from the flickering light of their lantern, her glare was enough to make the heartiest of men quail.

But not him. He could face her disdain. He could not face her leaving him and never knowing if she were safe. "We have a lot to take care of here."

"Such as?"

He released her to count on his fingers. "Stone and his cohorts need to be taken into custody. Unless you left a note before you were taken, my mother is likely frantic with worry. Not to mention your family needs to be updated on what happened to Lady Alexandra."

Mention of her family got to her. She sunk into herself and pulled away from him. "I'm not so sure I want to see them."

With a finger under her chin, he tilted her head so he could look her in the eye. "Then you don't have to. But what about my mother? And Prudence?"

"Prue?" she said in a tiny, wavering voice. "Yes. Miss Crawford said she was all right, but I really would like to check on her myself. I never intended to leave without saying a proper goodbye first."

"Miss Crawford?" What part had she played in this? Cold had seeped through his backside. His legs ached from his awkward position and the jagged rocks he sat upon. "It appears we have much to discuss. Let's get out of here. We'll take care of Stone first and then head back to Tyndale Manor. We can talk there in comfort."

"What if Nicholas and Alex come back through the portal? We can't leave." Her voice rose at the end.

"As soon as we get home, I'll send someone to watch over the portal. We'll keep a twenty-four hour guard. Since they didn't come back right away, we have to assume Oakleigh has found a way to get Lady Alexandra the assistance she required. He won't leave her until he can be certain she is safe."

"How do you know that? Maybe he'll get her to the hospital and come right back."

"Trust me, I know."

"But how?" she insisted.

"Because he loves her. And there's no way in hell I would walk away from you."

****

Charlotte reluctantly preceded James away from the portal. Her head was fuzzy, her limbs shaky, and the burn marks around her wrists from the rope stung. A part of her was grateful James had decided to take charge of the situation. She'd be more herself later. For now, the evening's events were beginning to take their toll.

She stumbled frequently, but each time James was right there to keep her from falling. When they reached the larger cavern where she and Alex had been held, she stopped short with a gasp.

James immediately stepped up beside her. "What's wrong?"

"Cantor! We tied him up." Her hand shook uncontrollably as she pointed to the empty space. "We left him there. He should be right there."

"Damn." James searched the cavern, returning after a few seconds holding a pile of rope. "He must have had a knife on him. These ropes were cut clean." He held up one end of the bindings which had clearly been cut through.

"Bloody hell. We didn't think to check him. We knocked him out and tied him up. I took the gun he threatened us with, but that was it." She cursed her stupidity. She'd watched enough television to know she should have checked him. Her eagerness to get out of the damn dark made her act foolishly. She shivered. Speaking of which... "Any idea how long we've been down here? Who knows how long he's been gone."

"Long enough." James had her gun out. He grabbed her elbow with his other hand. "I'm going to make sure he's not waiting at the surface to ambush us. Can you stay here?"

She shook her head vigorously. "No. We only have one lantern. I can't, James. I just can't."

He gave her a quick kiss. "Do you know that's the second time you've called me by name? I like it."

So did she.

"Fine. We'll go together. When we get closer to the entrance, though, I want you to stay behind with the lantern while I go ahead. All right?"

She bristled at being treated like a child, but now wasn't the time to debate women's lib with him.

"Fine."

They made their way slowly to the surface, using the lantern only enough to guide their way, while trying to conceal the light from anyone who might be lying in wait for them. When sunlight from the exit finally filtered in, James doused the light and held a finger to his lips. He pointed to a spot that would provide her some cover. She nodded and tucked herself against the wall while he continued on silently.

Screw that, though. Seeing Cantor had escaped reminded her of the gun she had tucked into her pocket. She pulled it out and sidled her way closer to the exit, careful not to make any noise or let James see her.

He crouched behind the bushes, gun ready and swinging slowly side to side as he searched the area just outside the cave. From her stance behind him, she couldn't see much. When he carefully made his way around the bush, out into the open, she took his place. She scanned the area, searching for any danger that might take aim at him.

The gun shook so badly in her hand, her chances of hitting anything were slim. She was probably more likely to hit James by accident. But she could at least threaten to shoot. As far as backup went, she would not be anyone's first choice, but right now, she was all he had.

Thankfully, she didn't see anything out of line.

The smaller of the two carriages was gone. Cantor must have freed Lord Stone, and the two of them made a run for it. James let the gun drop to his side as he made his way over to the other carriage. He checked on a lump near the wheel. She started, realizing the lump was actually Timmons. So Cantor and Stone hadn't bothered saving the old man. There's gratitude for you.

She scanned the area one more time, and judging it safe, marched over to James's side.

He swung toward her. "Damn it, Charlotte. I told you to wait inside the cave until I called."

She propped her fist on her hip and glared back at him. "Yes, you did. I elected to help you instead. Deal with it."

A slow smile took over his face. "Yes, my lady. Don't mind me, I shall learn my lesson soon enough." He turned back to Mr. Timmons, squatting to get in the old man's face. "Where has Lord Stone gone off to?"

"I don't know now, do I. 'e done left me here."

James continued to question Mr. Timmons while she searched the carriage. If she could just find something to write on, she could leave a message for Nicholas. Let him know to wait, and someone would come here to meet him. Whenever he came back. If he came back.

Nothing. She shouldn't be surprised. Just because she always kept a small notebook and pen on her, didn't mean she'd find anything of the sort here. Paper was a much more precious commodity in this time than she had grown used to in the future.

Stupid not to have made arrangements before Nicholas and Alex passed through the portal. But she'd been so frazzled, she hadn't thought past the immediate need of getting Alex to someone who could help her.

She should have gone in Nicholas's stead. He knew nothing of the modern world. How would he handle all the questions the doctors would ask? She paced between the carriage and the cave entrance. Was she risking Alex's life by not being there? Should she follow now, find out what was going on?

Not knowing was killing her.

"I know what you're thinking. And the answer is no. Let Lord Oakleigh handle this."

She jumped. She hadn't noticed James's approach. "So you're psychic now? How convenient. Since you know so much, tell me what's going on with Alex. Did she survive long enough to make it to the hospital? Is she in surgery? Did she lose too much blood? Can Nicholas understand a word the doctors are saying to him, or are they walking all over him and letting Alex die while no one is there to be her advocate?" Her voice neared hysterical levels, but she couldn't stem the tide of panic overtaking her.

He rested his hands on her shoulders, holding her at arm's length and forcing her to keep her chin up to maintain eye contact. "Lord Oakleigh may not know what you do, but he does know how to command attention. Your doctors will bow to his demands and ensure Lady Alexandra's safety if only for fear of what he will do to them should they fail."

"If she was too far gone, there's nothing they can do to save her. It won't matter what threats Nicholas uses."

"Then your presence will not make a difference."

All her strength flooded from her limbs. She slumped, thankful he was there to catch her before she could fall to the ground. He swept her into his arms and placed her gently in the driver's seat of the carriage. He shoved Timmons in the passenger area and slammed the door shut before swinging up to the seat beside her. Warmth surrounded her as he placed his greatcoat over her shoulders. She clutched the front together and tucked her chin into the folds of the collar. His scent surrounded her, providing a modicum of comfort.

He squeezed her hands. "I don't wish to make light of your worry. I understand how difficult this must be for you. However, at this point in time, we must allow Lord Oakleigh to see to Lady Alexandra. As her fiancé, it is his right and his duty."

"And what of my duty as her sister? Shouldn't I be there? Nicholas knows nothing of the future. Sending him there to take charge was foolish. I'm much more capable of taking care of Alex there. He has no idea what he's dealing with."

He shook his head and took hold of the reins. With a flick of his wrists, he sent the horses surging forward.

"Wait, we need to leave a message. What if—"

"Nonsense. Lord Oakleigh would only return today were he to fail. He will not. And as for you being more capable in the future, I might agree with you were circumstances different."

"What circumstances?" What was he talking about? What would make Nicholas deal better with the future than her?

"This Sawyer you spoke of. A man such as you described would hardly be swayed by appealing to his better nature. I can assure you that Lord Oakleigh did nothing of the sort."

Maybe James had a point. Hadn't facing Sawyer been the reason she'd yet to make an attempt at returning?

Unfortunately, knowing all this did nothing to ease her anxiety or improve her situation. The man who wanted her dead had escaped. Her sister was at death's door, she had no way of knowing what was going on with her, and she still had no idea what she was going to do about her own life.

****

James drove the carriage home in silence. The horses had already been pushed nearly to their limit, so he kept them to a more sedate pace than he preferred. He supposed he could have arranged to switch horses at *The Rambling Inn*, but he elected to avoid what was sure to be a bustling business at this hour of the morning.

Scandal from the night's events would be unavoidable, but he had no wish to court more than his fair share. He needed time to think through all that had happened before facing those who would spread rumors that may or may not be based on the actual facts.

His first order of business was to take care of Charlotte. In the light of this new day, he could tell she'd been through quite an ordeal prior to his arrival. Then to have the sister she'd been so anxious to see shot in front of her...

Her very brief brush with hysterics was understandable. He wanted to get her home, where he could be ensured of her safety and allow her time to heal from her trials.

The question was whether she would allow him to take care of her as he wished. Charlotte was a strong woman. A trait he'd grown to admire. He'd never thought highly of strong women before, other than his mother.

Her strength was part of her appeal, yet he could wish her able to let down her guard for a moment and allow him to take care of her. He feared the moment his back was turned, she would run back to the portal with

237

all due haste and leave him without a word.

Would she do such a thing? He'd like to believe she'd at least take Prudence into consideration before leaving them. If he were not mistaken, he believed her to be quite enamored of his child. He might even define her actions toward Prudence as motherly.

Or perhaps he only saw what he wanted to see.

They arrived at Tyndale Manor in due time. Max, a wide bandage wrapped around his head, ran to greet them. James tossed him the reins so he could relinquish control of the carriage and see to Charlotte. Despite having his great coat wrapped around her, he flinched at the icy touch of her fingers.

"Max." He kept hold of Charlotte's hand, preventing her from proceeding to the manor's front door without him. She needed his support right now, whether she wished to acknowledge it or not. "There is a Mr. Timmons tied up in the carriage. He is responsible for abducting Miss Evans last evening at the behest of Lord Stone." He acknowledged Max's shocked gasp with a nod. "I will explain all that has transpired later. Please see Mr. Timmons does not escape. Send someone for the constable right away. Then see me in my study. Gather several men we can trust to keep these events to ourselves. There are many errands that must be seen to."

Max nodded, then rushed off, shouting for the assistance requested.

Seeing his commands being met, he led Charlotte to the house. Worthing opened the door immediately. James had never seen his steady retainer so shaken. His face was pale, and worry lines ran deep in his forehead and around his fierce frown.

"My lord, Miss Evans!" He grabbed hold of Charlotte's other elbow, lending additional support. With his other hand, he signaled something to another servant, who immediately scurried away toward the back of the manor. "We have been worried. When you did not appear at the evening meal last night, we all feared an accident of some sort. Then Max was discovered with a terrible knot on his head and informed us of his attack. The staff has searched through the night. Are you well? Shall I send for the doctor?" He led them into the drawing room, the nearest room with a convenient place to sit.

"No. I don't need a doctor." Charlotte snapped out of her stupor, a horrified expression on her face.

Knowing what he now knew, he'd gained a new respect for her dislike of the man. Their ways must seem barbaric to someone with knowledge of future medicine.

"Thank you, Worthing. There will be no need for the doctor. I have asked Max to—"

"Miss Evans." His mother burst into the room. Dark shadows haunted her eyes, she clutched a shawl to her chest, and her normally pristine clothing was wrinkled and splattered with dirt along the hem. He'd not seen her so distraught since the months following his father's death. She rushed to the sofa and gathered Charlotte into her arms. "Oh, my dear. We were so worried. Where have you been all evening? We feared the worst."

Charlotte straightened her spine and attempted a smile, though her eyes glistened with tears. "I am so sorry I worried you. I'm fine."

His mother leaned back and scanned Charlotte

from head to toe. Her eyes widened when his greatcoat slid off Charlotte's shoulders and her blood-splattered dress was revealed. She gasped. "Oh my goodness. Are you bleeding? We must send for a doctor right away."

Charlotte grabbed his mother's hands, preventing her from rising. "No. I'm fine. It's not my blood." She then covered her face with her hands, leaned forward and burst into tears.

Eyes wide, his mother sent him a questioning gaze as she gathered Charlotte in her arms and patted her shaking shoulders.

"It is a very long story, Mother. Perhaps best not rehashed at the moment. Miss Evans and I will explain all at a later time. For now, I must see to a few details. Will you please stay with her?"

"Of course, dear."

Reassured Charlotte was in excellent hands, he crossed the hall, intent on setting the search for Lord Stone into motion. He wouldn't rest easy until the man had been taken care of and he could be assured no one was left who would seek to harm Charlotte.

****

"Are you quite all right, dear?"

Charlotte shook her head as Lady Tyndale's question penetrated the fog that had descended upon her mind. "I…I'm sorry. I'll be fine. I'm still reeling a bit from everything." Exhausted and heartbroken, but nothing the lady needed to worry over.

She perched on the edge of a small, upholstered bench at the end of an enormous four-poster bed, Lady Tyndale beside her. The room was overwhelmingly pink. The bedding, all the chair cushions, the wallpaper. Even the carpet had pink woven throughout. Pink had never been one of her favorite colors.

They'd moved from the drawing room to a bedroom in the family wing, a few doors down from James's room. Apparently, news of Charlotte's family had spread quickly. Lady Tyndale insisted Charlotte move out of the governess's quarters and stay as their guest rather than servant. She also made a point of mentioning that she slept in a different wing, giving James ample privacy. There was a dowager house on the property, but Lady Tyndale was not ready to remove herself quite yet, though the implication was there that she would consider moving once James settled down with a new bride. Charlotte suspected James's mother of playing matchmaker.

Lady Tyndale gave her a soft, gentle smile and held her tighter to her side. "We're all a bit unsettled. Would it help to speak with me about last night? I know I spend much of my time talking, but I'm quite a good listener as well."

Charlotte chuckled. "Thank you. I don't even know where to begin." Lady Tyndale knew nothing of her history. And she definitely wasn't up to explaining the future without anything handy to prove her point. She was fond of James's mother and cared what she thought of her. Acting like a lunatic wasn't the impression she wanted to leave with the lady.

"I've always found the beginning is a good place from whence to begin one's tale."

So she explained about Mr. Timmons and Lord Stone, Alex and Nicholas, the caves and her kidnapping fifteen years ago. If Lady Tyndale noted the gaps where Charlotte left out anything pertaining to the future or where she'd been the past fifteen years, she was polite enough not to push for answers. She simply listened, gasped, and made comforting noises when appropriate.

Charlotte didn't know how long she rambled on, but by the time she finished, her stomach rumbled and her head ached, but her heart felt lighter for sharing her burdens.

A soft knock sounded on the door. "Enter," said Lady Tyndale.

Theresa nudged the door open with her hip, her hands full with an enormous tray. Tea for two, along with a mouthwatering assortment of pastries. The delicious aroma set Charlotte's stomach growling like a monster truck. She jumped to clear space on a small table before the fireplace. This room Lady Tyndale had insisted on moving her to was quite luxurious compared to her previous accommodations.

"Thank you, Theresa." Once the tray was settled, she asked, "How is Prue? Did she wonder where I'd disappeared to?" She twisted her fingers together. Had the poor girl thought Charlotte abandoned her? She'd always made it clear she'd be leaving one day, but she never intended to leave without a proper good bye.

Theresa curtsied. "She's well, mum. Eager to see you when you're ready."

"I shall send for her shortly, Theresa," Lady Tyndale interrupted. "If you would leave us now, I'd like Miss Evans to have a bite to eat before she gets too settled."

Theresa curtsied and then left.

Charlotte suppressed her dismay. She shared Prue's desire to get together. She wouldn't be happy until she could see for herself that Prue was all right.

"Please, sit, Miss Evans. Have something to eat.

You will see Prudence shortly, but..." she let her voice trail off with a slight frown as she stared into space.

"But?" Why did Lady Tyndale want to keep her away from Prue? "Prue's all right, isn't she? They didn't..." Her voice cut out. She couldn't continue. If Mr. Timmons or Miss Crawford had done something terrible to that wonderful little girl...

Lady Tyndale placed a hand on her knee and squeezed. "Prudence is fine, dear. Don't you worry. However, you don't look quite yourself. Have a little something to eat while I have a bath drawn for you." She paused, then resumed gently, "I fear Prudence would worry were she to see you in your current state."

Damn. Her hands flew to her cheeks. Her nails were jagged, her fingers black with muck and dried gore. Her dress was ripped to shreds, and she was splattered with Alex's blood.

She was certain she didn't smell particularly nice, either. And here she'd been crying away on Lady Tyndale's shoulder when she should have gone straight into a bath and freshened up.

Coming back to her senses sucked. Her wrists stung, her skin itched, and she didn't want to think about the creatures that probably crawled in her hair and in the folds of her clothing. The idea of sinking into a tub of hot water was heavenly. "A bath sounds like a brilliant idea, thank you."

Lady Tyndale poured her a cup of tea, but Charlotte didn't reach for it. Instead, she shuffled over to a basin and poured it full of water from the pitcher nearby. She shivered, the chilly water quickly became murky from her mess. Getting her hands completely clean was out of the question without copious amounts of soap, but she did the best she could. She'd scrub herself raw in the bath later. For now, she just needed her hands clean enough to eat without spoiling the food.

While she ate, Lady Tyndale directed the filling of the tub. Pretty soon, the bath was full, and steam could be seen rising from the heated water. She didn't want to be rude, but she couldn't wait to be alone.

"I'll leave you in a moment. Let me help you remove your dress."

"No, that's not necessary. Thank you."

Lady Tyndale was not to be dissuaded, so Charlotte gave in, wondering at the lady's frown and hesitant manner. Lady Tyndale was usually one to come right out and say what she meant or come up with some seemingly innocent remark to set someone in their place. Yet she remained virtually silent, except for giving a direction here or there.

"Is there something you wished to say to me?" Charlotte finally asked.

"Yes, dear. Yet, I'm afraid I don't quite know how to ask. It is a—delicate matter."

A delicate matter? What was that supposed to mean?

Lady Tyndale cleared her throat. "I wonder whether you have told me everything that occurred last evening?" She paused and gave Charlotte a searching gaze. "I sense that you have kept something back from me."

Shit. What could she say? The bath called to her, and by the time she explained the entire truth to Lady Tyndale, the water would be cold. She trusted the dear lady, but she was so tired. Convincing Lady Tyndale she wasn't a nutcase would take much more energy than she had. "It's nothing. Really."

"You may view me as an old—"

"No, I would never—"

"—lady. However, I'm well aware of the terrible things that can happen to a woman in this world. I would like you to know that I would never think the less of you had the men who took you—"

It suddenly dawned on Charlotte what Lady Tyndale was worried about. "No!" She shook her head vigorously. "Nothing like that happened. Mr. Timmons was strong, but thankfully not interested in anything other than pleasing his lord by capturing me. I have no doubt had I been left alone with the coachman something like what you're thinking might have occurred, but he had to rush to London to inform Lord Stone of my capture." She squeezed Lady Tyndale's hand. "You don't have to worry. Other than being tied up and left in that dank, dark cave, I wasn't hurt. Not physically."

Lady Tyndale let out a loud gush of air. "I hated to even think such a thing might have happened, yet were you hurt in that way…"

She gave the woman a hug. "Thank you. I appreciate your concern."

"Do not worry overmuch about Lord Stone and his servant evading capture. Even now my son is taking care of everything. The culprits will be apprehended in no time. Meanwhile, you have returned to us safely, and I couldn't be more pleased." She gave one last tug on Charlotte's chemise and the neck gaped wide.

Charlotte grasped the fabric together to cover her breasts, a furious blush heating her entire face at being practically naked before James's mother. Not to mention the heartbeat tattoo she had on her ribcage in memory of her parents. That would take some explaining.

"I believe you can manage the rest on your own. Please know that you are welcome to stay as long as you wish. Perhaps, one day as more than a mere guest." With that parting remark, she left.

Charlotte dropped her chemise and stepped into the steaming hot bath. She completely submerged, grateful to block out the surrounding world. If only she could avoid Lady Tyndale's less than subtle hints as well.

Chapter Eighteen

Two days later, James paced his study waiting on Charlotte's family to descend en masse. And before they did, he had to let Charlotte know they were on their way.

He had to get her out of her room first. Her new room. Upon learning her family name, his mother had moved Charlotte into the rose room, two doors down from his. Having her so close had kept him awake most of the past two nights.

Yet he'd seen little of her despite their proximity. He had informed her of his intention to send word to her parents, so that her family soon being with them shouldn't be entirely surprising.

So why were his palms sweating and his stomach churning at the thought of breaking the news to her?

He wiped his hands down the sides of his breeches. His mother was speaking with Charlotte now. Whether she would accompany Charlotte to his study, mention the Creswells' imminent arrival, or simply inform Charlotte to come see him, he had no idea.

As the minutes ticked by on the mantel clock, he found himself staring at the door, eagerly anticipating her company at any minute. His heart picked up its beat with excitement to be near her once more. He'd missed her the past couple of days.

What was that saying he heard recently? A

watched pot never boils? He sat at his desk, forcing his attention to the ledgers before him. Each set of numbers had to be reviewed multiple times to be sure he didn't make any errors. His mind refused to focus on the job at hand.

Where was she? If she didn't come down soon, her family would arrive with no time to warn her. And he wouldn't be able to spend any time with her before her whole family was here to plague them.

The door burst open, and his mouth stretched in a welcoming smile. Which fell almost immediately when Sebastian strolled into the room.

"What the hell are you doing here?" he burst out.

Sebastian's mouth gaped open, his eyes wide, his eyebrows raised. "While I appreciate the warm welcome, I can come back later if now is not a good time."

James ran his hand through his hair. "I apologize. I have been most anxious about the arrival of Miss Evans's family. I worry how she will react to seeing them once again. It is my understanding she holds them in some disfavor." And he had yet to figure out why. His intention had been to question her about the issue as soon as she emerged from her room, yet the opportunity had not occurred. In those moments he'd managed a glimpse of his elusive love, either his mother or daughter was present, allowing no room for the discussion he sought.

"I was but a child of six when all that occurred, so never knew the story. I learned much during the past few days."

"It is a shocking tale. Lord Stone has much to answer for. Did anyone explain why Charlotte holds her family in such disregard?" He should be asking such questions of Charlotte, not his brother. However, if she was to continue to make herself scarce, he had little choice.

Sebastian shook his head. "They are unaware of any such rift. The first they heard all was not well with Lady Charlotte's feelings toward them was when you mentioned it the night of the ball."

"Have you spoken with them since that night?"

"I relayed the message of Lady Charlotte's safety as soon as your letter arrived. They had already set to packing the morning after the ball. I urged them to give her a few days to prepare for their arrival. They apparently had difficulty with that direction as I ran into them an hour ago at *The Rambling Inn*. I offered to ride ahead and inform you of their imminent arrival in case you did not receive their missive informing you of their intent to visit."

"I was aware. They're at *The Rambling Inn*?" He studied his reflection in the looking glass, straightened the knot in his cravat. "Damn. I had hoped they would not set out quite so early in the day. I must go find Miss Evans and see that she is prepared to receive visitors."

"How soon will they get here?"

James swung toward the door. Charlotte stood with one hand on the jamb, the other tangled nervously in her skirts. He and Sebastian bowed in her direction. "I didn't hear you enter." He strode over and offered a hand. Her soft, cool grip trembled slightly. He led her to a chair and urged her to sit. "They will arrive at any moment."

Sebastian strode to her side, took her hand, and pressed a kiss to her knuckles. James considered smacking him on the back of the head but restrained himself. "It's a pleasure to finally meet you, Miss Evans, or should I say Lady Charlotte Creswell?"

Charlotte flashed a quick smile. "Miss Evans will do nicely, thank you."

James tipped his head toward the door. "Sebastian, if you don't mind, I'd like a moment alone with Miss Evans."

"Not at all. I shall see you at the evening meal." He bowed and strode to the door. "Dinner is sure to be entertaining." With a smirk, he left, closing the door behind him.

"Scapegrace." James shook his head, then took the seat next to Charlotte rather than sit across from her with his desk between them. He took her hand, enclosing it within both of his. She shivered. "Will you be all right, Charlotte? I wish I could put off this meeting with your family, yet I can't help but understand their wish to see you as soon as possible. Were I separated from Prudence in such a manner, I would not rest easy until she were returned to me. I can't begin to imagine your parents' agony these past fifteen years."

Her smile trembled. "Yeah, well, Prue is special. But not all parents feel the same toward their children."

What was she saying? Did she think her parents cared nothing for her? "Do you—are you saying your parents don't love you? I can assure you, what little I know of Lord and Lady Downing indicates they care deeply." Whispers had followed the Creswells for years. Personally, he'd been at school when the event occurred, but he'd still heard all about it. And whenever Lord or Lady Downing were discussed by the *ton*, there was a brief, "They're the couple whose children were taken so many years ago. You remember..." and the whole event was rehashed.

"I wish I could believe that."

****

Charlotte closed her eyes. She couldn't look James in the face as she admitted what she'd thought of her parents all these years. And despite Alex's assurances, a part of her still couldn't wrap her head around the idea that she'd been wrong.

With James watching her with such sympathy, and disbelief, in his gaze, she had to fight furiously against the tears that burned against her eyelids. She didn't want to break down in front of him.

"Alex—" She gulped. Thinking about her sister didn't help matters any. "Alex assured me I was wrong, but I just can't brush aside what I've believed all these years."

"And what is it that you believe?"

"My memories of the kidnapping, the first one I mean, are fuzzy. Flashes of a nightmare. I remember Mr. Timmons grabbing us." She rubbed her arms. "I was covered in bruises when I fell through the portal. He pinched my arms so tightly. I remember crying for my mum. I remember all the blood..."

"What blood?" he asked.

"Alex's. We ran down that tunnel. We were so scared. But the last part of that tunnel was rough, narrow, and with uneven footing. Alex tripped. And when I fell through the portal after her, I landed partially on top of her. Her head..." She put a shaking hand to her mouth. "There was so much blood."

Strong arms wrapped around her. She hid her face

in his cravat, let the fabric soak up her tears. "But before we ran, I overheard Timmons and Lord Stone talking. Alex says I misunderstood, but…" She shook her head.

"Go on. What did you think you heard?"

"I heard Timmons tell Stone that our father had given us to him in exchange for his vote."

James gasped. "Impossible. Besides how devastated your father appears over your disappearance and how concerned for your welfare, what reason could he possibly have for wanting to get rid of his daughters?"

"I don't know. Alex thinks I misheard. That Timmons was just making an offhand comment about how easy we were to kidnap."

James shifted, leaning back and pulling her with him so she rested more comfortably against his chest. His warmth and manly scent seeped into her consciousness. Without needing to ask, he arranged them into such a comfortable position she could quite happily take a nap. The emotions of recent days had taken their toll. She was exhausted.

"I believe Lady Alexandra's theory is correct. I'm confidant you will feel the same once you've had a chance to discuss these circumstances with your family."

Her heart lightened at his words. The feeling that he and Alex just might be correct had her anticipating her family's imminent arrival rather than dreading it. Resentment had played so heavily on her mind, for so long, her spirit would be lighter for getting rid of that awful weight. "I hope you're right. I remember some of my childhood. We were a happy family." She laughed.

"Alex and I got into trouble all the time."

"Quite the little hellions, I take it?" Amusement rang in his voice. A deep rumble vibrated through his body, snapping her attention back to him.

"You could say that." Reluctantly, she disentangled herself, leaned back, and tried to put her clothing into some semblance of order. Her parents would be here soon, and she shouldn't be caught lying in James's arms as if she had a right to be there. After all, she had said no to his proposal.

His gaze bore into her as he continued to lounge against the corner of the little sofa they shared. He crossed his legs, but not before she caught sight of the bulge in his breeches.

Her cheeks heated instantly. If she'd agreed to his proposal, his body's reaction to her proximity would delight her, but given that she'd refused…well, matters had become much more complicated. Giving into her desire when she wasn't sure what their future could possibly hold would just make their situation all the worse. She needed to keep a clear head on her shoulders. Having sex with James, which undoubtedly would be amazing, wouldn't help her figure out what she needed to do next.

She jumped off the couch. "I should freshen up. They could be here any minute, and I don't want to face them looking like such a slob."

"You are beautiful, as always, and I don't think your parents will care one whit whether your dress is wrinkled." The smoldering gaze he sent her reassured her that he didn't think she looked bad at all.

The way he lounged back, one arm over the back of the sofa, hair slightly tousled, desire burning in his eyes, tested her resolve.

The sound of carriages on the gravel drive interrupted her carnal thoughts. She gasped. "That must be them."

James stood. "Go. I'll see them first and give you a moment to set yourself to rights." He stepped up to a mirror hanging next to the door to fix his rumpled cravat.

She couldn't resist. His consideration warmed her heart as much as her attraction to him warmed her body. Before she could think better of it, she dashed over to him, gave him a quick kiss on the lips, then scurried from the room.

****

Charlotte fled like a frightened fox, her kiss warm on his lips. Her tale had shocked James. That she'd believed for the past fifteen years that her father had sold her made his own resentment of his mother's background and the gossip it caused feel ridiculous in comparison.

He couldn't imagine that were true, but he'd make sure of it before letting the Creswells within five feet of Charlotte. She may not have accepted his proposal yet, but he was determined to gain a yes from her before much more time had elapsed. As her future husband, it was his duty to see to her welfare. Determining the truth of this matter was paramount.

He tidied his appearance as best he could while Worthing made the guests comfortable in the drawing room. Albert would dress him down later for the sorry state of his cravat, but there was no time to fix it now.

Once the commotion in the entry died down, he closed his study door behind him and made his way to greet his guests.

His mother stood and swept to his side as he entered the room. "Tyndale, dear. There you are." She faced the room at large. "You all know my son, I believe?"

Lord Downing and his sons bowed, each befitting their station in comparison to his, while the ladies kept to their seats but nodded politely. The tension in the room was palpable.

Lady Downing wrung her hands until they gleamed white in her lap. "I apologize if I appear rude; however, I am quite anxious to see my daughter. Where is Charlotte?"

"I'll send for her right away," his mother responded.

He held out a hand to forestall her. "Wait a moment, Mother. We have a few issues to clear up before Miss Evans—"

"Her name is Lady Charlotte Creswell. Please refer to her as such." Charlotte's brother, Viscount Creswell, stepped forward, his fists clenching and unclenching at his sides.

He reminded James strongly of Sebastian, though he doubted Sebastian had ever been quite so on edge. Lord Creswell appeared ready to lash out at a moment's notice.

James nodded his acknowledgment of Charlotte's true heritage, yet he didn't think their insistence upon her switching names would go over well with her. "I understand. However, I would caution you to approach this issue carefully. Lady Charlotte views herself as Miss Evans. She feels great loyalty to the family that raised her."

Lady Downing's face drained of color while her son's flooded red. Lord Downing rested his hand upon his wife's shoulder, standing at the side of the chair upon which she sat. "We understand." He gave his eldest son a silencing gesture when the boy moved to argue. "Thank you. You showed great concern for our daughter when you approached us in London. And your brother has intimated that you have shown a marked affection toward her. He believes of a permanent nature. Is this correct?"

This was not where he'd planned to take this conversation, but there appeared to be no way to avoid it. "Yes. I have asked Charlotte to marry me."

"And her response?" asked Lady Downing.

He gave his mother an apologetic glance. He had failed to heed her advice and run off to London before securing Charlotte's affections. Of course, he'd had no reason to believe Charlotte wouldn't be here when he returned. With all that had happened since, he'd yet to resume his pursuit of Charlotte's hand. "No."

"This appears to be a habit of my daughters," Lord Downing quipped.

"I have not, as yet, received any offers. I shall endeavor not to follow in their footsteps unless absolutely necessary," Lady Mary returned.

The tension lessened slightly with their amusement only to come crashing back when Charlotte said from the doorway, "I'm so sorry to be such a disappointment," her tone icy with disdain.

Everyone jumped to their feet and began talking at once, denying her statement. Lady Downing surged forward, but Charlotte held out a hand and stopped her in her tracks.

His mother stood by Charlotte's side, their hands entwined, but mostly hidden in their overlapping skirts, they stood so close. Lady Downing's face fell.

He couldn't blame her. Charlotte appeared to be choosing his mother over her own. He cursed beneath his breath. He'd hoped to have all doubt about her parents' part in the original kidnapping laid to rest before Charlotte came face to face with her family.

He moved to flank her other side.

"Charlotte?" her mother whispered, her voice cracking midway.

Charlotte's eyes misted, but her spine remained stiff. "Lady Downing." She nodded at her, then toward her father. "Lord Downing. It's been a long time."

****

Charlotte's hand shook so much, Lady Tyndale's arm was likely to vibrate right off. Her heart ached to run into her mother's embrace. She could tell that was exactly what Lady Downing had expected, or at least, hoped would happen. A pang of guilt hit her chest.

If Alex was right, then this family had suffered through an unspeakable loss for the past fifteen years. And here she was ruining what should be one of the happiest, most bittersweet moments of their lives. She studied each face, trying to find answers.

Lady Downing's whole form screamed of her need to run forward. Charlotte remembered that her family had never been quite so reserved as some of the other members of the *ton*. Her parents had always shown their love for their children, even when they were snot-nosed little brats defying their nannies and driving everyone crazy. Her friends' families, not so much. True, she'd learned how to behave properly formal in public, but home had always been another story.

Lord Downing stood a step behind his wife, one hand gripping her shoulder. Charlotte hid her wince. With his knuckles white as chalk, Lady Downing was likely to have a bruise when he finally let go, but her mother didn't appear to notice.

He gave the impression of a weary man with only a tenuous grip on his dignity. The need to stay strong for his wife the only thing keeping him from sagging to the floor. He didn't look like a monster.

Then again, do monsters ever really look the part?

Alex trusted him, James seemed to as well. But could she?

A rustling of skirts directed her attention to the other side of the room where three younger people stood in a cluster. The oldest man was familiar. Gregory? Yes. The resemblance to their father was remarkable. He no longer had the starving air of a boy growing too fast for his own skin, but she recognized him.

Her feelings on him had flip-flopped numerous times over the years. Sadness warred with jealousy. Over the years, she'd wake up sobbing from nightmares where Gregory lay all bloodied in that cave right next to Alex. On those nights she was convinced that Gregory had been sold to Stone as well and hadn't had the good fortune to stumble upon a time portal.

Other times, when she was feeling particularly sorry for herself, her jealousy would grow to extreme heights. Father had loved him best. Of course Father would never harm his only son. Must be nice to be born with a penis. In her old world, that particular appendage meant the difference between being loved and cherished versus sold as a bargaining chip. A number of her female friends had fathers who barely acknowledged their existence other than to bemoan their need for a dowry.

Those thoughts of her brother always led to a great deal of self-loathing. Nothing that had happened to her had ever been Gregory's fault. "I see you're not so scrawny anymore," she said to him in a light, teasing voice. She used to love comparing him to the older boys who'd already grown into manhood. "You're so different. All grown up."

Gregory's lips twitched. "Same could be said of you," he said, pretending to scrutinize her dress. "Or at least, you haven't had a chance to ruin your dress yet today."

Charlotte chuckled. True, she'd been known for staining her clothing the minute she stepped out of her room. If she wasn't running off on some adventure or other with Alex, she'd manage to spill food into her lap or get spit up on while playing with baby Mary.

Who was now a young woman with a striking resemblance to Charlotte. Mary's hair was a little lighter, and her eyes were a light blue rather than green, but the similarity was striking. "Hello, Mary. You probably don't even remember me, but you used to love to drool on my shoulder."

Mary's face blushed beet red, but she smiled. "Mother and Father have told me all the stories about you and Alexandra, so I feel as though I remember you quite well. I've always admired the portrait of us all from the year I was born. I was an ugly little thing, but I had hopes of sharing the beauty my sisters already promised at only ten years. I can't tell you how often I wished to know you. Wished that I had grown up with my sisters rather than two annoying brothers." With that, she elbowed the youngest one in the room.

He flinched and poked her back before a stern glare from Lord Downing stopped them both.

Her parents had had another boy after she and Alex disappeared? He resembled the Gregory from her memory, though a few years older. He would soon fill out in proportion to his height, but for now he was tall, gangly, and awkward. He showed promise of being as handsome, if not more so, than Gregory. Her heart twisted a tiny bit. At least she had memories of Mary, but this boy—she didn't even know his name.

"I guess you've been told who I am, but...what's your name?"

"Myles, Myles Creswell. It's a pleasure to meet you at last." He bowed, and his gaze slid to their parents. "We've all missed you."

"You don't even know me."

He nodded and gulped, his Adam's apple bobbing up and down. "I'd like to. Gregory told us all the stories Mother and Father knew nothing about. You and Alexandra were devilish hoydens. All the crack from what I hear."

Gregory and Mary stifled laughs behind their hands, her parents gasped with wide-eyed glares at Myles, while Charlotte tried to remember what that term meant. She gave it up for a lost cause. Given the way Myles's head had nearly vanished between his shoulder blades, she wasn't going to get an answer out of him. His tone indicated it was meant as a compliment, though, so she smiled. "I think that was meant as a positive thing, so, thank you, Myles."

He shuffled his feet, but she was pretty sure his lips twitched into a brief return smile.

Back to her parents. No more avoiding her real questions. She'd daydreamed this reunion so many times in her head, and each time she was filled with righteous indignation at these two people who had been so callous, so unforgivable. Her father for selling them, and her mother for allowing it.

Now she wasn't so sure and struggled with what to do next.

"Tell me what happened."

Warmth touched the small of her back. The weight of James's hand settled against her, his heat spreading through the thick fabric of her dress and all the necessary Regency era layers.

"Why don't we have a seat? This could take quite some time. We may as well be comfortable."

"Yes," Lady Tyndale chimed in. "Please, make yourself at home. Tea should be here at any moment." A knock sounded at the door. "Ah, that must be Mrs. Sterling now. Perfect timing."

She opened the door wide, but Mrs. Sterling wasn't there with the tray as expected. Worthing stood there instead, a worried frown on his face. He bowed. "Excuse me, my lady, my lord." He stepped forward and spoke quietly in James's ear. "I apologize for my intrusion, my lord, but I felt certain you would wish to know of our latest arrival immediately."

Charlotte made no attempt to disguise her relief at this interruption and eavesdropped intently.

Worthing scanned the room, obviously noting everyone's eyes trained on him. "Ah-hem. Shall I show him into your study, my lord, or do you wish him to join you here?"

"Who is it, Worthing?"

A shadow fell across the room, and in strode a large man, exhaustion plain on his heavily scarred face.

"Lord Oakleigh," James exclaimed.

Chapter Nineteen

Sorrow ravaged Oakleigh's face. Hair mussed, eyes bloodshot, his scars stretched tight by his fierce frown. James had never seen anyone so forlorn. The icy prick of fear pierced his veins. "Lady Alexandra?"

"She lives," Oakleigh replied.

A collective sigh sounded around the room. Lord Downing stalked over to stand before his would-be son-in-law. "Has she not returned with you? Was she not well enough to travel?"

Oakleigh laid a hand upon Downing's shoulder. "She will be well, of that I promise. But she will not be returning to us. The danger was too great."

Lady Downing burst into sobs, collapsing onto the sofa. His mother, along with the Creswell children, ran to help the distraught woman. James watched Charlotte.

Face white as a ghost, she stood steady, white knuckled hands twisted together. The hard look on her face gave him pause. Eyes wide, staring at Oakleigh as if her mind were elsewhere.

"Charlotte?" He approached her cautiously, suddenly nervous what her sister's failure to return might mean for Charlotte. He'd had a hard enough time keeping her from storming through the portal. What would she do now that her sister had elected not to return?

She blinked. Her gaze met his briefly before she

swung toward Oakleigh. "What state was she in when you abandoned her there?"

James gasped.

Oakleigh's fists tightened. A tic pulsed in his jaw, his lips drawn to a tight white line. His scars blanched a mottled white, the rest of his face red. "I did not *abandon* her. I left her in the care of her dear friend and your modern day doctors, who assured me she will recover fully. When she wakes—"

"When she wakes?" Charlotte sputtered. Knuckles clenched, her entire body visibly shaking. "You didn't even discuss it with her first?" Charlotte stormed up to him, inches from his face. "Why the bloody hell didn't you wait with her?" She drew her arm back and slapped, no she punched, Oakleigh in the face.

Oakleigh's head rocked back—more from shock than force of the blow. James jumped forward before she could pull back and strike again. She struggled in his arms. "Charlotte, calm down," he repeated himself until gradually she stilled. He spun her around to face him.

Tears streaked her face.

"She's all right, Charlotte. She survived. Oakleigh saw to it."

She sniffed. "Then he left her there. The man she loves abandoned her when she was at her most vulnerable."

"I did it for her own good," Oakleigh yelled. "Do you honestly believe I wanted to leave the woman I love two hundred years in the future where I will never see her again?" He sank onto a chair, burying his head in his hands. "I had no other choice. Traveling through that portal is dangerous. Life, now, is dangerous. How could I force her to give up her safety, all those luxuries… How could I compete with the wonders of the twenty-first century?"

"The for-her-own-good argument has never, in the history of the world, been a valid one. She's a grown ass woman. She should have been given the chance to make that choice for herself."

"Leave him be, Charlotte. Can't you see he's devastated." Guilt and self-doubt riddled his insides. *He'd* laid those ideas in Oakleigh's head. On their trip to save the ladies. He'd gone on and on about how difficult it would be for their women to give up all that the future offered. If one trip to the future led the over-confident Marquess of Oakleigh to decide his woman was better off alone in the future than with him in this time, the future must be more extraordinary than James had imagined. He was sorry he'd ever mentioned the possibility in the first place. Considering his wish to keep Charlotte with him in this century, he now feared he was being horribly selfish.

"What is all this nonsense about Lady Alexandra being two hundred years in the future?" his mother asked.

Damn, he'd forgotten she was in the room. "I shall explain all to you later, Mother. It's an extraordinary tale and best left to another time."

His mother bit her lip but nodded.

He sighed. Exhaustion hit him hard. How was he to explain? On top of the madness of the day, his evening would be occupied with explaining the entire mess to his mother. If only she would allow him to put such unpleasantness aside until the morrow. He would not lay odds on that occurrence.

Charlotte turned into his arms, burying her face against his shoulder. Enough worrying about himself, he must see to her needs. She was his priority.

Reuniting her with her family could perhaps ease her pain as well as provide additional reason for staying within his century. Though he wished he were enough, such did not seem to be the case.

****

Depression hung heavy in the air. Charlotte's tears gradually eased allowing for a deep breath. James's warm body bolstered her flagging spirits. The steady beat of his heart thudded gently in her ear, and she realized how inappropriate it was for her to be leaning upon him so heavily.

What were her parents thinking?

Her parents. Shit. What was *she* thinking? She had to get her head back on straight. Alex was safe in the future. Nicholas may have broken Alex's heart by leaving her there, but her body would mend. He was a chauvinistic idiot, and Charlotte had no idea what Alex saw in the bastard, but he had been true to his word and saw her sister to safety. That had to be enough for now.

She needed to figure out her own path. And that started with her birth parents.

Keeping close to James's side, she snuck a peek at them.

Lord Downing sat beside his wife, one arm wrapped supportively around her back. Lady Downing wasn't the only one in tears. While he didn't sob like his wife, silent tears made a slow trek down his cheeks. He'd aged a decade in the moments since Nicholas made his entrance.

Could he be that skilled an actor? Working in the

hospital, she'd seen people lose children before—one of the reasons she'd decided pediatrics wasn't to be her specialty—and her parents looked just like any of the others she'd once consoled over their loss. Alex was alive, but for all intents and purposes, they had lost her. Again.

She switched her gaze to her three siblings. Mary sat on her mother's other side, one hand clenched tightly to her mother's. Myles had sunk back into a corner. He shuffled his feet, glancing up every few seconds but not making eye contact with anyone.

Gregory glared at Nicholas. Spine straight, chest puffed out—he clearly did not like Alex's fiancé. Ex-fiancé? What exactly was he now that Alex had returned to the twenty-first century? Whatever the case, something had clearly gone on between those two. Alex had left out some details of her time here.

Not that it was any of her business. And, frankly, she didn't care. Nicholas wasn't high on her list at the moment either.

She returned her attention back to her parents and found her father's sad gaze upon her.

"Perhaps we should move on to more pressing matters," he said. "We can all be reassured that Lady Alexandra, while we shall miss her terribly, is safe. I understand wounds that would be fatal in our time can be healed in the future. That knowledge will have to sustain us."

Lady Downing gave a loud sniff but nodded. "I apologize for my unseemly display."

"Nonsense," Lady Tyndale said. "While I do not entirely understand what has happened to Lady Alexandra, I have gathered that she has recovered from her injuries but will not be returning now or in the future?" At James's nod, she continued, "Therefore, it is not unseemly at all. I rather think such a display is to be expected. But to make you more comfortable, we shall all endeavor to pretend we notice nothing amiss."

Charlotte grinned. Lady Tyndale was a blessing.

A knock at the door made Charlotte jump, but Lady Tyndale simply called out, "Mrs. Sterling. At last. Please, do come in. James, that tray is much too heavy, please relieve her of it and set it here." She indicated a small table set up for just such a use.

James made haste to do her bidding. Wise boy. His mother had taken control, and woe to anyone who stood in her way.

Once the tray was placed to Lady Tyndale's satisfaction, Mrs. Sterling left, closing the door behind her. Lady Tyndale served tea.

"Can I help, Lady Tyndale?" Charlotte reached toward the pot but got rapped on the knuckles for her trouble.

"Nonsense. I won't hear of it. You shall have a seat and enjoy your refreshments." She leaned in close as she handed her a cup. "Do be gentle with your mother, my dear. In times of loss, wouldn't we all do better to cherish those we have left to us?"

Charlotte wrapped her hands around her lukewarm cup and smiled her thanks. Lady Tyndale patted her arm and continued serving.

Her point was valid. She could compare this sitting room with any number of waiting areas where she'd had to deliver bad news to patients' families. The worst were those that had no family to lean on.

If she could put aside her misgivings, she didn't

have to be one of those. Alex's story made so much more sense than the one she'd grown up believing. Could she finally give up the hate that had burned inside her for so long?

She wanted to. Deeply.

Watching her family huddled around Lady Downing, she truly wished to be a part of them once more. She'd shoved all her good childhood memories of this century so far down, she had a hard time dragging them back up.

Maybe she had to work at it, little by little.

How to start?

Lady Downing rose shakily, Lord Downing supporting her with a hand at her elbow. "I believe I shall retire for the evening."

A chorus of voices rose to inquire into her well being, whether she needed anything. Lady Tyndale summoned a maid stationed outside the door to see the lady to her room.

Charlotte took a deep breath and stepped in front of her mother, barring her way to the door. James stood at her side, the warmth of his hand at the small of her back gave her some much needed courage.

The Creswells stared, mixed emotions flitting across their faces. Soul deep sadness mixed with love and hope. That's what Charlotte saw, though she wasn't sure if it was real or only what she wanted to see.

She trained her eyes on her mother's hands, twisted together before her. "Well." She cleared her throat. "Um, maybe we can talk some in the morning." Before she could lose her nerve, she took a quick step forward and hugged her mum.

Lady Downing gasped. Her arms raised, but

Charlotte wasn't ready for more. She pulled back quickly, whispered, "Good night," and fled.

****

Charlotte ran from the room. The Creswells appeared stunned, but slowly smiles lightened their tear streaked faces. James struggled whether to follow Charlotte or see to her family.

His mother tucked her hand around his elbow. "See to our guests. I will check on Miss Evans—er, Lady Charlotte. I am certain she will appreciate your care for her family while she is indisposed." She nudged his side. "And it never hurts to endear yourself to your future wife's family," she whispered.

He grinned. Maybe he would get the chance to put off the whole future conversation with his mother after all. Curiosity fell to the wayside when a potential daughter-in-law was at stake. And his mother looked upon Charlotte with a favorable eye.

At his nod, his mother slipped her arm out from his. "If you will excuse me, I must check with our housekeeper to ensure everything is ready for your stay. Lady Downing, if you are ready to retire, I can show you to your room."

Lady Downing nodded, and the two women swept from the room.

"I should attend to my wife, if you'll all excuse me." Lord Downing bowed and turned to leave.

Lady Mary placed a hand on her father's shoulder. "I am rather tired as well. I will check on Mother and then retire myself. You should stay here and discuss matters with Lords Oakleigh and Tyndale." She kissed her father on his cheek and followed the ladies.

"Perhaps something a little stronger than tea is

called for," James suggested. At the enthusiastic nods he received in response, he stepped to the sideboard, selected a decanter of scotch, and poured healthy servings for everyone.

He raised a brow and tipped an empty glass to young Myles. Lord Downing nodded while holding his thumb and forefinger less than an inch apart. James poured a small serving and handed it to the young man who puffed out his chest and nodded solemnly when he accepted the drink.

James kept an amused eye half on the lad, barely restraining his laughter when the boy took a healthy sip and turned nearly purple with his efforts not to cough.

Gregory slapped his brother on the back. "You'll get used to it soon enough," he said with a laugh.

They settled into their respective chairs, and silence reigned for several moments.

Oakleigh finally broke the tension by clearing his throat. "I apologize for my failure to bring Alex back to her family. I know how upset you must be. However, please believe me that I would not have done such a thing if I did not believe it to be in her best interest."

"I have always wanted what was best for my daughters," Lord Downing replied. "I had given up hope of ever finding out what truly happened to my girls. If I can be assured she is safe and happy in her future world, I can at the least take comfort from that fact, though I shall miss her until the end of my days."

"As shall I," Oakleigh whispered.

James felt for the man. His head hung low, his features haggard. Were he to lose Charlotte, he was certain to look quite similar. He knew not what to do to comfort Oakleigh. Lady Alexandra was not dead, but she may as well be. The result was the same. They'd never see her again.

The question heavy on his mind, of course, was whether Charlotte would choose to join her sister.

"Can you tell us much about the world in which my sister now resides?" Myles asked. On the verge of manhood, his voice wavered between a deep baritone and a faltering tenor.

At the same time, his father asked, "How did you know to come here rather than returning directly to London?"

Myles blushed and sank back in his chair holding his glass to hide his face. Ah, those awkward years. James didn't miss them.

"Had Lord Tyndale not sent word of all that occurred that night, we would be in doubt even now as to whether our daughters survived Lord Stone's treachery. I could wish your first thought would be to inform us of all that transpired." There was more than a hint of reproach in the older man's voice.

Oakleigh acknowledged the rebuke with a nod, but James broke in, "I must take the blame for that, my lord. I posted servants at the cave entrance with strict instructions to bring Lord Oakleigh here directly should he return. Had you not already been on your way here, I would have made sure to keep you informed. Lady Charlotte has been extremely agitated waiting for news of her sister, and I feared she might have taken it upon herself to seek out answers were Lord Oakleigh to not return straightaway." Now with Oakleigh's return, he still worried she would leave him at any time.

"I did, indeed, plan to return directly to London to assure you of Alex's well-being. But upon ascending from the depths of the cavern this morning, Tyndale's man, Max?" He raised a brow in question, and at James's affirmative nod, he continued, "Informed me that I should make my way to Tyndale manor. That, in fact, Alex's family was set to arrive at any moment."

"This morning?" James asked. The clock had struck eleven only moments ago. Oakleigh had not arrived until late in the evening, and the journey from the cave should not have taken longer than an hour, two at the most. The hairs on the back of James's neck prickled his skin as they rose in trepidation.

Oakleigh nodded. A fierce frown pulled at the scarring on his left side, making his harsh, haggard appearance positively foreboding. "We were delayed on our trip. I'm afraid we made a rather gruesome discovery near the cave."

"What?"

"We found...the body of a young woman. She'd quite obviously been murdered."

****

Lord Stone paused in the act of opening the door from the back room of *The Grey Goose Inn*. Had someone just said his name?

He pressed his ear to the door, hoping to overhear the conversation. His name on anyone's tongue was cause for concern.

"Yes, Gabriel Stone. He may be accompanied by a scurrilous fellow named Cantor. Have you seen either?" A large, intimidating fellow leaned against the bar. Stone recognized him from the Downing ball. Oakleigh's man.

Damn that fool, Cantor. First, he steered them toward this godforsaken place where, it turned out,

Lady Alexandra Creswell's lover was known to frequent. Then, he got himself killed playing it too rough with one of the harlots down the street.

He should have parted ways with the cur directly upon reaching the docks. He'd thought his wicked retainer would be useful, but Cantor had grown more and more surly as he realized Stone was mucked out. Several missives sent to Miss Crawford had yielded no answer, so his hope of regaining his wealth through blackmail were sadly disappointed.

Now, he was stuck in this rat-infested hole until he could afford the passage to his estate in Jamaica. Time was of the essence that he reach his holdings before word of his difficulties reached his younger brother's ears. Stone may hold the title, but his brother kept their finances afloat. He was already displeased with several bad investments Stone had incurred and would cut him off the instant he learned of recent events.

This was the second time in a week that Oakleigh's man, Grayson was his name, had come close to discovering Stone's whereabouts. The man appeared to have contacts in just about every tavern at the docks. The barman wasn't likely to keep his tongue and would be pointing Grayson his way any second.

The back door squealed as Stone tried to sneak out unnoticed. He winced, hoping the ruffians in the common room were loud enough to cover his escape. He didn't wait to see but slipped out into the back alley.

He stumbled on a pile of rotten refuse, flinging out his hands to catch himself against the building. His hand met with something foul, and he cursed as he wiped the muck off against his breeches.

Any hope of maintaining the pristine state of dress

he was accustomed to had long since fled. Without his valet to see to his needs, he was afraid he appeared as unkempt as the rest of the motley crowd that frequented such places as *The Grey Goose Inn.*

He dashed down the alley toward a brothel he'd visited upon occasion before his current troubles. He knew the layout well enough he could easily slip through without detection. At this hour, the women would be in their rooms, preparing for the evening's coming work.

None of them would be servicing him this night, more's the pity. The last of his coin had gone to the inn keeper who'd insisted on payment for the past few nights' lodgings. A situation desperately in need of modification.

One of the trulls' brats spotted him the minute he stepped into the bordello. He glared at the child, who wisely kept his silence, lowered his gaze to the floor, and sunk back against the wall.

Hmm. Tyndale has a brat.

An idea began to take shape. A way to gain the money he needed and exact a measure of revenge against Tyndale at the same time. Perfect. He continued on, a renewed vigor in his step.

Chapter Twenty

Nerves on edge, mind whirling, Charlotte knew there was no way she was going to get to sleep anytime soon. She made her way up the stairs toward Prue's room so she could peek in on the little darling, who should be sound asleep at this time of night, but in the off-chance Prue was awake, reading a story or two could help her unwind a little. Prue was anything but relaxing, but being around her always lifted her spirits.

They hadn't spent much time together since the incident at the cave. Charlotte had struggled almost constantly against tears and hadn't wanted to spread her sadness to Prue, so other than checking on her at bedtime or asking Theresa for updates on how she fared, they'd barely come into contact the past few days.

The door was open slightly. Charlotte stepped up to spy through the wedge, checking to see if the little girl was awake or not.

Theresa flitted about the room, straightening toys, clothing, and anything else she found out of place, while Prue lay propped up in bed. She had a book in her lap but didn't seem to be reading. Instead, she stared out the large window, gaze vacant like her mind was a million miles away.

Charlotte nudged the door wider. "Prue? Still awake? Mind if I come in?"

Prue's head jerked up and toward the door. She popped out of bed and ran to her. Charlotte entered the room and dropped to her knees to gather Prue into a bear hug.

Over Prue's head, Charlotte smiled at Theresa, who smiled back and quietly left them alone.

Charlotte breathed deep, inhaling the flowery scent of Prue's soap. Damn, but she'd missed the child. She smoothed her hair and then released her, holding her at arm's length to get a good look at her.

Tears threatened at the corners of Prue's eyes, but she blinked against their falling. "I'm sorry for whatever I did. If I promise not to do it again, will you play with me again?"

A pang of guilt hit Charlotte square in the stomach as her selfishness nearly knocked her over. "Oh, Prue, sweetheart. I'm so sorry." She pulled her back in for another hug and spoke into her hair, "You didn't do anything wrong. I was upset about something that had nothing to do with you, and I didn't handle it well. I'm so sorry. Can you forgive me?"

Prue leaned back. "You're not upset with me?"

"No, of course not." She bit her lip, at a loss on how much to explain. "Something bad happened, and I didn't want to worry you, so I stayed away. That was stupi—foolish of me. I promise I won't make the same mistake again."

She frowned. "Were you hurt when the bad thing happened?"

"No. My sister was, but I found out tonight that she's going to be all right."

"Can I meet her?"

Sadness weighed her down once more. She bowed

her head. "No. I don't think I'm ever going to see her again. She left me."

Prue's little hand ran along the back of Charlotte's head, stroking her hair as Charlotte had just done. "It will be all right, Miss Evans. I won't leave you. Please don't cry."

Charlotte brushed the tears off her cheeks and forced a trembling smile. "I didn't realize I was." She laughed. "I'm afraid I'm a bit of a mess, Prue. But don't you worry. Everything will work out. I love you, sweet girl."

Their hug lasted several minutes and calmed Charlotte's nerves. She had to be strong, if for no other reason than to be here for the little girl doing her best to comfort a woman who was supposed to be taking care of her.

"All right. Enough of this nonsense. Time for bed."

Charlotte helped Prue into bed and read from one of her books for far longer than she should have at this hour in the evening.

"Good night, Miss Evans." Prue kissed Charlotte on the cheek, then rolled over. She was asleep within minutes.

Charlotte relaxed in the chair by the bed watching the even rhythm of Prue's breathing.

Had she really considered leaving Prue? She loved the little girl more than she'd have thought possible. And Prue wasn't the only one she loved.

Seeing Nicholas's devastation over leaving Alex in the future drove home to her how she would feel leaving James. She couldn't do it.

But it broke her heart. Not only would she never get to know Alex, but what about Steven? How could she leave him? He'd be all alone.

With the death of their parents, they'd been left without any family. All they'd had was each other, but now she had a whole new life, new love, and...family. While he would be left in the future with nothing. How could she do that to him?

She could only hope that Alex would reach out to Steven. It would make sense, right?

But then again, she didn't truly know Alex anymore. Would she seek Steven out, or simply slide back into the life she'd almost left behind.

The question was going to drive her crazy. Somehow, she had to find a way to connect with the future. If only to say her goodbyes.

****

James cursed under his breath. "Stone."

Oakleigh frowned. "How could Stone be involved? We had him trussed up like a Christmas goose."

"His coachman escaped while we saw to Lady Alexandra. They were gone by the time we made our way topside." He flinched at the scowl Oakleigh threw his way.

"Never mind how Lord Stone managed his escape," Downing chimed in. "Did you recognize the woman?"

"She was not known to me. However, your man appeared to recognize her. I trust he will have notified the authorities by now."

A woman Max recognized? Yet, he'd had no tales of missing servants at his estate. Someone from *The Rambling Inn* perhaps? "I have had people at the caves since you left. Why was her body not discovered earlier?" Could Stone be hiding in the caverns? There were other caves in the area, was that how Stone was evading the authorities who had been searching for him these past two days?

"She wasn't easy to find. Her body was partially buried in a copse of trees near the cave's entrance."

"Then how did you stumble upon her?" He was missing something.

"You'll recall Alex was worried for her sister's safety?"

James nodded. They'd discussed it briefly as they ran to the caves to save the ladies.

"Her fear was based on a report that a woman was murdered in the vicinity of the caves on the night of May the twenty-ninth. She believed the article was referring to Lady Charlotte."

"Yet you were aware that Lady Charlotte was uninjured. So what prompted you to search for a body?"

"The logistics of time travel have kept my mind in a whirl ever since I first began to contemplate the subject."

James held back a snort. "I know precisely how you feel."

"It occurred to me to wonder whether it is possible for us to change the future. One would suppose that having the ladies disappear when children and return fifteen years later would greatly upset the order of time. Yet, in the future their presence, and lack, in their native time is a foregone conclusion. As far as the twenty-first century is concerned, nothing has changed. I began to wonder whether our actions are predetermined or whether we can affect the future. So I set out to determine whether or not a murder had, in fact, occurred."

"And discovered that it had, indeed," Downing said. He downed a good third of his drink, then asked, "So who died, and was she the original victim or did all our deeds change the course of history, causing some innocent to die in my daughter's place?"

A knock sounded on the door.

"Enter." James turned to see who entered. "Ah, Max. We were just about to summon you."

Max bowed and stood just within the door, shifting nervously from foot to foot and wringing his hat into a wrinkled mess.

"What say you, Max?"

"I beg your pardon, my lord. The news is terrible." Max took a deep breath, while James held his own. "The woman we found...Miss Crawford."

James fell back into his chair. Miss Crawford? How could this be? He was no longer enamored of the woman as he'd once been, but he most certainly did not wish her dead. He recalled Charlotte mentioning something about Miss Crawford the day of the kidnapping, but he hadn't had the chance to question her further. How was Miss Crawford connected to this mess? "Have Mr. and Mrs. Crawford been informed?" The idea of informing parents that their child had been murdered...

"The magistrate wishes to have a word with you first, my lord." He bowed in Oakleigh's direction. "And with my lord Oakleigh, as well. I believe they wish to determine whether Miss Crawford's untimely death is connected in some way to the Ladies' abductions."

"Yes, certainly." He leaned forward, head in his hands. "Please inform the magistrate that I will be down directly. See him to my study."

Max bowed and then backed out of the room.

James took a deep breath and stood. "If you'll excuse me. It appears I have a difficult matter to attend to."

"I shall accompany you," Oakleigh said, rising to his feet and taking a step toward the door.

Lord Downing looked to his sons. "I think it best we retire for the evening. I trust Lords Tyndale and Oakleigh can handle this new situation." He nodded toward James. "We shall speak again in the morning. Thank you for your hospitality."

James bowed. "My pleasure." He spotted Mrs. Sterling hovering outside the door, probably in expectation of their guests needing direction to their rooms for the evening. "Mrs. Sterling will see you to your rooms."

"This way, my lords." Mrs. Sterling gestured toward the stairs and led them away.

James sighed. His own bed was a long ways away, and he was exhausted. No help for it though. He waved a hand toward his study. "Perhaps this will not take as much time as I fear."

Oakleigh snorted. "Unlikely."

****

Charlotte made her way down the stairs, thinking about the harm she'd done to Prue the last few days. Guilt riddled her. So consumed with her own issues, she hadn't spared any thought for how her actions affected Prue.

A good night's sleep might give her a clearer outlook.

She yawned and took the last step. And stopped short, face to face with her father. "Father."

"Charlotte." Her father shuffled his feet, his gaze trained somewhere around her knees. But then he raised his head and looked her in the eye.

She fought the urge to hide her face in return. She kept her head up, met his gaze head on. Shoulders back, posture as stiff as she could get, she asked, "What happened back then? Alex told me the kidnapping wasn't your fault, but…"

What little color he had in his cheeks faded. "You thought *I* was responsible?" He clutched his chest, staggering back a few paces.

She leapt forward and grabbed his elbow, now fully convinced of his innocence. No one was that good an actor. "I'm so sorry. Are you all right?" She tucked his arm against her side and led him to a small bench a few steps from where they stood. "Here, have a seat." She nudged him until he sat and then perched next to him. She wrapped her hands around his and leaned forward so she could gaze into his eyes. "Please, forgive me. I was stupid. I never should have believed you were involved."

His eyes watered, but he'd regained some of his color. "Why would you ever have thought such a horrible…"

"I don't know. I overheard Timmons say how easy it was to snatch us, how you'd practically given us to him. And I was so scared. And then we fell through the portal. And Stone's awful roar was ringing in my ears. And there were all these strangers. And Alex—" She choked, stumbling out of her rambling. Sorrow washed over her in a gush of emotion that stemmed the words flowing freeform out of her mouth.

He slid his hand from hers and patted her

comfortingly. "No need to continue. Your sister informed us of the injury that incapacitated her and robbed her of her memory." He leaned back against the wall, letting her hands drop, his head tilted against the wall as he gazed up at the ceiling. "I cannot imagine the horror. And to add the belief that your own parents were responsible…"

"I don't think I did. Not *really*," she said, surprised to realize she was telling the truth and not just trying to placate an old man. "I think…I think it made it all easier somehow. If I could hate you, then I didn't have to miss you." She blinked back tears and stared at the ground.

"We missed you as well." His voice was scratchy, his tone soft, but the love shone through loud and clear. "I suppose I can't begrudge you your hate if it gave you comfort. But please understand…we were devastated by the loss of you and Alexandra. Not a day has gone by that we haven't thought of you both, nor will one ever."

"Thank you," she said, yawning in between words.

Her father stood and offered her a hand up. "Perhaps we can spend some time together tomorrow? Alexandra shared her experiences with us. We'd love to learn more about the years you spent in the future."

"That would be lovely, yes."

"Then let us get some rest so we shall be refreshed come morning."

He escorted her to her room, standing watch until she shut the door behind her.

The overwhelming pinkness of the room didn't grate on her nerves as it had the past two days. Instead, the fluffy bed called to her. She wanted to crawl right under the covers, but sleeping in a corset was nearly impossible.

No matter how she twisted, she couldn't manage to untie the laces threaded up the back of her dress. She'd have to wake someone.

She hated to do it. She was well aware of how early the servants would be up in the morning. Waking someone in the middle of the night seemed cruel.

Better to search out someone still awake. She straightened her dress and set out to find help.

Voices echoed up the stairs. She peeked over the railing. James and Nicholas spoke with a gentleman she didn't recognize. He carried his hat in his hands and nodded repeatedly as James spoke.

"I will find out more in the morning. Lady Charlotte Creswell has already retired for the evening. As you can imagine, she has been quite overcome by her ordeal. We must treat this information with care and delicacy. She will be most distraught."

"Yes, milord. I quite understand."

Worthing opened the front door, and the stranger departed. "May I be of further service this evening, my lord?" he asked.

James clapped him on the back. "No, thank you, Worthing. You may retire. Lord Oakleigh and I will be in my study for the time being."

"Yes, my lord." Worthing bowed and swept away.

James and Nicholas drifted back toward the study.

"I must say, I could wish you had yet to return to us, Oakleigh. Such news is never welcome, and I hate to be the one to disseminate such ill tidings."

"Could not someone else inform Mr. and Mrs. Crawford? I fail to see your obligation to do so. You are not family, after all."

"No, yet I feel obligated to seek them out. They are insufferable people, yet no one deserves to learn of their daughter's death from a stranger."

Charlotte gasped. "Miss Crawford's dead?"

James and Nicholas swung toward her, heads tilted to see up the stairs.

The grimace on James's face was all the answer she needed. The knot in her stomach that had only just begun to ease, gripped her tight. She leaned forward, resting her forehead on the cool, slick wood of the banister.

Footsteps pounded on the stairs to the beat of her heart, and then James stood beside her. "I meant to tell you in the morning."

"Where? What happened?"

"By the caves. Oakleigh found her. I planned on telling you in the morning."

"That stupid, stupid bitch!" Charlotte whispered.

James drew in a sharp breath.

"I told her to run. I told her. Why didn't she listen?"

Chapter Twenty-One

Finally settled on a comfortable sofa in his study, James handed Charlotte a glass of brandy. After the events of the day, the strong liquor seemed appropriate.

Oakleigh had retired for the night shortly after recounting the details—many more than James wished—of the body he found. Charlotte had insisted. Both men had been taken aback by her demand.

"Why, in Heaven's name, did you wish for such details about Miss Crawford's condition?" he burst out, unable to contain his curiosity a moment longer. He'd held back remarkably well with Oakleigh in the room, but now he had her alone…

"I wanted to know what happened," she stated simply. As if that was an actual explanation.

He raised an eyebrow and stared.

She rolled her eyes. "Fine. I figured if I knew exactly what was done to her, I would know whether Stone had her killed, or if she was murdered for another purpose."

Now she had confused him. "For what other purpose might she have been done in if not to obtain her silence? And what makes you believe Stone did not kill her himself?" He and Oakleigh had agreed it likely Stone was too weak to commit the actual murder, but curiosity made him wonder how Charlotte had drawn that conclusion.

"Stone's a coward." She shrugged. "I doubt he'd have the balls. And he'd think it was beneath him to get his hands dirty. That's why he has Cantor."

He choked when she said 'balls,' but she grinned unrepentantly.

"I wouldn't think Stone would have her killed, though. As far as he's concerned, Miss Crawford was dealt with the minute I was out of the way. Giving him up would implicate her as well, so she'd keep her silence. Besides, she had her payment so she had no reason to give him away."

Payment? "You have yet to explain Miss Crawford's involvement in this entire sordid affair."

"Sordid affair? Really?" Charlotte shook her head, then took a sip of her brandy. She coughed delicately. "If you must know, that stupid girl sold me out. And when I tried to warn her she was in danger, she ignored me, convinced getting me out of the way was her ticket to…"

He waited for her to continue, when she didn't, he urged, "Her ticket to…"

"You."

He reared back. "Me?" Had he not been clear enough that his intention toward Miss Crawford was no longer as it once was? "How is that possible? What did she do?"

"Do you really want to know?"

He nodded. "Yes." *No.* But he must.

She sighed. "Fine. She lured me into a trap by saying Prue had been hurt."

Fury clouded his vision. "She threatened my daughter?" If she weren't dead already, he'd kill her.

"No," Charlotte insisted. "Prue was never in any

danger. Miss Crawford wasn't that foolish." She took another sip of brandy. Deeper this time. "Ah. That's good. Anyway, Miss Crawford knew I'd do anything for Prue. So, she lied, said Prue had been hurt down by the stables. I didn't question her. I just ran to help. When I got there, I found Max knocked out with Timmons leaning over him. Cantor was there, too. Once they had me, Miss Crawford bragged that when I was out of the way, you'd come around and she'd be the next Lady Tyndale in no time."

He sat, dropped his head into his hands and groaned. "Stupid was an understatement. After that fiasco where she tried to compromise herself in order to gain my proposal, how could she possibly think I would ever take her to wife?"

"She's a spoiled brat who's never been denied anything she wanted. And she wanted to be a viscountess. Before I came along, you were on the verge of proposing. Without me around, she had no reason to believe you wouldn't just—" She snapped her fingers. "—fall back in line."

"What a pleasure to know I'm so easy to command."

She laughed. "If that were the case, you would have been married long before now. Rumor has it you were taking your time popping the question."

"And yet, Miss Crawford had it as a foregone conclusion."

"Did I mention she was a spoiled brat?" Charlotte's smile dropped. "She still didn't deserve what happened to her. I tried to warn her."

His own humor faded. "Yet you don't think Lord Stone was the cause of her demise." Oakleigh's descriptions haunted his thoughts. He thanked the lord he hadn't been the one to find Miss Crawford's body. Hearing the tale was difficult enough. Oakleigh had left out a few details in recounting the story to Charlotte. Better she not know the full extent of what had been done to the poor woman.

"No."

"Explain, if you please."

"Cantor." She shuddered and grasped his hands.

She trembled so fiercely, he held her close and tucked her head under his chin, against his chest. "I'm sorry. We don't need to discuss this. It's much too upsetting." Had she guessed what Oakleigh declined to say?

"No. It's all right. I'll probably have to go over this with whoever is searching for Stone and Cantor anyway. It might help to talk it out before then." She cleared her throat, then straightened, pulling out of his embrace. "Like I said, I don't think Stone would have considered killing her. Cantor, though. He has a look about him." She waved her hand as if reaching for the right words. "I don't know how to describe it. He just gave me the creeps. So when he insisted that Miss Crawford come with us to see Lord Stone... I don't know. I didn't buy it. I think he took her to..." She paused, took a deep breath, and continued, "to...have his way with her. And when she fought back, he must have—" She broke off.

Bloody hell. Despite Oakleigh's reticence, Charlotte had drawn an accurate conclusion of what had happened. He would have spared her the knowledge could he have done so. "We can't possibly know what happened."

****

She scowled at him. "Oh, come on. I'm not bloody blind. I could see the looks passing between you and Nicholas. It wasn't hard to fill in the blanks." Did he really think she was that naïve?

Probably. That's the way they liked their women in this day and age.

She shoved off the sofa so she could stomp across the room. "You don't need to protect me, you know. I'm a grown woman. I can handle it." Keeping her back to him, she grabbed an iron rod from the stand by the hearth and sent sparks flying as she poked the dying fire. Smoke billowed up. The scent of burning embers so strong, she sneezed.

James grabbed the poker. "Let's not set fire to the manor. I believe we have enough to worry about."

She resisted for a second, then let go with a huff. "Fine." With the mood she was in, he was wise to take the poker from her. She didn't need a weapon in her hand. No matter how satisfying it might be, she'd eventually regret bashing his head in.

"I know I don't *need* to protect you. However, I can't help but wish to shield you from pain whenever it is within my power."

She sighed. She supposed she couldn't blame him. Hadn't she considered not telling him about Miss Crawford's motivation? Wasn't that the same thing he wanted to do by not letting her know what really happened?

"Please, forgive me. It pains me to admit but I am unfamiliar with the ways of twenty-first century women. You are the first I've known."

That forced a laugh out of her. "Yeah, I suppose

we're not all that common around here."

He stood so close she couldn't resist leaning into him. His normally clean scent was tinged with smoke from the fire and hints of brandy on his breath. So strong. Leaning into him was a pleasure she didn't want to deny herself.

Maybe she was due a little comfort. She tilted her head up. He gasped when her lips touched his, but before she could spring back in embarrassment, he recovered from his surprise and returned the kiss. She sighed with pleasure.

They'd kissed before, but something about this was different. The passion was there, oh yeah, but there was something deeper going on in this moment. Love, understanding, comfort. A swirl of emotions accompanied their kiss. Her heart fluttered with love for the man in her arms.

He groaned, and after one last taste, pulled away. With a shaky laugh, he said, "Perhaps it would be best if we retired for the evening."

"Brilliant idea." She wrapped a hand around his neck, rose onto her toes, and continued their kiss while backing toward the door. Despite the late hour, there would be people still awake in the manor. Best to go back to his room. She bumped into the wall and searched for the doorknob with one hand while maintaining a steady grip on the hair at his nape with the other. Despite her desperation to get the damn door open and get to a truly private spot, she couldn't find the will to break the kiss.

He pulled away again with an even deeper groan than before. "Rest well. I shall see you in the morning." His arms dropped from around her, and he walked away to stand before the fire. Head tilted down, he propped one hand against the mantel and studied the fire as if it contained the answers to all life's problems.

She blinked stupidly for several seconds as she took in what had just happened. "So, when you said 'retire for the evening' you meant, sleep? As in, alone? You're not coming upstairs with me?" He couldn't be dense enough not to realize she had completely different plans for the night ahead, could he?

"I think that would be unwise." He ran a hand through his hair and twisted his neck to gaze back at her. The heat in his gaze put the fire in the hearth to shame. "I fear I would be unable to keep my hands off you. Neither of us would find our rest for many long hours."

"Exactly what I was thinking." She hooked her thumb over her shoulder toward the door. "We're on the same page. Let's go." Okay, so she sounded a bit desperate, but seriously…she'd wanted him for months. Now that she'd finally decided she couldn't leave him, she saw no reason to deny herself any longer. And that kiss had definitely put some urgency to her plans.

His jaw dropped, eyes widened, but then a slow grin spread across his face. "Are all modern women as bold as you?"

She smiled back. "No. *I'm* not even this bold. Normally. But I'd say these are extraordinary circumstances. So, be a gentleman and don't keep a lady waiting."

He stalked toward her, and she met him eagerly. After another scorching kiss that set her blood boiling and her skin humming, he said, "Quite extraordinary. I suppose it would be terribly rude of me to deny the wishes of such an extraordinary woman."

"Damn straight. Let's go."

****

James woke, the feeling of a well-satisfied night put a smile on his face. He kept his eyes closed, memories of the evening fresh in his mind. With so little to smile about in the past few days, he never would have guessed he would be so close to meeting his goal today.

After last night, he had no doubt he'd soon call Charlotte his wife. He simply needed to ask her once more and set his mother, and hers, the task of planning a wedding.

He rolled over, groping at the blank space beside him, still warm from her body.

"Charlotte?" he called in a loud whisper. He had no intention of bringing attention to their night together. His future family might not appreciate the bedding preceding the wedding as much as he did.

Nor would he make Charlotte feel as though she were forced into marrying him. He wished to start their wedded bliss under entirely agreeable circumstances. His future wife would not take kindly to being manipulated into marriage, no matter how she might wish for just such an outcome.

When she didn't answer his call, he opened his eyes. His room was empty. The fire gone cold. The drapes shut tight. The door to his bathing chamber was open, and he could see it was empty. Where had she gone?

The door opened, and Albert strolled in. "Good morning, my lord. I hope I didn't wake you. I thought to set out your clothing for the morning." He indicated the pile of clothes he cradled in his arms, an uncharacteristically wide smile on his face for so early in the morning. Albert was not fond of mornings.

James said a thankful prayer Charlotte had woken early and left. Albert would never betray his lord, but James would not wish to put Charlotte through the awkwardness of such a situation.

"Thank you, Albert." He waited until his valet left before rising to get himself dressed. He'd call Albert back in when he needed his cravat tied. Albert allowed him the leeway to don his breeches and shirt himself but would never permit him to tie his own cravat or shrug into his waistcoat without assistance. He had not the skill for it and going out with a poorly tied cravat would be a great embarrassment for his manservant.

Not wanting to keep Albert waiting too long, he quickly donned his clothing and then approached the door that led to his late wife's old bedchamber. That would be the easiest escape route for Charlotte. From there she could quickly make her way to her own room. He suspected she'd left only minutes before he woke, and since Albert entered only moments later, she might have been trapped in the room next door. She wouldn't want to be caught leaving his or Harriet's room. She may have been raised in another century, but she was well aware of the rules that governed this time.

He nudged the door open. "Charlotte?" he whispered. Light from a dying fire flickered around the room. Shadows wavered making the furniture appear to move, but he couldn't tell if she was there.

"And just what would Lady Charlotte be doing in this room?" his mother's voice spoke out of the darkness. "I could have sworn I put her in the rose room."

Bloody hell. "Hello, Mother. What are you doing in Harriet's room?" He should have realized something was off the moment he noticed the fire laid upon the hearth. Since Harriet's death, this room remained all but abandoned. The servants kept it free of dust, but little else. There was no reason for a fire unless the room was in use.

Fabric rustled, and a dainty shadow separated from the poster bed. His mother made her way to the hearth, added a log, and poked until the fire bloomed once more. Even with the candles his mother lit around the room, the light was deceptive. He couldn't tell whether she was pleased or irate to have caught him searching for Charlotte in his deceased wife's chambers.

"We were supposed to have a talk, you and I. Don't you recall?"

He should have known he wouldn't be able to avoid telling his mother everything.

"I grew tired of waiting for you to retire and lay down in Harriet's bed for but a moment. Next I can recall, you had returned to your room, but it was quite obvious your mother would not be welcome."

Shame heated his face. He'd known inviting Charlotte into his bed before he secured her hand in marriage was wrong, but he hadn't imagined his mother listening in the next room.

"Oh, do wipe that ridiculous scowl off your face. I am the last person to berate you for allowing the bedding to precede the wedding." She lit the last taper and settled into a chair before the fire. "Especially when I desire Charlotte for my daughter-in-law almost as much as you desire her as a wife." She patted the seat beside her. "Now, tell your mother the secrets you and Lady Charlotte have been keeping from her these past few months."

He took the offered chair, wishing it were still evening so he could calm his nervous qualms with a good draught of whiskey. From the determined look on his mother's face, he was going to need it.

Chapter Twenty-Two

Charlotte opened James's door the smallest crack possible in order to get a quick peek into the corridor. She had to make it back to her room before the rest of the household woke, or she'd be in one hell of a mess.

To the left, clear. She inched the door open a little more to check out the right. Albert balanced a pile of clothes in one hand, his other hovering at door knob height, astonishment on his face. He quickly masked his surprise and bowed. "My lady."

"Bloody hell," she whispered under her breath. After a quick glance back into the room showed James lay still, snoring quietly, she slipped out the door and shut it behind her. "Good morning, Albert. I don't suppose we can keep this between us?"

He smiled. "Of course, my lady. I shall be glad to assist the future Lady Tyndale in whatever capacity I may."

Her mouth gaped open as he gave her a quick bow and then entered James's room, shutting the door quietly behind him.

The sound of James's voice startled her back into motion. She made her way swiftly down the corridor to her room. Thankfully, no one witnessed her indiscretion. Her mind was made up to stay, and that meant she planned on accepting James's next marriage proposal, but that didn't mean she wanted anyone to think she didn't make the choice of her own free will. That her acceptance was a foregone conclusion by the staff irked her, but she supposed she couldn't get too annoyed. They were right, after all. Not their fault she didn't particularly like being so predictable.

The fire in her room had yet to be lit, so she hurriedly got undressed and slipped into bed, messing up the covers as if she'd tossed and turned throughout the night.

The upstairs maid was likely making her rounds. Fires had to be prepped so all the bedrooms would be toasty and warm when their residents opted to get out of bed. It was still early, but sometimes she wondered if the staff of this house ever actually rested. People rushed around the manor at all hours of the day and night getting their jobs done while striving to make it appear as if the house stayed clean by magic.

Bed sufficiently mussed, she got up to select a suitable outfit for the day.

Getting into her favorite sky-blue, empire waist gown with the puffy little sleeves that thankfully didn't pinch her arms took only a few minutes. But a quick glance in the looking glass told her she needed to seek help to get her corset on correctly. Even with the soft drape from the high waist of the dress, the bumpy lines of her inexpertly tied undergarments showed through. Darn.

A scream shattered the air. Charlotte whirled to the door and ripped it open. James and Lady Tyndale burst out of a room just down the corridor.

"Did you hear that? Where did it come from?" she asked.

James strode to her side. He gripped her shoulders

in both hands and stared into her eyes. "Are you well? I heard the scream…" He winced. "I was afraid…"

She smiled that his first thought would be of her. "I'm fine."

Their relief was short lived. They still had no idea who made that awful noise.

"I'm going to go check on Prudence. If she heard that scream, she'll be scared," James said.

Prue's room was directly above them, and she slept so soundly she probably hadn't heard a thing, but a tightness in her gut prompted her to go with James and check regardless.

Charlotte nodded, and they all started toward the stairs, meeting up with Lord and Lady Downing and Lord Oakleigh at an intersecting corner.

They were all in varied states of dress, or undress really. Seeing them all not impeccably put together gave her an unsettled twinge. "Is everyone all right? Anyone know who screamed?"

No one had a clue, so they decided to split up with her and James heading up the stairs to check on Prue. They made it to the top step before they saw something that had her steps falter and her heart thunder in her chest.

Theresa lay sprawled on the floor to the side of Prue's door. Her face pasty white, blood splattered across her temple. A fireplace poker abandoned less than a foot away.

"Theresa!" Charlotte ran to the girl's side and bent to check her vitals. "She's alive," she said, after finding the thready pulse of her carotid. She ran her hands along Theresa's stomach, pleased when the baby gave a strong kick back in response to the pressure.

Theresa's eyes fluttered open. "Miss Prudence," she gasped out. "There was a man…"

The resounding *bang* of the door slamming open startled her. James quickly disappeared as he ran into his daughter's room. "Prudence? Where are you?" his voice had a frantic edge to it that scared her even more than Theresa's still form.

Charlotte sprang to her feet and into Prue's room. James ran about the room, checking all the usual hiding spots. He knew them as well as she did. Prue delighted in springing out at them. Charlotte had all but perfected her surprised shriek the past couple months. "Prue? Come out, sweetheart. Please." She sobbed. "Come out, now." It was no use. She'd known from the moment they found Theresa in the hall.

She dropped to her knees. *No. No. No.*

****

James paced the length of his daughter's bedroom. This couldn't be happening. "Damn it." He slammed his fist into the wall. His knuckles came away bloody, but the pain helped to slow the panic threatening to take over.

Charlotte was on her knees by the door, apparently thinking the same thing he was, repeating, "No. No."

Shit. He was stymied. What the bloody hell was he supposed to do next? How was he going to get his daughter back? All he could think about was what Prudence must be going through. Was she scared?

He actually hoped so. Because if she wasn't scared, then she was…

No. He couldn't stand the thought. He balled his hands into fists, wincing at the pull on his split knuckles. He embraced the pain. He had to clear his head, think logically. Prudence depended on him.

"Search the grounds. Everyone. Find her." The servants that had gathered outside Prudence's door scrambled to follow his orders. At least that was something.

He slowly studied the area, taking in every aspect of this room he knew so well. Nothing out of...No. Bunny was missing. Mary had sewn the toy while *enceinte*. His daughter cherished it.

He approached the bed. The sheets were messed, the pillows tossed. The villain must have struck before Prudence arose from her sleep.

Something lay on the bed, half covered by the pillow. He plucked up the tri-folded piece of parchment, grabbing a deep breath when the paper shook in his hands.

The warmth of Charlotte's hand upon his shoulder gave him some measure of calm. "What does it say?" she asked, her voice wobbling.

He flipped the paper over. Anger flared brightly at the sight of Lord Stone's seal upon the paper. "Stone." He broke the seal, tilting the paper until he could read the few words scrawled across the page.

"Join me at noon this day, and we shall discuss the terms of your daughter's release. Our usual meeting place will suffice. Bring the Ladies Creswell. Regards, Stone."

He crumpled the sheet in his fist. "He wants me to meet him at the caves."

"Not you," Charlotte said, her hand pinching his shoulder. "Us."

"No." He shook his head.

"Don't be stupid. He wants me there as well. Don't

you dare think there is anything I wouldn't do to see Prue safe. We can't risk my *not* going."

What the bloody hell was he supposed to do? How could he risk the woman he loved to the hands of a madman who'd almost seen her demise not once, but twice, already?

How could he not? The man had his daughter. He couldn't risk angering him by not bringing Charlotte. "He says, 'the *Ladies* Creswell.' He wants you both."

Charlotte bit her lip, her brows scrunched, eyes narrowed. "There's not much we can do about that."

"I can go in her place."

He and Charlotte swung about in surprise to see Lady Mary standing quietly at the door, an earnest expression on her face. She supported a shaky Theresa, who held one hand to her bloodied temple and the other to her swollen stomach. He hadn't heard them approach.

Charlotte leaped to help. Together the ladies installed Theresa in the chair where Harriet used to rock Prudence when she was but a babe. Charlotte took care of Theresa's injury with a swift, confidant energy. He greatly admired her poise, while he felt as though he were falling apart.

He needed to do something. A thought struck him. He lay a hand on Charlotte's shoulder. When she looked up, he asked, "Is she well enough to speak? I must ask her some questions."

Charlotte nodded while continuing to bandage Theresa's head.

He crouched at her side so she wouldn't be forced to crane her neck to see him. "Can you tell me what happened? We heard a scream. Was that you? Could he still be here?"

Theresa's response was weak. "I…I came to see if Miss Prudence was awake. A m…man hovered over her bed. I screamed, grabbed the fire iron, and hit him about the shoulders. He wrested it from my grasp. I ran. He chased after me." She placed a hand to her temple where a fresh white cloth covered her wound. "I don't remember… Then Lady Mary Creswell stood beside me, helped me up… Did you stop the man? Where is Miss Prudence?" Her voice reached an hysterical pitch.

Charlotte put her hands on Theresa's shoulders and mumbled in a low tone he couldn't make out, but did something to calm Prudence's nurse.

After several deep breaths, Theresa said, "If my screams alerted you, then he can't have gone far."

The urge to run from the room and capture the cretin burned in his gut. He stayed, knowing the household was awake and alert. Running off without knowing the proper direction would be less than useless. He needed to know more. "How did he appear?"

"Dirty, unkempt. As though he had not slept in ages."

"Do you think it was Stone or Cantor? Where could they have been all this time?" Charlotte asked. "Why would Stone do this? What does he hope to gain?"

"He has been cut off from his estate. His property seized. Doubtful he had much money with him when he fled and given his part in your abduction is now well known, he would have little access to the funds necessary to make good his escape. He most likely plans to extort money in exchange for Prudence." He clenched his fists. Stone was lucky James hadn't walked in on him abducting his daughter. He'd have ripped him limb from limb.

Still might.

"Then why would he want me and Alex?"

"Revenge." The thought chilled him further. Stone must intend to kill the ladies.

James would not allow that to happen. To prevent whatever trap Stone had laid out, James needed to find the son-of-a-bitch before those plans could be set into motion.

****

Charlotte softly shut the door to Theresa's room. She held a finger to her lips, then motioned Mary to follow her down the hall so they could talk.

There was no way Mary could go with them to face Lord Stone, but the girl would not be easy to convince. Thankfully, she had an idea. They slipped into an empty room.

"Mary, I'm going to need you to stay here and look after Theresa."

Mary shook her head. "Absolutely not. This monster that took Miss Prudence has requested both you and Alexandra be present. I may not be our sister, but provided I stay back somewhat, we can surely pull the wool over the cad's eyes."

Charlotte smiled at her young sister's courage. "I'm sure we could, but I'm serious about Theresa. She needs someone to look after her. She took a serious blow to the head. She needs to stay awake for a while. Plus there's always the possibility the baby might come. She's due any day now."

"Mother's with her."

Good point. *Shoot.* "She can't be expected to handle this on her own. Everyone else is out searching the grounds for Prue and Lord Stone. Please, Mary."

Mary bit her lip, her hands twisted in her skirt. "Mother can handle herself. Father will see to it someone is around to assist her. I feel strongly that Miss Prudence will best be served by my attending you on this rendezvous with Lord Stone."

Charlotte sighed. She didn't want to risk Mary, but she was torn. "All right. But I must insist that you stay in the carriage, in the shadows. You'll be safer and less visible. Stone will probably think it odd that Alex would hide, but there's not much we can do about that. Come on."

She grabbed Mary's hand, and they raced down to the entryway. Worthing stood guard over the open doorway, occasionally giving orders as a variety of servants ran up to him with their reports. He radiated a calm, self-assuredness that belied the chaos of the moment. Charlotte hoped she hid her panic half as well.

"Any luck?" Charlotte asked as she and Mary slid to a halt next to the efficient butler.

"My ladies." He bowed to each of them in turn. "My lord hastened off but a moment ago. Max found evidence of the baron not far from here."

Her heart pounded in her chest, a knot formed deep in her gut.

Mary squeezed Charlotte's trembling hand. "Did he go alone?"

The butler shook his head. "No, my lady. Your father and brothers attended him along with Lord Oakleigh."

"Which way did they go? We'll follow."

"I am under strict instructions not to allow you to follow, my lady."

She fisted her hands. "Excuse me? You won't allow—" A noise from the stairway cut her off.

Lady Downing gestured urgently for them to join her. "Charlotte. Quickly now. I believe Theresa's time has come."

Charlotte cursed under her breath and ran for the stairs, Mary right behind her. Worthing said, "I'll send for the midwife."

She was tempted to tell him the midwife wasn't needed. Charlotte had delivered babies before, but always in the safe, sterile confines of a labor and delivery room. If something went wrong…it might be a good idea to have someone around with more on-the-job training than she had. "Send me two of the upstairs maids. Have them bring extra linens. And if there are any footmen not already occupied with the search for Prue, have them fetch some boiling water and soap." Warm water would be enough to clean up, but with the iffy water quality, boiling first wouldn't hurt. So what if she sounded like a clichéd movie doctor, no one here would notice.

Theresa was pacing the confines of her small room when they burst through the door. Charlotte wanted to insist the mother-to-be lay down and get some rest, particularly after the nasty bump she had taken to the head earlier but had learned during her foundation years that it was usually a good idea to take her cues from the expectant mother.

She scanned the room for hazards instead, just in case Theresa tripped or fainted, but there wasn't much to worry over. She barely took four or five steps before spinning back the other way. The bed took up the majority of the space, with a small dresser under the window and a rocking chair in the corner.

Just the essentials, since the room wasn't used regularly anymore. Theresa used it only when anticipating Prue might have a rough night, or when there were strangers in the house and James wanted someone there to see to it Prue wasn't disturbed. Otherwise, Theresa lived with Max in a quaint little house not far from the stables.

Lady Downing, *Mum*—she had to get used to thinking of her that way—stood near the foot of the bed, hands out each time Theresa brushed past.

Theresa grimaced and bent double. Charlotte's mother rushed to one side, Charlotte to the other. "Help me get her to the bed," Charlotte said. They got Theresa to lay down and made her as comfortable as possible before Charlotte began her exam.

Damn. The birth was imminent. Charlotte wanted to run to help find Prue, but with Theresa so close to having the baby, she couldn't possibly leave. "Okay, Theresa. The baby's coming."

As Charlotte talked Theresa through the birth of her first child, she tried to keep her mind off Prue and James.

Please, please let them be all right.

****

James cursed silently. Stone struggled to keep Prudence from leaping off the horse while he attempted to mount the stallion behind her.

When had Prudence become such a fighter? Had she learned that from him, or more recently from Charlotte?

Oakleigh's hand on his arm kept him from charging forward. It damn near killed him, but the gun Stone slipped from his pocket proved James had to take a moment to think through what he was doing rather than charge ahead.

They had a modicum of luck that Stone had picked that particular horse for his escape. Whiskey was an ornery beast, not inclined to sit still while mounted. That Stone hadn't taken the time to saddle him properly was an added bonus.

If not for Stone's poor choices, he might have been far away with Prudence by now instead of fighting to remount the horse who'd apparently stopped at his favorite watering hole for a drink. Whiskey wouldn't be moved until he'd had his fill or he received the proper signal. Getting him to continue away from the barn so close to mealtime wouldn't be much of a picnic either. James silently gave thanks to the animal's odd training. A fine beast, but not one for a mediocre rider.

Good.

They crouched behind a downed tree, with plenty of foliage to block them from Stone's view even if he were to spare a glance for his surroundings. Still occupied with the unruly horse, he made no attempt to ensure he remained alone.

Slowly, a plan started to form. "Can you distract him?" he whispered to Gregory and Myles.

Both men nodded. Myles dug around in the dirt at their feet a moment, then held up a handful of small stones. He pointed to Whiskey.

James nodded. Good idea. Whiskey would spook, but with the way Prudence held onto the animal, he felt certain she could maintain her seat. With Stone trying to get the animal under control, they'd have room to move in.

Lord Downing held up his pistol. "I shall endeavor to find an opportunity to dispatch with the...the black guard."

Glancing toward Stone to be sure he hadn't heard their low-voiced conversation, James nodded his agreement. Their plan so far had all of Charlotte's family well back from danger.

"You take care of your daughter," Oakleigh whispered. "I'll handle Stone."

James agreed. Gregory and Myles headed round toward Stone's left, while Oakleigh made his way behind. Stone's cursing, Prudence's cries, and the running water of the small brook muffled any noise the men might have made.

Within moments, Whiskey snorted and danced to the right, kicking up his hindquarters and knocking Stone off balance. Prudence clung tight to his mane, leaned forward, and buried her head to the side of the horse's powerful neck. Good. If Whiskey reared back, she would be spared the pain of being hit in the face by the animal's head.

"Drat you, you mangy, cursed fiend," Stone cried out as he stumbled. The horse blocked any view he might have had of Oakleigh leaving the shelter of the trees.

James prepared to spring into action. Stone yanked viciously on the reins and used the pistol to smack Whiskey's rear end. If only he would put the damn thing away, they could use a more straightforward approach. But Prudence remained in danger.

Whiskey shied again, this time rearing back and

then dancing forward a few steps. The reins yanked from Stone's grasp. James whistled. Whiskey's ears perked forward, and he broke into a quick trot.

Stone was left alone and in the open. He spun in a circle, arm out, gun shaking. He spotted Oakleigh, stiffened his arm.

"Stone," James called as he stepped out into the open, drawing the bastard's attention.

Stone twisted his head, gun still trained on Oakleigh. "Tyndale," he sneered. "You're early. We were to meet at the cave entrance. Where are the Creswell chits?"

James scowled. "Home. What exactly was your plan, Stone? Kill the women? Kill me? Your deeds are known. There is no escape, no returning to the time before. You're finished." He took a few steps to the right. After his initial burst of energy in response to James's whistle, Whiskey had come to a stop several yards away. He munched on a sprig of grass, not a care in the world.

Prudence's head popped up. "Father!"

Stone swung the gun to point at Prudence. "Lovely girl, Tyndale. Don't force me to do something you shall regret."

James clenched his fists. With Prudence in his peripheral vision, he faced Stone. He forced a calm tone. "Everything will be all right, darling. Stay with Whiskey. I need to speak with Lord Stone for a moment." He had to keep Stone talking and calm. The minute the man thought he'd lost the upper hand, there was no telling what he might do.

Stone appeared as unhinged as one would expect. Used to the luxuries of his class, he had not fared well without them. His clothes were encrusted with filth, his face unshaven, eyes sunken and rimmed red. He had not done well on his own.

"Where's your coachman?" His own servants were spread out in these woods. Had they caught the churl, or could he possibly sneak up on them while they dealt with Stone?

"Cantor? The fool. Got himself killed at a bawdy house. I barely made it out myself. The cock bawd demanded recompense for the damage he inflicted on one of the bunters."

One less worry. "I'm not surprised. After what he did to Miss Crawford..." James shuddered. "Nothing less than he deserved."

"What did that cur do to her?" The gun shook in Stone's hand. Surprise colored his voice.

"She's dead."

Stone cursed. "That would explain why she never responded to my request for assistance. Poor sighted of Cantor. We could have used the gel."

"Blackmail for her part in Lady Charlotte's abduction, I assume." Stone's dismissal of Cantor's misdeeds as a mere inconvenience to him turned James's stomach.

"But, of course." He waved the gun but kept it pointed in Prudence's direction. "Now you shall have to finance my departure from this country all on your own." Stone glanced behind him. "Or perhaps Oakleigh can contribute. I shall let you work out the details. I'll be leaving now—with the young lady." He took one measured step toward Prudence. Two. His gaze swiveling between him and Oakleigh.

James froze. He couldn't let Stone escape with

Prudence. But with the gun pointed in her direction, he couldn't risk startling Stone. The gun could go off and hit her accidentally.

Whiskey whinnied. He'd finished his patch of grass and pawed the ground, his morning meal long overdue.

Stone flinched, his gaze swinging toward the horse, the gun rising to take aim at Prudence.

A shot rang out.

Chapter Twenty-Three

Charlotte leaned her head back and watched Theresa nurse her newborn, William. The scent of blood hung in the air, despite all the soiled linens having been removed and the floors cleaned. Theresa could barely keep her eyes open but smiled contentedly.

The birth had not gone easy, and Charlotte was thankful she'd been there to unwrap the umbilical cord from around William's neck. The midwife had declared the child dead without a thought to giving aid. It was touch and go there for a few minutes, but Charlotte's training saw them through, and William would be just fine. He scored well on the quick and discreet Apgar test she performed.

Damn, he was adorable.

Watching the new mother and her baby had Charlotte thinking and worrying about Prue. The men had left in pursuit over twelve hours ago, and there had been no word since. She may not have given birth to the sweet girl, but Prue had become lodged in her heart as though she were her own. If anything happened to her...

"You should try to get some rest," Lady Downing said.

Charlotte's hand jerked where it lay on the rocking chair's arm. She'd forgotten her mother was still in the room. "Theresa's almost done nursing William. I

314

should lay him down so she can get some sleep," she replied in a hushed voice. Theresa's eyes had closed, a soft snore fluttering from her lips.

"I shall see to it." Her mother gently lifted William from Theresa's slack arms. She cradled the child against her shoulder. He gave a soft burp and then sighed contentedly. "There, there."

"Great, thank you. I'm going to see if anyone's heard from James, but William needs to be watched for a while. I'll ask Mary to come relieve you. You've been up just as long as I have. Let Theresa sleep, but wake her when William needs to nurse." She rattled off a few more instructions, then turned toward the door.

Her mother stopped her with a whisper, "She'll be all right. I'm certain of it."

Charlotte nodded, even though she hardly felt as convinced. She left, closing the door behind her, and went in search of her sister.

She found her picking at a lonely meal in the dining room. Her head perked up when Charlotte pulled out a chair on her right.

"Has Theresa delivered the babe?" she asked.

Charlotte smiled. "Yes. A boy."

Mary clapped her hands together and clasped them under her chin. "That's wonderful. Has she named him, or will she wait until her husband returns?"

"They had names already selected. William, after Max's father." She slumped into the chair and picked a biscuit off Mary's plate. "Mother's sitting with the baby now while Theresa sleeps, but she's exhausted also. Would you mind checking in with them when you're done eating?"

Mary had broken out into a huge grin. "That's the

first I've heard you refer to her as *Mother*. Does this mean you have forgiven our parents for their failure to protect you and Alexandra?"

"Nothing to forgive." Charlotte grimaced. She felt like an ass for sticking to her belief for so long. It all seemed so ludicrous now. "It wasn't their fault. I'm just trying to adjust to this new way of thinking." She crumbled pieces of the bread between her finger and thumb.

"I would imagine that to be a difficult task, given that this time is so very different from that in which you grew up."

Charlotte gave a little start. Right. She forgot. Alex had explained time travel to their family, and they had believed her. "You have no idea." Mary appeared interested in pursuing this line of questioning, but it wasn't the time. She needed to find out what was going on with Prue, or go crazy. "Any word from James—Lord Tyndale, I mean—or the others?"

"No, I'm sorry."

"Bloody hell."

Mary's eyes widened.

"Sorry. I don't usually curse all that much, but I feel like I've been doing it nonstop since I got here." She rubbed a hand over her eyes. Damn, she was tired. No way she'd get any sleep until she knew what was going on with Prue, though. She used to curse her cell phone when she was on call at the hospital, now she cursed its lack. They could be on their way right now, Prue safe and sound, and she wouldn't know it because they had no way of calling ahead. "I can't just sit here. I need to do something."

"Have something to eat. You have been at

Theresa's side all day. You must be famished."

Charlotte's stomach took that moment to rumble. Mary hid her smile with a raised hand, while Charlotte's face flamed bright red. "I know I should eat, but…" Nerves battered her insides. "I think I'd be sick if I tried to eat anything right now."

"Have a little wine at the very least. Small sips to settle your nerves." Mary lifted a thick-cut crystal decanter and poured a dark red liquid into a delicate glass.

The smell made Charlotte wrinkle her nose, but she took a sip to please her sister. The fruity overtones of the wine weren't to her taste, but the liquid flowed easily over her dry tongue. She placed the goblet back on the table. It wouldn't do to drink too much. She needed to keep her wits about her and her hands steady. If anything happened to Prue, or James, or… She blinked back tears realizing how much she had to lose.

****

With the gunshot ringing in James's ears, he raced forward, yanked Prudence off Whiskey's back, and put himself between her and Stone, confident the others would see to the evil lord's demise. He had to be certain she wasn't hurt in any crossfire. He hadn't seen where the shot originated, whether Stone had pulled the trigger or someone else, but he couldn't risk his daughter.

He ignored the shouting going on around him until he had Prudence tucked safely behind a closely grouped crop of evergreens. He tilted the crying girl's face up. "Are you all right? Were you hurt?" When she continued to cry without answering, his alarm grew. "Prudence, darling, please. Answer me. Were you hurt?"

She sobbed uncontrollably. "N…no, F…Father," she cried, hiccupping.

He had to brush his own tears of relief out of his eyes.

"Tyndale?" Oakleigh called.

"Here." Keeping Prudence behind the tree, he twisted to get a view of the clearing. Stone was out of sight. Downing and his two sons stood near Whiskey, with Oakleigh striding toward him.

"Stone's dead," Oakleigh called out. "It's safe to bring Miss Prudence out."

James turned to his daughter. "You're safe now. Come." He held out his arms, and she launched herself against his chest. He held her tight. The constriction in his chest slowly loosened.

The nightmare was finally over.

He stood, cradling Prudence in his arms, her head tucked against his chest. Her tears had subsided, but he worried at her silence. His happy, talkative little girl was unnaturally quiet.

Keeping her head facing away, he examined the scene before him.

Stone lay on the ground, hand outstretched, eyes wide open. The gun lay several feet from his open hand.

Lord Downing gripped his gun, still pointed at the baron's dead body. His sons on either side, hands on his shoulders lending support.

"What happened?" he asked Oakleigh.

"I was making my way behind Stone, hoping to catch him unaware. The horse startled him, and when he raised his gun arm toward Miss Prudence, Lord Downing shot him."

They strode over to the Creswells who remained huddled around Stone.

Lord Downing lifted his head when they approached. "This man caused such pain for my family. I can't find it in myself to forgive him or regret what I have done."

James cradled Prudence. Hand on her head, he looked Downing in the eye and said, "Had you hesitated, my daughter might not be alive." He gave a slight bow, all that he could manage with his daughter in his arms. "From the deepest reaches of my soul, I thank you."

Downing nodded. "We should return to the manor. The hour grows late, and the women will worry."

James noticed the growing dark for the first time. Damn, it had grown late. He feared Charlotte and his mother would indeed be terribly worried. "Then let's make haste to return."

"Is Miss Evans still at home?" Prudence piped up in a tired voice. "The bad man said I would never see her again."

Rage fired in his gut, and James would have kicked Stone's lifeless corpse if given the opportunity. "Yes, she awaits us at the manor. She will be anxious to see you are well." He whistled, and Whiskey trotted to his side.

A trio of horses pounded into the clearing. Sebastian leaped from his horse and ran to James's side, grabbed Prudence, and swung her around in a bear hug. "Prudence, thank God."

Prudence giggled but quickly reached back for her father. James gratefully hugged her to him once more. Her weight reassuring against his chest.

Max and the constable dismounted. Downing called them over, and they spoke in hushed tones over Stone's body.

"Can we go home now, Father?"

"Of course, darling." He turned to Sebastian. "I should get Prudence home. She's had a trying day."

"Indeed." Sebastian lifted Prudence out of James's arms. "I shall pass her up to you." He kissed her on the forehead as he waited.

James mounted Whiskey, then took Prudence up before him. He called out to the group around the body, while carefully keeping the gruesome sight from his daughter's view. "I must return to the manor. I'm sure you will have many questions, Constable. Please see me at my home at your earliest convenience. I will make myself available."

"Yes, milord." The constable gestured toward Sebastian. "Mr. Tyndale was kind enough to apprise me of Lord Stone's reappearance this morning when he fetched me. With Lord Stone dead, the urgency of my investigations has decreased. Seeing to the young lady's comfort must take precedence."

James nodded his thanks.

Downing motioned to his sons. "Myles, go with Tyndale. You can assist with carrying Miss Prudence if necessary. Inform your mother and sister of all that happened this day. We shall return with all due haste."

"Yes, Father," Myles responded and mounted.

With Prue cradled in front of him plus Sebastian, Myles, and Max following behind, James commanded Whiskey to a canter, and they headed home.

****

The sound of pounding hoof beats approaching the

front sent Charlotte running. Worthing threw open the door, allowing her to pass through without pause.

Horses trotted up the drive, but the light was too dim to distinguish the riders. She wrung her hands, straining her eyes to see into the darkness. Four horses was all she could determine. Was James on the first? She couldn't be sure.

"James?" Lady Tyndale rushed to her side. She clutched a shawl around her shoulders and a shaky hand to her throat. "Prudence?"

Together they ran down the front steps to meet the riders on the drive.

Lady Tyndale was correct. The first rider was indeed James, carrying a prone Prue.

"Prue." Charlotte gasped. Her gaze flew to James's face. Was the girl injured, or merely sleeping?

James's happy expression answered her fear, and the tension drained from her body, leaving her weak and exhausted, but beyond happy and relieved. "Oh, Prue. Thank God." She hugged Lady Tyndale as the men dismounted.

Prue woke as James handed her over to Sebastian in order to dismount. "Uncle? Where are we?" she asked with a distinctly tired lisp.

"We're home, sweetheart," he responded, shifting her so she was more upright in his arms.

Charlotte ran forward. "Prue!" She jerked to a stop right before the little girl. When Prue reached out her arms, Charlotte grabbed her and tucked her in to a hug. "Oh, Prue. Ssh, ssh," she soothed as Prue dissolved into tears. Not that she didn't have just as many streaming down her own face. "It's all right. You're back. We're together now. It's all right, love."

Lady Tyndale hovered next to them, no doubt eager to embrace her granddaughter as well. Charlotte reluctantly passed Prue over, wanting desperately to keep her solid body in her arms. To feel that reassurance that the little one was alive and well. But Lady Tyndale must be feeling the same and deserved that comfort.

So Charlotte contented herself with placing a hand on Prue's head and stroking her hair away from her face. Lady Tyndale wiggled her hand, and Charlotte took that as an invitation to wrap her arms around them both.

They stood that way for a few moments until Sebastian chimed in. "Perhaps we should continue into the drawing room? I'm sure we'd be much more comfortable, and I could use a bit of a draught."

She let her arms drop and stepped back. "Yes, of course." She used her sleeves to mop up her face as best she could.

James pulled her into his arms, and she rested her cheek against his chest. She pushed back and swiped at the wet spot she left on his crumpled cravat. "Oh, sorry."

"I'm afraid I find myself without a handkerchief to offer. Perhaps you would settle for my hand in marriage for now, and I shall endeavor to be better prepared in the future."

She blinked up at him in astonishment. *Did he…?* "Did you just ask me to marry you?"

"I did." He nodded. His lips tilted slightly into a sober smile. His gaze darted back and forth from her eyes to her chin to her forehead. She'd never seen him so unsure.

Her heart swelled to bursting. What a ridiculous time for an engagement. But, somehow, it was perfect.

Crickets dominated the background with their overloud chirping. The moon beamed down brightly, and thousands of stars shone in the sky. Lady Tyndale had set Prue down, and the little girl that had become a part of her heart gazed at her with such hope, such love, that tears returned to Charlotte's eyes.

Charlotte winked at Prue, who clapped her hands and bounced in place. Lady Tyndale broke into a smile.

James cleared his throat, and Charlotte gazed once more into the eyes of the man she adored. "I suppose I should give you an answer, then." She took a deep breath and stood on her tiptoes so she could whisper against his lips, "Yes, I'll marry you."

He *whooped* and lifted her off her feet to swing her around. She let her head fall back as she laughed. Prue ran to join them, and he swept her up in their embrace. They were soon surrounded by well-wishers, and the crickets were drowned out by the sounds of their joy.

But throughout all the hugs and well wishes, Charlotte couldn't help thinking of those who weren't there, and may never be. The possibility that Alex would return was fairly high in Charlotte's opinion. If she were able, she'd return to be with the man she loved. Wasn't Charlotte making the decision to stay for that very reason?

Steven, though...she'd never see him again. A piece of her heart was missing and it was entirely of her own doing. Would she ever be able to forgive herself for abandoning her brother?

Chapter Twenty-Four

Charlotte stood and stretched. She'd been sitting outside the cavern entrance for over an hour. Three months had passed since James proposed, and the wedding was in four weeks. She should be deliriously happy, but the portal and the future cast a pall over her happiness.

Max's head rose with her movement. "Are you ready to leave, my lady?" He twitched Miss Bea's reins so she gave up nibbling on a patch of grass.

"Not yet." Guilt for dragging him out here so often made her stomach twinge. His new son was a handful, and neither Max nor Theresa had been getting much sleep lately. But James insisted Max accompany her whenever she spent time at the portal.

Even though Lord Stone and his evil henchman were dead and couldn't possibly bother her again, James didn't want her wandering the countryside on her own. He never said anything to her, but she suspected he feared she might disappear through the portal. She tried to hide it, but she couldn't help how depressed she was at the thought of never seeing Steven and Alex again.

She often wondered what Max would do if she decided to go in the cave rather than sit pathetically outside it. What exactly were his instructions for these outings? Was he to follow her? Prevent her from going any closer than she currently stood?

Not that she was likely to do anything of the sort. Merely peering into the mouth of the pitch-black cave set her legs to wobbling. She doubted she'd make it ten feet into the dank hole.

Maybe Lady Tyndale was right. Sitting here was a useless endeavor. What were the chances that *if* Alex chose to return to this century, Charlotte would just happen to be here at that exact moment?

James had made sure a lantern and suitable clothing were available both at the portal's entrance and at the cave mouth. Charlotte had included a letter among the items so Alex would know where she was.

Everything was perfectly set up. There was no earthly reason for Charlotte to spend this time waiting for an event that was extremely unlikely to happen. But a tiny nibble of hope tickled the back of her brain, or was that her heart? She couldn't dash the thought Alex would return. Granted, she didn't know a whole lot about her sister's life in the future, but her impression was Alex didn't have much. No family. Few friends. Working her way through college, but not with a specific goal in mind. As far as she knew, Alex was only interested in anything that might afford her a more comfortable lifestyle.

So why would she stay in a future devoid of emotional bonds when she could live in the past with the man she loved and a family who missed her terribly? The more Charlotte thought of it, the more she was convinced her twin would return. Alex had expressed a great love for Lord Oakleigh in the few hours they'd spent in the caves. No way would she give up on that without a fight.

If Charlotte had learned one thing about her sister, it was that she was most definitely a fighter.

The only thing that might keep Alex from returning was her health. She'd have to be sufficiently recovered before braving the portal again. Over three months had passed. She should be out of the hospital by now, but likely still recovering. The real question was how long Alex could live without Oakleigh.

Charlotte would be hard pressed to go so long without James. She could only assume Alex would feel similar. That left her return to occur any day now. And given the cave's distance from London, the sensible plan would be to get there early in the day in order to find shelter before evening.

So Charlotte had made a habit of visiting the cave for an hour or so each morning.

James didn't understand, and she regretted that immensely. If only he could trust that her love for him was strong enough to keep her happy in this century.

Her decision was made, and she was going to stick with it. She had little choice. She'd be miserable without James. And Prue, she couldn't forget the little girl who had come to mean more to her than she could have thought possible.

Neither could she dismiss her parents and siblings. Knowing what they'd gone through when she disappeared, she couldn't put them through that again. They already suffered so much with Alex's absence.

Oakleigh had returned home months ago. James made a point to visit whenever he had occasion to go to London. From what he reported upon his return, the marquess was dealing with Alex's absence even worse than Charlotte. Reports of heavy drinking and an obsession with his investments that, while likely wonderful for his income, left little doubt the time was not passing easily, worried Charlotte. At least when he'd been at Tyndale Manor, he'd been involved in the search for Lord Stone. But with the threat to everyone's safety alleviated, there was more time to dwell on their missing loved ones.

There was little Charlotte could do to help. She might have liked the chance to talk to Oakleigh, find out some of the details Alex had neglected to share about her time in this century, but he'd made it clear that seeing Charlotte was too painful. They did, after all, share the same face.

She spoke of Alex often with her parents. Memories of their childhood before the kidnapping were rehashed over and over, but no one knew much about Alex's life during the twenty-first century. All they'd learned to this point was that she had not had an easy time of it. Which played into Charlotte's theory that Alex would likely return.

But Steven, poor Steven, would be left all alone. And that tore at her heart. Charlotte had been something of a wild child as a teen, and Steven was a large part of getting her through those difficult years. They'd grown even closer when their parents died. Now she was abandoning him when he needed her.

Miss Bea whinnied a greeting, and Charlotte turned to see who approached. Her depressed spirits lightened as James trotted up on Whiskey.

He hopped off his horse with a grace born of a lifetime in the saddle. Not a wrinkle marred his coat, but a light coating of dust covered his boots. She smoothed a hand down her dress, certain she looked a mess after sitting on a tree stump for so long.

She'd left him reviewing the accounts in preparation for a meeting with his steward this afternoon, while Lady Tyndale played dolls with Prue. The majority of Charlotte's family had returned to their own country estate a few weeks ago to be sure the wedding banns were read properly in their home parish. Only Gregory had remained, but he seldom rose before ten, so she hadn't expected anyone to miss her for another hour at the least.

Max took Whiskey's reins from James. "Max, see Whiskey and Miss Bea are comfortable, and then you may head back to the manor. I'll accompany my lady home."

Max bowed. "Yes, my lord." He made quick work of securing the horses and took off at a fast canter.

Charlotte laughed. "I don't think I've ever seen him quite so eager to leave the horses in anyone else's care."

James returned her grin. "I cannot fault his desire to be at home. I felt much the same when Prudence was first born."

"I wish I had known her then," she said wistfully. "I'll bet she was adorable." How could she not have been? Prue was the most amazing little girl. "Oh well. I may be a time traveler, but I fear that is beyond even my power." The cave loomed behind her, and she turned to peer into its dark depths.

****

James grimaced. The wistful smile on Charlotte's face caused great unease within him. What did she see as she stared day after day into the black depths of that damn cave? Did she consider returning to the future?

She'd grown more and more distant the past few weeks. Each morning spent on her own, thinking God knew what as she kept her own counsel on the matter.

She wasn't much better at home. Mother assured him Charlotte was simply preoccupied with wedding preparations, but he knew better.

She mourned the loss of her sister and brother.

And he could do nothing to ease her pain.

Were they dead, she could experience the pain of their passing, and move on. But they were not. They lived, breathed, had lives separate from this time. And so Charlotte was unable to stop imagining how they fared.

"Do you ever think about what *is* in your power?" he asked.

She tilted her head and frowned. "What do you mean?"

He nodded toward the cave entrance. "The portal. It's your path to Lady Alexandra and your brother."

"Are you saying you want me to go back?" Her tone of voice echoed his surprise that he'd ever suggest such a thing.

He hadn't meant to say anything. In fact, he'd come here to whisk her away from the damned place with all due haste. Yet he nodded slowly. "Yes, I do believe that would be best."

She fisted her hands on her hips and glared. "Are you bloody well joking? Having a good laugh at my expense?" She poked him in the chest. "We're to be married in less than a month. Have you changed your mind already?"

He grabbed her by the upper arms and held her close. He got right in her face and said, quietly, "I love you, Charlotte. More than I could ever have imagined possible. I can't bear to see you so unhappy, and I suspect you will remain so until you have resolved your feelings regarding your departed siblings. So, no. I'm not *laughing*. I'm very far from doing so." He took a deep breath. His heart pounded in his chest. "Use the portal. Visit with Lady Alexandra and your brother. Devise a solution that will enable you to come back to me with your whole heart."

He kissed her on the nose, swung around, and grabbed Whiskey's reins. He focused on the leather in his grip, the whitening of his knuckles as he made a fist. Anything but look back at his love. "I ask only that you first write a letter to explain yourself to Prudence so that she may understand should something—" he cleared his throat "—prevent your return." He nodded toward Miss Bea. "There should be paper, quill, and ink with the items gathered for Lady Alexandra. Leave your missive with your horse and then set her free. She will make her way back to the stables. She knows the way. A servant will be assigned to keep watch for your homecoming. I trust you will return in time for our wedding. If not, I shall know how we stand."

He mounted Whiskey and steered him toward home.

"James," Charlotte called to him, but he refused to look at her.

"Go, Charlotte. Don't think any more on it. We both know this is something you must do. If you don't go now, I won't have the strength to do what's right in the future. I wish I could go with you, but I can't take a chance on my daughter losing both of us." All his strength was needed to not grab Charlotte in his arms and take back his words. He did not want her to make the trip.

He did not doubt her love for him. She'd accepted his proposal, and he could not believe she would have done so if she did not desire to marry him.

But what if, upon returning to the future, she discovered the life that called to her from beyond the portal was infinitely better than life in the past? He'd seen her minor trinkets from the future and listened to her stories of marvels he could but barely imagine. What if their pull was stronger than her love for a nineteenth century widower and his daughter?

And should their love prove stronger than any lure from the future, there remained the very real possibility she would be unable to return through no fault of her own.

****

James galloped away. Tears stung Charlotte's eyes. Whether of anger or despair, she couldn't decide. How could he demand such a thing of her? Return through the portal? As if that were a mere walk in the park. He knew how dangerous such an action was. For all his talk of protecting her, he was quick to urge her toward danger.

Uncontrollable shivering racked her body as she stared into the dark depths and inched closer. A cold draft wafted up through the cave mouth. It would be several degrees colder down there. Her short, puffed sleeves would do little to protect her arms. Crouching her way through the tunnel while wearing a corset wouldn't be any fun either.

If she returned to the manor to grab a shawl, she'd never have the courage to come back. If she ran into

Prue, or her mother, or caught a glimpse of Theresa and the baby, then she would find excuse after excuse not to go through with it.

She hated to admit it, but James was right. This was something she needed to do.

The package for Alex was just inside the entrance where her sister couldn't fail to find it were she to pass this way. She found the writing supplies just as James had said. She chewed a fingernail ragged as she thought of what to write to Prue. She pressed quill to paper a dozen times before writing as quickly as possible.

Dear Prue,

There's something I must do. I don't plan on being gone more than a few days, a week at most. Should something prevent my return, please know that it was not my choice. I could never leave you. I will love you and your father, always.

With all my love,

Charlotte Evans Creswell

A tear dropped onto her signature, blurring the ink. She waved the paper in the air to dry, then folded it once over and tucked it into a small pocket attached to Miss Bea's saddle. She threw the reins over the horse's head and steered her toward the manor. After a good slap on the rump, Miss Bea trotted off. James was right. Miss Bea loved nothing more than returning to her stall at the end of a ride. The Tyndale horses were treated well.

Her task complete, she faced the cave once more. The lantern they'd kept at the mouth was all ready to go. Once it was lit, she took a deep breath, gathered her skirts and the bag of supplies in her left hand, the lantern in her right, and stepped tentatively into the cave.

The light flickered, casting shadows against the jagged walls. The scent of mildew tickled her nose. "Bloody hell," she whispered, and her words echoed back to her.

Trekking her way down to the portal left her breathing heavily. Every so often a drop of moisture would plop onto her back or her cheek, and she'd jump as if it were acid. The echoes of her steps and labored breathing made her feel like she was being stalked through the increasingly narrow tunnel.

And then, the faint humming of the portal. Gooseflesh raised all over her body. She stashed the bag of supplies so she would be able to find them easily when she returned.

She took a deep breath, coughing on the exhale. She did not want to do this.

Which didn't matter one bit. She had to. "Steven," she whispered, and his name echoed back to her. She could never be happy if she didn't say good bye. This was her chance. "Come on, Charlotte. Get a grip. There's no point sitting here in this Godforsaken hole in the ground."

She bit her lip, gathered her skirts, and stepped through the portal.

Chapter Twenty-Five

Charlotte stepped into the room that had haunted her dreams for months. It didn't seem too different from what she remembered. There was an obvious patch job on the ceiling above her, but that was the only evidence of her flight from Sawyer back in March.

The bright white fluorescent lighting switched suddenly to a pulsating red. Sirens blasted her eardrums. Charlotte slapped her hands to her ears, cringing. The lantern crashed to the ground.

"Hands up." Two soldiers trained their guns on her. The one shouted his demand again when she didn't respond immediately.

She thrust her hands in the air. Of course she knew this was an option, she'd just hoped she was wrong. Her hands were jerked behind her back, and plastic cut into her wrists as one of the guards used a tie wrap to bind her arms painfully behind her back. "Ow."

Not surprisingly, no one rushed to loosen her bonds.

She was shoved into a chair while one of the guards slapped a button near the door. She breathed a sigh of relief as the terrible wailing of the alarm ceased. She flexed her jaw, wishing she could rub the ringing from her ears.

The guards stared at her, guns trained in her direction.

She cleared her throat. "I gather the restraints mean you're not going to just toss me back through the portal. What are you waiting for?"

An intercom near the door buzzed, and one of the guards slapped a hand on the response button. "We have a traveler. Send for Sawyer."

Charlotte rolled her eyes. "Bloody hell. Just the person I *don't* want to see."

"Quiet."

She leaned back in her chair, but the bindings on her wrists made that too uncomfortable. She pitched forward to take the pressure off. The one guard still paying attention flinched. "Relax. I'm trying to get comfortable. You tied these things a bit tight." She twisted her hands to the side so he could see.

The door banged open. Sawyer strode through, flicked his hands, and the guards relaxed their stance.

"Ah, Miss Evans. I've been expecting you for a while now. What took you so long?"

Charlotte stared. "What are you on about? Why do you sound so pleased?" He had something up his sleeve. The grin on his face did not fit her expectations. Her gut twisted with anxiety. She didn't trust him. If he was so pleased to see her, she had made a serious mistake in coming through the portal.

He slipped a knife out of his pocket and flicked it open as he approached her. She flinched, but he merely circled around behind her and cut the plastic tie wraps squeezing her wrists together so painfully.

Her arms shot apart. She held them in front of her and massaged her wrists while Sawyer sauntered around to stand before her.

He motioned for the guards to leave the room.

They shot uneasy glances between themselves but followed his order.

The silence screamed at her. Speaking to the jerk was better than sitting around wondering what the hell he was up to.

She opened her mouth to say who knew what, when Sawyer spoke, "I imagine Lord Stone is dead, and life has settled down some?"

"H…How do you know about that?" she stuttered.

"I can read."

Charlotte bit her lip to keep from yelling. Seriously? She'd just burst through a time portal, leaving the love of her life and the family she'd only just come to accept, and he was going to get all flippant on her? "You can read? That's your answer?" She stood, hands fisted in front of her. If she didn't deck him it would be a miracle.

Sawyer held his hands up in front of him to ward her off. "Relax, relax. Sorry if I'm coming off a bit too self-satisfied, but this whole mess hasn't exactly been easy to manage, you know. I had to get you and your sister back at just the right moments, and neither you, nor your sister, are precisely easy to deal with." He frowned. "I trust you're here to coax dear Alex to return home with you? I shall look forward to your success. Your sister has been an enormous pain in my ass since her return."

Charlotte smiled for the first time since coming through the portal. "And I'm glad to hear it. How is she?"

"Recovering. She left the hospital a few days ago."

She breathed a sigh of relief. If Alex was out of the hospital, she must be doing well in her recovery. She might still have a ways to go, but Charlotte's spirits lifted. A tiny pinch of the tension squeezing her stomach eased. But it didn't go away entirely.

Wait a minute. His comment on getting them back at the right moment registered an alarm in her head. "You knew? You knew what was going to happen to us, to everyone?" The smug smirk on his face confirmed he did. "You bloody bastard. People *died,* and you could have stopped it." She shook her head thinking of the article about Miss Crawford's murder. "No. Not even. You caused it. If we'd never gone back, none of it would have happened. What the hell is wrong with you?" Her anger warred with the part of her that was happy she'd gone back. If she hadn't, she wouldn't have found James, or Prue, or made peace with her family and their complicated past.

But guilt over the deaths knotted her stomach. Stone, Cantor...they were horrible men. She couldn't mourn their deaths. But what about Miss Crawford? She was a bitch, for sure, but she hadn't deserved what happened to her. And Charlotte was going to have to live with her guilt over that for the rest of her life. Sawyer should share some of that pain.

"I didn't cause anything. Not really. I simply ensured history occurred as it was supposed to do."

****

Lady Tyndale burst through James's study door, panic on her face. "James! Miss Bea returned to the stable. Alone." She clutched a hand to her chest. "Something must have happened to Charlotte."

Max followed close behind. He waved a small, folded piece of paper in the air. "I found this note tucked into her saddle. It's addressed to you and Miss

Prudence."

James let his head drop until his chin met his chest. She'd done it. She'd left him. He'd all but pushed her through the portal, but he'd half hoped she would defy him. He held out a hand to take the letter from Max. "Thank you. I am aware of where Lady Charlotte has gone. Do not be alarmed."

Max didn't look entirely satisfied with that answer but bowed and backed out of the room.

"Where could she possibly have gone? Without a horse or companion? Do you expect me to believe she simply *walked* off without a word to anyone?" His mother settled into a chair before his desk. She looked none too pleased as well, though the scowl on her face was much more pleasant than the fear of a moment ago.

"She has returned to her own time, Mother." He twisted the paper in his hands, not wanting to see what Charlotte had written moments before stepping through a portal that could possibly take her away from him forever. "She had to go. I *made* her go." He put his head in his hands and leaned forward, elbows on his desk. "It was the right thing to do, wasn't it?"

The warmth of his mother's hand gripped his shoulder. Her rose scented perfume comforted him as it always had in moments of doubt. He stared up into her worried gaze.

"Oh, darling. I don't understand. Why would you do such a thing?"

So maybe that look was more condemnation than concern. "What was I to do? You must have noticed her spending more and more time at that damn portal. Was I to let her continue in such a manner indefinitely?"

"Certainly not. Charlotte merely needed time to

mourn the loss of her previous life. A little more time was needed, not banishment to a place from which she may never be able to return."

He groaned. "Thank you for your kind reassurance," he ground out. "Of course she'll return, James," he said in falsetto, mimicking his mother's high-pitched tone. "She loves you, James. Nothing could keep her away from you, James."

She smacked him on the shoulder. "Don't be so chuckle-headed." She bowed her head, then returned to her chair across from his desk. "I apologize. I should not have implied she may not return."

"Thank you." He placed the folded letter on his desk before him, letting his hand rest on top. He could not read it. Not yet. "Please, take this. If she has not returned within a week, we shall open it then. I do not have the heart to read her farewells."

His mother took the letter and stood. "Very well. I shall go rouse Lord Creswell from his bed."

"Why?" The last thing he wanted to do right now was face Charlotte's family.

"For Charlotte to wander off alone would be scandalous. However, were she to decide to spend time with family, she would need an escort. We'll claim Lord Creswell saw to her safety. He can return in a few days and await her return."

He nodded. "A good plan, you think of everything. Now, I must hold out hope that she will come to terms with all that she must leave behind in the twenty-first century and see that her future is in this century—with us."

****

Charlotte fumed as she paced the length of

Sawyer's office. A six foot-something behemoth guarded her only way out. Guess Sawyer hadn't gotten word he wasn't allowed to hold people hostage whenever the mood took him. The wait was driving her insane. What was he doing?

She'd tried logging into his computer to see if she could at least find out what the world had made of her disappearance, but his laptop was password protected, and she didn't know how to begin to guess it. The stupid guard had shaken his head rather menacingly when she attempted to rifle through his drawers in search.

She bit her lip, hating that she'd been intimidated into obedience, but seriously, the man was huge.

"You know, he could at least have told me where he was going, or how long he'd be gone," she said to Gigantor. "Any clue how long I'm supposed to be held prisoner here?"

Gigantor merely shook his head, then continued his steely stare-down.

She rolled her eyes back at him. The least she could do was be as obnoxious as possible without crossing any lines that might get him mad. She stuck her tongue out at him for good measure.

To her surprise, he actually cracked a smile. "I really am sorry, miss. Mr. Sawyer instructed me to see you remained in this room and stayed out of trouble. He doesn't bother explaining himself to the help."

Her brows rose. So Gigantor wasn't a fan either. "Did he give instructions not to talk to me?" She tilted her head and tried to gauge whether she might be able to dig up some info after all.

Gigantor's smile increased. "He didn't mention it,

no."

"Brilliant. So you're free to answer a few questions?"

He nodded. "Sure thing. And I'll do my best to answer provided the information isn't classified."

She frowned. "Classified? What exactly is Griffin International involved in that would be classified?" She'd known it was a large corporation, but the men with guns seemed way out of place for a private organization.

"Classified. Sorry."

"Hmph." She should have known that line of questioning would get her nowhere. "Do you know what happened to my sister? She came through the portal back in May."

"I was here that day. Kept watch on the big guy while she was in surgery." He folded his arms across his chest, glanced up and down the hallway, and then leaned against the doorjamb. "Sawyer wasn't at all pleased she returned. I heard he took some shit over that mess, but since he'd accomplished his main mission, they weren't too bent out of shape. They've been pushing hard for him to get rid of her though."

Her breath caught in her throat, and she shivered from the chill his words sent down her back. "What does that mean?"

He waved a dismissive hand in the air. "Not what you're thinking. Despite appearances, the board doesn't condone killing anyone. They may press some legal and ethical boundaries, but they're pretty careful about crossing them."

"So you think kidnapping me and forcing me through a time portal doesn't cross any lines? I'm fairly certain a lawyer would think differently."

"They might. If you'd been born in this century. Fact of the matter is, you never should have been allowed to stay."

"So why did I? Why didn't they just force us right back through the portal?"

"Above my pay grade." He shrugged. After a glance over his shoulder, he leaned forward and whispered, "Rumor has it, your survival was necessary for the timeline. Sending you back was too risky. Had you gone back and died…well, the theory is, you needed to return at a specific time."

"Rumor, theory?"

"Yeah, it's all I have for you. My fiancée works in research. She let a few things slip when your sister came back." His lips pursed in a disapproving scowl. "I suppose I was having a bit of an existential crisis. Your sister was in bad shape. Her man was upset—to put it mildly—and all the while, Sawyer was fuming that she should have been sent back through the portal. One of the guards was fired for relaxing her post to help. I considered quitting, going to the press… I wasn't sure what to do. Then Sarah, my fiancée, told me what she knew about your background. I don't want to give away too much, but she convinced me what we were doing was a necessary evil, so to speak."

Charlotte shook her head, a dull ache pounded right behind her eyes. "So, as far as you're concerned, my sister and I are just a part of history. Screw what we want, our lives are already decided."

"It sounds harsh, I know, but yes. Exactly."

Gigantor straightened abruptly.

Sawyer sauntered into his office. "Ah, Miss

Evans." He held up a hand to stall her when she opened her mouth. "I have a surprise for you." He swept his hand toward the door.

She peered through the open door out into the hallway.

"Charlotte!" Alex burst through the door and straight into her.

Charlotte had to brace herself by grabbing onto her sister and returning her embrace. "Alex. You're all right. I was so worried. Sawyer said you were recuperating, but..." She looked good. A bit off color, but good. Charlotte hadn't expected anything else given how recently Alex had undergone major surgery. Recoveries always seemed to take longer than expected.

"Yeah, I wouldn't trust him either," Alex said with a scowl and a tipped chin to the man in question. She twisted back around and smiled full force. "So let's get out of here. I know someone who's dying to see you."

****

Charlotte held her breath as Alex knocked on Steven's front door. Her chest threatened to burst with excitement. She'd missed her brother like crazy. She couldn't wait to see him. "Does he know I'm here?" she whispered.

Alex shook her head. "No. He's probably not even expecting me." She leaned against the door. "I'd already made the decision to return when Sawyer called me this morning. When I told Steven I was going to Sawyer's office, I'm sure he figured he'd never see me again."

What was taking him so long to answer the door? Charlotte's hands shook. "He was okay with that?"

"He's the one who told me I should do it."

Charlotte chuckled. That sounded like Steven all right. He was always telling her to go for what she wanted. He'd been the one to convince her she was capable of becoming a doctor whenever she doubted herself.

The lock turned with a soft click, and Steven called out, "Coming."

Alex stepped back, leaving Charlotte in the doorway to be the first person Steven saw.

Charlotte smoothed a hand down the front of her gown, wishing she'd stopped to clean herself up before rushing over. Sawyer's limo driver had studiously avoided looking at her, but his eyes widened when he first saw her getup. She must be a sight.

The door opened. The expression on Steven's face was priceless. Welcoming, followed by a hint of confusion, and swiftly followed by joy. His crooked smile always warmed her heart, and this moment was no exception. "Charlotte!" Rather than retreating into his flat, he joined her in the hallway, grabbing her up and swinging her around in a giant bear hug. They both laughed.

He let her down and leaned back to stare at her. "You look fantastic. Here I've been worried sick, and you look like you've been away at the spa."

Guilt hit Charlotte hard, and tears burned behind her lids. "I'm so sorry, Steven. I never meant to…"

"Oh, shut up. Can't a guy tease his little sister?" He tugged on her hand. "Let's go inside." He smiled at Alex. "I'm glad to see you, too. I thought you were all set to return to that prince of yours."

"Marquess," Alex replied, and she swept past them into the flat.

It wasn't a large space, but luckily Steven wasn't into 'things,' so the place remained fairly uncluttered. They sat facing each other on an overstuffed leather couch, while Alex perched on a wing chair across from them. Once they were settled, Steven patted her hand and said simply, "Tell me."

And the entire story poured out. She held nothing back. And, damn if it didn't feel really good to get it all off her chest.

Alex sat quietly through it all, though she bit her lip in what appeared to be a mighty effort not to curse when Charlotte told of Stone's escape and all that transpired after Alex's return to the future. It was pushing midnight by the time she finally finished and sagged back to rest her head against the sofa cushions, exhausted.

Steven held out another beer, and she leaned forward to take it, twisting and peeling off the label in strips. Empty bottles littered the coffee table. She set hers on a coaster and then dipped a chip in the salsa Steven had set out. The extra spicy mixture set her tongue on fire and made beads of sweat pop out on her upper lip. He'd broken out just about all her old favorites throughout her tale. She was fit to burst, but eating was a distraction she sorely needed. The longer she was back in the future, the more she realized she belonged in the past.

She sighed. "I miss James. And Prue." She fought back the tears. "But I missed you so much. I can't stand this."

Steven leaned forward and squeezed her hand. "It's okay, sis." A sheen of tears sparkled in his eyes. He sniffed and swiped a hand across his cheeks. "You belong back then. This James of yours sounds like a good guy. Am I right?"

"Absolutely. He's wonderful."

He nodded. "Good. Because two hundred years is an awful long trip to kick his ass if he mistreats you." He gathered up the bottles and walked away.

Charlotte stared at Alex, the sound of the bottles dropping in the rubbish bin coming from the kitchen.

"He's right, you know. We belong there. The fact that both of us are miserable here proves it." Alex bit her lip. "I need to at least try to make it work with Nicholas. I'm scared out of my mind that he's not going to want me as much as I want him, but I have to take that chance."

"Oh, he loves you. And the sooner you get back there, the better. He's a wreck."

Alex shrugged. "You say that, but..."

"No buts."

"*But...* I won't feel sure until I see him again. I mean, he left me here. If he loved me, why would he do that?"

"Why wouldn't he?" Charlotte asked. "I'll admit. I was pretty cheesed off when he got back and said he didn't even have the decency to say goodbye—" She cut herself off to answer the daggers her sister was flinging her way with her eyes. "Oh, come on. You have to admit it was a dick move."

Alex huffed and leaned back in her chair.

"We have to cut him a little slack." She'd given this not a little amount of thought the past few months. "He was trying to be noble. He failed miserably, but he had good intentions. Mansplaining, chauvinism...those weren't even concepts back then. Not like we know them. For a man of his time, he's actually pretty decent. He may be a bit chauvinistic, but he was trying to do what's best for you, and that's something. You can teach him not to be such an ass."

"Who's a chauvinistic ass?" Steven sauntered back in. His eyes were red, but his lips were tilted up in his typical goofy grin. "I hope you're not talking about me, because I have a great respect for the weaker sex." And he ducked just in time to miss the pillow Charlotte aimed at his head. He didn't dodge the one Alex threw but caught it against his chest with a laugh.

"Brothers." Charlotte rolled her eyes and laughed along with both her siblings.

"It's getting late," Steven said. "Why don't we get some sleep? I know you're both eager to go back through the portal, but maybe you can spend a little time here? A week, at the most."

Charlotte and Alex both nodded.

"Yeah," Charlotte said. At least with her mind made up, she could spend the next week enjoying some time with Steven before she left and never saw him again. "We can do that."

Chapter Twenty-Six

"Will Miss Evans return to us today, Father?" Prudence asked. Her lips quivered, and tears pooled in her eyes. "I miss her."

"I don't know." James wished he had a better answer. Bloody hell, he wished he had any answer that could bring the happy light back into his daughter's beautiful face.

Miss Bea poked her head over the stall door and nudged his arm. He absentmindedly stroked her nose as he contemplated how to explain the situation to his daughter. Charlotte had been gone for a week already, and he hadn't had the courage to read the note she left for him. Had she wished him goodbye? Had she decided, at that last moment, never to return?

No. He had to believe she would return. "I miss her as well, but we must be patient. She needs to spend some time with her family. I believe she misses us, and I do not doubt she will return to us as soon as circumstances allow." *And what if it's not possible?*

He couldn't let himself think such things.

"Now, give your father a hug and then help Max get Muffin ready for your riding lesson. It's important you know how to take proper care of your mount."

"Yes, Father." She flung herself at him full force, almost knocking the breath out of him.

She shifted so quickly from little lady to hellion, he

sometimes forgot to brace himself. He exaggerated his stagger, and she laughed delightedly before running off to the far end of the barn. She disappeared into Muffin's stall, and Max immediately began his instructions. The man was a wonder with the horses and his daughter. Prudence would be a strong rider in no time.

Miss Bea whinnied for his attention. Or, more likely, for the sugar cube he had in his pocket. He dug it out and fed it to her before heading outside where John had Whiskey saddled and ready.

"Thank you, John." He mounted quickly, eager to return to the cavern entrance as he'd done every morning for the past week. She would return early in the day. He was sure of it. Just as she'd held vigil in hope of Lady Alexandra's return, he returned each day to wait upon hers.

He refused to give up hope, though the servants must wonder at his odd behavior. Convincing everyone she'd gone to visit her family had been relatively easy. Viscount Creswell made a quick trip to London to corroborate the story and returned two days later.

As if his thoughts conjured him out of the air, Creswell appeared on the path from the manor. "Tyndale. Good, you haven't left yet. Wait a moment, and I shall accompany you."

"Of course. I will be pleased of the company," he lied.

Creswell was mounted in no time, and they headed out. Neither spoke much on the journey, preferring to take in the crisp fall air in silent contemplations. James's thoughts were consumed with hope that Charlotte would be awaiting them. He didn't doubt

Creswell's were much the same.

His hopes were dashed within moments of reaching the cave entrance. Nothing had been disturbed since the previous day.

"Damn," Creswell breathed.

James nodded.

They dismounted, and each found a comfortable spot to perch on the boulders littering the clearing in front of the cave. "I really should have a set of chairs brought out here." He sighed.

"That wouldn't raise any eyebrows, I'm sure." Creswell laughed. "The servants are already questioning our sanity."

James shrugged. "They'll gossip no matter what we do. But they're loyal. Their talk remains on the estate."

"Excellent." Creswell shifted with a grimace. "But let's hope our vigil here is limited, and more comfortable accommodations will prove unnecessary."

James nodded, and they settled in to wait.

****

Charlotte clung to Steven's hand in a tight grip. Bloody hell, she was going to miss him. The portal loomed in front of them. She shivered from a distinct chill in the air. At some point, someone mentioned they kept the room cool so none of their equipment overheated. She hadn't noticed it quite so much before. Now that she knew exactly what she faced, all the small details loomed larger in her head.

"No one's going to create a scene, are they?"

She bristled at Sawyer's condescending tone, but Alex beat her to a response.

"Shut up, Sawyer. No one wants to hear from you

unless you plan on finally telling us what this whole thing has been about."

Charlotte held her breath. They'd been trying to get the story out of him all morning, but he'd kept mum.

Alex propped her hands on her hips and glared. The ill-fitting clothing Sawyer had provided should have made her look ridiculous, but her sister pulled off defiant anger in a way Charlotte never could. She'd enjoyed spending time with her this past week and was glad they were going through with this together.

"Tell us, and I'll give you my word I won't make any more trouble for you," Steven pitched in. "I'll even get Jim at *The Times* to give up the story. We've gotten quite close these past few months. He'd listen to me if I said there's nothing to find."

That was news to Charlotte. She'd heard about the reporter that Alex's friend had pitted against Sawyer but hadn't realized he'd come in contact with her brother.

Sawyer grimaced and then settled into a folding chair in front of a bank of blinking, whirring computers straight out of a sci-fi movie. He waved a hand at Gigantor, and the guard set out chairs for each of them.

The three of them aligned their chairs in a straight line with Charlotte in the middle, facing off against Sawyer. The guard took up his post near the exit doors.

"It's simple, really. As I mentioned before, you weren't meant to stay in this century. Your place is in the past."

"Then why not just send us back immediately. Why wait until we'd settled into our lives here? It took you fifteen years to realize we didn't belong?" Alex asked.

"I'm getting to that." Sawyer sneered.

Alex's lips twitched. She'd confessed to how much she liked baiting the man. It was amazingly easy to do. Charlotte suppressed her own chuckle. It felt good to know they got to him, even if only a tiny bit.

"I suppose the easiest way to explain would be to give you one missing bit of information." He paused with a lifted brow and surveyed each of them.

Steven huffed. "Get on with it. We don't need the drama."

Sawyer scowled. He hadn't been particularly pleased when Steven insisted on tagging along with them in the first place. Having her brother burst his dramatic bubble didn't help. Charlotte grinned and squeezed Steven's hand.

"Fine." Sawyer huffed. "Gabriel Stone died before producing an heir. So upon his death, his title and all his lands passed on to his younger brother."

"I'm not following," Alex said.

"Gabriel Stone made several bad investments, so his fortunes were rather depleted, yet he'd managed to keep himself afloat with some rather nefarious dealings, a bit of help from his younger brother, and his position as a member of parliament. His brother, however, was a man of many talents but lacked connections."

"He was the brother of a baron. That didn't get him anywhere?"

Sawyer shook his head. "No. The brothers didn't get along. The younger brother left England to seek his own fortune shortly after their father died. He did quite well. Even stepped in on occasion if his brother showed danger of losing the family estate, etcetera."

"So this is the simple explanation?" Charlotte

asked, sarcasm heavy in her tone. A clock ticked in the background. She was almost sorry they'd asked. So close to the portal, she was suddenly eager to get the journey over with. James and Prue must be worried sick with her gone for so long.

Sawyer all but growled, shoulders tense, lip curling. Months ago, she'd have been frightened, but now she was just annoyed. She wanted to go home.

"Fine. I'm as eager as you to finish with this business once and for all." He crossed his arms and leaned back. "The brother's name was," he paused for dramatic effect, "Griffin Stone."

Charlotte's jaw dropped.

"Griffin…" Alex whispered. "Holy shit."

Sawyer nodded, his smile smug. "Yes. Griffin Stone took the title, leveraged his new status, rebuilt the family fortune, and eventually started a small company that today bears his name."

"So you know so much about Charlotte and Alex because of their connection to Gabriel Stone's death. Did you know all these years, or did you send them back this year because you just figured it out?"

"We've known for a few years. We had some difficulty finding Alex when it became apparent both of you needed to return."

Charlotte darted a glance at her sister, but Alex appeared to take this news in stride.

"An American couple had sought to adopt her, but the adoption fell through after Alex had traveled to the US, and Alex was lost to the American foster system. We were quite pleased when she contacted us just when we needed her to return." He gestured toward the guard.

Gigantor marched over to a filing cabinet, rifled

through the top drawer for a few seconds, and then withdrew a leather-bound book. He handed it over to Sawyer and winked at Charlotte on the return to his post.

Sawyer flipped the pages, then held it aloft in his right hand, shaking it back and forth. "This diary, uh, lets say, *came into* our possession about four years ago. It told us everything we needed to know. When you ladies went back, what had to happen—"

"Had to happen?" Alex leaned forward, elbows on knees, and rested her head in her palms. "Jeez. If I wasn't so eager to go back through that damn portal, I'd totally kick your ass about now."

Charlotte agreed. She would forever feel the weight of Miss Crawford's death on her shoulders.

"Whose diary is it?" Steven asked.

"Charlotte's."

Alex bolted upright in her chair, mouth hanging open.

Charlotte's eyes began to water, and she forced herself to blink. *Bloody hell.* "Mine?" she asked, voice cracking. She had been keeping a diary of sorts but had been careful not to mention the portal, time travel, or anything that might get her thrown in an asylum if someone were to find it.

Sawyer nodded. "Very informative. Once you fill in the blanks." He waved it in the air again. "And you have so much more to write. You really should be heading home."

Steven lunged up, towering over Sawyer, and grabbed the diary out of his hands. The guard started forward, but Steven held him off with a gesture. "Wait. What if Charlotte goes back and burns the thing. Why risk it? If you didn't have this book, none of this would have happened."

"But she won't. First, time travel's tricky. I already have the diary, so I know she will go back, and I know what she'll write. It has to happen. Second, she won't risk not getting sent back. After all, we're all here right now because both girls want to return home. Now. Give me back my book."

Steven snorted. "No way. I'm not sure how you got this, but you're not keeping it."

Sawyer's face purpled with rage. Before he could begin shouting, Charlotte and Alex both stood. Alex said, "Forget it, Sawyer. You have no right to Charlotte's diary. I have no idea how it *came* to you," she said, with air quotes emphasizing came, "but I'd wager to guess it wasn't yours for the taking."

When Sawyer didn't argue, Steven made to hand the diary to Charlotte. She shook her head. "No. I don't think I should take that." She pushed it back toward Steven. "I don't want to know. You keep it."

Steven nodded and held the diary against his chest. Tears glistened in his eyes. "It'll be like I can still talk to you."

The tears started in earnest. Charlotte had to blink rapidly so she could still see her brother. "Are you sure you're going to be all right once I'm gone?" she asked him for about the thousandth time that day.

Steven squeezed her hand. "I'll be fine," he answered, his normally cheerful voice, rough and gritty. "Give us a minute," he said to Sawyer.

They drifted closer to the portal, while Sawyer stood near the guard. Steven put his arm around them both. They all leaned in close. Steven whispered,

"Check in at the portal every once in a while. I've been talking to Jason. He's agreed to play mailman for me."

"Who?" Charlotte asked, puzzled. Who could Steven possibly know at Griffin International?

"You call him Gigantor."

She gasped and quickly slapped a hand over her mouth. She didn't dare look toward the guard.

"Could I send messages to Jessie through you?" Alex asked.

"Maybe. We'll have to see how it goes. He thinks he can send a message through pretty easily without being spotted, but picking one up could be dicey. You'd have no way of knowing whether he's actually here, and we wouldn't want anyone else to intervene."

"Aw, bloody hell, that makes sense."

"Now, you ladies better get going. I don't know how much longer I can take this," Steven said with a rough laugh.

He straightened, and Charlotte spied the diary still clasped in his hand. "That's it." She snapped her fingers and swung toward Alex. "A diary. You can keep one, too. We'll figure out a way to pass it on to your friend. We'll have plenty of time to figure out how."

"Brilliant," Steven said. "Now, go." He gave them both hugs, first Alex, then her.

Charlotte clung to him, reluctant to let go. "I'm going to miss you so much, big brother."

"I'll miss you, too. But knowing you're going back to a big family and this James guy, will help. I just want you to be happy, sis."

"I will be."

As she and Alex suffered through the crossing, she knew in her heart what she'd said was true.

****

Charlotte groped along the cave floor until she found the extra lantern James had placed there. Her sister nudged her from behind, both of them straining away from the strength of the portal. "There should be a bag around here somewhere," Charlotte muttered. The clothes Sawyer had supplied for Alex wouldn't do.

"Damn, Sawyer," Alex cursed. "You'd think he'd at least let us have the lantern you brought with you. But, no…"

Charlotte snorted. "Yeah, he's a prince all right." Her fingers finally contacted the lantern, and she struggled to sort out their supplies by touch. It took her a few minutes, but she finally managed to get the thing lit. Light flared, causing spots behind her previously blind eyes. "Bloody hell. There's not one thing I like about this stupid hole in the ground."

"It brought us together, so I'll own a tiny bit of gratitude myself, but I won't be sad to never come here again," Alex said.

Charlotte turned awkwardly and returned Alex's hug. "Yes, same here." She blinked until her eyes finally adjusted to the flickering light, then gestured toward the surface. "Ready?"

"More than," Alex responded. "Let's go." She grabbed the lantern and headed out.

Charlotte followed a few steps behind. They stopped to catch their breath when the tunnel opened up into the larger cavern. "Do you want to change here, or get to the surface first? James said he'd have someone watching for my return, so you might not get the chance to change if we head up."

Alex placed the lantern on a relatively flat jut of

rock, so Charlotte tossed her the sack. "I've changed the outfit in there more than once. I added a spencer last time, so you should be pretty comfortable."

"Thanks."

Charlotte tried to give her sister as much privacy as possible while also helping with her dress. It wasn't easy, but they finally managed to get her sufficiently clothed.

"How do I look?" Alex held out her arms and watched Charlotte with an expectant look on her face.

"Lovely. Wrinkled." Charlotte giggled. "But lovely."

Alex grimaced. "Well, at least it's better than that monstrosity Sawyer saddled me with."

They both scowled at the pile of cloth now lying at Alex's feet. "Not sure what he was thinking with that mess." The chemise was about five times Alex's size, the corset two sizes too small, and the skirt fell just below her knees. Showing up out of nowhere would have been nothing to the nasty reception she'd have received if anyone spied her dressed like that.

"He was thinking how much he hates me."

Charlotte grunted. She was probably right. Sawyer hadn't exactly liked Charlotte, but he seemed to absolutely loathe Alex. "Was your friend, Jessie, that much of a pain in the ass?"

Alex chuckled as she stuffed the awful outfit into the satchel. "Yup, she sure was. Gotta love her. But the reporter was the real issue. I wonder if he'll give up now, or what? I feel kind of bad having Steven blow him off, but what could we say?"

"Nothing he'd believe." Charlotte took the lantern. "Ready?"

"To get out of here? Absolutely."

"I get the feeling there's more to that answer, and I'll expect details when we reach the surface." Charlotte led the way, her attention only partially on the path, the rest on the waves of uneasiness radiating off her sister. She intended to push for an answer, but hoped Alex trusted her enough to take her into her confidence.

"What if he's over me already?" Alex finally whispered when a gradual lightening of the shadows indicated the entrance was almost within reach. "It's been months. His mother's probably been trying to hook him up with someone this whole time. What if he found someone else?"

Charlotte paused. "Not possible. You didn't see him when he returned. He tried to act normal, but the man who returned was a shell. Tracking down Lord Stone gave him purpose for a little while, but once that was done, he just..." She waved her free hand in a circle. "I don't know how to describe it. He just, wilted, I suppose is the closest I can come. And since then, James tells me he's inconsolable. It's a good thing you've returned before he drinks himself to death."

And what would James have been doing this past week? She couldn't wait to see him. Going back to the future, seeing Steven, taking hot showers, catching up on her favorite TV show, had all been wonderful. A nice vacation. But the trip had made it perfectly clear that her home was here. With James, and Prue, and her birth family.

"I need to get back to him real quick then," Alex said.

"We'll head back to Tyndale Manor and get a carriage to take you to London." She could sense

Alex's impatience. It mirrored her own. "If Mother and Father have returned to the manor, they may wish to accompany you."

"I can't wait to see everyone. How long will it take to walk to the house?"

"I doubt we'll have to walk." They reached the entrance and stood, blinking until their eyes adjusted to the bright sunlight. She expected to see Max, or one of the other grooms, but the tall figures she spied sitting on a pair of rocks, were much more beloved. "James," she breathed.

His head popped up. The next second, he leaped to his feet and she ran forward, straight into his waiting arms.

****

His name was but a whisper, but it brought James's head up with a snap. Charlotte. He leaped toward her.

And then she was in his arms. Where she belonged.

He held her tight, buried his nose in her neck and inhaled. And promptly sneezed from the dust coating her hair.

They sprang apart, laughing.

Charlotte beat at her clothes, raising even more dust. "Ugh. I hate those tunnels. I'm a bloody mess."

He grabbed her hands to still them before he too was coated in dirt. He wasn't about to step far enough away to avoid the flying debris. "You're beautiful. Dirt and all." His hand trembled as he brushed the hair away from her face. Tears sparkled in her beloved eyes. He lowered his head toward hers…

The sound of a throat clearing startled him. He whipped his head toward the sound. "Lady Alexandra," he cried with a mix of emotions swirling in his head. He settled on joy. Annoyance at this interruption seemed ill advised.

"Alexandra, Charlotte," Creswell cried. He ran to Lady Alexandra and swung her up into a hug, twirling her around the clearing, both of them breathy with laughter. They stopped less than a foot away, and Charlotte reached toward him, thankfully without leaving James's side. Creswell grabbed the offered hand and leaned close to kiss her cheek. Their smiles rivaled his own.

James recalled the last time he saw Oakleigh. Thank the lord Lady Alexandra had returned. Oakleigh would not last long at his current rate of alcohol consumption. "Lord Oakleigh...well, Lord Oakleigh will be beyond pleased to see you. For his sake alone, I would be grateful for your return, but the happiness I know your presence will bring to Charlotte... I can't thank you enough." He bowed in her direction without releasing his highly improper hold on Charlotte. He was not ready to let her far from his grasp.

Lady Alexandra curtsied in return. "Nice to meet you." She glanced back over her shoulder and pointed a thumb behind her. "I, uh, think I dropped something back there. Gregory, can you help me find it? We'll, uh, be back in a minute."

James didn't believe her for a moment, but he smiled his thanks as Charlotte's siblings disappeared down the tunnel entrance. "I see your trip to the future was a success?"

"Yes." Charlotte stepped closer, the heat of her body pressed against him. "Did you miss me?"

"With all my soul." He didn't waste any time but pulled Charlotte into his embrace and brought her lips to his in a deep kiss.

She met him with enthusiasm, and he was lost. All he could think was that he had Charlotte, his Charlotte, back in his arms.

And all was right with the world.

Epilogue

May 1819

James tipped his glass of champagne to Oakleigh. "All's well that ends well, as they say."

His friend returned the salute. "They do indeed."

The two leaned against the drawing room wall at Oakleigh's London townhouse while dancers whirled around the room in a brightly colored rainbow. Oakleigh had spared no expense to make this ball the event of the season. While his sister, Lady Meghan Somerville, already numbered her beau in the dozens, she had yet to express a clear preference for any one man. Oakleigh was pleased, not wanting his sister to rush her choice and settle for anything less than what he shared with his wife.

He'd lay odds Oakleigh's gaze was as glued to Lady Alexandra as James's was to his own wife.

Charlotte danced with Myles, who surprisingly hadn't stepped on her toes once. His shy demeanor had disappeared the moment he stepped onto the dance floor. The boy was coming into his own. Several young ladies followed his progress with interest.

"Good thing the lad hasn't noticed his admirers." He nodded toward a trio of young ladies who giggled behind their fans whenever he passed them by.

Oakleigh chuckled. "Indeed. Care to wager on the

shade of red his face will turn at the moment of enlightenment?"

James's grin faded as the song ended, and Charlotte caught his eye. Her gaze trained on him, she linked her arm with Myles's before heading his way.

"Ah, song's over," Oakleigh said. He straightened, his focus on Lady Alexandra as her father escorted her off the dance floor to their side of the room.

James waited eagerly for Charlotte to reach him. He couldn't resist taking the last few steps to hurry their reunion. He nodded to Myles and with a wicked grin, said, "I see your dancing skills have not gone unnoticed by the fairer sex." He tilted his chin toward the giggling gaggle of girls whose gazes had not left Myles for the duration of the dance.

Myles's face turned a deep crimson, and James had difficulty restraining his mirth.

Charlotte hit him with her fan. "Stop it, you." Her eyes shone with amusement.

He bowed to his wife as the orchestra began the waltz. "I believe I have this dance?"

"You do indeed." She curtsied in return and then took his proffered arm as Oakleigh swept her sister in the opposite direction.

"They look happy, don't you think?" Charlotte asked, her gaze following the blissful couple.

"Indeed they do," he murmured, distracted by the scent of oranges. He sniffed lightly, trying to be discreet. Her hair smelled of flowers, not citrus, yet the scent was strong.

She ran a finger along his jaw. He leaned into her touch, his eyes drifting shut to focus on the sensation. "Are you playing with me, my dear, or are you ready to go home?"

Her low-throated chuckle had his eyes popping open. "Just playing, then?" He sighed.

"I was just trying to help you get a better whiff."

He wrinkled his brow. *What?*

"Oranges. On my hands. I peeled one earlier, and the scent lingered."

He'd completely progressed beyond scent as his body focused on touch. "I was not aware Oakleigh was serving the fruit this evening."

"He isn't. His mother has a tree in her greenhouse, so I asked for one. It's a precaution." He must have looked as confused as he felt, because she explained, "This many people...all crushed together in a hot room..." She passed her hand under his nose. "When certain other...odors become overwhelming, this helps." She shrugged.

"Clever." The clean, tangy scent of the fruit did mask the more pungent odors that formed a backdrop so common at events of this order. "I've heard of scented handkerchiefs, but never hands."

"It's something a friend used to do." Her eyes glazed over with that faraway look they got whenever she thought of her previous life in the future.

He maneuvered them through the open doors onto the patio. A fresh breeze cooled his heated body as he whisked her to a semi-private spot along the balcony. Couples gathered in the shadows, keeping their faces turned discreetly away to avoid recognition.

They leaned against the balustrades. The sun had long since set, the full moon casting its light upon them. He faced her, though she continued to gaze out upon the garden bathed in moonlight.

Damn, she was beautiful. He would never tire of gazing upon her profile.

Did she feel the same? Was she having second thoughts about staying here with him? Did she miss the future? She reassured him repeatedly that she did not, but moments like these caused him concern.

"You still miss that life? Miss the future?" he finally asked. The question had burned within him for far too long, he should have asked her long since. Yet, he'd been too afraid of her answer. He'd been so happy upon her return, he hadn't wanted to waste a moment with her worrying over the damn future.

"Sure."

His heart sank. "Will you always? Can you ever be truly happy here? Will you need to return one day?" He closed his eyes. He couldn't bear to watch her voice one of his greatest fears.

"Return?"

The surprise in her voice gave him pause. His eyes shot open to find her staring at him. And not all dewy-eyed and love-struck, as the poems tended to describe a woman in love. She looked ready to start a round of fisticuffs. He held up his hands to hold her off before she actually took a swing at him.

Before he could think of anything to say, she raised her fist and shook it at him. "You are so annoying." She grabbed his hand and tugged. "Come with me."

She dragged him along the outside of the house, through the kitchen gardens, and in through a door at the back of the home. Servants scurried around these back rooms, but without fail, stopped in the midst of their duties to greet Charlotte with a smile and an inquiry as to whether there was anything she needed.

She thanked everyone but continued on their way until they entered the privacy of the family sitting room on the second floor. They'd spent quite a lot of time with her sister here and knew the home well.

To say she shoved him into the room and slammed the door behind them would be an exaggeration, but though she was gentle in her motions, he was left with the impression her restraint was hard won.

"I did not mean to anger you." And he was at a loss to figure out what he had done to warrant such a heated display.

"And yet, you did, you stupid, doubting prat."

"Prat? Stupid?" This is what she thought of him?

"How can you think, for even a second, that I would leave you now? After all we've been through? Bloody hell, we're married. Do you really think I would have married you if I was going to up and leave you someday?"

When she put it like that...

"And not only you, but my parents, my siblings, Prue?" her voice cracked. "How can you think I would ever leave her? Or..." She hesitated, and a small smile pulled at her lips. "...take her brother away from you?" She placed a fist against her flat stomach.

He stared at her hand in a fog. Was she saying...? "Brother?"

"Or sister." She shrugged. "Without a sonogram, I guess we'll just have to wait until November to find out."

He let out a whoop of joy, grabbed her up in a bear hug, and swung her around until her feet flew from the floor. She could explain what a sonogram was later. They laughed together and ended with a searing kiss that left him breathless and eager to return home. He was a fool for ever having doubted her. It was high time he stopped questioning his good fortune and accept that Charlotte was here to stay.

"Have we stayed long enough this evening? Might we return home now?" he asked. "I know you want to be here for Lady Meghan, but surely we've put in a good show? It is after midnight." Early for an event of this nature, but if he didn't get his beautiful wife home soon, he was likely to create a scandal the likes of which society would be speaking of for decades.

She leaned into him, her hand curled over his arm, and her head on his shoulder as they slowly made their way down the stairs. "I am rather knackered."

"Then I shall see you straight to bed."

"Perfect."

Yes. Exactly what he was thinking. He kissed her one last time before they came within view of the myriad guests milling about Oakleigh's home, then together they ran to their carriage for the short ride to their London townhouse. If they didn't wait until arriving home to consummate the passion running hot between them, well no one was the wiser. And had they been caught, they could weather any scandal.

Together.

A word about the author...

Emma Kaye is married to her high school sweetheart and has two beautiful kids that she spends a ridiculous amount of time driving around central New Jersey.

Before dance classes and scouting entered her life, she decided to write one of those romances she loved to read and discovered a new passion. She's been writing ever since.

With her loving family, a playful dog, and two extremely patient cats, Emma's living her own happily ever after while making her characters work hard to reach theirs. http://emma-kaye.com